Praise for Lexi Blake and Mercenaries

"I can always trust Lexi Blake's Dominants to leave me breathless...and in love. If you want sensual, exciting BDSM wrapped in an awesome love story, then look for a Lexi Blake book."

~Cherise Sinclair USA Today Bestselling author

"Lexi Blake's MASTERS AND MERCENARIES series is beautifully written and deliciously hot. She's got a real way with both action and sex. I also love the way Blake writes her gorgeous Dom heroes--they make me want to do bad, bad things. Her heroines are intelligent and gutsy ladies whose taste for submission definitely does not make them dish rags. Can't wait for the next book!"

~Angela Knight, New York Times Bestselling author

"A Dom is Forever is action packed, both in the bedroom and out. Expect agents, spies, guns, killing and lots of kink as Liam goes after the mysterious Mr. Black and finds his past and his future... The action and espionage keep this story moving along quickly while the sex and kink provides a totally different type of interest. Everything is very well balanced and flows together wonderfully."

~A Night Owl "Top Pick", Terri, Night Owl Erotica

"A Dom Is Forever is everything that is good in erotic romance. The story was fast-paced and suspenseful, the characters were flawed but made me root for them every step of the way, and the hotness factor was off the charts mostly due to a bad boy Dom with a penchant for dirty talk."

~Rho, The Romance Reviews

"A good read that kept me on my toes, guessing until the big reveal, and thinking survival skills should be a must for all men."

~Chris, Night Owl Reviews

Love the Way You Spy

Other Books by Lexi Blake

ROMANTIC SUSPENSE

Masters and Mercenaries
The Dom Who Loved Me
The Men With The Golden Cuffs
A Dom is Forever
On Her Master's Secret Service
Sanctum: A Masters and Mercenaries Novella
Love and Let Die
Unconditional: A Masters and Mercenaries Novella
Dungeon Royale
Dungeon Games: A Masters and Mercenaries Novella
A View to a Thrill
Cherished: A Masters and Mercenaries Novella
You Only Love Twice
Luscious: Masters and Mercenaries~Topped
Adored: A Masters and Mercenaries Novella
Master No
Just One Taste: Masters and Mercenaries~Topped 2
From Sanctum with Love
Devoted: A Masters and Mercenaries Novella
Dominance Never Dies
Submission is Not Enough
Master Bits and Mercenary Bites~The Secret Recipes of Topped
Perfectly Paired: Masters and Mercenaries~Topped 3
For His Eyes Only
Arranged: A Masters and Mercenaries Novella
Love Another Day
At Your Service: Masters and Mercenaries~Topped 4
Master Bits and Mercenary Bites~Girls Night
Nobody Does It Better
Close Cover
Protected: A Masters and Mercenaries Novella
Enchanted: A Masters and Mercenaries Novella
Charmed: A Masters and Mercenaries Novella
Taggart Family Values
Treasured: A Masters and Mercenaries Novella

Delighted: A Masters and Mercenaries Novella
Tempted: A Masters and Mercenaries Novella

Masters and Mercenaries: The Forgotten
Lost Hearts (Memento Mori)
Lost and Found
Lost in You
Long Lost
No Love Lost

Masters and Mercenaries: Reloaded
Submission Impossible
The Dom Identity
The Man from Sanctum
No Time to Lie
The Dom Who Came in from the Cold

Masters and Mercenaries: New Recruits
Love the Way You Spy
Live, Love, Spy, Coming March 5, 2024

Butterfly Bayou
Butterfly Bayou
Bayou Baby
Bayou Dreaming
Bayou Beauty
Bayou Sweetheart
Bayou Beloved

Park Avenue Promise
Start Us Up
My Royal Showmance, Coming June 4, 2024

Lawless
Ruthless
Satisfaction
Revenge

Courting Justice
Order of Protection
Evidence of Desire

Masters Of Ménage (by Shayla Black and Lexi Blake)
Their Virgin Captive
Their Virgin's Secret
Their Virgin Concubine
Their Virgin Princess
Their Virgin Hostage
Their Virgin Secretary
Their Virgin Mistress

The Perfect Gentlemen (by Shayla Black and Lexi Blake)
Scandal Never Sleeps
Seduction in Session
Big Easy Temptation
Smoke and Sin
At the Pleasure of the President

URBAN FANTASY

Thieves
Steal the Light
Steal the Day
Steal the Moon
Steal the Sun
Steal the Night
Ripper
Addict
Sleeper
Outcast
Stealing Summer
The Rebel Queen
The Rebel Guardian
The Rebel Witch, Coming November 7, 2023

LEXI BLAKE WRITING AS SOPHIE OAK

Texas Sirens
Small Town Siren
Siren in the City
Siren Enslaved
Siren Beloved
Siren in Waiting
Siren in Bloom
Siren Unleashed
Siren Reborn

Nights in Bliss, Colorado
Three to Ride
Two to Love
One to Keep
Lost in Bliss
Found in Bliss
Pure Bliss
Chasing Bliss
Once Upon a Time in Bliss
Back in Bliss
Sirens in Bliss
Happily Ever After in Bliss
Far from Bliss
Unexpected Bliss

A Faery Story
Bound
Beast
Beauty

Standalone
Away From Me
Snowed In

Love the Way You Spy

Masters and Mercenaries:
New Recruits, Book 1

Lexi Blake

Love the Way You Spy
Masters and Mercenaries: New Recruits, Book 1
Lexi Blake

Published by DLZ Entertainment LLC
Copyright 2023 DLZ Entertainment LLC
Edited by Chloe Vale
ISBN: 978-1-942297-87-1

Sign up for Lexi Blake's newsletter
and be entered to win a $25 gift certificate
to the bookseller of your choice.

Join us for news, fun, and exclusive content
including free Thieves short stories.

There's a new contest every month!

Go to www.LexiBlake.net to subscribe.

Family Trees

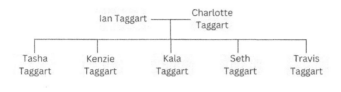

Ian Taggart — Charlotte Taggart

Tasha Taggart | Kenzie Taggart | Kala Taggart | Seth Taggart | Travis Taggart

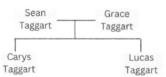

Sean Taggart — Grace Taggart

Carys Taggart | Lucas Taggart

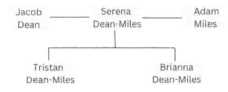

Jacob Dean — Serena Dean-Miles — Adam Miles

Tristan Dean-Miles | Brianna Dean-Miles

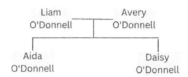

Liam O'Donnell — Avery O'Donnell

Aida O'Donnell | Daisy O'Donnell

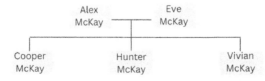

Alex McKay — Eve McKay

Cooper McKay | Hunter McKay | Vivian McKay

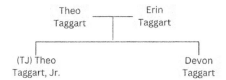

Theo Taggart — Erin Taggart

(TJ) Theo Taggart, Jr.   Devon Taggart

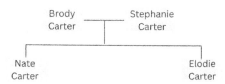

Brody Carter — Stephanie Carter

Nate Carter   Elodie Carter

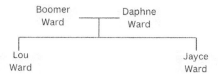

Boomer Ward — Daphne Ward

Lou Ward   Jayce Ward

Acknowledgments

It is hard to believe how fast time goes. I swear it was yesterday I wrote the first draft of *The Dom Who Loved Me*, and now I'm writing books about the kids. Writing, it turns out, is a lot like life. It goes fast and sometimes we're not ready to keep up, but it's here anyway and we have to deal.

I thought it would be weird to write these kids as adults. After all, in some ways, they're my babies, too. Didn't I want to keep them young and sweet and innocent? As with many of life's events, writing this book had an unintended outcome. I felt young again. I felt new. This world I've spent so much of my adult life building was suddenly fresh, and I found myself happy to dive in each day. I've talked a lot about grief, written a lot about the process. In some ways I thought that dealing with grief and loss might be the center of the rest of my career. But Tash and Dare showed me how much joy is left. Writing Ian and Charlotte handle getting older, becoming grandparents and handling their adult children helped me handle my own.

It wasn't weird to write the intimate scenes. I want that for my kids. I want them to have full, amazing, messy lives because we find meaning when we fumble. When we fall we learn who is there to help us up. When we fail, we figure out who loves us simply for who we are, who will stand by us not matter what happens. We learn to keep trying, and that is the most important lesson of all.

So this one is for the kids who are growing faster than we could have imagined. For the kids we worry about, the ones we're really certain can't possibly live in the real world. They can. They will. And they will take the torch we pass to them and build something amazing.

As always for Dylan and Lindsey and Zoey, but friends are family, too, so for Sarah and Jake. For Eli and Elizabeth. For Max. For Glen and Jack. For Éilish. For Chloe and Kayla. For Caleb and Cece and Camden and Casey. For Gabe and Karlina.

Here's to a whole new generation so our stories never end.

Special thanks to my team – Kim, Kori, Stormy, Riane, and Maria. And thanks so much to my Aussies – Khloe Wren and Erin Lewis who helped make this trip down under as fun and real as possible.

Chapter One

Tasha Taggart looked over the rowdy bar and wondered for the one hundred and thirtieth time what the hell she was doing. She wasn't this girl. She wasn't the girl who stepped into a bar looking to pick up a guy because she needed affirmation.

She wasn't a girl at all. She was a woman, and she wasn't looking for affirmation. She was a whole-ass grown woman who ran a CIA team. And that CIA team included her twin siblings who were smart and also terrifying to handle and no one had even died yet. Well, no one who wasn't supposed to.

She was about to start a mission where she would subsist on takeout and hide in the shadows of whatever safe house the Agency was willing to put her up in, so she deserved some sex. She deserved a night out before she went back to the shadows. Tomorrow the op would start in earnest, and she would spend all her time staring at a computer screen and trying to keep everyone alive. Yes. That was why she was standing here in a slightly disreputable bar in Sydney wondering if her boobs looked good.

"Just so you know, your boobs look great," a cheery voice said.

She looked at one of her wingmen for the night. Louisa Ward hadn't taken the same ridiculous care with her appearance that Tasha had. Lou wore jeans and a T-shirt that proclaimed *Never Trust an*

Atom...They Make Up Everything. Her hair was in the same messy bun she always wore, and she hadn't bothered with her contacts. Her brown eyes were framed by overly large glasses that looked like they could have been worn by Sir Elton John himself.

Such an adorable dweeb and so deeply important to the whole freaking world, though no one really knew it. Lou had left a life of academia to join the team, and she'd already changed the way the Agency worked by adapting tech to fit their needs.

"Of course her boobs look great. Who do you think dressed her? You should have let me dress you, too."

Sometimes she wished Lou wasn't so great at tech. The glasses Lou wore were a part of the high-tech communications tool she'd helped create. It allowed the sister who was not there to just keep commenting anyway. Kenzie was stuck at base, so she'd made sure she could keep up via Lou's glasses and the microphone that would allow them all to hear her. She touched the earpiece her sister had insisted that she wear. "Hey. I thought this was for emergencies only."

Kenzie's voice came back over the line. "This is an emergency. I am bored and Coop and Tris are watching something called rugby, and I thought it would be more interesting than it is because I read a thing where sometimes the players shove a finger up the opposing player's butt to throw them off a little, but you can't see that. And if it's happening, then these dudes are seriously excellent at handling butt stuff because their faces do not change. They are like the most experienced subs at The Hideout on butt-stuff night."

They didn't actually have one of those. Tash was fairly certain that every night was butt-stuff night at the club a couple of members of the team had formed. It had started in the unattached garage at the rambling house Cooper shared with two of his best friends, and they'd recently pooled enough money to buy a building they were renovating. She loved The Hideout.

"Is she talking about the rugby rumors again?" Kala leaned in, whispering in Tasha's ear...or rather her earpiece. "You are such a perv. I can't believe I'm considered the wild one."

Kala and Kenzie were her sisters. They were fourteen months younger. Perfect twins. If one looked at them, they wouldn't be able to tell the two apart. Right up until their mouths opened, and then it was righteously clear who was who.

Kenzie was sunshine and puppies and yes, a smidge of sexual perversion—who could blame her—while Kala spoke mostly sarcasm and genuinely enjoyed knife fights. Seriously. Tash had seen her start a couple because the op was taking too long. There was not an ounce of patience in Kala's bones.

It wasn't easy being their handler. It was as easy as breathing to be their sister.

Sometimes. Now was not one of them.

"You know I didn't want any of you to come with me. I'm just getting a drink before we start the op," she said quietly.

Kala's brow rose, and for a second she looked so much like their dad it hurt. "Sure you are. That's why you let Kenz pick your look-at-my-boobs top."

God, she was so glad her father was hours and hours away sitting on a beach in Loa Mali, probably perving on their mom because that was what he did when he wasn't running his highly successful security company or working for the CIA.

Lou frowned Kala's way. "You know why she's wearing it. She's had a rough time, and she needs to get back on the horse. It's been months. This is the perfect scenario. Whoever she meets tonight she will have zero chance of seeing again because we're about to go into the not-so-fun dungeon for the rest of the op."

Lou would be sitting right beside her in the safe house listening to whichever twin wasn't out in the field moaning about how bored she was.

"Kala, don't be such a bitch. You know how hard the last couple of months have been on Tash," Kenzie complained into her ear despite the fact that Kala wouldn't be able to hear any of what she was saying. "She has the right to walk into a skanky bar and find a dude to ride for a couple of hours before she ditches him heinously and moves on to the next. Tash is transitioning into her slutty phase, and I am here for it."

Put like that, this whole thing sounded like a horrible idea. Not that there would be a *next* for quite a long time. Lou was right about that. "I want to get a drink and have a night of fun before the op begins. That's all. If I find a nice man to spend the night with, so be it. I'm away from the hotel. I've got wingmen to make sure if I happen to pick a serial killer, at least you'll know who killed me, and hopefully the boys don't figure it out because the last thing I need is Cooper McKay riding in like my big brother."

The team included her two sisters as the main operatives, Lou working tech, and their childhood friends, Cooper, who could fly or drive pretty much anything, and their computer whiz Tristan, who dealt with all things communications. Zachary Reed handled the military side of their ops. Tristan would laugh and tell her to get laid and have fun. Cooper would give her a lecture on situational awareness and probably talk to her about the fact that she was having an emotional reaction to what had happened to her. Zach knew where they were, and he was totally fine with the idea of a fun night out before a long mission.

It wasn't so surprising she'd had some emotions connected to finding her fiancé fucking a gorgeous MSS agent. He'd claimed he was doing it all for the op he'd been on, and that was likely true. Her father had rules involving what he called Honey Pot Ops. Flirting was fine, but he wasn't going to allow any operative under his command to fuck for information. He claimed it was because he knew how it felt, but she wondered if he would have the same convictions if he wasn't in charge of his daughters and a group of men and women who'd called him Uncle Ian all their lives.

Her fiancé's handler had no such rules. He'd promised her it meant nothing and she should understand because she was Agency, too.

It meant something to her.

And it meant something to the MSS agent who had damn near killed both her and Chet Whittington because she'd rapidly figured out what was happening. Tash had blown an op, and she was pretty sure it was only her dad who'd managed to keep her from being fired.

"No one is saying a word to the boys," Kenzie assured her. "Though you should know they told Chet that he can't come to poker night anymore. They are shutting his ass out. And he's not allowed at The Hideout. Coop revoked his membership."

Tash felt her eyes roll. The club Cooper and the twins had founded had never been Chet's favorite place. "Like I care. We still have to work with him."

"Not if he dies in the line of duty." Kala was dressed to kill, and she had a look on her face that let Tash know she wouldn't mind some wet work tonight.

"Operatives die all the time," Kenzie assured her.

Tash shook her head and looked to the most reasonable of her group.

Lou simply smiled. "It's sad when they die. I heard the big boss suggested he get an assignment in Antarctica."

The big boss was her dad. Ian Taggart. Yup. She was the lucky girl who had been adopted into a whole family of spies. Sometimes they could be scary. She didn't want to know what thoughts had gone through her mother's head when she'd told her the wedding was off. Her mom had once been a real-life Russian mob assassin, and she'd probably thought about coming out of retirement. Her dad would have held the sniper rifle for her and gotten her tea and told her how hot she looked when she killed assholes.

Her parents were weird, but damn she wanted that kind of love. She hadn't found it with Chet.

"I don't want him dead. I want to move on with my life. It was stupid to think it could work." She should have known it wouldn't work when he'd told her his name was Chet. She'd known how much her father loved her when he'd taken that news with a silent nod even as his face had gone red with the desperate need to let his sarcasm flow.

Her dad hadn't even complained about the twenty-two thousand dollars in deposits he'd lost. Another sign of his love. She'd overheard him gleefully telling her mom he would have paid any amount of money for her to not marry that douchebag.

Kala's blue eyes widened in that "you're a dumbass but I still love you" way of hers. She had a lot of those looks, and navigating them was an important part of Tasha's life. There was *you're a dumbass but I love you. You're a dumbass and I'm barely tolerating you. You're a dumbass and I'm a messenger of Darwinism sent to take you out of the gene pool.* That one came up way too often.

"Of course it couldn't work. His name was Chet. I have zero idea how he got into the Agency with that name. Someone's not doing their job." Kala was totally their father's daughter.

"Because Kala is so normal," Kenzie said in her ear.

Kala got her "my sister is a dumbass and I know what she's saying even though I refuse to have her in my ear because I wanted to wear my hair up" look. When Lou had tried to give her a comm device, she'd refused. "Tell her Kala is awesome and it stands for something awesome, and she was named after some chick who had nice shoes."

"And fought for the Earth." Kenzie could hear Kala perfectly well thanks to Lou's excellent communication devices.

Family lore had it that Mom had named Kenzie after some chick in a Sci-Fi TV show and Dad had used an acronym for Kick A Little Ass to name Kala.

Tasha believed it.

Sometimes she wondered what they would have named her if she'd been their biological child. But it was only a passing thing. She thought about her bio parents often and hoped they were together wherever souls went after death. It was odd. She'd never once felt the complex longing other adopted kids did. Somewhere deep down she knew they'd loved her. They'd lost her. Somehow they'd made sure she'd gotten to the best place she could.

It was a weird feeling but one she'd never tried to deny. Her parents had loved her. They'd put that love into her soul and then when the universe had taken them, she'd managed to land straight in the arms of the Taggarts.

"Well, this looks like a heap of trouble right here. Welcome, ladies. You're going to elevate this piece of piss pub," a deep voice said. "You girls from out of town?"

Tash turned and saw the man behind the bar. He was roughly six foot, with a beard to rival Santa Claus and a grizzled face softened by kind eyes. Even on a night off, she had a cover to keep. "Yes. My sister and I are visiting my cousin."

Kala nodded his way. "They came all the way from America to spend a couple of weeks in my flat in Revesby. I thought I'd bring them down here to enjoy a few brews. It's okay. The short one doesn't drink much."

Every word that came out of Kala's mouth was pure middle-class Aussie. One of the things her sisters were excellent at was mimicking accents.

They'd spent months preparing for this op, and it had included them all learning the local dialect.

Some people thought guns and self-defense were the most important subjects an operative could possibly master. Tasha knew the truth.

It was languages. She spoke three herself fluently. Russian had been her native tongue, and then she'd learned English. Mandarin had been more of a stretch, though it hadn't hurt having a whole group of people she lived with immersed in it, too.

"I'm the quiet type," Lou admitted with a grin.

Kala slapped a hand on the bar, but it was a friendly gesture. "We'll have two pints and a middy."

The bartender nodded as he pulled down a pint glass. "It's quiet tonight. I'll bring these out to you. There's some nice seats by the windows if you like."

They thanked the man and then Kala walked through like she already owned the place. It was a tactic that worked time and time again for her. Sometimes she wished she had half of her sister's confidence.

Tash followed along, noting the pub was about half full at this time of the evening. It wasn't late. The sun had barely set. She was certain before too long the place would get louder. She counted five guys at a table in front of the big screen which seemed to be playing the aforementioned rugby match. There were two couples sitting in a booth playing cards, and another who sat staring at each other sullenly.

"You getting all of this, Lou?" Kala asked, sticking to the accent.

"Is there anyone interesting?" Kenzie asked in her ear.

"I'm getting everything," Lou promised as they approached the table Kala had selected. It was close to an exit, and she would be able to see everything from her seat.

Kala took the chair that had her back to the wall and Lou took the one closest to the window, leaving Tasha staring at the exit. "Oh, he could be interesting if he wasn't such a douchebag. I can tell from here. That guy thinks he's god's gift to women."

That got Tasha's head turning. She glanced over and...holy hotness. He *was* god's gift to women.

She wasn't sure how tall he was, but suspected he would be

about six six. He had golden-colored hair and ridiculously blue eyes and a jaw carved from granite. Sensual lips tugged up as his companion said something, and then his eyes caught hers and she looked away as fast as she could.

Oh, Kenz had talked about her getting back on the horse, but that one was a thoroughbred.

"Lou, send me something," Kenzie begged. "I want to see."

Those glasses of Lou's weren't merely a salute to Sir Elton. They were smart glasses she and Tristan had been working on for years. Those suckers connected to their personal systems and allowed Lou to access an enormous amount of data. Including facial recognition and the handy photo function the FR used. It made it easy for Lou to glance around the bar and send Kenzie what she longed for.

"He's gorgeous," Kenzie breathed.

He was. He was almost too beautiful to look at. The man didn't belong in this slightly seedy pub in a working-class Sydney neighborhood. He should be in Milan making one of those commercials that made no sense but seemed to sell perfume.

"He's a manwhore," Kala said quietly. "I assure you that one is a player."

"That's exactly what you need," Kenzie replied. "Oh, Tash, you should put on the glasses and seduce him."

Such a perv. "I am not doing that. Lou needs those so she can tell me if I'm about to hit on a criminal. Or a married guy."

It was handy to have a wingman who could background check a guy right there on the spot.

"His name is Brian Peters," Lou said quietly, turning her head away from the seriously gorgeous man's table. "His friend's name is Darren Nash, if anyone's interested."

She'd barely looked at Darren, but it was good to know who was with the hottie she intended to spend the evening with. Well, if he was single and ready to mingle that was. And if she was his type. And if she found a way to actually do this.

She'd faced down foreign operatives and been taken hostage for a full forty-eight hours before. Luckily it was by people who were terrified of her father and his Russian mob connections, so they'd mostly let her watch *Love Is Blind* and fed her French fries, but it had been a trial nonetheless. She'd done a lot of scary things, but walking over there was another thing altogether.

"I'm on his socials," Kenzie said in her ear. "Damn, Tash, he's stunning. I kind of wish I was there to fight you for him."

She glanced back over and there he was. The man practically had a halo, like the light in the room was drawn to him. He said something to the Darren guy. He wasn't bad either. He was a bit smaller than Brian's Greek god status, but it was obvious the man worked out. She was sure she would have paid more attention to him if he hadn't been sitting next to Brian. "I'd win. All I would have to do is threaten to let Kala stay in the field for a couple of days and you'd let me have him."

The twins shared their cover. They'd been doing it since the conception of the team. As far as she knew, no one outside the Agency was aware Ms. Magenta was actually two people.

"I might be willing to give up a couple of work days for that one," Kenzie admitted.

Whichever twin was stuck at the safe house always complained. Always.

"You know, he's not all that," Tasha said, rethinking her position on the gorgeous guy. Her sister was far more important. There was something about the wistful tone in Kenzie's voice that made her want to back off.

"Don't you dare," Kenzie replied. "It's been a while for me, and Dad won't let me take out my sexual aggression on the enemy. Who thought this was a good idea? Why couldn't we have gotten a handler who didn't care what we did as long as the job got done?"

She wasn't about to point out that their enemies rarely looked like this Brian guy, and Kenzie would be hella upset if this handler who wasn't her dad told her to sleep with some stinky politician.

"He's not married," Lou continued. "He works with a banking group that funds a lot of medical research. He was born in Dayton, Ohio. Very exciting. He's been working in Toronto the last couple of months."

"I bet he plays a lot of sports." Kala sat back, utterly uninterested.

"He plays a lot of sports," Kenzie said in her ear. "According to his socials, he's active in his local amateur basketball league and…oh, he's a big brother. Not like family wise. It looks like he's an only child. He sponsors a kid in his hometown."

Kenzie sounded half in love with the guy.

"You girls should stay away from the blokes watching the telly. That big group of them?" The bartender set down two twenty ounces for Kala and Tash, and a ten in front of Lou as he gestured to the rugby fans around the big screen. "Those boys are known for getting in trouble."

"What do you know about the two in the back?" Kala asked, pulling the beer close. "The cute fella and the male-model looking arse."

The bartender chuckled and gave Kala a big smile. "You remind me of my daughter. Smart as a whip. They've been in here a couple of times. I'm pretty sure they're tourists. I think they're staying somewhere close. Honestly, they both seem like pretty nice fellas, though I like the Canadian better. The American's a little brash for my tastes, though he does attract the ladies. But from what I've seen they don't start fights."

"Have they picked up anyone?" Kala seemed deeply determined to embarrass the hell out of her.

The bartender shook his head. "Nah. They come in and have a couple of pints and leave. Not that the ladies haven't tried to pick them up. I thought they might be…well, together, but then I heard them talking about the dark-haired one's divorce, and it was obvious they were discussing a lady." His lips curled up. "Well, well. Looks like they were just waiting for the right ones. You girls yell out if they give you any trouble."

He stepped away and that was when Tasha realized she wasn't going to have to make the decision whether or not to hit on the hottie.

He was right here. Right next to her, and his friend was beside him. Tash looked up, ready to smile his way.

"Hey there, gorgeous. Can I buy you a drink?" Brian Peters said, his voice deep.

And he was looking at her sister.

Not her. Kala. He was hitting on Kala.

Tash took a drink. It was going to be a long night.

* * * *

Dare Nash couldn't take his eyes off the brunette. Oh, he could absolutely appreciate the stunning gorgeousness of the woman with vibrant pink hair and a classically lovely face, but it had been the brunette's warmth that drew him in. The shorter, curvy girl was sexy, but not the way the brunette was.

"Hey there, gorgeous. Can I buy you a drink?" Brian asked in a deeper voice than he'd heard his friend use.

That must be the dude's seduction voice. Dare was pretty sure he didn't have one of those. At least he hoped he didn't.

His seduction "voice" would be to get private with that brunette and order her to take her clothes off, to offer her breasts up to him, to let him take her anyway he wanted.

You're a monster. You just hide it under a nice-guy surface. No woman wants what you want. You want to treat me like a whore.

His ex-wife's words slid over his brain. He had to keep telling himself that she'd been looking for a way out of the marriage and she'd found one when she'd gotten him to admit his sexual desires. And then she'd happily taken most of everything and moved in with her coworker.

Still, it was good to remember that there was a reason he'd kept those needs in check for almost thirty years. The brunette looked young and vulnerable, and he would have to be gentle if he managed to get her in bed.

Manage being the operative word here because she wasn't looking at him. She was looking at Brian, and he saw the moment she realized Brian was talking to her friend.

"I have a drink," the pink-haired woman said with a twist of her lips. It was part smile, part smirk, all challenge.

"Well, then maybe you should buy me one." Brian seemed ready to take her up on it.

Brian wasn't catching the same vibes he was. The woman was not interested in him. Not at all. He'd never actually seen a woman look at his friend that way. They usually melted at the sight of him. This one looked like she would rather kick him in the balls than play with them.

It had been so long since anyone had played with his balls.

Masturbation was getting boring.

"Would you two like to join us?" The third woman at the table looked greatly amused at the scene that was playing out in front of her. She was cute, and he would bet she was smart. She looked like she belonged in a lab or teaching a class at university.

He was about to turn them down and make a hasty retreat. This situation was not what he'd been expecting when Brian had announced they needed to be more social. He'd been perfectly ready to stare at the brunette most of the night and then go back to his suite. Soon he would move to the conference hotel, and it would be all work for a few weeks. Yep. They should wish these beauties a good night and run as fast as they could.

"Would love to," Brian said, pulling the fourth chair out and sliding it closer to the object of his desire. Who might also be the person who killed him given her look of disdain.

He hadn't expected Brian to be a masochist.

In the months he'd worked with him, Brian had been the happiest of all go lucky men. Brian was easy to be friends with. He took everything and everyone as they came and was excellent at making the people around him feel comfortable. Pink Hair didn't look comfortable. Or rather she did, but in a deeply predatory way that Brian did not seem to be picking up on.

"I'm perfectly willing to let a woman buy me a drink," Brian was saying.

"Then you should find one who wants to," Pink Hair replied.

"I think we should probably call it a night." The brunette started to stand. She wore a pretty yellow top that showed off the curves of what looked like generous breasts and jeans that clung to her hips.

He wished she'd glanced his way, but it looked like he wasn't catching any breaks this evening. "We'll go back to our table. I don't want to interrupt your evening."

"Not at all," the one with the glasses said. "We were recently discussing how much fun it would be to meet some new people."

She was obviously American. Pink Hair sounded like she was straight out of Sydney, but Glasses and the Brunette had flat American accents, the kind that likely meant they'd been raised in large cities where accents rounded out due to the amount of diversity found there.

"I thought we were doing fine on our own," Pink Hair argued.

Glasses frowned her way, and the two seemed to have a silent argument. Which Glasses won as Pink Hair sighed and nodded his way. "Please join us. It looks like it's my shout. I'm Kara, by the way."

Her sister would give her hell about having to buy the drinks, but she proved she knew how to Aussie. A shout was a round, and her sis was paying.

"Brian." Brian held out a hand, and Dare watched as Kara barely managed to avoid rolling her eyes before she shook it. "Brian Peters."

He said it in an almost James Bond way. It was good to know his friend could lose his mind over a woman. He'd kind of thought Brian was impervious.

It still felt weird. He looked down at Glasses, who seemed to be the only one enjoying herself. "I don't want to intrude."

"I'm Lou." She grinned up at him, and she was adorable. "This is my sister, Tasha. We're in town visiting Kara, who happens to be our cousin. It's our first night here. We thought it would be fun to hang out at a pub and meet the locals."

"They're not locals." Kara managed to make the words an obvious complaint.

He should introduce himself. It felt like he should. Like it was the polite thing to do. He pulled over a chair and placed it a distance from the table in between Lou and the brunette who was named Tasha. A pretty name for a gorgeous woman. Who wasn't interested in him.

"My name is Dare Nash, and I'm not a local. I'm in town for work. Brian and I work together," he explained, though he wasn't going into the ins and outs of what they did. It was a lot of boring banking stuff, and women tended to get glazed expressions when he detailed how investments moved the medical world. Being the guy who connected doctors to the funds they needed for research wasn't the sexiest job.

Tasha turned those soulful dark eyes on him, and he actually had to catch his damn breath. "It's nice to meet you, Dare. That's an interesting name."

Yep. Now that she was looking his way, all the thought of

leaving kind of flew out of his head. Sure she'd wanted Brian, but maybe she would settle for him, and then he would show her she wasn't settling at all. He would show her exactly how good he could be.

Gently. Without the nasty dominance he feared he required.

"It's far more interesting than my actual name. Darren," he admitted. "I'm afraid I come from a long line of Darrens. My family isn't creative. We use four names, recycling them over and over. The Nashes are all Johns or Darrens or Edwards or believe it or not, Hugos. Lucky for us we've never had more than four boys in a single family, but it can get confusing at family reunions. Apparently the Hugo comes from an ancestor who was a nobleman in England. Let me tell you that name might be fine if you live in medieval England and own all the land you see, but it's hell in a Toronto primary school. Ask my cousin."

Her lips had curled up slightly, her eyes brighter than before. "I thought Canadians were always polite."

Ah, she bought the myths. He could show her how polite he could be. He could politely order her to spread those long legs of hers and take his cock. Which was starting to ache, and he was kind of pissed about that. He wasn't the type of man who rubbed himself against any woman who came along. He was discriminating. A little picky, to be honest. "Oh, I can assure you Canadian kids are still kids, and they can be assholes when they want to. Tasha is a pretty name. Is it short for Natasha?"

She nodded. "Yes. My parents were interested in Russian literature."

Lou leaned in, a mischievous look on her face. "She's lying. They watched a lot of *Rocky and Bullwinkle*."

He was at a loss. "I'm sorry. That must be an American thing."

Tasha chuckled. "Not at all. It's a super-old thing that almost no one knows about anymore. My sister is a weirdo who watches a lot of old shows about…squirrels and their moose friends."

He was almost certain she'd been ready to say something else, but she took a drink of her beer and seemed to relax, so he wasn't about to call her out. Besides, he had some questions of his own. "Where are you from?"

"Dallas," Lou replied.

"Our mom's brother married a woman from here in New South Wales, and that is how we came to visit our cousin, Kara," Tasha finished, and she glanced over at the other end of the table. "Should we do something about that?"

Cousin Kara was staring at Brian like she was going to eat him alive, and not in a good way. Intimidating young woman.

Lou cleared her throat, and Kara suddenly leaned forward and put her chin in hand and managed to look like she was interested in what Brian was saying.

This was an odd group, and yet he couldn't quite make himself get up.

"So you're from Canada," Lou prompted. "Tasha loves Canada."

Tasha's nose wrinkled in the most adorable way. "I actually do. I went on a trip as a kid… Well, I was fourteen. My mom had some business there and we went to Toronto and she took us all over the city. We went to the CN Tower and to all the museums."

"We got lost at Casa Loma and our mom freaked," Lou reminisced. "But what Tash loved was…"

"…the crêpes," they both said with smiles.

Oh, he liked the sisters very much. He settled in as they started talking about their travels and realized it was okay if she wasn't into him. He was going to enjoy talking to her.

Two hours later, he pushed back his chair. Kara and Brian were at the dart board and she hadn't even stabbed him, so that seemed to be going well. Lou had walked outside because she'd gotten a call she said she couldn't refuse.

It was getting late, and Tasha had been incredibly gracious with her time despite the fact that she was simply entertaining the guy who was attached to the guy she was interested in. "I should get going. I've got a lot to do in the next couple of days. And let Lou know it was lovely talking to her. Both of you. Thank you for the nicest evening I've had in a long time."

He didn't want to go, but he'd caught Lou yawning behind her hand and stretching a couple of times as though she was ready for bed. Tasha was probably tired too, and honestly, he was feeling melancholy because she was the most intriguing woman he'd met in forever and she wasn't into him.

Looking at her kind of hurt because now he was absolutely certain he could be into her. She was funny and smart and had an interesting career. She worked with her sister at a security company, and they'd had the most amusing stories about the highs and lows of that world. He'd liked listening to her, liked being around her, and that made him a little sad.

He'd thought he was almost resigned to being alone, and Tasha made him feel it all over again.

"It was good to talk to you, Dare," she replied and held out her hand. "I hope your business here goes well."

He'd almost gotten away without touching her. He reached out and sure enough, he felt a spark go through him. Her hand was small and warm in his, and he couldn't resist covering it with his other hand so she was surrounded by him. "And I hope you enjoy your visit with your cousin."

He expected her to drag her hand away, but she stayed where she was, her eyes wide as she looked up at him. It was like she was seeing him for the first time. "I don't know if you'll be able to get him away from my…cousin. They seem cozy."

He was the one to let go of her hand. He liked holding it too much. He managed a half smile. "I don't know. I don't really think she's into him."

"Kara's hard to read sometimes." She stood up, and he realized she came to roughly his nose. She wasn't tiny but she looked that way to him. He knew in a logical way that she wasn't petite, but in that moment he felt like he could easily pick her up and run away with her.

And that was an excellent reason to walk away now. "And Brian apparently doesn't understand a good thing when he sees it. Good-bye, Tasha."

He turned and started to pull his cell out of his pocket. It was obvious Brian was going to keep trying to make time with the pink-haired beauty, but Dare was all tried out for the night. He would text Brian and let him know he would see him back at the hotel. Luckily they weren't rooming together so he wouldn't have to worry about Brian actually landing Kara. He wouldn't have to listen to those two go at it, and that was a good thing because he kind of thought it might get violent. And not from Brian's end.

Kara might be the kind of woman who didn't mind playing out a domination fantasy. Though he rather thought she would be the one dominating.

"Dare, wait." A soft hand found his elbow, causing him to stop.

Tasha. He turned and she was standing there, her head tilted up and eyes on him. "Yes?"

"I don't want you to leave," she began and then shook her head as though making a decision. "That's not exactly right. I don't want you to leave without me. I want you to take me back to your hotel room and let me get to know you better."

Fuck. It was the only thing he wanted to do tonight, and he suddenly worried he was on the edge. It had been so long since he'd indulged in sex. "I don't think that's a good idea."

A brow rose over her eyes, a clear challenge. "Because I was attracted to Brian first?"

He reached out, smoothing back her hair. He barely stopped himself from twining his fingers in the soft stuff and giving her a good tug. "Because what I want from you might be too much. Tasha, you might have wanted Brian, but I knew the minute I laid eyes on you that I wanted you. I wanted you in my bed, under me, over me, doing everything I tell you to do to me. I'm not like most of the men you know."

Her lips spread in the widest grin. "I think you're exactly like most of the men I know. Shall I call you Sir or do you have a different kink?"

She winked as she turned and strode boldly out the door, her hips swaying in a way that made his damn mouth water.

Holy shit. For a second, Dare stood there letting her words wash over him. And then his dick was hard as a rock and insistent on following her.

He was letting his dick lead the way.

What could possibly go wrong?

Chapter Two

Tasha made sure she was out the door before she brought her hand up to her earpiece.

"Hey, what was that?" Kenzie asked. "Are you going for it? Have Lou let you borrow the glasses."

Her sisters were so weird, and that was not happening. She did not need her sister watching in on what she hoped would be a steamy night. "Tell Kala and Lou I'll see them in the morning and not to track me. Bye."

She managed to toss the earpiece into the planter before Dare walked out of the pub, the lights and sounds swooshing closed behind him so all she could see for a moment was his big shadow.

He might not be as massively overgrown as Brian, but he was a big guy. And she'd been mistaken. Brian might be hotter at first glance, but she'd talked to Dare all night, and there was no way to deny she was more attracted to him. Her eyes were one thing, but they could be easily led by other instincts. After half an hour of talking to Dare, she'd forgotten about Brian. Dare was funny and sweet and apparently a top.

She liked a top. She wouldn't say she wanted a truly dominant partner in her normal life, but she appreciated being able to sink into submission. It was what she'd been missing with her fiancé. Well, that and actual love that included faithfulness and the fact that her parents and siblings and friends loathed him.

She wasn't thinking about him tonight.

"What did you mean by calling me *Sir*?" Dare's tone was far more demanding than she'd heard this evening. And he suddenly looked taller than he had before.

It was good to know she could surprise him. "I'll tell you everything you want to know if we can walk away from here right now. Unless you want my sister to tag along. Because she will."

He would think she meant Lou, but Tash was far more worried about Kala. Lou would retrieve her earpiece from the plant and probably go back to the safe house and be quiet in that way she always was after she talked to TJ. Tash was almost one hundred percent certain his was the number that had flashed on the screen of her cell phone. Lou'd had a massive crush on Tasha's cousin TJ Taggart since they were kids, and TJ was an asshole who kept her on a string. That was probably harsh, but TJ always gave Lou just enough to keep her close.

Lou would trust that she knew what she was doing, but Kala would follow her and watch her like a freaking hawk, and Tasha had done a lot to have one last night of freedom.

"I do not." There was a tightness to Dare's tone as he put a hand on her elbow and started to lead her away. When they got to the street, he held out a hand to hail a taxi. "Now tell me what you meant."

He was going to be so serious. It was funny because he hadn't been in the pub. He'd been light and focused on her in a way that made her flirty. She wondered how the other half of the man would look at her, how the Dom would focus on her like a predator about to catch a hearty meal. The thought made a delicious shiver go up her spine. "What club do you play at?"

"Club?" His hand fell and a taxi drove by. He practically growled and seemed determined to catch the next one. "Are you talking about a D/s club? How do you know about D/s clubs?"

She found it interesting that he referred to it as a D/s club and not a BDSM club. There was a difference between Dominance and submission and a club that focused more on bondage and sadomasochism. It was good he seemed to understand the subtlety because she was definitely more on the D/s side. Not that she'd had much D/s sex. Or sex at all. She was a founding member of a club—and it was not a rat-infested hellhole like her father said—and she'd only been a dozen times. "I pretty much grew up in one. Well, not in one. That sounds weird. I didn't like hang out there when people were playing. I did make a lot of money babysitting for those people though. My parents are a D/s couple. Not 24/7, but it's definitely part of their life."

A silver taxi pulled up and just in time because she caught a glimpse of Kala stalking out of the bar, her eyes narrowed as she started to look around, searching for her.

Dare opened the door and Tasha slid inside, scooting all the way over so he could tuck his big body in next to hers. "We're going to the Dolphin."

So he was staying at a hotel on the beach, and a nice one at that. There would be lots of CCTVs there for her sisters to track her on, and she had no doubt they would. She was sure Kala had already figured out where she was going. Not that she needed to ask. They all had trackers implanted in various places on their bodies at the insistence of their overly protective father.

I track the puppies I don't give a shit about, Tash. I'm damn straight going to track my daughters. You could have avoided this if you hadn't wanted to be a spy.

She wondered about that. She wouldn't put it past her father to have secretly implanted a tracker on her as a child.

Still, she felt some sense of independence as the driver took off, turning down the road that ran right past the pub. Her sister shot her the bird as she drove past. Tasha merely waved as Kala rolled her eyes and stalked back inside.

So she would keep her distance. For a while.

"You didn't answer my question." She was ready to focus on Dare. "Do you have a home club?"

"Home club?" He settled into his seat. "Like in my house?"

"No, I meant like a club you belong to," she corrected. "Like I belong to a club called The Hideout, but there are other clubs in other cities that honor my membership and would let me play there if I happen to be visiting."

She didn't mention that it wasn't The Hideout those other clubs honored. Their club was new and didn't have much of a membership yet. But the club her father had founded with his friends was known throughout that world. Sanctum.

Someday The Hideout would be every bit as respected as Sanctum. No matter what her dad said.

Dare frowned, and his voice went low. "Maybe we should talk about this when we get to my room."

"Why?" She didn't lower hers.

His head tilted toward the driver. "We're not exactly alone."

"I don't think the driver cares," she pointed out. Taxi drivers heard everything. And she didn't really care. It was their business, and she didn't see why some driver who overheard five minutes of their lives should care either.

"I care." His jaw went tight.

She studied him for a moment and realized this man didn't have a club at all. He was one of the two kinds of Doms her father had taught her to stay away from.

The fact that her father actually had a talk with her and her sisters about the types of tops and bottoms to avoid was proof that she had a weird family. Taggart Family Rules. There was a list of them, and while many of them were totally normal—clean up after yourself—there were some that probably didn't show up in other families. There were two types of tops her father had told her to avoid. One was the top who simply used the power exchange to control his or her partner without any thought to what the submissive needed. For some reason her dad called these the Storms of the world. She'd also been told to stay away from anyone who called themselves Storm.

The second was the top who was ashamed to be a top. There wasn't a lot of use for shame in her father's world.

The good news was she wasn't about to have an actual relationship with this man. She didn't have to save him from himself and teach him that his instincts weren't some evil thing that needed some sweet vanilla princess's love to vanquish them. All she wanted from this man was to have a great night and move on and hope he figured out a way to be comfortable in his skin, that he found the woman who helped him do that.

So she needed to decide if she wanted to spend the night with him or to pass and take this taxi right back to the safe house and the vibrator that would never once try to shame her.

Her mom had been the one to tell her what to look for in a vibe. That had been one deeply uncomfortable conversation, but that's what happened when your parents were the world's most sex positive couple. You got embarrassing discussions and conversations about birth control that she wished her brother would have listened to.

She sat back and respected Dare's boundaries on the short trip to the hotel, her mind going through all the options and how to handle this situation. He tried to make some awkward small talk about the pub they'd come from and how nice it was to be by the ocean. She murmured at the right times, but she had a decision to make.

It was no more than five minutes and they were there. He paid the fare as she stepped out and realized he'd been absolutely right about the ocean. She could feel a cool breeze on her skin, smell the salt in the air.

In a couple of days she would be stuck in the safe house with Lou. She would be careful, so careful. She wouldn't be able to focus on her body's needs. All that would matter was ensuring the mission went off without a hitch.

Because this was the first time she was running the op without her parents or her Agency bosses looking over her shoulder.

"Do you want to get a drink?" Dare stood in front of her, the doorman holding the ornate door for them. "We can talk about it in the bar if we keep it quiet."

She wasn't about to keep it quiet. A long sigh went through her, and she wondered if she shouldn't have given one of the rugby guys a try. She probably could have had a nice couple of hours by now, but no, she had to find the complex one. Not tonight. "I think I'm going to pass. I hope you have a good night, Dare."

Maybe she would walk on the beach for a while and that would settle this restlessness she felt. She could walk and then head back to the house and order pizza with Lou and they could watch whatever old spy show she was into at the moment and tomorrow she would settle into work. When they got back to Dallas, she would go to The Hideout or The Club and find a hot Dom and play to her heart's content.

"Why?" Dare's handsome face had gone a polite blank, but there was a wealth of ache in the question.

He really was a lovely man. Brian was a work of art, but Dare's rugged masculinity actually called to her more. It was the difference in appreciating a painting and being drawn to a real person. "I don't think you want to talk about this in front of the doorman, and I think I should walk away now."

"If I stand here and let you talk as much as you like, will you tell me? I'm sorry. I didn't mean to sound harsh. I'm used to keeping things like this private."

From everyone it seemed. "You're not comfortable. I understand. The problem is I am. I am perfectly comfortable talking about sex and what I want out of it. I'm not ashamed of my needs, and I won't apologize for them. I like some fairly rough D/s sex. I have a home club, and I've been to a couple of others. I've had three boyfriends over the years, though I only slept with two of them, and there was a guy back home I had a friends-with-benefits agreement with. So my body count is exactly three, though I've played with more tops than that. It doesn't always involve sex. I recently came out of a relationship that ended poorly, and I thought it would be nice to have a fun night with a guy I'm attracted to. No strings attached, but I've learned that men who aren't comfortable with themselves often throw that discomfort on their partners. So I'm not going to risk that."

"What do you think I would do?"

"Oh, any number of things. Disrespect my boundaries. Hurt me more than I want to be hurt. Call me all sorts of names. Make me feel used because if I'm a whore, you don't have to accept that the instincts you have are actually natural and okay. You can keep hating the instinct, but for a night you don't have to hate yourself because you can hate me."

He reached out and smoothed back her hair, an infinitely sad look coming over his face. "I would never think that, Tasha. Never. I'm sorry. This is a touchy subject for me. My ex-wife divorced me over it. I have gone to a club. There's one in Toronto, and do not make a joke about polite Canadians. I assure you I can be nasty if I want to. If you want me to. Please come upstairs with me. I think if you don't, I'll regret it for a long time. I'll honor your boundaries. Hell, I'll keep it vanilla if you don't trust me enough to play. Come up to my room and let me show you how good I can make you feel. Remind me how fucking good it can be when I'm not thinking about anything but how much pleasure I can give my partner."

He was staring down at her, and she no longer had to wonder what the man looked like when he was focused on sex. Her breath caught in her chest, and she could feel her nipples go hard.

She was pretty sure no walk on the beach would ease the ache she suddenly felt. It was low in her pelvis, but also somewhere close to her heart. How long had it been since she'd felt this deep longing? It wouldn't last for more than a night, but she wanted to sink herself into it, to revel in it and let herself float for a couple of hours. Submission could be like a drug, but the safe kind she could easily shake off when she needed to.

"That sounds like a right good offer," the doorman said with a nod and a smile like they'd been talking about going to brunch and not upstairs to fuck like rabbits.

Or maybe both were just damn fine offers.

Dare's cheeks were stained a light red, but he straightened up. "See, Tash, Giles here thinks you should."

He was trying. She could reward that, but she needed him to understand a thing or two. "Fine. I'll come upstairs with you, but you should understand that if you don't treat me well, I know how to twist a man's balls off and stuff them down his throat. Your dick and I can be friends or we can be something else."

"Fuck, Tash. Why does that do something for me?" His hand was at the back of her head, fingers slipping in and lightly twisting.

Had he forgotten they were in public? She didn't care. It honestly sent a thrill through her, and she didn't mind the idea that she could make this man forget all his uptight ways. She could also answer his question honestly. "Because you need a sub you believe will speak up when you go too far. I'm that sub, Dare. I can take care of myself, and you if I need to. Don't think your physical superiority will save you from me if I feel I'm in danger."

She might run the team from the shadows, but she'd been put through all the same training as the rest of them. She and Lou might look like the lightweights, but that's what made them excellent secret weapons.

"Friends," he whispered as he leaned over and his mouth moved in on hers. "I think we should definitely be friends. And Tash, call me Sir. I do have training, and I assure you I can control myself. That's what it's all about, isn't it? Exquisite control that leads to exquisite pleasure. Give over to me tonight and that's what you'll have, you magnificent brat. I'll make sure of it."

And then he kissed her, no mere brushing of lips. A hungry kiss that devoured her mouth, his tongue pushing inside, demanding and offering. Dominance and pleasure in exchange for submission and trust.

She could do that.

Her whole body went soft, her mind letting go of any notion of leaving him tonight. Tasha let her arms drift up around his neck as he pulled her close and kissed her over and over again, the soft sounds of the busy Sydney streets a soundtrack in the distance.

He pulled back, though his hands tightened around her waist. "Will you come up and play with me, Tasha?"

He was holding her like he was afraid to let her go. Yeah, that did something for her ego, too. "I will, Sir."

When he turned to go this time, her hand was in his and she followed.

* * * *

Dare managed to not fuck her in the lift, but the thought had crossed his mind.

This was a woman who knew what she wanted and didn't feel a second's regret about it. This was the kind of woman he could have found if he hadn't been stupid enough to listen to his father, who'd blackmailed him in the cruelest of ways into giving up what he'd wanted.

He wasn't thinking about that tonight. He wasn't going to allow the past to fuck over what looked like a very nice present.

"Do you have a sock?" Tasha asked as they stopped in front of his room and he tried not to fumble for the damn key card.

She was so fucking gorgeous, with her dark eyes and hair that still looked mussed from how long and hard he'd kissed her.

He wasn't sure he'd ever kissed a woman the way he had Tasha... "I don't know your last name."

"Smith," she replied.

Such a common last name. Probably why they'd named her Natasha and her sister Louisa. She'd asked him a question. "Why would I need a sock?"

His brain whirled, trying to figure out a sock kink.

"To let Brian know not to come in," she said, those full lips of hers curling up into the sexiest smile. "Unless that was your plan. Is ménage a kink of yours?"

He needed to make a few things plain to her here and now. She was a pixie brat who loved to tease him, and he could take that for the most part. He buried a hand in her hair because he'd noticed she enjoyed having it pulled. Her nipples had poked through that thin shirt of hers the minute he'd tugged on her hair. "No, it is not a kink of mine, Tasha. I don't share my partners. I certainly would never share my sub. That would be a hard limit for me."

Her eyes sparkled like she'd expected that response. "I think I can handle that, Sir."

Of course she could. This young woman seemed to be able to handle anything. She'd told him she worked for her father at his security firm, though she'd made it sound like she was more in an admin role. Whatever she did, Tasha came off as calm and ready for anything that might come her way. It was incredibly sexy to him. "Yes, I think you can, too. I'm not bunking with Brian. He's down the hall, and I already texted him to let him know I won't be up early."

He got the door open and she walked in, a hint of a smile on her face. "Presumptuous of you. This might all be over quickly and you could be asleep by ten."

She was asking for it, pushing all the right buttons, and he could feel something sweet and warm pierce his veins. It was hunger, but not overwhelming. The beast inside him suddenly knew it was going to finally be fed and was content to enjoy a slow, leisurely meal.

He was fucking comfortable with her, and he knew it was far too soon, but he was going with it tonight.

The universe had sent him so much shit, so much tragedy and heartache. Maybe he was due some small amount of joy.

He followed her inside and carefully placed the *Do Not Disturb* sign on the door before locking it. It was kind of the high-class version of a sock.

His heart was pounding in a low-key pleasant manner, his cock tightening. Simmering. Not exploding. In control. He felt perfectly in control.

Why did he even question himself? He'd never attacked a sub. When he was younger he'd been on a path to being an excellent top, and he'd let life derail him.

He hadn't *let* anything derail him. He'd had no choice.

"Dare, do you want to talk about it?" Tasha stood in the entryway of the big suite that had seemed ridiculous at the time and now felt perfect because he could show her how nice it might be to be his sub.

Except you would have to hide her or your father would find a way to destroy her.

"I don't, sweetness." He shoved all the bad shit to the back of his head. "It doesn't matter tonight. All that matters is you and how fucking gorgeous you are. Can we agree that once you walk into the living area, we're playing and basic rules apply?"

For a moment she looked like she would argue, would demand that they pick at that wound that never seemed to close, but then her shoulders relaxed. "I never did like basic, Sir, but I can handle that this evening. I prefer to have options, so I would like to use the stoplight system, though if I say red I mean it."

She wanted the opportunity to slow him down. He would like that as well. But she should understand a few things. "I won't make you even come close to saying red. It's been a long time since I played. I'll be extremely bossy during sex, but I won't go far past that. I'm afraid I don't even have a kit anymore."

"I think you could be creative if you wanted to, but I'll take what I can get," she replied, moving into his space. "How about we D/s light for the evening? You be your bossy self and understand that I enjoy a bite of pain. That thing you did with my hair was perfect. I'd like for you to twist my nipples, too."

He hissed as his cock went full-on eager puppy and all the blood in his body seemed to go right to his groin. "You're going to kill me, Tash. I don't think I've ever met a woman like you."

"See, if you'd stayed at your club, you'd probably be surrounded by them and I wouldn't be such a glorious revelation." Those dark tresses shook as she smiled and turned and walked purposefully into the big living area of the suite.

Because she was a woman who knew what she wanted, and fuck all, he was happy she wanted him tonight. She was exactly that. A glorious revelation. He'd kissed the hell out of her right in front of anyone walking down the street, and he hadn't thought about anything but how soft and hot her mouth was and how those luscious lips would feel wrapped around his cock. The world had floated away, or even if it hadn't, he hadn't given a damn what anyone thought.

It was freeing.

He followed her into the living area. The room had obviously been cleaned and turned down because the shades were drawn, but during the day they opened and gave a spectacular view of the beach. He wondered what she would look like wrapped up in a robe, drinking coffee as they stared out at the beach in the morning.

His company did some business in Dallas. This didn't have to be a one-night stand. She was here in Sydney for a couple of weeks. Maybe he could stretch his time here, too.

She glanced around. "You're not some low-level employee, are you, Dare?"

He didn't want to go into his family. If he had his way, she would never get anywhere near those sharp-toothed sharks. His family was proof that not all Canadians were kind and pleasant to be around. They could be ruthless as well. "I do okay. This was kind of a last-minute gig, so we took what was available. Take your clothes off, Tasha."

"Impatient man," she murmured. "I thought you wanted to have a drink and talk about things."

"That was before you pushed my every button, so now I want you naked." Was she going to push him even further? He wasn't sure he could stand it if this all turned out to be one big tease.

Did she know who he was? Who his family was? Hell, she could have been sent here by his family. It wouldn't be the first time one of the fuckers tried to control him through blackmail. Or sent in a woman to spy on him.

The sweetest smile hit her face, and she started to unbutton her blouse. "Yes, Sir. I think we've talked enough."

When she smiled like that, all his suspicions flew out of his head. When she smiled, he didn't care who'd sent her as long as he got to have her.

She removed her blouse, carefully folding it, and then her shoes and the jeans that hugged her every curve. She was wearing a lacy pink bra and some nothing underwear, and she looked like she was a package wrapped and waiting for him. The best present ever.

He knew he should wait, but he was working on impulse tonight. He moved into her space, letting his hands run down to her hips as he kissed her again. Her head tilted up, mouth softening and allowing his tongue to slide along hers.

"I didn't mean to push your buttons," she whispered as he kissed her cheek and up to her ear.

He nipped her lobe, a quick bite that had her gasping and shivering in his arm. "I think you did. I think you knew exactly how to get me to do what you wanted."

"I wanted you to loosen up," she replied. "That was all. I wanted you to see that we can meet our needs and it doesn't have to be drenched in shame. Whatever we do together is okay. As long as we both want it."

"I want you. I want you more than I've wanted anything in a long time." He didn't mention to her that he rarely allowed himself to want anything at all because wanting something, loving something or someone, gave his father another hold over him.

"I want you to do that again." Her eyes had gone soft. "I want you, too."

It was all he needed. He pulled his shirt over his head and tossed it aside before leaning over to pick her up. She was a sweet handful in his arms. He'd intended to get her on her knees, but he couldn't wait. The cautious, wary man he usually was had fled, and in his place was this hungry Dom who wanted nothing more than to taste his sub.

He kicked the door to the big bedroom open.

Tasha's eyes were wide as he moved into the space. "You picked me up."

"It's the easiest way to get you where I want you," he admitted.

"No one's ever picked me up." She'd flushed and for the first time seemed the slightest bit unsure.

"Ah, so those Doms at your club aren't the smartest in the world because my first thought when I saw you was that I should throw you over my shoulder and carry you off into the night." He'd thought maybe it would be good to simply run away and leave behind all the weight of his responsibility. Even if only for a day or two.

"I…" she started and then her mouth closed. "I like it."

He set her down on the bed and loomed over her. "That's not what you were going to say."

She stared up at him with gorgeous, innocent eyes. "I'm smart enough to know not to say what I was going to say."

She wasn't tiny. She was actually kind of muscular, but she would always have curves unless she starved herself. "You're not heavy, Tash. At least not to me. I know I'm not crazy muscular like Brian, but you'll figure out I'm more than strong enough to carry you around like the submissive princess you should be. Take off the bra if you want me to play with your nipples."

She had that bra off in seconds, and those breasts were every bit as gorgeous as he'd thought they would be. Tasha had tan lines, golden skin fading to lighter where the cups of her bikini top would be. It made her breasts stand out, the dusky pink nipples tight and puckered.

Her legs opened, letting him move between them. He was the one who dropped to his knees, putting his mouth right where he wanted it. His body felt electric as he leaned forward and licked one nipple. "Lean back and don't move."

The sweetest whimper came out of her mouth, but she did as he asked, thrusting her breasts out and offering them up to him.

He traced the nipple with the tip of his finger and loved the moan she made. His cock was hard as a rock, and it would have to fucking wait because he wanted her every bit as hot for him as he was for her. Another touch and then he pinched down, twisting lightly.

Her whole body jerked and she gasped, and her feet moved against him as though she needed the contact.

"You like it when your Dom twists these pretty nipples any way he wants?"

"Yes," she said between clenched teeth. "I like it. I love it."

He moved to the opposite nipple and gave it the same attention, and that was when he felt how wet she was. Her pussy rubbed against him, right above his belt buckle, and those pink undies of hers were already soaked.

Fuck, if that didn't make him feel ten feet tall.

How would she like it if he put those pretty nipples in clamps and made them bounce as he fucked her hard? They would get so red, and he would have to soothe the ache with his tongue. He would have to give her so much sweet aftercare.

He pushed up a breast, weighing it in one hand before licking around her areola. Then he set his teeth and gave her a nip.

"Fuck," she said, her legs tightening around him.

"Such a filthy mouth," he whispered as he moved back to the other breast. "I'm going to have to find a way to occupy it."

"Yes." The affirmation was out of her mouth quickly. "Absolutely, Sir. You should put something in my mouth. Something big and hard. That will teach me."

He couldn't help but chuckle. Such a brat, and she wasn't getting that tonight. He wasn't sure he could last tonight, but in the morning he would put her to work before he brought them breakfast and treated her like the princess she was. His pretty princess. "Lie back. All the way, Tasha."

A growl came from her throat, but she did as he asked, allowing him to kiss his way down her torso.

He breathed in the scent of her arousal. Damn, but she smelled good. Like sex and longing.

He moved back and then dragged the pretty panties off her hips and down her legs.

She wouldn't need them.

He didn't have to be anywhere this weekend. He might keep her naked the whole time.

He leaned over, ready to begin.

Chapter Three

Tasha sank her hands into the soft duvet and gritted her teeth as Dare spread her legs wide.

He was going to kill her.

It had been way too long since she'd had a lover who actually took his time with her. This was something else that had been missing. Sex had been good, but this felt like something else. This felt like she was the center of the fucking universe, a goddess to be worshipped and adored.

And teased and tortured.

When he'd picked her up and carried her across the room... That moment had been so sweet. He was the perfect amount of nasty Dom and sweet potential boyfriend.

He's not going to be your boyfriend, Tash. You have a job to do. Tonight is all you get.

But did it have to be?

Warmth suffused her as he lowered his mouth to her pussy. She'd taken care earlier with grooming, and now she was damn happy because she could feel his breath on every inch of her bare flesh.

"This is a pretty pussy," he whispered, the words rumbling across her skin.

She was feeling pretty. Pretty and sexy and so, so submissive. She wished he had a kit because she would let him tie her up and push his cock inside anywhere he wished. If he blindfolded her, she wouldn't know where it would come from. She would be helpless and waiting to see where her Master would invade.

She had some pretty specific fantasies, and now she realized she'd kind of given up on them because they hadn't been interesting to her partner.

She'd given up a lot of herself. She'd gotten lost in planning a wedding when she should have been thinking about the marriage and what it would cost her.

And then she wasn't thinking at all because Dare licked her pussy, his tongue sliding through her labia and up to tease at her clit.

"Damn, sweetness, you are so fucking wet. It's intoxicating," he said before giving her another long lick of that strong tongue of his.

She gripped the duvet because if she didn't, she might float away. Or grab Dare's head in an attempt to force him to fuck her with his tongue. That would lead to him stopping and turning her over and slapping her ass for a while, and that sounded like fun, but maybe later.

Her body was taut and wanting, impatient for the release it had needed for months and months.

"You taste like heaven." His hands parted her labia as his tongue explored every inch of her sensitive flesh. He licked and sucked and nibbled as one big finger began to tease her opening.

He felt like heaven. She couldn't do anything but groan against the delicious sensation of Dare making a feast of her pussy.

She bit her bottom lip to keep from screaming out as he gently took her clitoris between his teeth and gave her a sweet tug that lit her up. Fire crashed through her, and he took that moment to fully seat his finger, curling it up inside her like the cock that would come soon.

"I want you to come all over my tongue. Give it to me." His tongue played with her clit while his finger pierced her pussy, rubbing her in all the right places.

She felt her back bow as the orgasm hit her. It sizzled along her spine and burst over her, making her vision go soft.

"That's what I wanted." He placed a kiss on her pussy before standing up and looming over her.

Without the overgrown Brian beside him for comparison, she could see how big Dare was. Big and strong, with a lean, muscular chest and beautifully made shoulders. He'd carried her like she didn't weigh a thing. Now he looked like some dark god standing over her, ready to demand his pleasure.

She would give it to him. The man had earned it. And she'd been serious before. She wanted his cock in her mouth, wanted to pleasure him every bit as much as he had her.

But this was a bossy Sir, and she would have to wait.

"Sit up, Tasha."

The deep timbre of his voice had her doing his bidding despite the fact that she could sink into this bed. She felt boneless from the orgasm, but she managed to sit up. She found herself right at chest level and allowed her hands to skim his lean waist as she nuzzled him.

"So affectionate," he murmured.

"Yeah. An orgasm will do that to me," she admitted, though the truth of the matter was she was an affectionate person in her routine life. She'd been hugged a lot as a kid, and it made her cuddly. "It's been a long time since I felt this good, Dare. I needed that."

The world and all her responsibilities had fallen away, and she could breathe for a moment. There was no anxiety in this place, no questions running through her head. She was able to focus on her body and his. Nothing else.

His hands sank into her hair. "I'm glad. Now you can focus on me."

She perked up, tilting her head toward him to show how genuinely enthusiastic she was. "I can do that."

His head shook, and he leaned over to brush his lips against her forehead. "You know exactly how to make me feel good. Now I want you to carefully lower the zipper of my jeans."

Her attention focused down on the fly of his denims. His cock was pressed against them, tenting the pants out. There was a reason he'd used the word *careful*. Gently she unhooked the fly and started to ease the zipper down. He wore white boxers under his jeans that contrasted with the tan of his skin. She let her fingers slip between the boxers and his hips, gently shoving them down and freeing his cock. His beautiful, straining cock.

His hands were smoothing over her hair as she let her fingertips brush over him for the first time. The muscles of his stomach contracted, but he managed to stay still as she explored him. She palmed his cock, loving the feel of silky skin covering that hard muscle she would enjoy soon. She stroked him, feeling him strain to stay still. When she looked up, his eyes were closed, jaw straight and tight. There was such power in this position.

"I think you're beautiful, Dare." It was only the truth. She'd been taught that it was important to be honest with her partner about what she didn't like and more importantly, what she did.

His eyes opened, an infinite warmth in his gaze. "I think you're everything, Tasha, and if you don't stop that, I'm going to come in your hand."

"I don't see anything wrong with that." She kept stroking him. Her hand moved from his plum-shaped cockhead to the strong base and back again. Leisurely. Like they had all the time in the world. "I bet you have a gorgeous bathroom in this monstrosity. We can clean up and then get dirty again. I'm in no hurry."

He stepped back and started taking off the rest of his clothes. He toed out of his sneakers. "We'll get to that bathroom, and yes, it is spectacular. But I'm not coming in your hand. I'm going to get inside you, sweetness. I'm going to make you come for me again and again until you fall asleep, and in the morning, I'll do it all over again."

That sounded perfect. Except for the morning part. She would have to leave. Maybe she could wait a few hours, get back to base around noon or so. She shoved the thoughts out of her head. There wasn't a place for them tonight. Tonight she didn't run a CIA team. There was no mission to prepare for, no targets to acquire. Tonight she was simply Tasha, Dare's play partner for the evening. The only thing that mattered was enjoying herself and ensuring his pleasure.

If he wanted to fuck her, she was ready. He'd made sure she was. Her nipples hardened again, and she felt a pleasant rush of arousal as she watched him go to what had to be the bathroom. He was back in seconds with a condom in hand. She moved up on the bed and spread her legs like the good sub she was, ready and eager for whatever her Master could give her. In this case, a spectacular cock.

He rolled the condom on and then stopped at the edge of the bed, staring at her. "Do you have any idea how hot you are? You are pretty much my every fantasy in one gorgeous package."

That made her smile. Not every man appreciated her easy sexuality. "Back at you."

"I doubt that, but you are mine," he said quietly, and then he was crawling up on the bed, covering her with his body.

He pressed her into the mattress, making a place for himself between her legs. He kissed her as his cock brushed against her pussy. His tongue invaded, and she shuddered because she could feel that kiss in her toes. And then she wasn't thinking about anything but how it felt to have his cock inside her.

He thrust up, making her gasp against his mouth and tighten her arms around him.

"That's what I want. You feel so good," he whispered against her mouth. "Knew you would feel perfect."

She was so wet, so ready that there wasn't any discomfort despite his size. There was only heat and the pleasant feeling of being stretched, and then he thrust back up and she wound her legs around his waist.

He pressed up and she matched him, his cock finding her sweet spot while his pelvis pressed on her clit. It wasn't long before she was flying all over again, this orgasm even stronger than the last. She held on as he gritted his teeth and held himself tight against her, giving her everything he had.

When he fell on top of her, she welcomed his weight. It felt good. Grounding. Like she was in a good place and she should stay right here.

He nuzzled her neck. "You are too good to be true, Tasha."

She wasn't, and he would find that out in the morning.

But for tonight, she simply wanted to revel in him.

* * * *

Tasha slipped out into the hallway, a tight feeling in her gut.

Dare was asleep in the room behind her. She'd stared at him after she'd quietly gotten dressed. He'd been on his stomach, his arm outstretched as though he was reaching for her. The sheet had barely covered that muscled ass of his, and his beautiful back was on full display. Her heart seized while she watched him sleep. She didn't want to leave him. He'd done everything he'd promised the night before. He'd picked her up—a move that did something for her—and carried her to a bathroom fit for royalty and indulged her every sense. After she'd fallen asleep, he'd woken her up and made love to her all over again, and the fact that she was thinking those words instead of using the word *sex* was a good reason for her to run.

Her hand held the door open, trapped between duty and what she wanted. As long as the door was open, she could sneak back into bed and pretend she'd never made the decision to leave him. She should wait until he was awake. She should crawl back into bed and spend the day with him. There was a chance she could see him again before she…

What? Moved on to the next mission, which would take her somewhere else across the globe? She would have to lie to him about almost everything in her life. He could never know her family, her real job, her friends. If he lived in Dallas, they might be able to have a relationship they kept to the club, but she doubted he would settle for that.

She didn't want to settle for that.

"You okay?"

She nearly jumped out of her skin, and the door snicked closed behind her, all choice now taken away. It was probably for the best because walking back in would have been a huge mistake. "Damn it, Kala. You nearly gave me a heart attack."

Her sister stood by the elevator, wearing exactly what she'd worn the night before. "That's why I'm here, big sis. Thought you wouldn't be in a proper frame of mind to get yourself home."

Or had there been something else behind it? "Did you stay with Brian?"

Kala's eyes rolled as she hit the button to call the elevator. "I let him buy me another drink and then I walked out on him when he went to use the bathroom. And I gave him a totally fake number. That man was trying too hard and totally not my type."

Kala's type was extremely specific. Cooper McKay. Always Cooper. Never Cooper. It was complex, and Tasha wasn't totally sure anyone knew the whole story beyond the two of them. It wasn't like they hadn't dated other people. They had. Technically they had never dated each other, but there was no denying the gravity that formed between them. Cooper and Kala were two planets who couldn't quite get out of the other's grip, and one day they would either be free or they would crash together and destroy each other.

"Did you sit outside the door all night?"

Kala shrugged. "Nah. I went back to base and slept for a couple of hours. I figured you'd be a while. He looked clingy."

He'd been amazingly clingy. "He's a top."

The elevator doors opened, and they stepped inside, Kala's lips curling up. "Seriously? Like a trained top? Way to gravitate toward our dad."

"Ewww." Tasha shuddered. "He is nothing like Dad, thank you very much. He's polite and nice. And you're talking, Mistress Kala?"

That earned an outright grin from her sister. "I simply find it interesting that you have all of Sydney to pick from and you find a Dom." The doors closed, and the elevator started the inevitable drop to the lobby. "You know that's the reason it didn't work with Asshat."

She should have known Kala would bring this up now. "I thought it didn't work with Chet because he was a cheater."

"Well, that, too, but even if he'd been the sweetest guy with monogamy in his heart, it wouldn't have worked with him," Kala argued. "Besides Kenz, you are absolutely the subbiest chick I know when it comes to sex. You're wired that way, and maybe you could have settled for less if you hadn't been raised by the Dr. Ruth of his generation."

She had to snort at the image of their six and a half foot, looked-like-he-ate-nails-for-breakfast father as a small German sex therapist in a fussy suit, but it was kind of true. "Well, you might be right about that. Dare Nash was exactly what I needed."

"And that's why I'm asking if you're okay," Kala said, her tone going serious.

She was quiet for a moment. "I was wondering if maybe it wouldn't hurt if I saw him again."

A low groan came out of her sister's mouth. "Damn it."

It was stupid, and she wasn't about to let her team down. "I know. I can't."

"Tash, you know how many great things I want for you, but I think it would be a mistake to try to live two lives in the middle of a mission. I should know because I only get to live half of one, and it's still hard as hell," Kala replied. "This is our first mission without heavy oversight…"

And Kala wanted it that way. They all loved their dad and mom, and Drake and Taylor Radcliffe were great liaisons with the Agency, but the team wanted some leeway. They'd spent two years with their parents directing their every move and Drake and Taylor supervising from Langley. This was the first time they were on their own. It was an easy op that could get real complex if she started fucking up. She took a long breath as the doors opened again. "You're right. The op is way more important, and it's not like I'm in love with the guy. He was great in bed, and I needed that. He was also excellent at stroking my ego. Now I'm absolutely sure of what I need, and when we get back to Dallas, I'll let Coop set me up with one of his friends."

"Good. We've got a couple of tops I really like," Kala said as they walked into the beautiful lobby. "And one of them is a doctor. Well, he's going to be a doctor. He's in the same residency program as Aidan and Carys. Oooo, everyone loves a doctor, Tash. Mom would be so proud."

She could see out of the front window that there was a car waiting, a convertible with a familiar driver in the front seat. "You called Tris?"

Kala shrugged. "Thought it would be more fun than taking a cab. And he's promised us mimosas. I thought Lou could use a nice brunch. She was quiet last night. Fucking TJ."

Tasha stepped out into the early morning light, followed by her sister.

Tristan Dean-Miles sent them a heart-stopping smile. He had curly dark hair and green eyes that sent almost every woman in a two-mile radius into a swoon. Lou was in the back, wearing a T-shirt and jeans and some sunglasses that looked designer and were almost surely Kenzie's.

"Hey, Tash. The walk of shame looks good on you. I hope you have a lot to be ashamed of," Tristan said with a wink. "So much shame."

There wasn't a whole lot of that kind of shame in Tristan's life lately. Tristan had been in love with her cousin Carys since they were kids. Despite his sunny smile, she knew the distance had put a strain on their relationship. Tristan, Carys, and Aidan O'Donnell had been something of a threesome since high school. Carys and Aidan had gone to college and then medical school together, and Tristan had joined the Army after they'd graduated and then the Agency team. And now they barely talked, and Carys and Aidan were planning a wedding that did not include Tris.

They were all fucked up. Maybe not Kenz, but the rest of them were all kinds of screwed up, and they needed her. This was her family. Her team.

Dare Nash was a magnificent man, but she had to focus on her team and the mission. She hopped into the back with Lou, letting Kala have the front. "I did many shameful things last night, brother, and I regret not a one. Now I was promised mimosas. How did you manage to get away without Kenzie?"

That girl loved a mimosa.

"Snuck out while she was sleeping," Kala revealed. "A little like you. She'll be pissed, but I'll bring her waffles. They have waffles here? It's not all kangaroo meat and Vegemite, right?"

So like their dad. "Dumbass. They have waffles. And Vegemite's not bad. You put too much on. You need a thin layer."

"I like their lollies." Lou seemed to perk up. "That's what they call candy."

"I like everything," Tristan announced as he pulled away from the hotel. "We've got sun and a beach, and the parents are either back at Langley or hanging out in Loa Mali about ten hours away. Freedom. I love it."

She didn't look back, though she'd lied about one thing. She did regret leaving him. Tasha worried she might regret that for the rest of her life.

* * * *

She was gone.

When he'd woken up, he'd thought she was in the bathroom or she'd slipped out of bed to watch the beach. It was kind of mesmerizing to watch the waves in the soft morning light. He'd gotten up and gone to join her, fully meaning to haul his wayward sub back to bed and give her a stern talking to about leaving her Dom all alone in the morning.

Except she hadn't been standing by the windows. She hadn't been in the suite at all, and that was when he'd realized her clothes and her purse were gone.

His cell phone buzzed, and it took him a moment to register the sound. Then he ran over to it like an eager puppy because it could totally be Tasha calling to explain why she'd had to leave.

Except she didn't have his number.

Fuck. Had he been played again?

He groaned as he realized it was his father on the other end of the line. Dare knew to take the damn call or his father would send someone on the hotel staff up to "check on him," i.e. force him to answer. He put the phone on speaker even though he knew his father hated that. "This is Dare."

No happy *hello, Dads* for him. He knew exactly how to talk to his father if he didn't want a lecture on how to be a real man.

"Dare, I know you're only supposed to meet with some clients at this thing, but something else has come up. I'm going to need you to step in for Lance, which means I'll need you circulating at the conference." His father wasted no time. "He's been cozying up to this doctor from Quebec. Runs a foundation. A couple of decades ago they were stationed in Toronto. He moved the whole operation to Montreal when he took over."

He knew it well. Dare walked back into the bedroom and slipped into his jeans. "The Huisman Foundation. Yes, I certainly know who Emmanuel Huisman is."

The man had become something of a celebrity in the last few

years. The Huismans were ultra-wealthy, but Emmanuel was the last of his line and had a rather tragic backstory. His father had been killed while attempting to commit a crime, and Emmanuel had been brought up by his grandparents in the shadow of that shame.

Now that he thought about it, he and Huisman might have a lot in common.

"Then you should know how powerful they are in the field of medical technology. I want to be in business with the foundation," his father stated bluntly. "He's going to be honored at the conference, and then there's going to be a big party for him hosted by some Aussie billionaire, and you're going to go in Lance's place. It's a house party over a weekend, so you should be able to spend some real time with him. You're going to figure out what Huisman needs and give it to him."

"What happened with Lance? I'm supposed to be back home next week." If he wasn't there, no one would go to his sister's school play. No one would make sure his brother had his shit together for class.

"I need you in Australia." His father had his stubborn tone on full volume. "We need to get in good with Huisman, and honestly it should be you. Lance isn't a Nash. He shouldn't have been representing us in such a fashion. I know what you're worried about. I'll hire someone to help Johnny if you do this for me. Someone full time. Someone you approve of and who has the right credentials, and I'll pay for a year up front."

Damn it. His brother was recently out of rehab and lived life on a knife's edge. A full-time sober-living companion would take so much pressure off Dare. His father always knew how to keep him on a damn string. "And Gina?"

"What about her? She's not a junkie who needs a mommy to keep her safe," his father said with a nasty chuckle and then a sigh. "Ah, you're talking about the play thing. Fuck all. I don't think anything is worth sitting through a bunch of teens doing *Romeo and Juliet*."

Not a surprising attitude from the man who'd missed his valedictorian speech because it sounded like a bore. "Then I guess you don't mind me not getting close to Huisman."

"I'll send Lauren," his father countered. They were in full-on negotiations now. This was his family life.

His stepmother was only a few years older than he was, but she actually did seem to care about Gina. Johnny was another thing altogether. She was always complaining about him, but she was okay with Gina. "All right, but she has to buy the recording. They'll sell it at the snack bar. If you do those things, I'll stay, but Brian stays with me, and he gets his per diem for the whole time."

He didn't want to do this alone, and despite last night, Brian was actually a pretty charming guy. He was a guy's guy and might have some good insight on how to handle Huisman.

Maybe she'd left a note. He hadn't thought about that. Something could have come up and she left a note.

"I'll let HR know," his father agreed. "Get this done for me, Dare. I want this, and you know what can happen when I don't get what I want."

His siblings suffered. Always. "I'll get it done."

"And when you get back, I've got a couple of women I'd like you to meet. You fucked things up with Audrey, but you're not getting any younger," his father said. "I want you married to a proper wife within a year, and this time no fucking around. She needs to be pregnant shortly after."

His gut tightened and he wanted to punch a wall, but that wouldn't help things. "Sounds like fun."

Any argument wouldn't hurt him. An argument would mean Johnny was out on the streets or Gina would be pulled out of the school she loved. His father had learned a long time ago they were the best way to control him.

"I know you hate me, son, but one day you'll thank me." His father hung up.

Dare threw his cell phone across the room, barely missing Brian, who was walking in.

"Whoa." Brian was dressed for the day and looking picture perfect. "That feels like a statement. I take it the date didn't go as well as I thought it had."

Dare shook his head, trying to regain control. "Not at all. The date went fine. How are you in here? When did I give you a key?"

Brian smiled and walked over to the couch, throwing his big

body on it while he held up a familiar-looking card. "Convinced the lovely lady downstairs I left something in here and desperately needed it. I knocked twice and when you didn't come, I used this. I was worried. Don't get her fired. I'm convincing when I want to be. Now if the date went so well, why was our luscious Tasha sneaking out at seven a.m.?"

"How did you know that?" He didn't ask the question he wanted to ask. How did she look? Happy? Sad? Where did she go? Did she say anything?

"I was down in the lobby when her cousin showed up. I might have followed her from a distance," Brian admitted. "Kara showed up around six thirty, and she and Tasha left just after seven. Do you think they were in here? Do you have anything they could have taken?"

He hadn't even thought about that, which proved what a moron he was. No wonder Brian had gotten a key. He probably thought Tasha had rolled him and he might have been looking for a dead body. "I've got a couple hundred in the safe. Everything else is credit cards."

"I'm not worried about them rolling you for cash, man," Brian replied. "You have access to some big bank accounts on that laptop of yours. You have information on some of the wealthiest men in the world."

The thought made his stomach roll. He hadn't thought of that either. "You think they were corporate spies?"

"I'm merely going through scenarios, Dare. I was surprised she didn't stay, and I watched her drive off with Kara, her sister, and some guy."

Some guy.

"Or she's a nice woman who wanted a fun night and then her family came and picked her up," Brian offered. "It's the more logical reasoning."

"My laptop is in the safe, too." She wouldn't have been able to get to it. Even if she had, it was encrypted. She would have needed way more than thirty minutes to break through his security.

He moved to the safe and ensured everything was there and as it should be.

And that was when he saw it. A folded piece of paper on the

desk against the wall. He picked it up, his heart breaking a little.

Dare,
Thank you for the best night I've had in a long time, Sir. I wish
you all the best and hope you continue to follow your instincts.
You're an excellent top, and there's nothing wrong with that. You
made this sub very happy for a night.
Much love, Tasha

He sighed and sank down on the couch beside Brian. She hadn't been here to steal secrets. Her cousin had likely been worried and come to pick her up. He had no idea who the guy had been, but somehow he didn't think Tasha would have cheated on a boyfriend.

She was open and honest. She was beautiful and comfortable with herself.

She was gone, and that was probably a good thing because his father would be watching now.

"You wanted to see her again?" Brian asked.

It was morning and that meant it was time to get realistic. "No. It was a nice night but it's time to get to work. My father called."

Brian nodded sagely. "Ah, that explains the cell phone as a projectile. What does he want?"

"We're staying here for at least an extra week. We're supposed to get close to Emmanuel Huisman."

"The Huisman Foundation guy? The one who wrote that book?"

"That very one," he agreed. "You're staying with me, so we should get to work. I need to know everything I can about him."

"I can help you there," Brian replied. "I'll order some breakfast and we'll hit the Internet. And don't count her out, Dare."

His friend was being a bit too optimistic now. "I think she has what she wanted out of me."

"And I think absence will make the heart grow fonder and we'll see her again," Brian countered. "Or hornier. Were you terrible?"

He shot his friend what the Americans affectionately called "the bird." "It was good. Better than your night. Unless a miracle happened, but I don't think so since you had to stalk Kara when she got here."

Brian's lips kicked up. "Oh, I would have such fun stalking that girl. It's the hair. Give me a magenta girl anytime, and no, she was not interested. But I can change her mind."

He seemed to have a death wish. "Or you could take a hint and leave her alone."

Brian shrugged. "How about I'll take another shot if she shows up again? Let's agree to that. Now let's figure out this Huisman guy. Do you want pancakes? Toast?"

Brian picked up the phone to order breakfast, but Dare's mind was on Tasha.

The one who got away.

Chapter Four

Tasha checked over her presentation. Everyone was in place with the exception of Cooper, which was surprising because it was usually Kala or Tristan who showed up late to a briefing. Kala did it to piss off their dad. Tristan sometimes got lost in his work, spending endless hours on the Dark Web. Cooper was almost always early, but not today.

"I get to go in tomorrow." Kenzie stared at her twin over the conference room table.

They were in this spacious house thanks to the Agency. Tasha was certain they'd selected this place for the fact that it had an actual conference room rather than the tiny bedrooms they all got to share.

"Nope. It's my day tomorrow," Kala replied.

Zach sat at the head of the table. He was a few years older than Tasha, making him the senior in the room at the ripe age of twenty-nine. Zach was a stunning man with dark hair that started to curl when he let it grow out and deep brown eyes more than one target seemed to get lost in. He was like an extra brother, and he groaned as the twins started to argue.

It had been two days since she'd woken up and walked away from Dare, and she hadn't stopped thinking about him for one single minute. Even as she was preparing for tomorrow's first contact with the target, she'd had Dare on her mind.

Had he gotten her note? Did he understand how sincere she was? Or had he not even cared because he'd gotten what he wanted?

"Yeah, but it was my day two days ago and you stole it and got mimosas and you got to meet Hot Brian, and all I've gotten to do is go grocery shopping with Lou," Kenzie shot back. "I should have gotten to be the one to comfort our sister when she lost the man she's obviously in love with."

Kenzie was overly dramatic. Tasha hadn't even thought the word *love*. She'd thought the words *adore* and *wild about* but not *love*. Yet. "I just met him."

Zach snapped his fingers and pointed her way, giving her an approving nod. "I can always count on Tash to be reasonable."

"It doesn't matter," Kenzie insisted. "You looked at each other across a crowded pub and you knew."

Her sister was also a bit of a romantic.

"Uhm, she looked across the pub and saw Brian and drooled a bit and then settled for Dare." Tristan yawned and sat back in his chair, placing a mug of coffee on the table. It would be mostly cream and sugar, but Tristan drank it every morning.

"I did not." She hadn't settled at all.

"That's what Lou told me," Tristan countered with a shrug. "And I think Kenz should get to go out tomorrow, but it's mostly because she whines when she's stuck inside."

"Do you want to know what I'll do?" Kala asked, menace in her tone.

Tristan sniffled, and his eyes drifted closed. "Probably stab someone. If it's going to be me, go for the ears then I don't have to listen to Kenz talk about dudes she's never even met before. Also, Tash, you are not in love with this guy. Like you said, you just met him. I'm glad the sex was good, but his family is a fucking mess and a half, so you need to run and fast."

"You did a deep dive on him?" It was surprising because she had been careful to avoid mentioning Dare since that night. She'd been all about the op.

He looked half asleep, but that was part of Tristan's act. He was the pretty boy no one thought had a brain in his head or a dangerous bone in his body right up until he snuck in and took out the bad guy.

He brought his head up and yawned behind his hand. "Of course. I know you. No matter what you say, you're never going to be casual about sex. If you slept with him, you're going to be thinking about him, and if you're thinking about him there's the chance that you'll want to see him again. It's not a good idea. I'm actually a little worried because he might be at this conference given his family business. He works for an investment firm in Toronto. They're known for investing in high tech, including medical tech and pharma. I had to work up a report on him. Lou's dive was more like a splash in the shallow end of the pool."

Lou frowned his way. "You try manipulating the Internet with your eyeballs in the middle of a pub. The glasses are a work in progress."

"They're brilliant," Zach assured her. He was dressed in what Tash liked to think of as his uniform. Dark jeans and a black T-shirt that showed off arms he'd perfected in the gym. "And I'd like to see anything we've found out about this guy if he's going to show up again."

"If Dare is going to be there, then Brian might be there, too," Kenzie posited, tugging her lower lip between her teeth.

"Yeah, and both of them have met you." Tristan took a sip from his mug. "And that could be a problem."

"Only if Kenz tries to climb Brian like a tree." Kala waved the thought off. "Look, I didn't give Brian Peters any information about what the Kara construct does for a living. If he manages to find the information we've seeded on the Internet, he'll discover I'm a pharmaceutical rep working here in New South Wales, and I'm thrilled my cousins are in town and sad I have to work. Oh, and thanks for adding in how much Kara loves reality TV. I had to watch four seasons of *Australian Survivor.*"

"You loved it," Kenzie shot back.

Tash suddenly had a knot in her belly, and she wasn't sure if it was nerves or anticipation or both. Dare might be at the conference? Her siblings argued about reality TV and who got to leave the safe house, but Tasha was looking through the data Tristan had sent to her tablet. It was a whole dossier on the man who'd so recently rocked her world.

He was rich. Not like her parents rich. The Nash family was

super-elite wealthy. His family owned banks and investment firms across Canada. He was probably here at this conference to make some big deals to invest in medical technology. Damn, Tristan was right. They should have caught this before she got close to him. All Lou had been able to do with the glasses was run through his socials. Which were minimal. They knew more about Brian, who worked for the same company.

"Hey, you didn't have enough data to work with," Zach said quietly. "You walked into a bar in a completely different part of town. I told you to go there. I vetted the place myself, so blame me. There are over five million people in this city. It's cool. They're expecting fifteen hundred attendees at this conference. I would bet he's here to attend private meetings for the most part. Middleton is the firm's face here. He'll be on the floor, meeting vendors and doctors and getting a real feel for what's going on. I would bet Dare Nash barely leaves his suite. Lance will likely send up potential investments, and Dare will be there to decide if they're worth it. Kenz and Kala will get close to Lance Middleton, get the invite to the party, and hopefully never see Nash or Peters. If they do, they've got their cover in place."

"I don't know." Lou shook her head as she stared down at her tablet. "I don't like it. Something feels off."

Tasha had learned to trust Lou's instincts. "What's wrong?"

"I don't know yet," Lou admitted.

"Nothing is wrong." Kala's jaw tightened. "It's a minor problem. Look, I made it clear to Brian that I wasn't interested. I didn't tell him Kara has a boyfriend. I didn't go to my usual 'I like chicks' excuse. As far as he knows, Kara is one more professional woman working in Sydney, and it shouldn't be a surprise when Kara flirts with someone at a conference."

"Except Lance Middleton is way less hot than Brian," Kenzie pointed out. "Lance Middleton is forty-five and has a pot belly going. Don't you think that's going to raise suspicions when Kara is all over him?"

"Lance Middleton is dead, so that's a moot point, Kenz," a deep voice said.

Tasha turned and Cooper McKay stood in the doorway. He was six foot four and all lean muscle. Where Tristan's lethality was masked, Coop's was on full display. He had a rugged masculinity that let a person know he could probably kill a man thirty different ways. Right now, he had a fierce frown on his face.

"What do you mean the target's dead?" Kala asked.

Lou flipped open her laptop, her fingers starting to fly across the keys.

Cooper moved into the room, taking a seat at the head of the table, across from Kala, who had the other end. "I mean, I've been in conference with Drake and Taylor, and the target didn't make it to Sydney. His flight was supposed to come in yesterday. When he didn't show up at Toronto Airport, they checked on him and discovered he was pronounced dead three hours before his flight was set to leave. Car accident. According to friends, he was on his way to the airport. The police reports state he lost control and died in a single vehicle accident. The roads were slick, and he was traveling at a high rate of speed."

"Shit." Zach moved his seat next to Lou's so he could look over her shoulder. "Did Drake send us the report?"

Tristan was already on his laptop, looking for information.

"Of course. It should be in our cloud, so you can all pull it down," Cooper said.

"All right." Tasha took a deep breath. "Why was he talking to you and not me?"

This was *her* team. Cooper and Kala might like to pretend they made decisions, but ultimately it was up to her. She ran this team, and she wasn't going to take a back seat. She'd learned early on she had to be firm about her place or the large personalities she was surrounded by would take over.

"I was already on the line talking to Taylor about the plane. They're nickel and diming me on the upgrades." Cooper was in charge of the sleek, high-tech Bond Aeronautics jet assigned to their team. He and Tristan split the logistics work. "Drake walked in with the new intel, and I was there. Trust me. You'll get a whole lecture sometime this evening, but it's late in the States so he talked to me. Apparently one of the boys is sick and they're working from home, so it's a whole thing."

Kala hadn't bothered to look at the new intel. "It's a setback but it doesn't mean the op is off."

Tasha wasn't sure she agreed. "The op is all about figuring out if Auggie Oakley is a bioweapons dealer, and why he's trying to get close to Dr. Emmanuel Huisman. Lance already had an invitation to that party. The other men we could have targeted are married."

"I can get into the party," Kenzie assured her. "I'll find a way."

"Security is going to be tight. We've already looked into getting one of the guys on Oakley's security team." Lou talked even as her eyes moved across the screen. "That's been a no go so far. He only works with Aussie ex-military, and I don't think Coop can pass. His accent is terrible."

It was awful. Coop spoke three different languages and sounded Texan in all of them.

"Hey, mate. I'm right here." Tris held up a hand.

His accent was perfect. Tristan and the twins had zero problems mimicking almost anyone they listened to for a brief amount of time. But there was a roadblock.

"Won't work," Zach pointed out. "You still have an identity in the US. I know you could fake SAS credentials, but if someone even skims the surface, they'll find the real you."

"Fine," Tris conceded. "We need a way in."

Zach had been trying to find that path. "I'm still working on the catering team. It might be our best way in, but we'll have limited access. Lance was perfect because his profile stated plainly he's looking for a long-term relationship and likely will accept moving slow physically. You know how your dad feels about honey pots."

Ah, the honey pot. It was a scenario when an operative used his or her physical attractiveness to get close to a target. Sometimes it was nothing more than a flirtation to distract a target. Their dad was okay with those. Sometimes it was a full-on sexual relationship.

He was a resounding *no* on those. It was one of his many commandments. God had only come up with ten. Their dad had way outpaced the Almighty.

Thou shalt not fuck for information.

"Dad's not here, and we can handle it," Kala assured them all. "We need to look for a new target. Let's go through Oakley's associates. Surely there's someone looking for companionship. We know he's inviting several people out for the weekend. Hell, let's take a look at Huisman. He's pretty young, and I don't think he's attached. That might kill two birds with one stone. Dad wants an eval on the dude."

"Shit." Lou had gone pale. "Drake already sent us the new target."

"He also offered to dump the op if we decide it's too dangerous," Cooper explained. "The new target might not be as easy to handle as Middleton. He belongs to a banking family known for being ruthless as hell. There are rumors about him abusing his ex-wife. I don't know that I like this guy. I think we should huddle up and decide on a new plan."

"We can handle whoever it is." Kenzie was in synch with her twin. They might argue constantly about a lot of things, but when it came to a mission, they were a united front. "Besides, it might be fun to see how the fucker handles a woman who can easily kill him."

Lou was shaking her head, and now Tristan cursed, too.

"What?" Tasha hated feeling like she was out of the loop.

Lou turned her laptop screen Tasha's way. "It's Darren Nash."

There he was, his handsome face staring out from the report Drake had sent. Dare was in a suit, standing in an office and looking so serious it made her a bit sad. This was Darren Nash, businessman. This was the man who was ashamed of his needs, not the Dom who'd reveled in their play.

Kala burst into laughter, and Kenzie slapped her twin on the arm, but not before she bit back a laugh of her own.

Cooper frowned. "What am I missing?"

"You know how Tash let off some steam the other night? Meet the man she vented on," Tristan said, waving a hand across the screen.

"What do we call a honey pot the target's already gotten a big old taste of?" Kala said between guffaws.

Hell. That was what she would call it.

Total Hell.

* * * *

"You're reading that?" Brian asked, sinking down into the seat across from him. "I did not take you for a pop culture guy."

Dare put down the book he'd been perusing. Sort of. He tried to read, but his head kept going back to Tasha. He would read a sentence and then the words would kind of swim in front of him and he'd be right back to her. He'd dreamed of her the night before and woken up to ruined sheets like he was a freaking fifteen-year-old virgin having wet dreams.

He was an almost thirty-year-old man having wet dreams, and wasn't that pathetic? Worse, he missed her. Genuinely missed her. How could he miss someone he'd spent one night with?

At least the conference started tomorrow, and he could put his mind on the business of making his asshole father even more money.

"Sort of." Dare stared down at the cover of Dr. Emmanuel Huisman's memoir. *Recapturing My Mind* was the tale of how he'd come to forgive his family for his childhood and work with the woman his father had tried to murder. Dr. Rebecca Walsh-Shaw was a renowned neurologist making massive breakthroughs in Alzheimer's and dementia. Once she'd worked for the Huisman Foundation until Paul Huisman had tried taking her research for his own.

Emmanuel had been a child, and he'd watched as his father had been killed.

It seemed to be a tale of forgiveness and moving on. That might be why Dare couldn't seem to get into it. He didn't want to forgive, and he wasn't even close to being able to move on.

Someone killing his father might be nice though. Goals…

Brian frowned at the book, a look of distaste coming over his handsome face. "I hate celebrity autobiographies. He probably didn't even write it himself. It's all for publicity."

"I don't know. I've heard writing can be a form of therapy." Dare was sure he might get something out of the book if he wasn't in such a shitty mood.

He was caught, and there wasn't going to be any way out until his sister was… What? Through college? She didn't have a trust fund. She and Johnny were utterly dependent on their father for money. Maybe if they both got decent jobs he would be able to walk away.

Or his father would find another way.

"I found her, you know," Brian said quietly.

There was no question who he was talking about. Tasha. "I told you, I'm not going to pursue a woman who doesn't want me. I'm not some creepy stalker."

He'd been accused of many things. He didn't need to add that to his list of supposed crimes.

"Her social media profile is public," Brian pointed out. "And so is her cousin's. Kara Trent. Finally got a last name. She seems way friendlier on her socials. And she has a weird thing for *Survivor*. Did you know they have one of those here, too?"

Americans. "Yes, other countries have their own shows. Canada has its own, too. And she might be friendlier on her socials because she didn't like you. I get it, man. You're a woman magnet. You can pick up almost any woman you want. Except that one."

"Maybe that's what I like about her."

Yes, that's what Dare was worried about.

"Yet you should still stay away," Dare advised. "Because it will shock you to discover that women get to pick who they want to be around. We've moved past the 'Neanderthal, club the woman you want over her head and drag her back to your cave' stage of humanity."

"And that is where we went wrong, my friend." The waitress came by and took Brian's order of whiskey neat. When she was gone, Brian turned back to Dare. "And I think staying away might be a real problem."

"It's not." He was proof positive of how easy it was to stay away from a woman he wanted. "I've managed to not even try to track Tasha down."

He'd wanted to. There was a part of him that was angry she hadn't even bothered to stay and tell him good-bye. She'd slipped out while he was sleeping and hadn't given him the barest chance of convincing her to stay with him. The thought had run through his head that he could call up someone in the company's investigations unit to send him a complete dossier on her. They dug up crap on potential clients all the time. He was fairly certain his father used the unit to do surveillance on the whole family.

That was precisely why he hadn't done it, though not being anything like his father wasn't the only reason he hadn't made that call.

He could have had at least a week with her. His father, for all his assholery, wouldn't care about him sleeping with a woman while he was away on business. Hell, that was practically expected of him.

You don't want to fuck your wife? She's not doing it for you? Go find someone who does, but not in one of those fucking clubs. It's one thing to cheat on your wife. It's another to be a pervert.

His dad was such a dick.

But he'd had a point. A certain amount of vice was expected in their world. It would be tolerated and ignored, but there was a line that shouldn't be crossed.

When he'd been with Tasha, it hadn't felt like crossing a line. It had felt as natural as breathing to pin her down and give her a nip that got her panting.

"Is this about your ex?" Brian asked, his gaze narrowing. "I've been trying to figure this part out. Tasha was obviously into you, and you're still thinking about her. Yet you easily let her go. I have to wonder. Is it because you're still in love with your ex-wife?"

Dare snorted. "I was never in love with her in the first place."

"Ah, I thought that might be the case. Did you marry her for family reasons?"

Dare took a drink of his beer. He'd spent a lot of time with Brian recently, but they'd never gone deep into his history. They'd had some great talks about politics and sports, but they'd avoided breaking this particular surface. "What's the sudden interest?"

Brian seemed to consider the question for a moment. "We're friends. I don't have a lot of those. Working in Canada has been a transition for me, and you've made that way easier. We've been hanging out for six months now. You've listened to me complain about everything from my dating life to my mom nagging me about when I'm going to get around to giving her grandkids. I thought you should know I'll listen too."

Brian was the closest he'd had to a friend in a long time. Too many times he got chummy with someone only to realize their families had close ties to his and therefore couldn't be trusted. It could be the same with Brian. He could be concealing his ties. Still, it wasn't like he was telling Brian anything his father didn't already know. "I married Audrey because my dad thought it was time, and

Audrey was the daughter of a business associate he wanted closer ties to."

"So it was arranged?" Brian huffed. "The rich really are different."

"Not so much. I assure you most rich people still marry for love or lust or something like it. My father still lives back in the time of the railroad barons. He would fit in there well. He rules with an iron fist and thinks of little but profits."

"Why did you go through with it?"

Now they were in the danger zone. This was something his father knew but wouldn't want anyone else to know. The Nash family was beyond reproach. Well, they had been. This was something Brian could report back to his father and cause trouble with. Still. He was feeling reckless. He'd lost Tasha. Did he have to be friendless? Did he have to view every single person in his life with suspicion? "Because I have two younger siblings. Half siblings. My father controls everything about our lives, and if I step out of line, he punishes them not me."

"Fuck, man. I'm sorry. I thought that might be the case," Brian admitted. "I'm observant and I've noticed you take a lot of responsibility for your brother and sister. Way more than an older brother normally would. So if you're not still in love with your ex, are you still bitter about the divorce? Is that why you're shying away?"

"I'm shying away because Tasha walked out. She left a note that clearly said she wasn't going to see me again." Was that really the only reason? He sighed as the waitress returned, placing the drink in front of Brian. Brian didn't seem to notice how she looked him over like she wouldn't mind serving him in another way.

"All I know is I've never seen you react to a woman the way you did Tasha," Brian said as the waitress walked away. "It seems a shame to not take advantage of the time we have here to get to know her."

"Maybe I am still bitter about the marriage, but not in a way that I would put on Tasha. I worry if I got close to her, she would end up getting hurt. Or at the very least hearing some unsavory rumors about me." He wondered. Brian had only been working for the company for half a year. The divorce had been finalized by the time he'd hired on, but gossip never died. "Have you heard anything about my marriage?"

"That I believe? No."

Damn it. Well, he should be happy Brian hadn't brought it up. "I never abused my wife. She found out that in my younger days I was involved in an alternative lifestyle, and she used that to get out of a marriage she hadn't wanted in the first place. I didn't blame her for wanting out. I wanted out. I blame her for cutting me up as she left."

"Now that is interesting." Brian's gaze had gone sharp, a look Dare hadn't seen on his friend's face before. "Does that alternative lifestyle happen to involve bondage and sex clubs?"

He felt himself flush and cursed the weakness. "It's not always about sex."

"No, it's about control and being honest about your sexual needs," Brian corrected himself. "Sorry. I've read up on the subject lately. I was interested in a woman who spends time in clubs like that. I educated myself a bit. Not that it helped me. I think I might be doing it wrong."

"Is it someone at work?"

"She's work adjacent," Brian demurred. "But the point is yes, I've heard some rumors. Most of the employees I know don't believe them, but you hold yourself apart enough that a lot of people don't know you."

There was a reason for that. "If I get close to someone, my father can use them against me, and that is why I should stay away from Tasha. I could manage a couple of weeks with her, but if I tried to have even a long-distance relationship with her, he would find out."

"Why not take the couple of weeks? Have a little happiness?"

Dare wasn't sure he would be allowed that. "It's out of my hands."

"It's back in your hands because guess who turns out to be a pharmaceutical rep and is attending the conference right here in this hotel?" Brian's lips turned up in a smirk.

"Tasha isn't a pharmaceutical rep. She works at her father's company. I think they're in security." He'd found out that much. She was close to her family, as evidenced by her visit here with her cousin, toting her sister along.

"No, but Kara is."

Her cousin would be here in this hotel? They'd switched over to the conference hotel the night before. It was a downgrade from his place on the beach, but his father had still ensured he had a large suite. Couldn't have a Nash stay in a room with two queens and a view of the HVAC system.

The room was meant for him to entertain clients in, to show how successful he was, how the Nash family could help their endeavors.

He'd looked at the big four-poster bed and seen Tasha tied to it, naked and waiting for him.

Just thinking about her, about how readily she'd responded to him, how she'd made him feel like he had something to give her...it made his dick hard and his stupid-ass heart ache. No. He should stay away. From her. For himself. "She'll be working. I doubt she'll bring her cousin up here. I think Lou mentioned they might visit the Blue Mountains. They'll probably spend some time up there while Kara is working the conference."

It might be why she walked away. She'd had a choice between spending time with him or with her sister and her sister won. He could understand that.

"Or she's hanging out in her cousin's flat and has nothing to do." Brian was starting to sound like the devil on his shoulder. "We don't have to go back right away. You could take her with us to the Blue Mountains."

"That's supposed to be work," he pointed out. "It's precisely why I'm reading this book. Like I told you, my father wants me to pitch to Huisman, and he'll be there at the house party."

"I don't understand the fascination." Brian had gone strangely still. "I know the guy supposedly has an MD, but I don't know that I buy he's some wunderkind. He likes the press too much."

"The Huisman Foundation is worth over ten billion dollars. That's all my father sees, and since they announced they were funding Dr. Walsh-Shaw's research, the businesses the family owns have seen their stock go through the roof. She's on the cusp of some real breakthroughs when it comes to degenerative neurological diseases. His reputation means nothing to my father. He smells money, and I'm supposed to go after it. I also think my father loathes Auggie Oakley, but then he hates everyone. If Oakley is trying to get in bed with the Huisman Foundation, my dad will try to get there first. So our job is to charm the guy. Get a feel for him."

"But the invite is for two, and we'll have separate rooms." Brian's fingers tapped against the tabletop. "That's an interesting twist of fate. Oakley's a big partier, and he loves a gorgeous woman. Wouldn't it be a bigger power move to show up with an actual date?"

He knew exactly where Brian was going. "I doubt Tasha would say yes."

"You doubt she would say yes to spending a weekend at a billionaire's house party?" Brian looked at him like he should know the answer.

"She's not like that," Dare replied. But that was naïve. "Okay, everyone is curious."

"She's on vacation. She's obviously an adventurous girl." Every word out of Brian's mouth contained a hint of temptation. "And you've established this is a casual, fun relationship, so you don't have to worry about anyone getting hurt. I think you should go for it. Live a little, man."

It would be weird to show up with Brian. Too businessy when he was trying to form a real connection with Huisman. Going in hard might not work with a man as seemingly sensitive as Huisman. Having a date would make him look more like a real guy a man could relate to than the relentless businessman he'd become over the years.

He could ensure Tasha got something out of it, too. Maybe he was looking at this all wrong. He was viewing this through a romantic lens when he should be all business. So he could look like he wasn't all business.

"You're overthinking this thing, man," Brian advised with a shake of his head.

He rather believed he was finally thinking properly. There were still problems. "I have to run into her first. I don't think Kara is going to give up her cousin's location easily."

"I'll work on her." Brian smiled like a man who'd gotten exactly what he wanted. Which was probably more time to annoy the hell out of Kara. "I can be persuasive. She just needs to get to know me better."

Dare wasn't sure about that, but he was willing to leave this to fate. If Tasha came back into his life, he would offer her a deal.

A devil's bargain of sorts.

A Dom's bargain.

He took another drink because suddenly life didn't seem so boring.

Chapter Five

"Okay, I am trying to fully grasp what happened here." Cooper sat back. "Someone piece this together for me because I do not understand."

Kala's lips curled up. "Tasha and the new target." She used her thumb and forefinger to make a circle which she pushed the forefinger of her other hand through back and forth while making squeaking sounds.

Such a bitch. "I didn't know he was the target."

"Hey, he wasn't the target then," Tristan pointed out.

Zach was staring at his cell, likely reading through the reports Drake had sent. Of all the people in the room, he looked the most grim.

"Tash couldn't have possibly known," Lou argued.

"Tasha slept with Darren Nash." Cooper seemed to need a moment to wrap his head around that reality. "When? I wasn't aware you were seeing anyone. When did you have the time to meet this guy? Did you know him back in the States? I thought he was Canadian."

Captain America was in the house, and she wasn't going to let him make her feel slutty. He didn't mean it. Coop had been raised like the rest of them to be open about all their needs, but he could also be overly protective. He reminded her so much of his father,

Alex McKay. Uncle Alex, though there wasn't a drop of blood between them. Kenzie had stopped calling him anything but Mr. McKay by the time they were ten and she'd realized the ramifications of the relationship. Like Tash herself, Cooper had been adopted and didn't look anything like his father or mother, but the gestures were so familiar they didn't need things like hair color or eye color to make it clear they were related.

Tasha enjoyed being told how like her mother she was. Her mom was the best. Her mom would know how to handle this situation.

"I didn't know him before. It was a one-night stand," Tasha explained. "Like you've had one-night stands. And the twins have had one-night stands."

"Mine ended in me stabbing someone," Kala admitted. "I didn't know he was a Russian operative. I just thought he was hot. I didn't actually get to sex, so it was more like a one-night violence. Kenzie is a true-love girl. Zach has had his share, but he's discreet. Coop is the manwhore here."

A light pink stained Coop's cheeks. "I thought we weren't going to use hurtful words anymore."

"Well, I've never had a one-night stand." Tristan acted like he was adjusting his halo. "As the purest person here, I'm proud of Tash for getting some."

"I didn't say she shouldn't have a good sex life, but it might have been nice if it hadn't been with the freaking target," Coop shot back.

"Hey, it's not Tash's fault, and this conversation is doing none of us any favors," Zach proclaimed.

Kala's expression had lost its humor, and Kenzie had gone quiet.

"Well, I think I'm probably purer than Tris since I've never had a three way." Lou filled in the awkward silence. "And I'm proud of Tash, too. He seemed like a great guy. I spent a lot of time talking to him. What are these rumors?"

Tasha wasn't sure she wanted to know the answer to that question, but here she was. "Cooper, can you give us a report on what you know about the target?"

She'd called Dare the target. It made her stomach roll.

But the op was important. It wasn't terribly dangerous. Not compared to some of the stuff they'd been through, but there was a reason this op had been selected as their first solo mission. It was supposed to be fairly easy, with Kenzie and Kala tag teaming a man profiled for his harmlessness. They were to listen and evaluate relationships. If they had a chance to gather more intel in a safe fashion, they had the go ahead. Easy peasy. In and out.

If this op went well, they would be allowed more freedom.

She might have screwed that all up.

"Dare Nash was born out of wedlock. Not usually a big deal these days, but it comes into play here. The Nash family has roots in the Toronto area that go back a century. They're old-school money," Cooper began. He glanced over at Tristan. "If Tasha had an…encounter with this guy, I would bet you looked him up. You might know more than me."

"Encounter?" Tris rolled those emerald eyes of his. "She had nasty, glorious sex and yes, I did a deep dive on the guy because our Tash is so awesome I figure he'll show back up for another taste. I wanted to be ready."

"Do you think he would be open to seeing her again?" Zach's gaze had gone hawklike, and it was easy to see he was trying to decide the best path to take.

"Oh, if he gets another shot at her, he'll take it," Kala replied surely.

"He was into her," Lou agreed. "I didn't get a sense that he was dangerous. I did have some weird vibes from Brian, though."

"Because he's a douchebag player," Kala said with a shake of her head. "All I'm saying is this doesn't have to be a bad thing. It's fortuitous given what happened to the previous target. We should look at this as an easy in."

"He was accused of getting rough with his wife." Tristan's words threw a chill over the room. "Or rather that was the talk going around in certain circles."

Her heart ached for him. "Was there a police report or are we talking about rumors? I'm not discounting what his wife said, but I know a little about him and I worry rumors can be overblown. Especially in this case because he was in the lifestyle at some point, and he's shy as hell about it now. He didn't even want to talk about the club he belonged to."

"No police reports," Tristan said. "He's never been arrested. Never been in any kind of legal trouble. Do you know what club he attended? I can make some calls. I'm certain one of our parents knows someone who could get us some intel."

"It might actually make Dad more comfortable if he knows Dare wasn't troublesome in a club," Kenzie mused. "Especially if we don't mention that it's Tasha who's involved with him. He knows damn well Kala and I can keep sex out of a D/s relationship. Seriously, this might be an excellent way to keep him from showing up."

Tasha used every bit of restraint she had to keep her face as blank as possible. "You're going to try to get Dare to invite you to the party with him?"

Her beautiful sisters, the ones who did look like their mom. Kenzie and Kala were perfect twins from their hot pink hair to their gorgeous faces and gloriously toned bodies. They were both five foot nine and topped out at six foot in heels.

Tasha was fit, but she never seemed able to lose her curves. Her sisters had them, but in a glorious hourglass fashion. A whole lot of her extra something landed in Tasha's backside, which didn't balance with her on-the-smaller-side boobs.

What would Dare do if he met Kenzie? She was exactly what Kala had described. Kenzie was submissive sexually, maybe more so than Tasha herself. Would he respond to that part of Kenzie? If he got a taste of her sister, would he even bother to look her way again?

"Uh, I'm pretty sure that wouldn't work," Kala was saying.

"It definitely wouldn't," Lou agreed. "I watched him that night. He was not into Kara."

"I wasn't suggesting we try to hit on Dare. Ewww." Kenzie's nose wrinkled like she'd smelled something terrible. "You know we have a code. You guys might happily pass your exes around, but we are hands off. Once you've slept with my sister, you belong to her." She suddenly sat up straighter and her eyes sparkled, a sure sign she'd come up with what she would believe was the best idea ever. "If Dare's around then Brian's probably staying, too, and we know he's totally into us. Why don't we make Brian the target?"

Everyone groaned.

"Because Brian's not the one with the invite to Oakley's party," Zach pointed out.

"It's Dare or nothing," Cooper continued. "I'm reluctant to send Tasha in if he's got a reputation for violence."

Tristan was staring down at his laptop. "Ah. This makes more sense. I'm reading through the NDA his ex-wife signed in exchange for two point five million. She states plainly that he never hit her and she will not mention anything about him in relation to alternative lifestyles."

"So she found out he had belonged to a club, freaked out, and used it against him in their divorce," Kala surmised.

Tasha was staring at Tristan. "How the hell did you find that?"

He gave her a jaunty grin. "Like it's hard."

Cooper leaned in, his voice going low. "Bet he called Aunt Chelsea."

Tristan looked offended. "I did not. I'm good enough to hack into a law firm's system. Give me some credit. All I'm saying is this is some solid proof that what we might be dealing with is someone using Nash's D/s connections against him rather than him being an abusive asshole. Unless you think he's a Storm."

They'd all gotten the same lectures. "He's not a Storm."

It would explain a lot about how he'd reacted to her talking in the taxi. He'd married a sweet vanilla princess and it hadn't ended well when he'd been open with her. Which he should have been in the beginning, but she'd met a lot of men who seemed perfectly satisfied with a woman who was comfortable with her sexuality for the short term, but when it came to wife material they wanted one with less experience. One who didn't know they were bad in bed.

She wasn't trying to marry Dare Nash. It was good to know that when he went looking for something serious, he'd selected a woman who wasn't in the lifestyle, likely hoping she could save him from himself.

None of this solved their problems, and they were putting off the inevitable. "We should call in. I'm not one hundred percent sure Kenzie couldn't reel Dare in, but I don't think we should risk it. We should bring someone else in. Someone he hasn't met yet."

There were several operatives who might work. Anna Jenkins

worked on Chet's team sometimes. She was sure she wasn't Anna's favorite person right now—teams stuck together—but she was a solid operative who did her job well, and she didn't work for her dad, so sex was probably on the table for her.

The idea of Dare in bed with gorgeous Anna made her heart hurt, but she needed to focus on the mission. Maybe seeing it happen would help her stop dreaming about the man.

She glanced up and realized everyone was looking at her. "What?"

Kala sighed and rolled her eyes. Kenzie looked to Tristan as though he had an answer.

Lou put a hand on her arm. "Uh, Tash, I'm pretty sure we have the perfect person to send in."

"I was thinking about Anna," she admitted.

"You are not letting Anna Steel Nipples take your man," Kenzie announced with a huff.

Kala grinned. "They are always on display, right? Like I don't know how she manages that. Those headlights are always blaringly on. It's distracting, and I don't even like boobs."

"Everyone likes boobs," Tristan said. "But hers are kind of scary."

"I think she might use them as weapons," Zach agreed. "Definitely not a good call. I think we've only got one operative who will work here. Tash, you've got to go in."

Pure anxiety poured through her body. "What?"

"It makes the most sense. You know the target. You're already close to the target," Kenzie argued. "The target is super into you, so he will absolutely invite you to that weekend getaway and you can almost surely bring your cousin for part of the party. Then you can distract everyone while Kara gets the intel we need. It'll be fun."

It did not sound like fun. "I'm not a field agent."

"You're perfectly trained, and you can handle yourself. This is an easy op," Zach replied, looking more confident than he had before. "I don't think we even need to call Big Tag. The parameters are the same, and Tasha is well equipped to handle herself in the field. Unless you want to call your dad and let him know we kind of fucked up."

Kala sat back, her combat boots making an appearance on the

table as she relaxed. "Lou can do all the overwatch stuff, and whichever Kara isn't in the field can help her out. What do you say, bestie? Think you can stare at a screen and tell Tash if the bad guy is coming up behind her?"

Lou gave her a thumbs-up. "Sounds like fun."

"I don't know. Maybe we should call Dad." Her father would say no. Her dad would get her out of this because the only thing she could think of that would be worse than walking out on Dare was trying to walk back in and getting rejected. Then the op would be blown, and it would be all her fault.

"We are not calling Dad," the twins said in stereo.

Tristan's head shook. "Nope. I'm with the Karas on this one. We open that door even an inch and the big boss will never let us close it again. He will breathe down our necks for all of time."

She looked to Lou and Coop, who were always the reasonable ones.

"Sorry, Tash." Coop sent her an apologetic smile. "Tris is right. You let Ian Taggart know we couldn't handle this mission on our own and it'll be five years before we're allowed off the leash again. And he can't call this a honey pot because the pot was fully invaded before the op even started."

"You know I like to call in Uncle Ian whenever I can," Lou began. "But in this case I think you should go for it. I think if you don't, you're always going to wonder. It's probably going to blow up in your face and you'll get your heart broken, but at least you'll know if it could have worked."

Lou's plaintive words made her heart squeeze because they were as much about Lou's situation as Tasha's. She glanced over at Kala, who was suddenly staring at her boots. At anything that wasn't Cooper.

"It would be better to know." She was surprised because those words had come out of Cooper's mouth. His gaze was steady on Kala for a moment and then he sighed. "Anyway, I vote we don't call in the bosses. We tell Drake we have things covered and let Ian and Charlotte enjoy their vacation. All in?"

Everyone's hand raised.

And Tasha knew she was screwed.

* * * *

Dare sat in the lobby and wondered if Kara had called her cousin. They'd met up at the coffee mixer that opened the conference. It had been a shock to see her even though Brian had warned him she would be here.

Kara had a completely different work personality. It wasn't surprising since she was in sales and would need to be a people pleaser to do her job. She'd been happy and bubbly and only the slightest bit standoffish when it came to Brian, who'd practically drooled all over her.

It had been hours since she'd walked right up to him and given him a hug like they were old friends and told him Tasha was hanging around her flat like a sad puppy.

Had she truly missed him? Had she decided it was a mistake to not see him again?

He was the one acting like a dumb pup. He knew he should have told her then and there that it was all for the best because he needed to work and wouldn't have time to see her again.

Here's my number. Tell her to call me if she wants to talk.

Yep. That had been his dumbass response. He should have played it cooler. He should have pretended like he didn't care what she was doing, but he'd had his card out, holding it like he would die if she didn't take it and give it to her cousin.

"You must be Eddie Nash's kid." The words were spoken with a strong Aussie accent. "Damn, but you look like him."

That was something he didn't like to hear. Dare turned and there stood Auggie Oakley in all his glory. He'd never met the man, but he'd seen him on TV and the covers of magazines. The billionaire financier liked to pretend to be a man of the people, pulling himself up from his family's hundreds of millions in real estate to build a couple of billion-dollar businesses. He wore jeans and a Henley and well-worn boots. His reddish hair was a bit shaggy. Only the hundred-thousand-dollar watch on his wrist bespoke of the money this man wielded like a weapon at times.

Oakley would be his rival in persuading Huisman. He stood and held out a hand. "Unfortunately, I am."

A booming laugh came from Oakley's mouth, and Dare found

his hand pumping up and down. "Oh, I like you. You're not an uptight arse like your father. Must be your mother's influence."

His mom. Fuck. He didn't like to think about his mom and liked it even less that Oakley knew enough to mention her. Or did he? It was a given that he had a mother. It didn't mean Oakley knew who she'd been and why his father went to lengths to pretend she'd never existed. "She was definitely more pleasant than my father."

He winked. "That wouldn't take much." He backed off and sat down in the seat across from Dare's. "I heard you're taking Lance's place. Sad about him. I've known Lance for years."

Thank the universe someone had thought to call and tell him Lance had died. His father had acted like the man had simply inconvenienced them all. He hadn't mentioned the car accident that had taken his long-time employee's life. "I didn't spend much time with him, but I know he did some great work for us over the years. I hope you don't mind if I attend in his place. I didn't realize the two of you were friends. My father made it seem like the invitation to your place was more of a business courtesy."

Oakley waved that off. "Nah. I knew him but we weren't mates. Smart lad, though. Always had his ear to the ground. I'm happy to know you're coming out to my place in the mountains. I like to size up my competition."

"Competition?" He hadn't expected Oakley to be so upfront about it.

"Sure. We're both going to try to get in good with this Huisman bloke, right?" Oakley sounded like they were talking about a football rivalry or a friendly bet they were making. "You looked over the foundation's financials?"

Of course he had. "They've done well the last couple of years. A lot of it comes down to backing medical grade-lasers they've started using in neuro. After they got FDA and EMA approval, the stock in that company went through the roof. The foundation got a nice slice of that pie."

"It was an excellent investment," Oakley pointed out.

"And you would like some of that money to fund your pet projects." Dare stated the obvious since it was exactly what his father wanted him to talk Huisman into.

"It's always better to invest someone else's money," Oakley

admitted. "And honestly, we don't have to compete. We can talk about joining forces. My biomed wing has some interesting projects going. Projects that could use some of the work your firm is funding. I think we've got pieces of a puzzle that we could bring together and make a lot of money with."

"I thought you were changing the world." It was what he always said in those interviews.

Oakley shrugged. "I can change the world and make money at the same time. I assure you that's what Huisman's doing. Huisman's flush with cash, and he seems to have a need to show off what a charitable man he is. Probably because his father was a complete bastard. You heard about that, right?"

Huisman had written a book about it. "You think he's trying to rehab the family image?"

Oakley nodded. "I would if I was him. It's hard to have that kind of scandal in the background. The good news for him is all the players are dead and gone with the exception of his father's victim, and she seems the forgiving type."

"He was a child. I don't think there's anything to forgive."

"I don't know about that. The sins of the father and all," Oakley murmured. "They tend to cling to a man. I know some families will do a lot to keep their name pure, but those histories have a way of coming out."

A chill went over Dare's skin. Those words somehow felt like a threat, and he was back to wondering how much the man knew about his real background. "I think we should focus on the future. The past doesn't make a man money."

Money was all these people understood. In his father's world the only thing that mattered was money, but no one could convince his father that reputation wasn't every bit as important, that they were no longer living in the Victorian age, that one small variance shouldn't cost them everything.

"Anyway, I saw you sitting over here and thought I would let you know you're welcome to come out and pitch to the man. I've only met him once, and he's an odd duck, if you know what I mean." Oakley sighed and slapped his hands on the arms of the chair before standing. "I've got to go and deliver some opening speech or something. Probably shouldn't have asked me since I'm just going to offer to shout a round of drinks and get this party going. I'll send you some information on the projects I'm interested in. Run them by the old man and see what he says, and we'll talk next weekend. Feel free to bring a date if you like. Hell, bring a friend, too. I've got lots of room. It's going to be a ripper."

He wasn't sure that was a good thing, but damn he liked the idea of bringing someone with him. The party would take place over the course of a weekend. That would mean at least two uninterrupted nights with Tasha.

If she called.

"Maybe you should invite that stunner there." Oakley gestured to a place behind him. "She seems to be watching you, mate."

He turned and nearly stopped breathing. Tasha was standing there wearing a yellow sundress and looking so out of place. Everyone in the lobby was dressed in dark colors, professional business suits that somehow seemed to go with the lanyards most of them had around their necks despite the fact that this part of the hotel was outside of the conference spaces. It was as though the serious medical world had taken over the whole hotel with the exception of one shaft of brilliant light standing twenty feet away from him.

"She's a looker. You know her?" Oakley asked.

He was going to play this cool. He was going to offer her his deal, and they would be on a proper footing. She'd been the one who'd left him, not the other way around, and falling at her feet the minute she walked back in wouldn't do. He needed to be in the power position when it came to this woman.

"Because maybe I was wrong and she's looking at me," Oakley added. "Now that I think about it, she couldn't actually see your face."

That was not fucking happening. He wasn't about to let the billionaire hit on her. Oakley wasn't a bad-looking man, and that money made up for a lot. "She's here for me."

She hadn't called. She hadn't waited to see if he would call. He'd talked to her cousin a mere hour before and here she was. She'd put on a pretty dress and done her hair and makeup. This wasn't a woman who was playing games.

"We can't know that until we talk to her, mate." Oakley

chuckled. "I think I'll invite her to join us and let her take her pick. We should get some champagne."

He could fix this right now. "I'll see you next weekend. She'll be coming with me. You can talk to her then."

It wouldn't matter then because Tasha would be his. He would make sure of it. All of the reasons he should leave her alone flew right out of his head. They had a few weeks, and he would take them.

His long legs ate the distance between them, and all thoughts of acting like a lofty prick flew out of his head. So did common sense and reason. Instinct led him now.

"Dare, I'm sorry…" she began.

He moved into her space, taking that pretty face of hers between his palms and lowering his lips to hers. Her hands immediately went to his waist, face tilting back so she could give him access.

Her mouth flowered open beneath his, and he felt her sigh against him.

Something about this woman brought out the beast in him, the one he had to hide, to lock up tight so it never ever threatened his father's white-picket-fence world. When Tasha was close, the beast ripped open the cage and took over. It felt so fucking good.

He took her hand and started for the elevator. She was here. She'd kissed him like she needed him to breathe. As far as he was concerned, they were going to pick right up where they left off.

"Dare." Tasha sounded out of breath.

He turned as they reached the bank of elevators. "Did you come back because you want to spend time with me? Because you want more of what we had the other night?"

Her chin came up in a sweetly stubborn expression as though she knew he was pushing her and wouldn't back down. "Yes."

"Then come with me. You walked out on me without a good-bye, and we're going to discuss that upstairs."

Her eyes flared as though she knew what that "talk" would involve. "I left a note."

The doors came open, and he marched her inside, waving his key card since this was a private elevator that only went to the upper floors.

A couple started to follow them.

"No." Dare wasn't going to share an elevator with anyone.

There must have been something in his expression because those doors closed without a single argument.

"Sir is impatient today."

Oh, there was that brat he craved. She had a saucy smile on her face that he was going to spank right off.

"Sir is annoyed that you left him. You could have woken me up. You could have left me your number. I would have taken you home, Tasha. You didn't need to call your cousin."

She frowned at him, and he couldn't help but love how full her bottom lip was. "How did you know Kara picked me up?"

"It wasn't just Kara. Who was the guy, Tasha?" He didn't like the jealousy creeping into his tone.

That saucy expression softened. "He's an American friend of Kara's. He's doing a semester abroad. He's a nice guy, but I'm not exactly his type. There's a reason he was out with three women having brunch, and he's not dating any of them."

He was glad to hear there wasn't a love interest hanging around.

"So now that we've settled that I didn't run off with another man, I think we should talk," Tasha began.

The elevator doors opened, and he didn't want to talk. Not here. He wasn't going to take her back downstairs for a civilized lunch where they discussed the parameters of their probably short relationship. The thought turned his stomach. But other thoughts…

He leaned over and shoved one strong arm under her knees and hauled her up to his chest. He was letting his caveman side out a little today, and damn, but it felt good. On this floor there were only four suites and the hall was empty.

"Dare, what are you doing?" Tasha had thrown her arms around his neck. "I came here to talk to you."

He managed to make it to his door and set her on her feet because he needed the key card. "Did you? You put on that dress to talk?"

A brow rose over her dark eyes. "I put on the dress because it's pretty and I feel confident in it."

Damn it. She brought out all kinds of instincts in him, and he knew it was better to bury them all. He was being an ass. He took a long breath and prepared to apologize.

Her head shook, and she got into his space. "I'm sorry. I did put it on because I kind of hoped you would take one look at me and decide to give it another chance. What is this, Dare? Is this another chance or some revenge?"

He was confused. He let his hands find her shoulders because she wasn't pushing him away. "Why would I want revenge, sweetness? We didn't have a contract. We didn't say anything at all about what would happen the next morning. I had my feelings hurt because I thought that night meant something that maybe it didn't to you. When you showed back up…"

"You read the room, Dare." Her hands came up to frame his face, stroking his cheeks. "I walked out because that night was everything to me and I was overwhelmed. I wanted to avoid the whole 'it was nice to know you, see you later' thing. I screwed up. When Kara told me she'd seen you, I knew I had to talk to you again, but maybe we communicate best like this."

She went on her toes and pressed her lips to his, and the beast came fully off the leash.

He managed to get the door open, to get her inside, and then she was pulling at the hem of his dress shirt. He heard the door close behind them as he pressed the straps of her dress down. He turned her and pushed her up against the wall, catching her wrists with one of his. He let his nose run along the curve of her neck, reveling in the scent of lavender and the stirrings of her arousal.

"I missed you every fucking second you were gone, Tash. I didn't like it."

Her round ass nestled against his cock, tempting and teasing him. "I missed you, too, Sir."

He ran his teeth over the shell of her ear and felt her shiver. "Did you miss me before or after mimosas with your friends?"

"I'm more of a Bloody Mary girl," she whispered.

That earned her a hard nip that got her panting, but he rather thought that was the point. "I'll note your preferences. How long are you here?"

"A little over a month," she replied as he let his free hand cup a breast.

So soft and sexy. Everything about this woman called to him, and he knew it was wrong, but he was going to have this time for himself. This time with her. If his father asked, she was nothing more than a hookup. Hell, the man would likely encourage him to get it all out of his system because soon he would be courting whatever dried up prude his father decided was pure enough to not sully the Nash name. "I'm here for two more weeks. Stay with me. Be with me these weeks."

"Yes." She didn't hesitate.

She wanted him, wanted what he could give her, what they could find together. He kissed the back of her neck and released her hands so he could tug at the zipper of her dress. She wasn't wearing a bra, so when she turned and allowed the sunny bit of fabric to slide to her waist, he could see how hard her nipples were.

"Damn it, Tash. I want to go slow."

She shook her head. "Go slow later. Fuck me hard and fast now, Sir. I missed you. My pussy missed the hell out of you."

And just like that he realized how dangerous she was to him. Her open and honest approach to sex was a breath of fresh fucking air to him, like he could finally fill his lungs after years. She was everything he wanted, and when he had to give her up, it would decimate him in a way nothing had before. And he wasn't walking away. She was a storm he would seek no shelter from.

He picked her up again, unwilling to wait a moment more.

"I love it when you do that," she whispered.

He loved that she relaxed in his arms, trusting he wouldn't drop her. He did, of course. Right on the big soft bed, and he pulled her down so her pretty ass was on the edge. He dragged the scrap of her underwear off, every muscle in his body tense in anticipation. His hands fumbled as he unbuckled his belt and shoved his pants and boxers down. She looked up at him, her legs spread for him, nothing in those gorgeous eyes but longing.

He found the condoms in the bedside drawer and somehow managed to roll it on. Then she was pulling at him, her legs winding around his waist. Greedy, gorgeous girl. "This is not how it's always going to be."

She rubbed against his cock, getting it wet because that sweet pussy was soaked. "I know, Sir. Later, there will be orders and protocols, and I'm sure you'll find a way to make me scream out in frustration when you keep me on the edge over and over again. So much punishment is coming my way. Give me this. Show me you want me as desperately as I want you."

That was an easy request to fill. He shifted his hips and then he was inside her. Good. It felt so fucking good. He thrust in and dragged out, her nails digging into his ass, urging him on. He could give her all of this. He watched as her tits bounced with the force of his thrusts, her mouth coming open as she whimpered when he managed to find the right angle so he was hitting her clitoris and that sweet spot deep inside her. It wasn't long before she tightened around him and drew him right over the edge with her.

The orgasm was so much more than he'd felt before, even more than he'd felt the other night. She was here with him. She'd come back.

She was his.

For now.

Chapter Six

Tasha looked out over the spectacular views of Sydney Harbour as the sun was beginning to set, the sky lighting in pinks and oranges. Dare knew how to live. This hotel wasn't as glorious as the last one, but the suite was something to behold.

"Here you go." Dare moved in behind her, offering her a glass of the Cab he'd ordered along with a ridiculously lush charcuterie board.

They'd fucked through lunch, and he had dinner with a potential client this evening, so snacks were the way they were going. It was perfect, really. Cheese and wine and sex and a comfy robe.

"Thanks," she murmured, leaning back against his bare chest. He was in a pair of pajama bottoms and nothing else.

It had been the most erotic afternoon of her life, and she wished it wasn't under false pretenses.

The way this man looked at her…and she was lying to him.

This was why her father told her to never fuck for intel. Because it took a piece of her soul.

She told herself she wasn't doing that. She'd gone to bed with Dare because she'd wanted to, and she'd absolutely wanted to see him again. But there was no way around the fact that she was in this room for a reason other than desire.

"You all right?" He nuzzled her neck. The man was proving to be deeply affectionate.

She had to stop wallowing in guilt and get to the job at hand. Really getting to know this man. The truth of the matter was he never had to know why she'd come back to him. He could go through the rest of his life believing it had been only because she wanted him. Because she did. So fucking much more than she was willing to let her team know. She turned and gave him a smile, tilting her head up. "I'm amazing. It's shocking what a couple of ridiculously good orgasms can do for one's state of mind."

The smirk on his face proved the man was pleased with himself.

It made her heart clench because she got the feeling this wasn't an arrogant man who always felt on top of the world.

"I'll remember that. Come here and sit on my lap." He tugged her back to the sofa, easing her down. "Now is probably the time we should have that talk. I meant it when I said I want you to stay with me. I know you're here to visit your cousin, but I want you with me as much as you can handle."

He was making this far too easy. "You want me to move into your suite?"

"Yes. I know it's fast, but we don't have a lot of time." His hand was curled around her hip. "Tasha, I don't want to lie to you."

It wasn't hard to figure out what he was talking about. "I live in Dallas and you live in Toronto, and we both have busy lives. Long distance is hard and probably wouldn't work, so what we have is these two weeks."

"It's more than that." He seemed to think for a moment. "The long-distance thing I could work on. It's my family. My father is a controlling son of a bitch, and I would never expose you to him."

That was news. She'd heard a bit about his father, but she'd thought he was talking about him as a boss. She often bemoaned working for her own dad, and he was all kinds of awesome. "What do you mean by controlling?"

A long breath came from his chest, and he looked weary.

"You don't have to talk about it," she whispered. "That's the great thing about a two-week affair. We can pretend to be anyone we like. You can be my Dom and I'll be your sweet sub, and that's all we have to know about each other."

"And if I want more?"

"I think you'll find your sweet sub is always willing to listen, but from what you're telling me we have an end date."

"What if I want all of it even though it does have an end date? Even if I know I'll regret leaving you behind for the rest of my life? Hell, maybe someone will assassinate the fucker and I'll show right back up on your doorstep."

"Assassinate? That feels like a harsh word to use."

"It's true. My father... He's had some shady dealings in the past. There are whole parts of our business I'm not allowed in. He says I haven't proven myself to be enough of a Nash yet."

She didn't like the sound of that, and yet it was a path she felt compelled to go down. The Agency was worried about Oakley. Maybe they needed to be worried about the senior Nash. "How old do you have to be to be enough of a Nash?"

"I've only been a Nash since I was nine. I lived with my mother for the early part of my life. My parents weren't married."

So Tristan had told her, but she'd like to hear the story from Dare. "Lots of parents aren't married."

"Oh, my father was married," Dare corrected. "Just not to my mother. Helena was his first wife. They didn't have kids, and he divorced her over it. He had started to date the woman who would turn out to be his second wife when he found out about me. My mom was a sex worker."

He said it like he was dropping a bomb he expected to explode.

"Okay. So your dad was a client, and he walked away from her when she told him she was pregnant? That seems pretty rude."

His lips curled up, and he smoothed back her hair. "I tell you my mom was a hooker and you call my dad rude. It doesn't bother you?"

"You were right the first time. She's a sex worker, and it's necessary work," she argued. "You should have figured out that I'm not a prude. There are men out there who have zero interest in a relationship, but they want sex. Isn't it better for them to be honest than string along some woman who does want a relationship? And some people are lonely and can't find what they need, so they buy it. There's nothing wrong with it. We need human interaction like we need food and water. Sex is a need. It's a complex need, something that should be easy and simple, but we're human so we warp it."

He leaned over and kissed her. She loved the way the man kissed. "You are a miracle, Tasha." He sat back. "I'm glad you don't find my background distasteful, but I assure you my father did. And my mom didn't tell him. When she found out she was pregnant, she walked away because she knew he would want the baby if it was a boy, and he wouldn't allow her to be in my life. So I had nine years with her. They weren't all great, but I knew she loved me."

"What happened?"

"She got sick," he said quietly. "When she knew she was going to die, she called him. Did a DNA test. He still didn't have any children. When she proved I was his child, she made a deal. In exchange for taking me, formally adopting me and giving me the Nash name, she could never see me again. I didn't know she'd died until years later."

Her heart ached with the sacrifice his mother had made. "She must have loved you very much."

"I know that now. Years and experience have softened my memories of her, but at the time all I knew was she gave me away to a monster. My father sat me down and explained that I was his son now and I would do things the Nash way. He said the only thing my mother had done right was to give me the name Darren, so he didn't have to change it. She did it on purpose, of course. She'd hoped he would accept me if I ever needed him if she followed the family naming conventions. My father would have taken any name she gave me, so I suppose it was a good thing. Anyway, I was to get the best grades, play the right sports, befriend the right people, and never, never be anything like my whore mother or there would be punishment."

Tears pulsed at the back of her eyes. How terrible to go from a loving home to a cold one. It was something she could understand. "Dare, I'm so sorry."

"Don't be. I survived. It even got easier when it turned out I was good at school and not terrible at sports and my brother, Johnny, was born, and later my sister, Gina. My father wanted children, but he didn't give a shit about any of us unless we weren't living up to expectations. As long as we were good, we were left to nannies and our own devices. For a while I thought I might turn eighteen and get away. He thought he could control me through money. I didn't care about money. I had a scholarship to study in Vancouver, and I was going to give my dad the finger and go live my life."

"What leverage did he use?"

"My brother and sister."

She should have known. It was exactly the way someone could manipulate her. "Asshole."

"Yes, quite a bit of one. When I announced I was leaving, he explained that if I did, he would stop paying for Johnny's tutors. He has dyslexia. He would put Johnny in a military school, and he would find a suitably rigid school for Gina. Couldn't have her turning out to be anything like my mother. Johnny would die in military school, and Gina loved where she was."

"So you stayed."

"I went to the college he wanted me to go to, studied business and finance, and now I work for him."

"You found the club when you were in college, didn't you?" It would make sense. Despite her parents' openness about sex, she hadn't seen the inside of a working club until she was twenty, and then it had been one her father approved of, and she'd gone into training at The Club with her sisters. Cooper and Tristan had joined the year before.

"I was looking for one place where I had control, and I had a roommate who went regularly. I soaked it all in. I found a mentor. He was great. He talked me through a lot of my problems and taught me how to control my urges and to be patient. I was happy there for almost four years before my father found out, and well, I had to give up a lot for him to be willing to pay for my brother's first rehab."

Poor Dare. She leaned against him, letting her head rest in the crook of his neck. "What did you give up besides your whole community?"

"I didn't think about it like that, but you're right. All my friends were there, all the people who I thought knew the real me. As to what I gave up, it was my freedom. My father decided I needed a wholesome, traditional marriage to counter my wicked instincts."

"Says the man who cheated on his wife with a sex worker, and please understand that is not judging your mother in any way. She wasn't the one who was married," Tasha pointed out.

He sighed and rubbed his cheek against her hair. "I have no idea why I thought I would shock you. Anyway, he arranged my first marriage, though that didn't turn out quite the way he wanted. Audrey was as controlled by her father as I was. We weren't in love, but I thought we were at least friends given what we had to get through. I guess I didn't know how miserable she was. I work a lot, and she was alone most of the time. At some point she met one of my old friends and put together the whole 'I was a Dom in the past' thing, and she figured she could use it to force my father to let us divorce."

Well, she'd known that, and it still hurt hearing the pain in his voice. "Obviously she got what she wanted."

He chuckled, though there was a bit of bitterness to the sound. "I assure you Audrey didn't get what she wanted. We didn't have a prenup. She thought it was because I trusted her. In a Canadian divorce, assets are always split down the middle. I know all of this looks amazing, but it's company money paying for it. I get a salary and nothing else. Not even stock. Surprised the hell out of my first wife. She assumed I had a massive trust fund because no one watched her spending. She didn't understand my father was paying for her credit card. When she realized she wasn't getting more than a couple hundred grand, she twisted the screws a bit, started a couple of rumors about how rough I can be."

She turned so she could look him in the eyes. "There is nothing rough about you."

"Oh, there is. You have no idea how rough I could be with you if I let myself."

"Somehow I think you would control yourself," she replied. "I don't think you would hurt me, and you would respect my boundaries. Like I told you before, I can handle myself."

"Not if I've got you tied up."

What kind of fantasies were running through his head? Did he want to tie her up and make her helpless and do all sorts of nasty, filthy things to her? He would have such a weird relationship with his own sexuality given what had happened in the past. Did the fact that he was willing to talk about the outer edges of his desires mean he felt closer to her than any other woman? Somehow that thought sent a thrill through her.

She was the girl who'd always played by the rules, and she was breaking them all for this man. If she wasn't careful, she could fuck up and bring her team down.

"You would be surprised what I can get out of." When you were the child of Ian Taggart, there were all sorts of weird lessons including how to get out of any kind of restraints. "Dare, why would you ask me to stay with you if you don't want to explore? There's a club here. We could go if you like."

His jaw tightened. "I would like, but you have to understand that my father is watching. I don't think he'll have a problem with me having an affair. He doesn't give a flying fuck what I do in my personal life as long as it doesn't cause a scandal."

"And going to the club could do that," she surmised. "Let me think about it. My cousin has friends here who can arrange a discreet entry. I told you my father works in security. He's taught me and Lou a few tricks over the years."

She wanted to give him some good memories. Her whole soul felt like it softened around this man. She was a realist. It wouldn't work between them because she could never tell him what she did for a living, and she couldn't leave her team behind. Her team was her family.

"So you'll stay with me? You should know something else. My father told me he's going to find me a new wife and soon," he admitted. "If that makes you change your mind, I understand."

He was trying to be fair with her. He couldn't know that there was little he could say that would make her turn away. After all, she had a party to attend, and he was her way in. She tilted her head up, giving him access to her lips. "We have two weeks. We know the boundaries. So let's talk about a contract."

There was a look of pure excitement in his eyes at the thought. "Yes. I think we should do that. But later."

He lowered his lips to hers, and all thoughts of guilt fled.

* * * *

"That went well," Brian said as he watched the head of a medical research team walk away looking perfectly satisfied.

Dare wasn't. He felt like shit because he knew damn well those doctors who were trying to change the world would eventually get screwed if they succeeded. They would have a lawyer look over the contracts that would give them almost ten million in funds to continue their clinical trials, but they would ignore the lawyer when he pointed out how the terms were drawn to give the Nash Group all of the advantages. They were wide-eyed and thought they could make humanity better and would never understand that if they did, Nash would take most of the profits.

He'd seen it a million times.

"Yes, they'll almost certainly sign the contract." At least he hoped they would have a lawyer look at it. Sometimes they thought because they were smart enough to get through med school, they were smart enough to read some words and understand the legal costs.

They were not.

He wondered how the Huisman Foundation worked. He'd been reading the man's book, and he seemed like a genuine guy, someone who knew how hard the world could be and yet tried his best to fight it.

"You don't seem happy. I think your father will be." Brian sat back, ignoring the women who sent him heated looks as they passed. He'd been a good boy this whole trip when Dare happened to know he was a playboy at home.

"I hate the fact that if they succeed, they'll lose it all. My father will call in the debts and sweep the tech out from under them and sell it to one of his many businesses that look legit but aren't anything close."

A brow rose over Brian's eyes. "What do you mean by not legit?"

He sighed and took a sip of his whiskey. He wasn't drinking much tonight because he was hoping Tasha was up in his suite when he got back. She'd told him she was grabbing some clothes and talking to her sister and would be back as soon as she could. He'd arranged for a key and let the hotel manager know she could have anything she wanted. "It's not not legit, but it should be. My father is excellent at skirting the rules. He has companies across the world who can use a country's laws against the people he signs a contract with. It's all complex, and I don't even get most of it. He keeps me in the dark, but I know damn sure he doesn't have anyone's interests in mind but his."

The truth of the matter was he was fairly certain there were non-legitimate parts of his father's business empire.

"I think that's mostly true of all the billionaire class," Brian replied. "You don't get where they are without either ruthless will or being born into it. The ruthless will leads you to protecting everything you have. The generational wealth makes you think you were chosen, that all this is your divine right."

"I don't think it's all billionaires. I've met some who do a lot of good."

Brian huffed. "If you're talking about Huisman, I assure you he's like all the rest."

"You sound like you know him."

"I don't, of course, but I've studied the man and I think all that syrupy sweetness is a mask. I'm pretty good at reading people, and I think he's lying to the world, and he's every bit the monster his father was."

Dare wasn't sure what Brian had against the guy. Especially since they'd never met. Brian had grown up in the States, and the Huisman family, up until recently, had only been famous in Canada and medical research circles. "Well, we'll get to make some serious observations when we spend the weekend with him."

Brian frowned. "I thought you would take Tasha."

He'd thought a lot about this and decided to trust his friend. "I will. Oakley offered me two rooms. The truth of the matter is I'm going to be distracted. I want you to spend some time with Huisman."

The barest look of distaste crossed his face and then it was gone. "Of course. I can handle the man while you take care of your new girl. You move fast, man. Are you sure this is a good idea?"

"I thought you would be cheering me on. Tasha staying with me means Kara will be around a lot."

"I will admit she was way nicer to me today. I think I'm making some ground with her." A sly smile turned his lips up.

Dare wouldn't go that far. "I think she's working and will likely go back to trying to kick your balls in when you get her in private."

"Or maybe she'll do something else with my balls," Brian said, throwing down his napkin. "Any chance we could invite her up to the suite? Have a little party? I wouldn't hate having some more time with Tasha's friends."

There was something about the way he said the word *friends*. "What are you not telling me?"

Brian stared at him for a moment as though trying to make a decision. "I just think you should be careful. I know she didn't take anything from you the other night, but it seems coincidental that her cousin shows up at the conference we're in town for and she's back."

They'd been over this. "If she'd wanted to roll me for some cash, she could have done it the other night."

"I'm not worried about cash. I'm worried about all that research you have access to."

They were back to her being a corporate spy. "Fine. You're so worried, do a background search on her."

A moment went by before Brian's admission. "Already did."

This whole conversation was making Dare antsy. He didn't want to think about anything but Tasha. He wanted to wrap them both up in a bubble for the next two weeks, one where reality couldn't touch them. "And?"

Brian shrugged. "According to what I can find, she's exactly what she says she is. She works for a small security firm in Dallas. She and her sister are account managers. Everything about them seems perfectly normal."

"And that bothers you why?"

"Because perfectly normal can be a mask, too."

Brian and his masks. "You've done your research, now leave

her alone. If you don't want to be around her..."

Brian pointed his way. "And that is worrisome, too. You've known this woman for what amounts to a full day and you're threatening a friend for simply asking you to be cautious."

Because Tasha brought out all of his protective instincts. He was practically made of them, and he had to negotiate with his father when what he wanted to do was show his father who the boss really was. He didn't have to negotiate with Brian. "I'm taking these two weeks with her. If that bothers you or you think I'm neglecting my duties, then you can take it up with HR."

"You are being entirely unreasonable about this woman." Brian's head shook. "I suppose it's actually a good thing."

It wasn't. He would still want her two weeks from now, and he would still force himself to walk away. "I'll tell you something even less reasonable. I think I'm going to let her get me into a club here."

Surprise was plain in Brian's eyes. "Seriously? You have to keep that quiet."

"I know. She thinks she can get me in without anyone knowing."

"I know you're not going to like me asking, but I don't want you going in only with her friends."

He pushed back and stood to go. He'd paid the bill, and it was time to get back to Tasha. "Absolutely not."

Brian followed him. "Be smart about this. Let me back you up."

Dare wasn't about to tell Tasha he needed to bring a friend to a club she was welcome to. If they were anything like the club in Toronto, they would protect their members carefully. "No. I'm happy for you to come to Oakley's party, but I'm not bringing you along to the club. I don't need a keeper."

He turned to go to the private elevator that led to his floor. Brian managed to slip inside before he could close it.

"Fine. Leave me behind. See where that gets you," Brian complained.

He wasn't sure what else there was to say. "She's just a nice woman. And where is this coming from? You were the one who told me to go after her."

Brian frowned. "Well, I thought you would, I don't know, date her or something. I didn't realize you'd move her into your suite. It's one thing to take her to a party, but another to let her bring you back into a lifestyle that could get you into trouble. She is a nice woman, but she's a nice woman who happens to be exactly what you need at a time when she can influence you in so many ways because you're away from your father."

"Or she's one good thing that happened to me." He wasn't sure what was going on with Brian. "I thought you wanted to hang out with her cousin? Are you afraid Kara's some kind of corporate spy, too? Did you pull her records?"

"Of course not." Brian held his hands up. "I'm done. I won't say another thing. Let's simply agree that I'm on the paranoid side and move on. To tell you the truth I think Tasha's lovely, and I'm happy you're getting some joy in your life. So let's party. We're young and attractive and perfectly free to spend time with whoever we choose. I'd like to choose Kara. Hell, tell her to bring all her friends up here. I was talking to Kara about this American guy she knows. He's the guy in the car's brother. Cooper something."

"Are you trying to figure out what the guy's last name is?"

Brian sent him a perfectly innocent look. "I already know it. Well, I did. I forgot it now. I'm feeling like a party. You're going to be with Tasha. I'd like someone to hang out with."

Or he wanted to check out all of Tasha's family and friends to find a connection to… He wasn't sure what. He was well aware there were corporate spies out there, but he wasn't sure what they would want with him. It wasn't like he kept top-secret research on his laptop. He had a lot of information, but it was all logistical and banking and legal work. He had overviews of all the projects they were funding, but most of that was available to the public.

He never would have thought Brian was a weird conspiracy theorist.

Or he had some damage he hadn't talked about. Like Dare himself.

"Fine. But could you not let my girlfriend know you're suspicious of her."

A brow rose over Brian's eyes. "Girlfriend?"

He was pretending for a while. "That's what she is for the next two weeks."

He had a contract and everything. They'd spent the time before his dinner going over soft and hard limits and banging out a basic contract, and then they'd just been banging.

He wanted to get her alone, but she'd mentioned she wouldn't mind him spending some time with her sister. He got the feeling Tasha and Lou had to watch out for each other. And they'd come halfway across the world to spend time with their cousin. It didn't seem fair to leave her out.

"I will be a perfect gentleman," Brian vowed.

Sure he would. The doors opened and Dare started to walk out.

That was when he realized they weren't alone on the floor.

A man in a ski mask held a gun in his hand. He pulled the trigger and fired.

Dare felt something hit him in the chest, heard a shout, and the world went dark around him.

Chapter Seven

"He's gorgeous. Even more gorgeous in person than he was on screen."

Kenzie was swooning over this afternoon's encounter with Brian Peters. She'd won the war of who got to play "Kara" simply by waking up far earlier than her twin and being in the hotel before Kala could stop her.

They were all in one of the townhouse's living areas, this one an open space that included the breakfast nook and the kitchen where Zach stood wearing a muscle shirt and looking irritated at the whole situation. "Don't pull that shit again, Kenz. I know I said I would always keep your secrets, but this one is bullshit, and you do it again and I'll call in the big guns."

The entire team was here for what would likely be a hearty dressing down. Cooper paced by the kitchen bar. Lou was set up with a laptop at the table with Tristan, and Kala was sitting in the living room. No one but Kenz looked happy to be there, which let Tasha know Zach had been doing his growly thing.

Kenzie simply sighed. "My mom would understand."

Their dad would not, and neither would their Agency liaisons.

Tasha looked over at her sister, who had thrown herself down on the couch in the living room and put a hand to her heart. She wasn't sure how Kenzie managed to look like a Jane Austen heroine when she regularly took out the bad guys.

Tasha put down the small suitcase she'd carried down the stairs from the room she'd been sharing with Lou and gave her sister a frown. "You know he's going to be confused. You didn't act like the Kara he's met before."

And that was a serious problem. She'd spent the whole afternoon in Dare's arms, and now she had to come back to reality. The minute she'd walked in the door, Zach had been all over her, detailing all the ways Kenzie had screwed things over.

Kenzie's eyes stayed closed as though she was remembering every detail of her time with the ridiculously handsome Brian. "I was a very professional Kara."

"You were horny-as-fuck Kara." Kala frowned at her twin and then looked to Tasha. "I can't believe you let her go down there."

Tasha barely managed to not roll her eyes. "She was up and out of here at five a.m. I didn't have a chance to stop her. I was sleeping. Like you."

Cooper looked to Zach. "Aren't you always awake?"

A slight flush stained the man's cheeks. "I was out. For a run."

Tasha rolled her eyes. "So he met someone and hadn't done his walk of shame yet. Nice."

"We need better security." Kala put her back against the wall.

Tristan looked up. "We have excellent security. I knew the minute Zach walk of shamed right into this building. He missed Kenz by ten minutes. Cooper went for a run at five ten, and Kala didn't even notice her sister was gone until after she snuck out to buy pastries that she didn't bring back to share with the rest of us. That was rude."

"I hate trackers," Kala said with a sigh. "Talk about rude. And I went for the coffee."

"Well, if you'd been a little earlier you would have noticed Kenzie slipping out," Tristan said.

Cooper stopped and leaned against the bar. "Let's look on the bright side. This could turn out to be a positive if we play it the right way. Lou doesn't like this guy. Kenz can get close to him and figure out if he's some generic douchebag or someone we should worry about."

"Do you think her vagina will tell us?" Kala asked.

Kenzie sighed. "My heart will."

Kala made a vomiting sound.

Cooper put a hand on his perfectly flat abs. "Normally I would tell Kala to be nicer, but I'm with her on this one. Kenz, you need to tap the brakes and hard."

"I don't see why. Tasha's vagina has already broken this case wide open." Kenzie turned on her side, propping her head on her hand with a completely unapologetic smile. "Think of what mine can do."

Zach moved over to Kenzie and stared down at her. "I will pull you and stop this whole fucking op if I think you're getting emotional about this guy."

Tash was with him on this one. Her sister was a menace. "I'll back Zach up, sister or not. It was a complete coincidence that Dare turned out to be the best new target we could find. I didn't plan this."

Lou looked up from her screen, the light casting across her face. "She really didn't. She couldn't have planned this. Though I'm starting to think the whole 'oops, the dude who was supposed to meet with Oakley happened to have an accident on his way to the airport' thing might not have been. A coincidence, that is."

Oh, she knew when to follow Lou's instincts.

"What's got you interested?" Kala was suddenly focused again. She moved to Lou's side, sliding onto the seat next to hers.

Tasha moved in, too, and Zach went back to the kitchen, pouring himself a mug of coffee. He always had a pot on.

Lou looked up, the lights from the computer shining on her round glasses, giving her a slightly ghostly look. Sometimes Tasha worried Lou would sink into the shadows and lose an essential part of herself, falling into a completely intellectual world. Tasha remembered a time when Lou had been a scared kid with no friends, valued mostly for her genius-level IQ.

"What do our records on Lance Middleton show about his connections to Oakley?" Lou asked.

Tasha had gone over and over the dossier Drake Radcliffe had sent them. "There is no connection except the fact that they travel in the same circles on a basic level. Oakley invests in a lot of the same medical research that the Nash Group does, and Lance is one of

Nash's representatives."

Had they missed something?

"I was curious," Lou began.

Zach whistled. "That always leads to something interesting."

A wistful smile played over Cooper's face. "Well, at least this time it probably won't blow up like the time Lou decided to play around with chemicals."

Lou frowned. "I was trying to show how chemicals react. I had no idea I was making mustard gas. I was fourteen."

"I still think that's what went wrong with Travis's brain," Kenzie quipped. Of all of them, Kenz was the only one who didn't seem interested in what Lou had found out. Probably because she was still thinking of Brian and his dreamy eyes.

Sometimes she thought the twins had split down the middle, each of them taking more than their fair share of "parts." Like Kala got all their rage, and Kenz all the dreamer. If you put them together, they might make one whole person.

"Please continue." Tasha was rapidly discovering when their parents weren't around, they all slid back into their kid roles, and that meant she had to keep things moving along.

"I found a bunch of pictures on Oakley's socials," Lou explained. "None feature Lance Middleton, but if you look carefully, he's in the background of a couple of them. According to the intelligence the Agency sent us, they're not close friends. So why was Middleton walking around in the background of a dinner Oakley threw for his father's eightieth birthday?"

Tasha looked down and saw the picture Lou had brought up. It was of Oakley and an elderly man smiling for the camera, with family members at their sides. And in the background a man was walking behind the group. He had his head down, as though trying to be inconspicuous, but the picture was taken at an angle that made facial recognition possible. "We're sure it's him?"

Tristan moved in behind her. "Did you run it by my dad?"

Tristan's father was one of the great innovators when it came to facial recognition technology. He and Tris's other dad, along with several of their friends, had formed a company that found missing persons and aided in finding fugitives. Normally Tris would have immediately taken the new intel and gone to him, but like all the people he loved, Tristan was avoiding his parents, too.

From what she could tell, Tristan was avoiding everyone he loved. She thought the only reason he hadn't dropped the five of them was because he wouldn't leave the team. The only one he really talked to at this point was Zach. They often held long meetings behind closed doors that never seemed to resolve the darkness that surrounded Tristan now.

"I used the software he gave us, and it's a ninety percent match," Lou replied. "The only doubt is because of the angle."

"Well, the fact that he knows to hide his face says something." Cooper sat down next to Kala, and Tasha caught the minute his hand almost came down on her thigh. His jaw went tight, and he moved it back to his lap. "How many different places did you catch him?"

"Three," Lou reported. "All in the last eighteen months."

Tasha didn't like the implications. "I think I probably need a full workup on Dare's father and the whole business. According to Dare, he's a real piece of work. I'll get right on it."

A brow rose over Lou's glasses. "When will you have time? I think you'll be taking care of the target. Besides, it's already done. It's why I said I needed to talk to you before you put yourself in harm's way again."

Lou had mentioned it when she'd walked into the safe house, but she'd been caught up in packing and Kenzie endlessly going on about how cool Brian was.

Zach set his mug down. "Lou and I got on a conference call with Drake earlier today. We think we might have missed a couple of connections, including some involving your boy."

She didn't like the sound of that. "Dare isn't involved in this. He wasn't even supposed to go out to Oakley's until Middleton died. I don't think he and his father are close."

Their relationship sounded toxic as hell. It had hurt her heart to hear him talk about it. For all her dad's faults—and there were shockingly few of them—he would never threaten to abandon any of his kids. Even when her youngest brother had told him he would be a grandfather long before he'd expected it, her dad had stood by him.

And called him a dumbass. A lot.

"I think we should be the judge of that, Tash." Zach's gaze was steady on her. "I know you're used to being on the analyst side of the table, but you're the operative here. You're also too close to the subject, and the warning I gave Kenzie goes for you, too. Dare Nash's family has ties to a couple of groups I find highly suspicious. I can't directly link them, but I have my instincts. I think he might have some mafia ties."

Cooper snorted at the thought. "Canadian mafia? Is Eugene Levy the head? What exactly do they traffic? Maple syrup?"

"The Rizzuto family, despite their Canadianness, managed to traffic drugs and weapons along with extortion, murder, and racketeering." Kala gave Cooper what Tasha thought of as her know-it-all smile. "I'm not sure if maple syrup was involved. There are also several gangs in Canada considered to be some of the world's worst. Don't let the friendly smiles fool you."

Kenzie sat up and suddenly looked serious. "She's right. Dad jokes about how harmless Canadians are, but I've heard CSIS has a couple of new teams on the ground, and they aren't playing around. The rumor is they've developed a new department. I've even heard some of our teams have started coordinating with them despite what Kala did."

Kala shrugged. "I found the intel. That dude just did some backup, and honestly not that much."

"I'll find out everything I can," Tasha promised. "In the meantime, I'd like an update on Huisman since I'm apparently going to meet the man."

"He's a slippery shit," Zach said with a frown. "I can't tell. He's got connections I think are disturbing, but I can also explain them away. On the surface he looks like a great man who overcame a lot in his life. He's brought the foundation to new heights, and by all accounts he's helped a lot of people."

"He's dirty," Kala said quietly. "And we should be careful around him because he has ties to us. To our family."

Kenzie shook her head. "Levi Green killed his father. Dad had nothing to do with it."

"Levi Green was working for the Agency when he killed Huisman's father," Tristan corrected. "If anything, he should want revenge on the Agency, not the Taggarts."

"But the situation had been set up because Ian Taggart sent his team to Canada." Cooper crossed his arms over his chest. "Without that action, the elder Huisman is still alive. I've heard of worse reasons to seek revenge."

"And yet the man wrote an entire book about forgiveness," Kenzie pointed out.

"Wouldn't that be an excellent cover?" Kala countered.

Before they could continue to argue about the confusing Dr. Huisman, Lou sat straight up, her eyes widening. "We have trouble. Shit."

Lou almost never cursed. Tasha moved around her, and then she was the one biting back a curse. Lou had a feed from the hotel on one of her monitors. She'd cut into the CCTV feeds early this morning, and that was how they'd found out Kenzie had pulled her fast one and wasn't, in fact, moping in her bed.

Lou and the guys had watched them all day, and when Tasha and Kenzie had returned, they'd switched to following Dare. Lou would have made careful notes about what he did and who he met, sending intel to Langley along the way.

Now the feed showed Dare and Brian in the elevator. The next camera was already up in one of the four corners of the monitor. Lou had written a program that tracked the primary target wherever he might go, bringing up the next camera as he approached. Now it showed what Dare was about to be confronted with.

"Is that a gun?" Cooper leaned in. They were all crowded around the screen.

There was a man in a ski mask standing outside the elevator doors. He was close to the edge of the screen as though he knew there was a camera somewhere and was trying to avoid it, but he couldn't quite. Tasha's heart threatened to seize, and she went for her cell phone. If she could warn Dare...

Kala's hand went to hers, stopping the motion. "Too late, Tash."

Her sister was right. The doors were opening, and tears pierced her eyes as the attacker moved into place, his arm rising. He hesitated for the barest second as though trying to figure out which man he was targeting and then he picked.

Dare.

He'd shot Dare.

Tasha could feel bile rising as she watched Dare's hand go to his chest and his knees hit the ground.

"It was a sedation dart." Zach sounded perfectly calm. "I recognize the gun he's using."

She had to stay as calm as Zach. If she gave away the crazy panic she felt, he would do exactly what he'd said he would. Deep breath. In and out. Don't give into panic. Fear wasn't the enemy, her father had taught her. Panic was. "That one isn't. That's a SIG."

Kenzie gasped because the man had tossed the dart gun aside in favor of one that held real bullets, pointing it at the target that was left. "Brian."

Brian calmly smashed the button to hold the doors open and held his hands up to show he wasn't armed.

Then proved he didn't need to be armed.

Brian kicked out, catching the man in the gut, and gracefully brought up his elbow to break his opponent's nose as he bent over from the kick. He slapped the gun out of the man's hand, sending it to the floor.

"That dude?" Tristan was sending Kenzie a what-the-hell look. "You thought that dude was some frat bro from Ohio?"

Kenzie's eyes were wide as she watched Brian fight. His opponent threw a punch he easily dodged, and then Brian wrapped an arm around his throat and squeezed. And squeezed. And squeezed until the man was dead weight in his arms and he let him fall to the floor.

His expression hadn't changed once. The minute Dare had been hit, the happy-go-lucky smile had fled and he'd gone stone cold.

"Yeah, that dude," Kenzie whispered, her lips curling up. "But he's not some frat bro."

He was obviously Agency. Or something like it. "We're not alone."

Zach was already on his cell, calling his contacts.

"He could be mob," Cooper said with a shrug. "They know how to clean up a body. What if Brian is Dare's mafia protector?"

"Or the mafia dude who makes sure Dare does exactly what he's supposed to," Kala mused.

She watched as Brian started to expertly handle the situation and realized she might be in deeper than she'd thought.

* * * *

"What the hell happened, Brian? And why isn't he in a hospital?"

Dare started to come awake to a familiar sound, though he'd never heard that heavenly voice rail at him the way she was at Brian.

Tasha. Tasha was here, and he seemed to be lying in bed. When the hell had he gone to sleep? His limbs felt heavy, and his brain was in a fog.

"I need to talk to Dare before I tell you anything, Tasha," Brian said in a calm tone. "The truth is I shouldn't have let you in here at all. You've known him for a couple of days. You can't imagine what his life is like."

They were so loud. Dare managed to sit up, his head throbbing. He was in his room at the hotel, but he had zero recall of how he'd gotten there. He'd been down in the restaurant meeting with some wide-eyed researchers and then…

"Is he regularly attacked?" Tasha demanded. "I'm not going anywhere. I know you think you can scare me off, but you can't. My family runs a security business. I'm not afraid."

Brian was trying to scare her off? His head was so fuzzy.

Attacked?

"Hey," he called out.

Tasha rushed into the room. Even through the discomfort and fogginess, she was the prettiest woman he'd ever seen. The minute she reached for his hand and knelt down beside him, the world seemed more focused. "Are you okay? Maybe you should lay back. We don't know what that person used on you."

"Of course I do." Brian stood in the doorway, his arms crossed over his chest. "I certainly wouldn't have left him lying there if I thought he'd been poisoned."

"Poisoned?" The words didn't make sense to him. And then he remembered arguing with Brian and the doors to the elevator coming open and… "There was a man waiting for us when the elevator opened."

"Yes, there was." Brian moved into the room, looking more serious than he'd seen him before. "He shot you and when I confronted him, he ran. He dropped his bag. That's how I know the dart he shot into your chest was filled with ketamine. The darts were precisely dosed. I knew it wouldn't hurt you."

"Why would someone do that?" He put his free hand to his chest, feeling the soreness there. "Why didn't he shoot you, too?"

"He wasn't well prepared," Brian said. "I believe he thought you would be coming up alone. The gun he was using to deliver the dart only had room for one at a time. I had to fight him. I'm sorry. He got away."

"How?" Tasha asked. "How would he get away when this is a secure floor? There's only one elevator, and it requires a key card to operate it. It should have closed and taken Dare down to the lobby. You should have been able to follow the attacker down the stairs."

His head still hurt, but his girl was making sense. "Yeah, why didn't I go down to the lobby? What did the cops say?"

Tasha's head turned Brian's way. "He didn't call them."

"I didn't call them because getting them involved means getting Dare's father involved, and I wasn't sure he would want that," Brian said quietly. "Not when we don't know who this guy is and what he wants."

"That's exactly why we should call the police," Tasha insisted.

Damn. Brian was right. Dare sighed and hoped he looked pathetic enough that Tasha didn't get too mad at him. "I didn't think about that. My father would surely be informed, and he could pull me out of Sydney and send someone else in."

That would mean no more freedom. No more Tasha. The idea of losing this time with her... He couldn't do it. He couldn't get on a plane and leave her right now. It was stupid. He hadn't known her for long, but he was willing to risk his life to get a couple of days with her. That probably said more about how crappy his existence was than he liked, but he couldn't ignore the feeling. "I'm fine, baby. Brian is right. My father might overreact and bring me home. He doesn't like it when things go wrong, and he tends to blame me whether I caused the problem or not."

"I don't understand any of this." Tasha shifted, sitting on the bed beside him. "How can you be so calm? Someone tried to kill you."

"I don't think murder was his point." Brian walked in and stood at the end of the bed, a weary expression on his face. "I think kidnapping might have been. Dare's family is wealthy. It's not unheard of for certain groups to kidnap businessmen in foreign countries."

"In Australia?" Tasha seemed intent on challenging Brian. "I could buy that if we were in a country where those groups work. Australia is one of the safest countries on the planet, with a healthy CCTV system in public spaces."

"And the world is changing," Brian shot back. "Criminal groups are getting more bold. Why else would someone send Dare to nap world? They were either planning on kidnapping him and selling him back to his family or they were going to rob him. The watch on his wrist alone is worth twenty grand, and I don't like to think about what someone with bad intentions could do with his laptop."

"It's password protected." He wasn't a fool.

"And it has a biometric get around. Your fingerprint can open it," Brian pointed out. "It would have been easy to take your key card and your finger and walk right out of here with a whole lot of information about sensitive medical research, not to mention all of Nash's financials."

He thought Brian was being paranoid, but then he had recently been taken out with a freaking tranquilizer dart.

"You need a bodyguard," Tasha said with a frown. "And don't tell me Brian is a bodyguard. He couldn't even catch this guy."

Brian's jaw went tight, and it looked like he wanted to argue. "He was fast, and I didn't want to leave Dare. I'm an account manager. I'm not some ninja. I thought I handled it pretty well. I assessed the situation and decided to keep things quiet."

"I'm surprised security didn't catch it." Tasha's hand squeezed his. "It's apparent to me the security in this building is lax. Maybe we should think about moving."

That wouldn't work. "Moving would require me to inform my father, and I would have to have an excellent excuse. He didn't want me to be the one to make contact with Oakley in the first place. He can yank me at any time, and I would like to figure out what my dad wants from Huisman."

"All right. Then let me find you a bodyguard," Tasha offered.

"I think I can handle it," Brian countered. "I'll deal with this for you, Dare. Don't worry. I'll have someone here in the morning."

"Or you could go with the person who actually has connections to the security business." Tasha looked down at him, her dark eyes practically pleading. "You have to take this seriously. I know it feels surreal and you're thinking it can't happen again, but I'm worried."

She would be with him. What if she'd been the one standing beside him? It was obvious Brian had scared the guy off, but what would have happened if Tasha had been confronted with the danger?

She was right. There was a big part of him that wanted to write the whole episode off as bad luck and worse timing. No one was coming after him, and if they were, he could take his chances.

But he couldn't take a chance she could get hurt.

He had the choice to send her away and protect her or protect her another way.

"Could you make some calls, Tasha?"

Brian groaned and threw his hands up. "Fine. I can see you've got this."

"Brian." He didn't mean to piss off his friend. "Thank you for the save."

Brian's expression softened. "I don't know that I saved anything, but I'm glad you're okay. That bodyguard better be good."

"I'm going to get a recommendation from my dad. He knows a lot of people," Tasha assured him. "You can sit in on the call if you like, and I'll make sure you have all the information you need to feel secure."

Brian murmured something under his breath, but he was all smiles as he headed for the door. "I'll be out here when you want to talk, Tasha. I think he needs some more sleep."

Dare wasn't sure he wanted Tasha to talk to Brian alone. Brian seemed suspicious of her for no reason at all. "I'm fine."

She stood and nodded Brian's way. He seemed to understand her and closed the door as he left.

"You took a full dose of horse tranquilizer. You are not okay," Tasha said firmly.

How long had it been since someone tried to take care of him? He was the one who had to constantly be on the lookout for his siblings. He had to be the voice of reason and sleep with one eye open. "I think I should be with you. Brian is being paranoid, and I don't want him to upset you."

She reached down, running a hand over his hair. "I think paranoid is not a word we should be using. As my father would say, it's only paranoia if they aren't out to get you." Her expression turned solemn. "I might not like that Brian is trying to cut me out, but I do understand him. We'll work this out and everything will be in motion tonight, so you don't have to worry. This is what I do. My company has a bodyguard unit, and I match clients with the right guard. I'll call in some favors, and we'll have someone here in the morning."

He thought he liked her when she was soft and sweet and submissive. He loved this side of her, too. When he'd imagined his perfect sub, he'd thought he would always be in control, that she would need that dominance from him. But he was so tired. His body didn't want to work. It wanted to sink into sleep. If she was dependent on him for everything, he would have to push through.

"I can handle this, Sir." It was like she could read his thoughts. Or maybe he wasn't good at hiding what he was thinking when he was drugged out of his mind. "Get some rest, and I'll be beside you in the morning. Brian and I will be fine."

He caught her hand again, bringing it to his chest and holding it there. "You should put some distance between us. I know it. I should tell you to go, but I can't."

She leaned over and brushed her lips against his. "That is one order I would refuse, Sir. Go to sleep."

He watched as she walked out and turned the light off.

And he sank into a peaceful sleep knowing they would take care of him.

Chapter Eight

Tasha closed the door behind her and got ready for the real fight. Dare had gone down as easily as she'd hoped. There had been the tiniest fear he would do the classic martyr, protect-the-women thing, but she'd batted that away.

She'd learned early on in this job that the way to manipulate a target was to fulfill their needs. Oh, there were some assholes out there who were utterly unmanageable, but for the most part if a person had their needs met, they tended to fall in line.

Dare needed to be taken care of. Not in a baby-him way. In a simple, human, needed-to-know-he-wasn't-alone way.

He was so much more vulnerable than he would ever believe, and she was taking advantage of him.

She took a deep breath and let her mask settle into place because she was fairly certain she was about to face off with another person who wanted to manipulate Dare Nash.

The question was why. She needed to figure out who Brian Peters was working for because it sure wasn't Dare.

"I'm sorry I was so aggressive. I'm worried about him, and I've had a rough night." Brian stood across the room from her, and he had his mask in place, too. He was giving her a charming smile, likely the same one he'd been giving her sister all day.

But she'd seen the real Brian Peters. So they were going back to playing nice? She could do that. They didn't have enough information to drag him out into the light. Yet. "I'm sorry I questioned you. I was worried, too. Of course you didn't take off running after the guy who tried to hurt Dare. I would have been scared as well. It's a perfectly normal reaction."

There was a little tic in his cheek that let her know he so wanted to respond. He didn't like being thought of as soft and somewhat weak. It was there for a moment and then gone. Brian shook his head and gave her a self-deprecating laugh. "I wish I'd had a different reaction. I've always thought I would be a fight guy. I didn't even go to the flight response. I froze up."

He hadn't. He'd coolly and calmly taken the man out, got on his cell phone, and twenty minutes later he'd had Dare in bed while he was passing the attacker off to a man who did know how to avoid facial recognition.

He had a team with him. Tasha needed to figure out if it was an intelligence team that was backing him up or if he had a mafia cleaning team helping out.

Who the hell was this man and why couldn't her team break his cover?

The fact that they couldn't made her lean intelligence—and a high-level one—but she couldn't discount what a well-run syndicate could do.

The important thing right now was *her* cover. Did this man know exactly who she was? Was that why he was suspicious? Or did he buy into her act? She'd found most men took women at face value.

"I think that's what happens when you've never had to face real danger before," she replied. "Training helps."

"So you think you could have handled it better than I did?" There was a hint of challenge in his tone.

"I've spent my life around military men and women." She had to be careful about revealing actual parts of her background. It was important to give this man enough that he was satisfied she was being open, but not so much he could put together pieces she didn't want made into a complete puzzle. "By the time I came on the scene my dad was out of the Army, but he mostly hired ex-soldiers. All of his friends were ex-military, so I was trained from a young age in how to handle myself in various situations."

"And have you ever been placed in one of those situations?"

More times than she could count now, but her mind had gone back to one in particular. She wouldn't tell this man about how young she'd been the first time she'd had to hide to avoid the man all the girls in the orphanage feared. She wouldn't tell him that she remembered the day they came for her mother and she'd been hidden in the cabinet under the sink and told to stay quiet as they'd murdered her the way they had Tasha's father.

She went back to a more recent memory, one that was relevant to this mission.

"When I was a kid I was dumb and got catfished by a man who wanted to hurt my dad," she said quietly. "He found me online and worked to gain my trust for months. I thought he was my age. I thought he liked me and was trying to help me out. I went to meet him and he pretty much did the needle version of what happened to Dare. I couldn't run, couldn't make any decisions at all. I was sure I was going to die."

She'd wondered if she'd see her biological mother and father again. In those moments when the rogue CIA agent named Levi Green had drugged her, that had been the only sweet thought in her head. The rest was anger and fear and a not small dose of shame because she'd known her family was going to be so sad.

"Did he kidnap you?" Brian's voice had gone soft. He was good at projecting empathy. "If you don't mind talking about it. You don't have to."

"He did not. He was after something else. I was nothing more than a pawn to slow my father down." She would never forget how she'd woken up. In her father's arms, his tears falling on her face.

She'd never once seen her father cry at that point.

"I'm glad to hear that." He sank down to the couch. "Maybe we started off on the wrong foot. Some things have been happening around Dare that make me worry I don't understand what's going on."

"And a new woman shows up in his life, and you have to wonder if I'm using him." She sat across from him. It looked like he was trying a new tactic with her. "I am, of course, but only for sex and companionship. I like him. If you want the truth, I walked into that pub looking for a man to spend some time with. I recently came out of a bad relationship. I wanted to get back on the horse, so to speak. It was a random bar to me. I don't know how to prove that to you. You should feel free to do a background check on me. I can put you in touch with my father."

Who would be played on this day by Zachary Reed. They'd set everything up because she liked the idea of bringing a bodyguard in—of their own choosing, of course. A bodyguard would be able to get into Oakley's estate, and no one would wonder why he was armed.

Now that she thought about it, attacking Dare was an excellent play to bring in someone.

But it hadn't been Brian's play, otherwise he wouldn't have felt the need to take out the attacker. He would have shaken the man's hand and called the police and pretended to be the great savior.

She wondered if the man had been alive when Brian turned him over.

"I've already run a background check on you," he admitted.

"That's fair. Dare's what we would call a high-value target in my profession. If I was working his case, I would background check anyone he got close to." She could play this game with him. "What did you find out? Anything you're worried about?"

"Sometimes security companies have ties to the military, like you said. I have to wonder if your father isn't interested in Dare's family."

She was intrigued at where his mind had gone. He must be feeling comfortable with her if he was willing to give up that kind of information. "Why would my dad be interested in him? Is it the stuff Dare's worried about?"

A brow rose over his eyes. "He mentioned his father?"

"Yes. I know you think all we do is have sex, but there's some talking in there, too."

"I'm surprised he told you about his relationship with his dad," Brian admitted. "I've been working with him for months, and he's only recently started opening up. He's got a lot of walls up, and there's a good reason for them."

But they'd connected in a way she'd never connected before, and Dare had felt it. There was something between them she couldn't deny.

Something that could easily die if he ever found out who she really was.

"Why would my father potentially be interested in Dare's? That's a question I ask sheerly out of curiosity because we're just a security company. We offer security systems and bodyguards and have an investigative team, but they work with businesses. We're not some front for...military intelligence? The CIA?"

They kept the two completely separate. Mostly. She was pretty sure a whole lot of the staff at McKay-Taggart had their suspicions. After all, she and the twins went on a whole lot of business trips.

"Well, I know the Agency sometimes uses outside teams," he said and then shrugged. "I read a lot. And Dare's father has his hands in some unsavory pies. At least I think he does."

"What does that mean?" She hoped she was keeping her tone totally clueless, but she wanted the answer to that question.

Brian glanced over at the closed door as though wondering how much he was giving away and whether it would hurt his friend. "It means the Nash Group is only part of the business. It's the only part Dare knows, but the family company has more than forty subsidiaries. When you put it all on a white board it's like one of those conspiracy theories. There could be more. They do what they legally can to make the connections as fuzzy as possible."

"Why would they try to hide?" She could come up with a hundred reasons, but she wanted to hear his.

"It could be as simple as tax evasion. Or it could be something darker. I don't know. I only know that whatever that man wanted from Dare, it wasn't his watch."

"You think they wanted his laptop?"

"I think they wanted him," Brian corrected. "I think they meant to take him into custody in an attempt to force his father to pay up in some way. The best-case scenario is they want cash. His father might pay up. Might."

"His father is an asshole." She couldn't imagine a father not doing everything to get his son back.

"Absolutely."

"And the worst case?"

"They want to trade Dare for something else. Something dangerous." It was obvious this was a scenario he'd been thinking about long before the events of this evening. "Medical research is necessary and saves lives, but like all new technology, it can sometimes be twisted. Medications can have side effects, and sometimes those side effects can be used for nefarious purposes. That's my worst case. That some group feels like they can potentially use a medication that's being tested for something bad. Or they could want a sample to push their own research through. It could be corporate espionage at work."

He'd neatly summed up most of what her team had gone over. With the exception of the mob ties. It was interesting that he knew so much but hadn't heard those rumors.

It was time to play dumb. "I don't know a lot about corporate espionage, but my father does. He's in the States, but I can get him on the phone. I want to look through our contacts and see if there's a bodyguard here in Australia we can work with."

"I can talk to him? Your father, that is?"

She could only imagine how her actual father would chew this guy up and spit him out. Especially if he knew Kenz was swooning over him and hadn't seemed to change her mind when she'd realized he was lying. That had only focused her attraction. But Zach would be pleasant and affable and oh so helpful. Pretty much the opposite of the man the world knew as Big Tag.

"Sure. It's late here, so it's morning at home. He's an early riser, so I think we'll catch him before he goes to work." She pulled out her cell phone. If he looked, Brian would see she was calling a 214 area code. Dallas, TX.

Location was so easy to fake, but she didn't mean to get tripped up by small details.

She dialed the number and switched to speaker. Not something she would ever do in real life.

"Hey, honey." A deep voice came over the line. Zach faked a yawn. "How is life down under? Kara keeping the crocs away?"

The man was barely thirty, but he had her dad's sarcasm

down. Probably because he'd been trained by the best.

"Dad, I'm in some trouble. Or rather I have a friend who is. I've got you on speaker. It looks like I need to hire a bodyguard."

She settled in as Zach worked some magic and Brian relaxed. They were in.

* * * *

Dare rolled over and stared at the digital clock for a moment. Nine thirty. There were two of those, but he rather thought it was the AM one since he knew it had been later than that when that asshole had shot him. Unless he'd slept the day away…

He put a hand on his chest, rubbing the sore spot. Fucker. That had hurt, and honestly, the nausea and foggy head he'd gotten from the drugs hadn't been a party either.

0 of 10 stars. Would not recommend.

Where was Tasha?

He managed to sit up and flick on the light. She wasn't next to him, but there was an indentation in the pillow that let him know she'd stayed with him.

Had she woken up and realized he was a shitty bet? What could he actually offer her? A couple of weeks in bed, some play sessions? He could buy her presents, but nothing like a car or wildly priced jewelry since his father would have questions.

He was so trapped and he hated it, but he'd never hated it the way he did now. He felt like a fucking child asking permission to breathe.

She would be right to leave him.

He hated this, hated being caught in a freaking shame spiral.

Someone had taken off his shoes, but he was otherwise still dressed in the clothes from the night before. He forced himself to roll out of bed, and the scent of coffee hit him. Someone was out in the living area, but he couldn't be sure if it was Tasha or Brian. Had Brian scared her off?

The sight of her suitcase tucked against the wall told him no.

She was the one in the living room. She'd called down and gotten coffee, and she was sitting out there waiting for him to wake up and explain why she should stay.

They'd talked about something the night before. He could remember her saying something about a guard or being on her guard, and Brian had disagreed at first.

He moved to the bathroom. He wasn't about to have this conversation with her until he was clean and somewhat clearheaded. Damn. He had meetings today. He needed to do some research so he would be ready to meet with Huisman later in the week and here he was desperately worried about whether or not a woman he'd known mere days was going to leave him.

He tossed off his clothes and started up the big shower.

The problem was it felt like he'd known her forever. There was a deep comfort in being around her that he couldn't quite explain. It was like something eased inside him when she was around, something that had been tight for so long he'd forgotten what it felt like to be comfortable.

He stepped in the shower and breathed in the steam, letting it start to clear his head.

Gina was sixteen. Two more years and she would be able to make her own decisions. Johnny made bad decisions no matter his age. He would always have to be there for his brother, but Johnny was also more capable of living without money than Gina was.

Sometimes he wished his mom hadn't made the deal with his father, that he'd never known his younger siblings so they wouldn't be a weakness to be used against him.

He could pay for Gina's college. He had some money, and he knew how to make more. He wasn't completely foolish. After the divorce, he'd opened a couple of accounts and started stashing cash away. Cash that could be used to support his brother and sister if they chose to leave with him. Johnny would in a heartbeat, but he wasn't sure about Gina.

Could he leave her? Or would he stay to make sure their father didn't torture her?

"Hey, you're up," a soft voice said.

He turned, ready to tell her he would be out in a moment, but his breath caught in his chest because she was standing there completely naked, her dark hair spilling around her shoulders and brushing the tops of her breasts. She wasn't wearing any makeup and was so gorgeous it hurt his fucking heart to look at her.

Longing. She made him long.

"We should talk," he began. "I'll get dressed."

"Why?" She moved into the shower, that impish expression he was coming to love taking over. "Does your mouth work better when you're wearing clothes?"

"My brain works better when you are." His cock was already threatening to take over. His cock thought this was the best idea in the history of time.

She got right into his space, her hands going to his waist as she tilted her head up. "Your brain doesn't need to work at all right now, Sir. You need to relax. The bodyguard is going to be here in a couple of hours. I'm picking him up from the airport myself. He's kind of a family friend, but I haven't seen him in a couple of years. My friend Tristan knows him better, though it's been a while for him, too. Nate's former SAS, and he happens to need a job. You'll love him."

"Bodyguard?" This was what they'd talked about before she'd smoothed back his hair and told him to sleep, that she would take care of everything.

That she would take care of him.

Her nose wrinkled. "I wondered if you would remember. Yes. Bodyguard. He's a big guy who makes sure no one else shoots a dart into you. Or a bullet. Really, he's there to ensure nothing goes into this hot bod that you do not approve of. I don't think he'll save you from my tongue though."

He was so hard he could barely breathe. Shouldn't yesterday's crap have had an effect on his libido? Not when Tasha was around. He somehow managed to put his hands on her shoulders, stopping her from dropping to her knees. "Tasha, we have to talk. Someone came after me yesterday."

"And Nathan Carter is going to make sure it doesn't happen again," she said with a breezy smile that suddenly disappeared in favor of a wince. "He's expensive. Sorry about that. I had to promise him almost twenty grand, but when you think about it, it's not so bad. It's two full weeks, twenty-four seven. The good news is he doesn't actually work for a company. He's in between jobs, so there's no company fees. This job would be thirty grand if you were going through my dad."

"The money is fine." Hell, he could expense that amount and his father wouldn't notice, but there was something else. "You're in danger if you stay with me."

Her head dropped back and she groaned, looking like the most gorgeous brat he'd ever seen. "Ugh, I thought we got through this part. I hate this part. It's boring and sexist and you handled it so well last night." Her head came back up, her lips turned down in the sweetest pout. "Are you sure you want to go through this again? We could forget you said anything and get to the fun part."

"What are you talking about?"

She frowned and rolled her eyes and grabbed the soap. "Fine. I'm talking about the fact that you are about to suggest that the world is after you and you can't stand the thought of my nail breaking, and so in order to save the poor, weak woman, you must send me away."

Well, put like that it sounded bad. "I didn't say you were weak."

"You implied it."

"I did not," he countered. "I think you should consider the fact that I'm in some kind of danger and we've got an expiration date. I'm supposed to get married soon."

"You mean your feudal lord is in negotiations for a brood mare he intends to shackle you to. You don't even know the name of this woman. You've never met her. He probably hasn't even picked one yet."

Well, at least she had a way with words. "Something like that, yes."

"And you're going to do it because you love your siblings."

"Yes." He shook his head. "No. I don't know. If there's a way out, I'll take it, but I haven't found one yet."

"Then let me help you look. This whole expiration date thing… It doesn't have to happen. There are phones and planes and ways to see each other." She sounded so reasonable. "And don't tell me your father might find out. I'll tell him I'm perfectly happy to be a mistress, and all I need are a couple of presents, maybe a car and a nice condo, and I'll ensure you do your duty. I can convince him I'm the best thing that ever happened when it comes to keeping Dare Nash in line. I'll be his ally while I wait to cut off his head. I mean that in a rhetorical fashion. I wouldn't really do that. I've been told that's a nasty method of execution if you don't have a handy guillotine. Sniping is the best way to go if we decide that's the better route."

He stared at her, trying to figure out if he was scared or aroused, and it was probably both. "You can't be serious."

"I am not a shrinking violet, Dare," Tasha announced. "I am a woman who knows what she wants and tends to get it. If I decide to take on your father, I'll do it."

He let his head drop to hers, cradling her face in his hands. "You don't know what you're talking about, sweetness. He's...he could hurt you."

"Then I'll show him why he shouldn't fuck with me. I know he's been the monster in your life since you were a kid, but I've faced down a couple of monsters in my lifetime and I've come to find they're not so tough when you shine a light on them. There is always a way out of a trap. You just have to know where to look, and you have to be ruthless enough to beat him at his own game," she said. "I will go if you can't handle me being here with you. But don't send me away because you don't think I can handle the realities of your life."

She was offering him something so much more than sex. She was offering him partnership. Real partnership. He wouldn't be alone in the fight against his father.

He mentally backed away from that thought. She was the sweetest, warmest person he'd met in a long time, and he wasn't going to expose her to his father's toxicity, but he also wasn't going to send her away for her own good. She was smart and capable and had apparently won the fight with Brian the night before.

And if she was staying, then their contract was in place, and he could take full advantage of it.

Actually, when he thought about it, that contract had been in place the whole time and she hadn't followed the rules.

He let his voice go low, feeling more in control than he had before. He let his fingers wind in all that soft hair, looming over her. He tugged the slightest bit, watching as her pupils went wide and her breath caught.

Her nipples tightened as she went on her toes.

"Tasha, what were the defined times and places where I'm in control and you're supposed to play your submissive part and respect me?"

That sexy bottom lip of hers was suddenly behind her teeth as she obviously realized the trap he had her in. "Anytime I'm naked and we're ready to play."

"And did I give you the option of talking about this in a more civilized fashion?"

"You might have offered that, Sir."

"If you had taken me up on it, then I couldn't spank you for rolling your eyes and acting like a brat. If you'd taken me up on my offer, we wouldn't have been in a play space and the rules wouldn't have been in place."

"I did not think about that, Sir," Tasha admitted. "We're a new D/s couple, and I've heard that sometimes allowances are made for new subs."

Thought she could talk her way out of it, did she? He gently tightened his grip on her hair, eliciting a breathy gasp. "You are not a new sub, and you knew exactly what you were doing. Now lean over, hands on the bench and ass in the air."

"Kiss me first."

"I'm adding ten for the demand." But he released her hair and wrapped his arms around her anyway. He wasn't the Dom who withheld affection as a punishment. After all, it wasn't really a punishment since she would enjoy it. Every sign her body gave him spoke of excitement and arousal.

He let his tongue play against hers, stroking his hands down her back to cup her ass and draw her close.

After a moment he backed away and she took her position, her head turning the slightest bit so she could see him. There was a hint of a smile on her face, and that glorious ass of hers wiggled invitingly.

She was going to kill him.

The shower was massive, as befitting the largest suite in the hotel, so he could easily maneuver into position. A pleasant hum went through his body. This was exactly what he needed. The night before had been shit, and he'd been reminded once again how out of control he was in his own life. But here...oh, here he was the king. And she was every bit his gorgeous queen.

He put a steadying hand on her lower back and brought the other down on her left cheek. Hard.

Her whole body tensed, and she gasped.

He didn't know her limits well yet. This was their first bit of discipline. "What's your safe word, Tasha?"

"My safe word is not going to come into play. Could you not take me out of the fantasy? I'm your poor serving girl and you are the lord of the manor who caught me sleeping instead of working, and now you're going to spank me and make me suck your cock. Don't you judge me. I started reading romance novels at a young age, and now I have specific fantasies."

He slapped her ass again. Tasha was unlike anyone he'd ever known, and he needed to understand that she was a force of nature. He didn't have to worry that she would let herself be abused. She would tell him if he hurt her and likely kick him in the balls so it wouldn't happen again.

He could trust her.

He spanked her over and over, watching as her ass turned a pretty pink, and then it was time to move on to the other part of her fantasy, the part his cock had been waiting for since the moment she'd walked in.

"Think you can sleep on the job...milady..." He wasn't sure about the proper terms. He hadn't grown up reading romances. "Well, I'll show you some work you can do on your knees and then I'll get you on your back."

She was grinning as she turned his way. "We'll work on it, babe."

She dropped to her knees and when she took his cock in hand, he was sure he'd died and finally found heaven.

Tasha didn't play. She gripped his cock and sucked him down.

It took everything he had not to come then and there. Her tongue swirled around his cockhead as she stroked him, the softness of her palm contrasting with the firm grip.

Soft and competent and sweet and sarcastic. She was a complete revelation.

It wasn't more than a few minutes before his balls tightened, and he couldn't hold back one second longer. He let himself go, fucking her mouth and filling it as she worked his cock until she'd taken everything he had.

She sat back on her heels, tongue swiping to make sure she caught it all. "That was fun, Sir. Now you mentioned something about me being on my back. I've got an hour before I need to pick up Nate. Why don't we get dirty before we get clean?"

She stood and walked out of the shower toward the bedroom.

And he realized he was hopelessly in love with this woman.

Chapter Nine

"Any word on our friend Brian?" Tasha was still feeling relaxed and loose when she managed to make it back to the safe house.

Despite what she'd told Dare, she wasn't the one picking up Nate from the airport. That would be Tristan, with Cooper along to brief Nate on the situation he was going into. Nate and Tris were friends from way back. Nate's father had once worked for the London office of McKay-Taggart, and he and Nate's mom were still very friendly with Liam and Avery O'Donnell. Avery and Nate's mom, Stephanie, had known each other for decades and kept their friendship up even when there were thousands of miles between them. The Carters had moved back to Australia when Nate was a kid, but the two families often visited.

Nate was friends with Aidan O'Donnell, and that meant he knew Tristan, since the two had been practically attached since they were…well, born. She couldn't remember a time when Tris and Aidan hadn't been so close they could be brothers.

She'd been surprised Tris had been willing to do the pickup. She'd half expected him to turtle the minute he heard someone who knew him from his happier days was coming.

Dare thought she was on her way to the airport with her sister and cousin. One more lie she'd told him.

Maybe she wasn't so relaxed.

Lou turned in her chair. "I've looked everywhere and cannot find a thing on this guy except what he wants me to see."

"I don't like it." Kala had played Kara today. She was in a chic business suit, her magenta-colored hair tied back in a neat bun, and she'd already stowed the suitcase she toted around complete with real information on new clinical trials Millhouse Pharmaceutical was running. "We should kill him."

A pillow shot across the room, which Kala batted away without even looking.

It had come from Kenzie, who was still in pajamas despite the fact that it was well into afternoon. "You are not killing him. What is wrong with you? You always go straight to 'let's kill him.'"

"It's the easiest way to ensure he doesn't kill us," Kala shot back.

"It also gives us no intel." Lou settled in her chair as though perfectly willing to watch the twin smackdown.

Tasha didn't have time for a smackdown today. "You two chill. No one is killing Brian. I'm still not convinced he's mob, and if he's intelligence, he could be a friendly. Hell, he could be one of ours. You know sometimes the left hand doesn't know what the right hand is doing."

The Agency wasn't the best when it came to cooperating—even with their own teams.

"Now I am worried about that," Lou said as the twins seemed to calm down. "Zach said he's heard something about another team in play here in Australia. He's making some calls."

That was the last thing she needed. Any other team would be more senior than hers, and they would try to take over. Not just try. They would likely be allowed to do it, and she could lose the ability to protect Dare. "What would they be doing? This is a surveillance mission. We don't need two teams."

"Unless they know something we don't." Kala shrugged out of the jacket she'd worn. "And they're using us to do the surveillance and intend to swoop in and pick up the prize."

"What prize?" It was the mystery she'd been thinking about all morning. Well, when she wasn't under Dare.

When she'd been under Dare, she hadn't thought about

anything but him. She'd let the world fall away, and she hadn't been an operative, hadn't been working him for intel. She'd simply been his.

"I don't know," Lou admitted. "You talked to Brian last night and he told you he's worried someone wants Dare for reasons beyond mere money."

Kenzie gracefully leapt over the back of the sofa and landed next to her twin. "I read the report. He thinks there's something in the Nash Group's portfolio."

After Brian had left, she'd ensured the suite was bug free and then written a quick report to let her team know what had happened and that she was in place and safe for the night. She'd detailed her conversation with Brian. "Yes. Did you look into the subsidiaries?"

"There are more than Brian found," Lou explained. "I've been able to tie forty-two smaller companies to the Nash Group, and of course there are many more they've invested in. From what I can tell they really enjoy investing money in cash-strapped researchers and then taking the majority of the profits when they inevitably sell. Their contracts are heavily favored to their side. In one case, they even stole the patent for the process from a group of technicians who found a way to make MRIs run better. I think we also have to consider the fact that Dare's family has a lot of enemies."

Kala's head shook. "No. This isn't revenge or we wouldn't have competing teams. The Nash Group is important in a way we haven't figured out yet."

"We're not here to solve that mystery," Kenzie insisted. "We're here to get close to Emmanuel Huisman and report back on our findings. That's all. Anything else is outside of mission parameters."

"So is you trying to hump the enemy," her twin shot back.

Kenzie gave her sister her middle finger and then looked back to Tasha. "We don't know he's the enemy, and I'm merely trying to be the voice of reason. You know what we've been taught. We're supposed to do the job and get out as quietly as possible. If there's another team on the ground, they're here for a reason. This isn't a game we're trying to win. We get close to Huisman, find out if Oakley is trying to manipulate him, and then let the 'rents figure out what to do next."

Kenzie was way better at following the rules than her twin.

Most of the time. And she was making sense. "You're right. This situation has already been made a million times more complex because I screwed up."

"You didn't screw up," Kenzie corrected. "You fell in love."

Kala made a vomiting sound and stood. "She fell into bed. Don't make more of it. I need a drink. Do we have enough food for the Aussie? I've heard he's massive."

The problem was she was starting to think Kenzie was right. "Whatever I did, I made this whole thing more complicated."

"I think feeding Nate is going to be Tasha's problem," Lou shouted to Kala before she looked Tasha's way. "And Kenz, I understand you want to simplify things, but the mission parameters changed the minute Dare became the target. We need information on him, from him. Zach and I have been talking, and we think we should download his laptop."

Her gut tightened. She'd known this could be a possibility, but she'd hoped to avoid it. "He's got nothing to do with his father's illegal businesses."

"We can't know that unless we see what he's carrying around. You should know that Kala already duped his phone." Lou made the statement in a no-nonsense fashion, but her jaw had firmed as though she expected trouble.

She was going to get it. "Kala did what?"

"I duped his phone while the two of you were saying good-bye." Kala leaned against the bar, a glass of red wine in her hand. "He very kindly left it out in the living area. Since you confirmed the suite's not bugged, I left a couple, so now we can say it is."

Anger rose hard and fast, and she confronted her sister. "You had no right to do that."

If Kala was concerned with her flash of temper, she didn't show it. "I had every right because he's the target. I have every right because two of my sisters are acting like we're on *The Bachelor* and they need to get a rose out of a man instead of being the operatives they were trained to be."

"If you have a problem with the way I'm doing my job, you should talk to me, sister." She got up in her space. Tasha was the reasonable one, but she knew how to throw down when she needed to. The idea of Kala calmly taking away all of Dare's privacy while she distracted him with kisses in the next room infuriated her. "What you do not do is go behind my back. I know I share charge of this team with Zach, but I will not have you going rogue on me."

"What would you tell me to do if Kenz or I were working the target?" Kala's expression stayed a careful blank. "Let's think back. A couple of months ago we were working a scientist in Romania. We got to be such good friends. I liked her. What did you order me to do, Tash?"

A flush flashed across her. They'd been trying to get the plans for a potential bioweapon, and the best way in had been one of the scientists working on a lower-level project. However, she was the sister of the lead of the project the Agency was worried about. She'd been lonely, and Kara had been a good friend.

"I had you bug her apartment but that was…" Tasha stopped because she'd been about to use the word *different*, and she wasn't sure it was. In fact, she was certain it was pretty much exactly the same scenario. Kala had genuinely liked the woman, had become friends with her. Kala didn't do that often. Tasha stepped back. "I'm sorry. You're right."

"I am, and you're too close to the target." Kala's expression softened. "There's a reason you run the team and don't go out in the field, Tash. Same with Lou. You two are soft, and I like you that way."

"I'm soft," Kenzie argued.

Kala's eyes rolled. "Yeah, you like to pretend to be, but not the way Lou and Tash are. You're perfectly capable of making the hard calls in the field. What would you have done if you'd been Kara today?"

Kenzie sighed. "I would have duped his phone and hidden a couple of bugs. I've been carrying them around in case I got the shot, but Brian was always there."

"He wasn't this afternoon," Kala explained. "So I did it."

Kenzie perked up like she'd found a way out of being lumped in with her twin. "But I wouldn't have told Tash, so she wouldn't have to feel bad."

"So she wouldn't know we're probably listening in on her doing the deed with Dare?" Kala asked.

Kenzie shrugged. "Now you've made her self-conscious, and

she might not be able to perform. Did you think of that?"

"I think she'll probably just be a little quieter," Lou offered.

She hated her sisters sometimes. Loved, loved them, but they made life weird. "You will tell me the precise location of every bug you planted."

"Someone finally bugged the suite?"

The door had come open, and Cooper walked in followed by Tristan and one of the largest men Tasha had ever seen. The last time they'd been in the same room together had been eight years before when Nathan Carter had come to Dallas with his parents for a visit. He'd been a tall, lanky seventeen-year-old with a sweet smile and a whole lot of Aussie lingo and plans to go into the military. The Army had packed the muscle on and turned the boy into a big old hunk of man.

"Tasha distracted the target, and I didn't have a Brian problem," Kala said, her attention going to the new guy as a smile slid across her face. "Nathan Carter, you grew up right, man. Welcome to the team."

Kenzie had leapt off the couch, giving Nate a big hug.

He looked so much like his father. Six and a half foot plus, and there had to be two hundred and fifty pounds of muscle on him. Kala was right. He was going to be as hard to feed as Lou's dad.

"Thanks for being willing to help." The confrontation with her sisters was still playing through her head. They were right, but it felt so wrong to know that they would be listening in on all of Dare's conversations. She was usually the one listening in. She or Zach. This time it would be Lou taking her place. Lou would be listening in on all of Dare's secrets.

"Happy to do it. I was sitting around the flat thinking about my next move. Didn't think I would be leaving the Army so soon." He might have spent his first years in England, but Nate was pure Aussie now. His sister, Elodie Carter, had been born in London, but she barely remembered living there. "I'll be honest. I was about to have my dad call yours to see if I could get on with MT, maybe. I think it might be good to get away for a while."

He'd been in some kind of accident. At the time he'd been SASR and on a classified mission. She was sure Lou or Tristan could get the full report, but they'd decided to respect Nate's privacy. If he wanted them to know what happened, he would tell them.

They wouldn't give Dare the same courtesy.

Because he's the target. Kala is right, and you're putting everyone in danger.

Professional. She had to stay professional.

"I bet I can make that happen for you," she promised. Her father was always looking to add to the group of bodyguards he affectionately—if sarcastically—called the "douche." He'd explained once that if a group of geese could be a gaggle, a group of bodyguards was a douche. There was always room on the douche. "You looking to work in London or Dallas? I would offer you a job at our African office, but Ten Smith nearly murdered the last one we sent out. I think the man is only capable of working with his kids at this point."

She'd heard the former CIA agent Tennessee Smith had once been a smooth operator who could manage anyone, but she'd only ever known the cranky guy who traded punches with her dad from time to time and told the craziest stories. And did not like to work with newbies.

"Oh, Dallas would be brilliant," Nate answered. "I thought it would be good to be near friends. I didn't keep up with the London kids the way I did you guys. I'm still close to Aidan, and I think it'll be fun to see what Daisy gets up to. Haven't actually seen her in years."

Well, he was in for a treat because the last time he'd seen Daisy O'Donnell she'd been an awkward teen with braces and greasy hair because she hadn't been big on the whole bath thing. Daisy was the definition of late bloomer. Nate was going to find out the girl he'd considered a kid sister was now a freaking bombshell who seemed to attract trouble.

"Daisy is the single hottest mess we have in the family." Kenzie was grinning. She loved good gossip. "She's a walking episode of *Dateline*, except somehow she always manages to find her way out of it. Like once she followed a guy she was dating into an underground club and almost got herself auctioned off and because of the social media post she'd made, the cops raided just in time, and she was celebrated for saving ten other women."

Nate frowned. "She did what?"

"How about the time when she broke into the county animal shelter because they were set to euthanize twenty-five dogs? She got caught by the police because she did not take my advice when it came to burglary," Kala said with a smile. "Instead of being arrested, they put her on the evening news, and that was how her parents found out their fifteen-year-old wasn't in bed."

"And all the dogs got adopted," Lou finished.

"Her dad talks about her like she's some kind of saint," Nate pointed out, shaking his head. "All Liam could talk about the last time he came out to see us was how Daisy could do no wrong. I thought she might be considering becoming a nun or something."

"Uncle Li is deeply confused about his kids," Tasha explained. "He's kind of got it backward."

"He talks about how Aidan doesn't have a brain in his head. Aidan got a near-perfect score on his SATs," Tristan grumbled. "He's literally in med school. He's...anyway, good to see you, man. I'm going to go find Zach. I've got some Deep Web searches I need to monitor."

They all watched as Tristan strode away.

Nate's head shook. "What the fuck happened to him? That's not the Tristan I know."

"You know how the work can change a person. Now how about we have a beer and talk about what you're going to be doing for the next couple of weeks." Cooper neatly changed the topic.

"Sounds excellent," Nate replied.

Nate could help solve one of her problems. She'd put off calling the BDSM club here in Sydney because she worried they might call her father, but she happened to know that Nate's parents had connections here, too. "Hey, I also need you to get us into The Station this weekend."

A brow rose over Nate's deep blue eyes. "You guys looking to play?"

"We need to download the contents of the target's laptop," Kala explained. "I don't want Tash to do it. The easiest way to get the job done is to take the target someplace he'll have to leave the laptop behind. He's got some excellent security on it, so we need a couple of hours of knowing exactly where he is. In the club he'll be contained, and we can monitor the situation."

"Does this bloke know he's going to a sex club?" Nate asked.

He was definitely going to fit in. "He's a top. He was a member of a club in Toronto, but his father's an asshole, and he's been out of the lifestyle for years now. I offered to take him to The Station, and he seems excited about it. It's an excellent way to keep him occupied while Lou and Tristan do their work. Even if he insists on bringing it to the club, he'll lock it up while we're playing. I'll make sure we play until we have what we need."

Every word felt like a drag on her soul. She was falling for this guy, and it wouldn't work out. What the hell was she supposed to do?

Exactly what you said you would. Take on his father. Play the game because you were taught how to play, and Dare has no idea how to truly handle a man like his father. He'd been thrown into a situation where he had to protect the ones he loved, but he'd been given no tools. *So you be his sword.*

She was being overly optimistic. If Dare ever found out what she was doing, who she worked for…

"Sounds like a plan," Nate agreed. "Heard there was an Oakley connection to this mess. You know the rumors about Auggie Oakley?"

"I know what I've heard. Or rather what we've been told." She would be totally upfront with Nate since he would be putting himself on the line. Also, she knew his dad still worked with Australian Secret Intelligence Service. He might have some intel they didn't have. "We're here to gather information on Dr. Emmanuel Huisman. Apparently a Canadian associate of my father's believes Huisman is some kind of threat, and the Agency decided to look into it. Whether he is or not, there are people in the US who don't like the idea of a man like Oakley potentially influencing Huisman. The man has enough power over the medical industry as it is, and we've reason to believe he might be working with some foreign governments against US interests."

"You mean he's taking money from China to put them on the forefront of medicine at the expense of Western countries." Nate proved he was more than a big, gorgeous hunk of man. "The need for new antivirals and antifungal meds are starting to outpace our ability to keep up. We've got a nasty bugger here that is rapidly evolving past what we can cure. Oakley is heavily invested in firms currently doing that research. If he takes it and sells it, we'll be at the mercy of whoever has it."

"And that is why we have to make sure Huisman isn't involved with him," Lou summed up. "The Huisman Foundation is currently working on several vaccines that could cover emergent viral threats, and they're funding the most advanced research going on candida auris. He's funding research on a whole new class of echinocandins."

The "super" fungus had recently been spreading through hospital populations, and the new strain was proving to be resistant to the antifungal medications on the market.

There were more ways to wage war than simply setting off a bomb.

"I think it's safe to say the Australian government is aware of the threat Oakley could pose. Or rather some of us are. He owns a whole lot of Canberra, if you know what I mean," Nate said.

Yes, she suspected there would be a lot of politicians in Oakley's back pocket. Canberra was Australia's capitol and the seat of political power. A billionaire could put off a lot of investigations.

"Have you ever met him?" She hadn't thought to ask the question.

Nate snorted. "Me? Dine with a billionaire? Not likely." He frowned. "Wait. Am I going to have to meet the bugger?"

She had so much worse news for him. "Yep. And you'll have to wear a suit."

A shudder went through the big guy.

A bright smile crossed Kala's face, the kind she almost never saw from her grumpiest sister. Kala gave Nate a pat and went into her best Aussie accent. "Sorry, mate. You thought you could get away with a budgie smuggler, thongs, and some sunnies."

Nate frowned her way. "I would not wear a budgie smuggler, thank you."

"It's a banana hammock," Lou whispered. "I think he would look good in one, but it's probably not right for this job."

"Fine." Nate started walking toward the kitchen. "I'll shove myself into a bloody suit, but if you think I'm wearing a tie, you're mad as a cut snake. And Kala, your accent's damn near perfect, girl."

"Ta," Kala said with a wave of her hand. "I'm getting used to chicken salt on my chips, too. We need to get some of that before we head home."

Kenzie started talking about all the things she loved about Australia and Lou chimed in while Cooper passed out some beers.

Tasha sat back because the one thing she loved most about Australia was the one thing she couldn't take home with her.

* * * *

"I've done a quick recon of the restaurant, and it looks like we're a go for this afternoon," Nate Carter said as he walked out onto the big balcony. "I've got your driver coming at one. That should put us there in plenty of time."

Dare was getting used to the big guy. It had been weird at first—having a bodyguard shadow him—but Nate seemed professional and easy-going, for the most part. Especially after he'd told the man he didn't have to wear a tie. That first day Nate had looked like he wanted to die, and he'd explained Tasha had dictated the slick-looking suit he was wearing was to be his uniform. Once Dare had declared a suit coat and button down was fine, Nate had relaxed. And given Tasha a bit of hell.

It was fun someone was able to because the woman was practically running his life one week into their relationship.

And that was the way he liked it.

"Excellent, and you've talked to the manager?" Today was probably the most important day of the whole damn trip. He and Brian were meeting with Huisman and Oakley for lunch. Though he didn't intend to inform those two of his trouble, he would have to let the manager of the restaurant know he would be bringing in personal security and needed some accommodations. Accommodations he would absolutely pay well for.

He'd taken Tasha out safely several times in the last couple of days. Nate had made that possible. He'd been excellent at staying in the background and seemed to know the city pretty well.

And tonight they were going to a place called The Station.

Tonight he would get Tasha in a real club. They would play and play, and he would let go of all his inhibitions and be himself for fucking once in his life.

"He's aware of our concerns, and he's going to allow us to use a private dining room. I'll be on the only entrance and exit," Nate confirmed. "I've also talked with Oakley's security, and we're in coordination. There are several security cameras, and they're willing to give us access. Huisman is coming alone."

"Seriously? I would expect Huisman to have a detail." Dare himself was the one who wouldn't typically need one. No one should know who the hell he was. He still wasn't sure he needed Nate Carter, but it made Tasha and Brian comfortable, so he was going with it.

"No detail," Nate confirmed. "He's traveling with an assistant, and that's all. I was told she won't be at the meeting. So it's you, Brian, Dr. Huisman, and Mr. Oakley. His guard will be with me on the door. I've vetted the servers, and we're comfortable with them."

"I'm afraid I won't be attending." Brian walked in from the suite. He managed to find his chair despite the fact he had his eyes on his cell phone. "We've had a problem with one of the accounts we signed. Apparently the fuckers got a real lawyer and they're demanding a meeting. Your father told me I need to handle it. I took the time to text Oakley and explain I won't be there. You'll be surprised at his response."

"His response? He doesn't want to do the meeting if you're not there?" Brian was kind of incidental. Brian had been going so Dare would have backup. He wouldn't be doing any real negotiating with Huisman.

Brian sat back, a wry smile tugging up his lips. "Oh, he wants the meeting. He just wants it with… How did he put it?" He looked back at his phone. "Tell Nash to bring that stunner of his so we have something nice to look at instead of his ugly mug."

"I don't have a… Does he mean a stun gun?" Dare was slightly confused.

Nate bit back a laugh. "I believe he's asking you to bring Tasha. And the other reference wasn't to a coffee mug."

Dare frowned his way. "I got that part."

"At least he didn't tell you your face is a bucket of smashed crabs." Tasha moved in behind him and tilted his head back, staring down at him with her impish grin. "He's got terrible taste. You're obviously a spunk."

She knew way more Aussie than he did. Probably what happened when a person had family here.

A bell chimed behind him, letting him know someone was at the door, probably Tasha's cousin, who'd started meeting them for what she called "brekky."

Tasha kissed him and sank down on the seat across from him. She was still in the big, oversized robe that sported the hotel crest. He happened to know there was absolutely nothing under that robe, and he had the wildest urge to order her to go get dressed because there were men here.

Which would likely get him in serious trouble because he was literally sitting out here in his robe, too. He'd made the decision because he had a couple of hours before he needed to shove himself into a suit. It looked different on Tash. On Tash that robe might completely cover her, but it also reeked of sex and sensuality and reminded him of the way she'd straddled him the night before. She'd ridden him like a stallion, and he'd been happy to do it.

When she'd gasped and come and her body had relaxed, he'd flipped her over, spread her legs, and fucked her hard.

And then he'd slept. Like a baby. He could sleep with her around.

He needed to keep his mind on the plans for the day or he would be sitting here with a massive erection, and his sub might actually try to take care of it for him. She was surprisingly comfortable with her sexuality.

A bad idea considering they had company. "I do not understand the language here."

"It is a different world," Brian agreed. He seemed more comfortable around Tasha now that they had Nate with them. He'd stopped complaining that she might be a spy. And started complaining that she was a distraction. "Looks like you're going to be working a bit today, stunner."

"I thought Dare was working." Tasha poured out some coffee.

"He is. If you can call having a power lunch with some of the most influential people in the world work," Brian replied.

"Yes. It's absolutely work." Dare didn't want to do it. Not at all. Brian seemed to think it was fun to talk business with sharks. It wasn't.

"Well, it's the first time in days we've managed to get you out there," Brian snarked.

He deserved that. He'd pretty much pushed all the work off on Brian so he could spend time with Tasha. He was useless, anyway. He'd tried that first morning, but the idea that she was sitting upstairs had blown all his concentration, and by afternoon he'd told Brian to go solo on the meetings and taken Tasha to the beach. They'd lain in a cabana and splashed in the waves and tried not to step on shit that could kill them.

Nate was good at telling them about all the things that could kill them.

"Sorry. I'll try to be better." He wouldn't try hard. He was already thinking about other things they could do. Maybe she would like a morning hike up Sydney Harbour Bridge. He'd been told it had fabulous views of the city. Was hiking romantic?

"At least I know you'll make this meeting because Tasha will be there," Brian replied.

"Why am I involved in this?" Tasha asked.

"Morn." Kara stepped out on the balcony and frowned at her cousin. "What are you doing? Can you not get dressed anymore? You look like sex, Tash."

Ha. Someone else could be the voice of reason.

Tasha merely sent her cousin her middle finger. "I'm perfectly covered, and Brian has zero interest in seeing my girl parts. Neither does Nate."

Nate shrugged. "I mean, I wouldn't look away."

"I only would because Dare would beat the crap out of me," Brian admitted. "Otherwise, I would absolutely look, but only for aesthetic reasons. You know I only have one set of parts I'd like to see."

Kara's eyes rolled as she sat down. She was looking perfectly respectable in her dark suit and killer heels. She reached for the coffee. "Well, let's hope there's no paparazzi floating around taking pictures that could get back to her dad eventually. Because she looks like a woman who recently had sex. Like two minutes ago."

That had Tasha sitting up straight and ensuring her robe was actually covering her. She also smoothed down her hair.

"I don't think there's paparazzi here," Dare assured her.

Tasha's head shook. "My s...cousin is being a dick. She's jealous because she's not getting any."

"But she could," Brian offered.

A bright smile crossed Kara's face. "Still might."

Those two were going to kill him. He wished they would hop in bed together because the sexual tension was so thick, he could cut it with a knife. Sometimes. Other times he got the feeling Kara couldn't be less interested. She was playing games, but Brian didn't seem to mind.

He was glad his Tash didn't play any games. She said what was on her mind and never prevaricated.

Tasha was a woman he could trust.

If Oakley wanted to ogle her, maybe that would give him more time with Huisman. She could flirt a little, provide some distraction. It would be perfectly safe because he wouldn't let her be alone with the man, and she could handle herself.

Shouldn't he be jealous? He wasn't. Tasha wanted him. Tasha cared about him. It was the weirdest, nicest sensation. "Oakley wants to flirt with you, sweetness."

She grinned. "If I'm flirting with that horny billionaire, you can talk to Huisman."

They were so in synch.

"I'd love to talk to Huisman," Kara said. "Any chance I can tag along?"

Shit. The answer was no, but he didn't want to disappoint Tasha's cousin. She was close to Kara. Closer it seemed than she was to her sister, Lou, who never came by.

"Absolutely not." Tasha sent her cousin a narrow-eyed stare. "You aren't going to ruin Dare's big meeting."

Kara's expression went totally "what me" innocent. "I can flirt, too."

"No," Brian said in a wholly serious tone. "This meeting is important. I honestly don't like sending Tasha into it, but Oakley asked for her and I can't go. You are not going in there to flirt with billionaires."

Kara wrinkled her nose. "Fine. I'll stay here and flirt with the regular people."

Kara seemed to flirt with everyone. Men, women, young, old. It didn't matter. She drew them in like flies to honey when she wanted to. And when she wanted, she could shut it all down and become distant and mysterious. Brian was obviously captivated by the contrast.

"Are you going to this secret place with them tonight?" Brian asked before digging into the eggs he'd ordered the night before.

This had become their morning ritual. Brian and Kara showed up, and they all had breakfast on the terrace overlooking Sydney Harbour. Like they were some kind of a family. A found one, but a family nonetheless. He liked it. Even Nate had become something of a friend.

"I thought the secret place was supposed to be a secret." Nate frowned his way before taking the sterling-silver cloche off the plate in front of him, revealing the full "fry up" he'd eaten every morning he was here. Smoky bacon, three fried eggs, toast, beans, grilled mushrooms and tomatoes, and a plethora of sausages and hash browns.

Dare took a long sip of his coffee. That was one of the things he loved about Australia. The coffee was surprisingly amazing. Australian coffee culture was something he would miss, though Canada had its own. "He knows, and I suspect Kara knows her cousin is a sub."

His sub.

"Of course I do," Kara said with a wave of her hand. "We pretty much tell each other everything. I'm going, too, you know. I don't belong to this particular club. It's way fancier than anything I could afford. We're only getting in because Nate's dad here used to work with the owner."

"Which is why we're going to be polite. He sent over a contract for visitor's rights." Tasha went still, as though waiting for him to argue with her. "There was a clause that allows you Master rights. I was surprised by that. That would mean he had a reason to give them to you."

She needed to know how far he was willing to go for her. When it was made clear that more than money was required to get the rights he needed, he'd made a decision. "I talked to Master Colin when Nate first reached out to him. He explained that we could be visitors and you would have all rights because Nate's father vouched for you, but he couldn't do the same with Master rights for me."

"I know. That's why I said we could watch the scenes," she said.

But he didn't want to watch. He wanted to play. He wanted to be with her in a place where they were free to do as they wished. The way he wanted the world to be. "Or I could give him the number of the man who runs the Toronto club I was a member of and let him vouch for me. I called Tom first and explained the situation. He's a kind man."

Tom had told him how much the group missed him and wished him well. How the door was always open.

He needed that door open. He needed the light from it so he could find his way out of the dark hole he was in.

Tasha was looking at him, her eyes pooled with tears. "You didn't have to do that."

"Do what?" Nate asked. "If it's call his old club, he already did because Colin's serious about his protocols. If he doesn't have Master rights, he won't be able to play, and that seems silly to go to all this trouble when you can't even spank your own sub."

Kara put a hand on his arm. "I think there's more at play here."

"Yes, like your father finding out." Brian summed up the problem neatly. "He lost his shit the first time he found out you were in the lifestyle. What do you think he'll do now?"

He'd weighed the risk and taken it. "I don't think Tom will talk. He's very discreet. My father found out the first time because he set a PI on me. I doubt he's got Tom's cell bugged. Nate is going to be watching to see if anyone is following us. So we can go to The Station and have a great night."

Tasha pushed her chair back and walked around the table, settling herself on his lap. She wrapped an arm around his shoulders and turned her face up to his. "Thank you, Sir."

His fucking heart squeezed. Any anxiety he'd had playing in the back of his head flew away the minute he saw that look on her face. He would do anything for her. "You're welcome, love."

"Owww." Brian stared at Kara.

"You were making a face, and my cousin is having a beautiful moment with the man of her dreams, and you will not make a face, Brian," Kara declared.

"I'm not making any faces." Nate had his head down, concentrating on his food.

Man of her dreams. More like nightmares, but she was settling in and he didn't care. She was soft and sweet and in his arms.

She was worth the risk.

The way she talked about her dad… He'd been thinking about it for days. She talked about her dad like he was larger than life and able to handle any problem that came his way. According to her, her parents were the kind of people who helped others.

Would they help a man who loved their daughter?

Or would he be ruining them, too?

"Hey, don't leave me," she whispered as Brian and Kara began to argue about why Brian wasn't allowed to go to the club.

He shook off the feeling and brushed his lips with hers. "Never."

But wasn't that a lie? He was starting to think it wasn't. He was starting to think she might be worth risking everything for.

He picked up a strawberry and put it to her lips and let things be for the moment.

Chapter Ten

Tasha stared up at the big man blocking the doorway. The restaurant seemed lovely and inviting when they'd walked through the main dining room. However, the mood had changed as they'd been led to the more private areas of the building. The long hallway was paneled with dark, rich-looking wood and antique mirrors and lighting. Oakley's big bodyguard stood in front of the door to the private dining room, his eyes covered in sunglasses even in the low light of the hallway.

She had to wonder if they were there so he would look cool or to cover a rough night, or if they were like Lou's and were sending back all kinds of data to someone sitting close by. If anyone could afford some high-tech toys, it was Auggie Oakley.

Precisely why she wasn't wearing any.

She had to go in completely naked. Well, naked when it came to weapons and a way to talk to her team. This big, rough-looking guy didn't seem to want to take her word for it though.

"You are not going to pat her down," Dare said in a deep tone, stepping in front of her.

The alpha male she knew lurked deep inside her man was making an appearance today. Dare wasn't one of those cavemen who talked about owning a woman. She was his partner, not his possession, but he took care of her, too. He was pretty much her perfect man.

And she was going to lose him if she didn't tell him the truth.

"No one gets close to the boss without being checked out," the guard insisted.

Nate moved in front of Dare, and he had a good half foot on this guy. "Then maybe the boss doesn't need anyone close. I thought we were friends, Jeffy. I gave you all the information you asked for. I assumed you would vet her. You really think she's some kind of assassin?"

Oh, she could be quite a good one when she wanted to be, but only when it was totally necessary, and mostly she was assassin adjacent. She was excellent at handing her sisters snacks while they waited in a sniper position for some homicidal megalomaniac to show up so they could do their job.

Not that she said that. She was far too busy giving the nasty-looking guard big, wide eyes and making sure her dress was smooth and pretty. "Do you need to look in my purse?"

Dare had a hand on her waist. "He doesn't need to look in your anything."

"I'm afraid I have to insist," the guard said.

He liked that she was being submissive. He probably enjoyed hurting women or simply humiliating them.

She turned his way. "I don't mind."

"He's not putting his hands on you," Dare promised.

She turned to the guard. "What exactly are you looking for? I'm afraid my boyfriend isn't going to let you do a pat down. Where would an assassin hide a gun?"

It was time for theatrics. There was a time to blend into the background and a time to be bold. It was time for bold. She'd learned men sometimes couldn't handle bold, especially the ones who liked to humiliate and manipulate. There was a chair sitting to the guard's left. Tasha moved to it, settling her left leg on the seat and pulling her skirt up to reveal her perfectly smooth and tan leg. She might not have her sisters' height, but her legs were nice and shapely. "Would I hide one here?"

"Tash." Dare's voice had gone Dom low, and she knew she was pushing his limits.

The good news was he could spank her to his heart's content tonight. "This way he doesn't have to touch me and you don't have to kill him, baby. Mr. Whatever your name is, do we agree I'm not carrying a weapon on my thigh? I'm wearing a thong. I don't think they've made guns small enough to fit between my cheeks yet. Should I show you?"

Nate growled but stepped back. "You're going to be the death of me, Tash."

She lowered her leg, pulling her skirt up to show him the other. The skirt of the airy Dior she wore was a vibrant blue, contrasting with her skin. They'd spent a half day shopping on Oxford Street. He'd bought her a couple of dresses and some shoes to die for, and a Cartier bracelet she was never going to take off. It shone in the light as she ran a hand up her leg. "Nothing here, either. I would show you my breasts, but I think my boyfriend would take offense."

"You're fine," the guard grumbled, having gone a bright red. "You should go on in. It's obviously fine."

Bold. Sometimes it was the only way to go.

Dare moved in behind her, that big hand grasping her arm as he leaned over to whisper in her ear. "You are going to pay for that, brat."

She would have told him she happily would, but the door to the dining room came open as a server came out. A familiar server.

Zach was coming through the door with an empty tray and nodded their way. They'd known about this meeting for a couple of days, but she'd been unaware he'd found a way in.

"Ma'am. Sir. I just dropped off the bread service. They're waiting for you," he explained in a perfect Aussie accent. "And there's a private washroom inside to your left, should you have need. We'll be in with wine momentarily."

"Thank you," she said.

Before she could push through the door, Dare leaned in, stopping her. "I should take you out of here. I don't like this. Something feels off."

Something was off, but she had everything in place.

For the hundredth time, she thought about telling him exactly what was going on. He wasn't involved in this. Hell, an investigation might lead to his father getting arrested, and that would be good for him. He might understand. He might forgive her.

Now was not the time. She wasn't sure when that time would be—if that time would be—but she had to talk to her team first.

And a member of her team had just told her where he wanted her to go. Kenzie could have warned her Zach was going to be here. They hadn't had much time before she and Brian had left for the conference, but she could have sent a cryptic text at least.

"It's fine. We're in the middle of Sydney, and we have a perfectly good bodyguard watching after us," she assured him. "I promise they can't hurt me. They won't even try."

And if they did, she would take care of the problem. If Zach was here, then he'd almost certainly hidden a couple of weapons for her.

She pushed through the door, taking the choice away from him. He needed this meeting and so did she.

The private dining room was filled with soft light. It still held with the old-school themes of the restaurant, but there was an airiness to this room that felt lighter somehow.

There were ten or so white-linen covered tables, but only one was occupied. Two men sat at a table near the windows, their backs to the wall so they could see when she and Dare walked in.

Oakley slid out of his chair and stood. He wore jeans and a T-shirt and sneakers, looking utterly out of place in the luxurious restaurant. But that might be his point. He didn't have to fit in. He was the king, and he could do as he liked. "Ah, you're here. I've been waiting for you, love. Never been so happy a bloke got called off to work. Come and join us. Meet Dr. Huisman."

A tall, lanky man stood, smoothing down his suitcoat. As casual as the billionaire looked, Huisman was his opposite. He wore a suit that had obviously been fitted to his athletic body. Huisman looked barely old enough to be in medical school, much less a doctor of his reputation. He was also way hotter in person than he was in photographs. His dark hair was slightly wavy and reached past his ears. He held out a hand, and generous lips gave her a smile. "It's good to meet you. Tasha, is it?"

Well, if he was a supervillain, he had excellent cover. His voice was soft but deep, and she felt completely unthreatened by the man.

Oakley was another story. She could practically feel the man

155

undressing her with his eyes. Now he was a man she wouldn't go bold with. He would take that as a challenge. She would have to walk a careful line with him.

"Tasha, yes. It's a pleasure to meet you, Dr. Huisman. Dare has been telling me about all the fabulous work you do." She shook the man's hand.

"Emmanuel, please." His voice held the faintest hint of a French accent.

"Your guard tried to feel up my girlfriend. I should have walked right out of here," Dare was saying.

Her Sir needed to relax or they would get into a fight. Did the man not understand Aussies? A fist fight was a perfectly acceptable way of communicating in some circles here. "I'm fine."

Oakley simply laughed, putting a hand on his chest. "I knew there was a reason I like that bloke. I told the bugger to make sure to vet everyone who comes through, and he uses that as an excuse to feel up a pretty lady." Oakley winked her way like casual sexism was all fun and games. "Sorry about that. I'll talk to him. You're not a threat to anything but my concentration. Please have a seat."

She wanted to because she wasn't sure she should leave Dare at this point, but Zach had given her an order. "If you would excuse me, I'm going to the ladies' room. Be right back." She went on her toes to brush her lips against Dare's. "Behave. Remember our plan."

She turned and walked away, praying he could tamp down the glorious alpha male she seemed to bring out in him.

It took her a second, but she found the hallway that led to the women's room and wondered what Zach had left her there. He couldn't follow her in, and if there was another way in it was through a window. So he must have left something behind he wanted her to have.

She pushed through the door of the small room marked *Ladies* and realized what Zach had managed to smuggle in. "Hey, Lou. You having fun hanging out? You know you're Lou in a loo, right?"

"That's terrible." Lou was dressed in the same dark pants and white shirt as Zach, though she had on a name tag that declared her name was "Nan," and there was a full mopping rig at her side. And a laptop open on the sink. Her normally shoulder-length hair was hidden under a blonde wig, and she wore far more make up than usual. Kala had been at work on her bestie, and she'd done an excellent job. "And I've been in worse places."

She had, and usually Tash was right there beside her.

"Is there a reason Kenz didn't tell me Zach got on the staff?"

"Didn't happen until about an hour ago. We were looking for a way in, but they were vetting everyone, and the manager seemed to be very cautious."

That could only mean one thing. "What did Zach dig up on him?"

"The owner is a Russian immigrant," Lou said with a shrug.

Tash could guess. "He's got Denisovitch connections."

Her mother's family happened to run a syndicate with fingers that crossed much of the world. She'd only met her cousin Dusan a few times, but he was the very stereotype of the mafia boss from romance novels. Ruthless as hell, no scruples at all when it came to business, but soft with his family.

He'd had a lot to do with smuggling her out of Russia and into the arms of the Taggarts.

But there was one problem with calling in favors with Dusan.

"He's going to tell my mom. Did Zach think of that?" Tasha would bet no one else in the history of the Agency had worried about their mom being called in. When Drake and Taylor had decided to bring together teams of agents who were invested in each other, they should have thought about that. James Bond didn't worry about his mom disapproving of his choices in the field. Or his dad showing up and finding out he was having way too much fun with the target.

Lou shrugged. "We have bigger problems. Kenzie followed Brian."

She'd worried about the moment when she would have to decide what to do with Brian Peters. "He said he was taking a meeting with a client."

"He lied. Unless the meeting with the client is in the building across from here."

Fuck. Tasha went to the small window. Given the time of day and how the sun was hitting the glass, he wouldn't be able to see inside. She peered out at the building across the street. "He's got this place bugged."

"I didn't find anything, but he could be using something I can't detect," Lou admitted. "There are some long-range hearing devices that don't require a physical bug. Or he could be doing simple surveillance, but according to Kenzie, he's on the third floor of the hotel in a room he'd obviously taken out in advance."

"He's known about the meeting for days. It wouldn't be hard for him. Did you get the name he registered under?"

"It wasn't Brian Peters, and he didn't register. He already had a key. The room is registered to John Smith. Why can't they be more creative? Throw in a *Mortimer* or *Luigi* every now and then," Lou murmured as she looked down at the laptop. "Kenzie's pulled back because Zach is worried Brian might see her and recognize her. Cooper's in place. He's watching right now, but he'll bring Brian in if we need to."

"I'd rather see what he does. Have Coop follow him. Brian doesn't know Cooper exists. And you need to stay out of sight. He might have someone in place. We know he's got at least one person he's working with," Tasha explained. She didn't like the fact that Brian had lied to Dare. It wasn't the first time, but the days had been so pleasant it was easy to forget what they'd seen the night Brian had taken out the threat to Dare. It was nicer to think he was some kind of guardian angel.

He wasn't. Brian Peters was working an angle, and it was time to figure out what that angle was.

"I was careful," Lou promised. "I don't think Brian would remember what I look like if I wasn't in disguise. I've got a couple of things for you. First, stick this in your bra."

Lou offered her what looked like a sticker, but when Tash took it she felt it was slightly thicker. "Recording device?"

"Yes, and we'll be able to hear everything in real time. Sorry, but I couldn't risk bugging the room. Oakley had his team do a sweep. Even if he did pat you down, he wouldn't find this," Lou assured her. "I'm screwed if they shut off the Internet, but we'll have a recording. And take this. That purse won't fit a gun, but this sucker is for emergency use if you find yourself in a tight spot."

Lou passed her another sticker-looking device, this one the precise color of Tasha's skin. A microdoser. It would be filled with a powerful sedative that would take an enemy down in a couple of seconds. The tiny needle had to be engaged in order to function, and it took more than simply touching the table or another part of her body.

"Do you honestly think I need this? It seems a bit extreme for lunch," Tasha said, taking the small device. When they'd trained on it, the boys and the twins had naturally found it fun to dose each other in an attempt to get better at counteracting the effects. Sometimes when the other person wasn't expecting it.

"Zach thinks so, and he's the military smarts of the team when your dad isn't around," Lou said with a shrug. "You'll have to squeeze your fist tight and you'll feel the safety pop off, then be careful."

Tasha placed the device halfway between the base of her thumb and her wrist, where she could reach it with her fingers if she needed to. "I need to go."

Lou nodded. "We're going to meet in the conference room at the club tonight. Nate will keep Dare occupied. Zach's heard some rumblings about a couple of intelligence operatives in town. Something big is going on, and I'm afraid we're in the dark."

The thought made her gut tighten. "Keep me updated on Brian."

"Will do." Lou closed her laptop and slid it into a hiding place on her cleaning cart. "Good luck with them. Oakley's a massive ass and Huisman... I can't put my finger on it, but there's something odd."

Given the trauma he'd gone through in his life, it wasn't surprising the man wasn't normal. "Will do."

She straightened her dress and got ready to play her part.

* * * *

Dare watched Tasha walk away and wished he hadn't brought her. That fucker outside wasn't the only threat. He'd seen the way Oakley looked at her. The problem wasn't that he thought Tasha would fall for his bullshit. She shouldn't be subjected to it.

Remember our plan.

Damn it. They had a plan. Tasha was going to be her vibrant, vivacious self, and he would be able to talk to Huisman and figure the man out a little. She knew what she was doing, and he had to trust that she would tell him when she didn't want to do it anymore. She wanted to help, and she wasn't a precious doll who needed a man to do everything for her.

"She's quite a stunner," Oakley said.

And she was his. That was what he had to remember. He couldn't act like she was his favorite toy and he was a ten-year-old desperate to keep it from being thrown in the trash so his father could teach him a lesson. The scared boy needed to take a backseat. Tasha was a gift, a partner who could hold his hand while he made his way through this storm he found himself in.

Damn it all. He was going to marry her.

"She is indeed. She's an amazing woman."

He sat down across from Oakley, leaving the seat next to him open for Tasha.

"What happened to your business partner? He was supposed to be here originally, right?" Huisman gracefully sank to his chair, dragging the black cloth napkin over his slacks. "What was his name? Peters?"

"Yes. Brian. He got called away on another meeting." He wasn't about to say they might lose an important investment partner.

"I hope nothing went wrong." Huisman took a sip of the water in front of him.

"I wouldn't be surprised if his meeting wasn't with that bombshell with the pink hair," Oakley said with a chuckle. He leaned over, giving Huisman a friendly pat on the arm. "You should see this beauty. She's with Millhouse Pharma. They're a nothing player in this industry, but I give them credit for sending her. I wouldn't mind spending a bit of time with that one. I might invite her along to our weekend and see what happens."

He knew what would happen. If Brian didn't kill him, Dare would have to make things clear to the man. "She's Tasha's cousin."

A brow rose over Oakley's eyes. "Really? That family has some nice DNA. Anyway, it's been fun watching poor Brian chase after her."

"She sounds intriguing," Huisman replied with the first real interest Dare had seen from him. "I am not much of a player, but I do enjoy the company of a vibrant woman. And I'm ashamed to admit it, but I enjoy a bit of drama. Yes, I think both Mr. Peters and

Tasha's cousin should come with us. I'm eager to relax a bit. I would like to meet Mr. Peters. I've heard he's an interesting man."

It was good to know Brian was making an impression. "I assure you he's at a meeting and not chasing a woman around. He's serious about his job and is looking forward to this weekend. It's been a bit of chaos for us here. I wasn't supposed to take the lead at all."

"Yes, it was supposed to be Middleton," Huisman murmured. "Sorry to hear what happened to him. I've met him a couple of times, and he knew what he was doing. But I'm sure you do as well. It's hard to start out a trip like this with a bit of chaos."

"Chaos can be good. Shake things up a bit," Oakley said, settling back.

Chaos was the enemy in his line of work. "I think I like things to play out in an organized fashion. It tends to keep the boss happy."

"The boss being your father," Oakley prompted.

"It is his name on the door." But did his father have to be his boss? The longer he spent with Tasha the more he asked himself if there was another way. He needed to sit down and figure it out because leaving her behind was rapidly becoming an option he couldn't consider.

"Oh, I've seen that door, mate. All it says is the Nash Group. There's more Nashes than your dad." Oakley's fingers played on the lip of the Scotch glass at his side.

"I assure you, my father has a firm hold on the board of directors. Don't expect a coup anytime soon." His father ruled them with the same iron fist he did his family.

"That's the funny thing about coups. They happen when you least expect it," Oakley mused. "See that's where chaos can come in."

"There's no amount of chaos my father isn't prepared for." What he needed was leverage.

"I understand the nature of a family business," Huisman said. "It can be especially difficult when the business or foundation has been in the family for longer than a generation. The Huisman Foundation was started by my great-great-grandfather. I suspect he intended for it to move down through the generations, employing all the Huismans. He brought the company to Canada from the Netherlands. He had three sons. Now it is only me."

Because his father had been an only child and he'd died young, having only fathered Emmanuel himself.

"I've got a couple of kids out there," Oakley admitted. "They live with their mum. Living the life high on my dime, of course, since she took half my fortune when we divorced. I doubt either will be worth spit when she's done with them."

Half of a couple of billion, and he'd made it all back in a few years. Money like that produced more money. Oakley couldn't spend it fast enough, but he was bitter his ex-wife was financially fine. He probably shouldn't show his disdain.

"I have a brother and a sister. I suspect neither will want to work with our father. My brother is something of an artist, and I worry my sister has caught the acting bug." He'd talked to her the day before, and she'd been so excited with how the play had gone. She would love Tasha. He'd wanted to tell his sister about Tasha so someone he cared about knew.

"Your half siblings, right?" Oakley asked.

Dare wasn't sure he liked this line of questioning. "Yes. They're from my father's second wife."

"You're from his first marriage?" Huisman asked. "My parents were divorced, too."

The server who'd greeted them earlier was back, pouring water into his and Tasha's glasses. He quickly took their drink orders. A beer for him and a glass of dry rosé for her. He knew what she liked in the afternoon. This evening she'd switch to a rich Cab, but she liked the crispness of a rosé for lunch.

"Nah, his parents weren't married. He's the bastard of the family," Oakley said quietly as the server walked away.

A nasty term, and one so few people used these days. It was a carefully chosen word meant to wound.

So he'd done his homework, and this was his play. Did he suspect he could put him in a bad position because of the circumstances of his birth? "Yes, I believe that's the term you would use if we were in Victorian England. Your point being?"

Oakley's big shoulders shrugged. "I'm merely stating fact. I find it interesting that your father pretends your mother never existed. She was a hooker, right?"

It was odd. A few days ago he was sure he would have gotten

emotional, but the only person he'd met who actually counted hadn't blinked an eye when he'd told her. Tasha hadn't been embarrassed for him. She'd wrapped her arms around him and asked him about his mom. He'd told her the stories he could remember and felt closer to his mom than he had since he was a kid. Tasha had reminded him that his mother had loved him, had sacrificed for him.

He didn't feel a bit of the shame he'd felt when he thought about her the last couple of years. Shame his father had instilled. That poison had slid right out of his veins.

"Yes, she was, and if you're going to insinuate that makes her a lesser human, I suggest you don't do it around my girlfriend. She won't take kindly to it." He needed to let this man know he couldn't use the knowledge that way. This might have been the exact reason he'd asked Tasha to come. The man had said he enjoyed chaos, but Dare wasn't going to give him any. "As to embarrassing me, you can't. I loved my mother. She was a good mother. You can probably embarrass my father if that's your goal, but you'll honestly only be hurting my siblings. If he kicked me out, I would cheer. If you want to hurt a twenty-year-old with substance addiction issues and a sweet high school kid, have at it."

"I don't think that's what Mr. Oakley meant." Huisman looked from Oakley to Dare. "He's a forthright man. Very Australian of him. If anyone has a relative they should be embarrassed by, it's me. My father was something of a villain. Are you going to try to turn that on me, Oakley?"

At least he wasn't alone in his surprise.

Oakley held his hands up as though to prove his innocence. "Not at all. I wasn't being nasty, Nash. I was making a statement of fact. You overcame a lot. And I couldn't use your past against you, Manny. You put it all out there for everyone to see. Smart man. Sometimes the best defense is to wound yourself first. Show everyone you can take a punch."

"My father was the one who wounded me," Huisman insisted. "The books I've written were all part of the healing process. I often wonder what my life would have been like if my mother had been allowed to raise me, but after Father was killed, my grandfather focused all of his time and will on me. It made for a difficult childhood. His death unfortunately gave me freedom. I've had to deal with that. Being open and honest about my pain has brought me great joy. My father was a criminal. He died as he lived. I shall do the same. I shall die as I live as well."

The difference being Huisman was doing good in the world. He'd been right. He and Huisman had a lot in common. Likely far more than he and Oakley. Dare had to wonder how much goodwill that might buy him. It was time to show his host he had a backbone.

"What do you want, Oakley? You brought me here for a reason, and I doubt it was simply to insult my parentage."

"Hey, you're hearing me all wrong. I was stating facts, that's all. I admire you. I got no problem with women like your mum. I'm sure she was a real nice lady. Your father is the problem and you could be the solution," Oakley insisted. "I think we could do some important work together, but your father insists we be rivals instead of friends."

What exactly was going on? "I'm afraid my father isn't good at making friends."

"You could be better."

"At being your friend?"

"I think all three of us could be friends," Oakley replied. "Look, the world is a dangerous place these days. Lots of threats out there, and I'm worried we're working against each other when we should be working together. For the good of humanity."

Dare wasn't that stupid. If Oakley wanted to work together, there was profit on the line. "Work together on what?"

Huisman studied Oakley for a moment. "I think he's referring to a project I've been funding. I'm heavily invested in a company that's working on vaccines for several emerging threats."

There wasn't a lot of money in vaccines. It made sense Huisman would be funding them. They were a nonprofit. The question was why was Oakley here. "And I can help how?"

"The Nash Group is funding a similar group," Oakley explained. "It's a small research firm. Tandy Medical. I think your company and Huisman's are working on the same puzzle, and you each have different pieces."

Tandy Medical wasn't one of his accounts. He would have to look it up. Brian might know more, but it wouldn't matter. "I'm afraid my father doesn't believe in team ups, but I can certainly look into it for you."

"Oh, he'd love to team up with Huisman, wouldn't he?" Oakley asked.

"It's not the same. Huisman isn't a rival," Dare pointed out.

"We'll see about that. And I meant what I said about chaos. There's opportunity in chaos. It's a lesson I learned from a young age." Oakley's eyes seemed to catch on something. "But this is a discussion we should have when you come out to my place. Right now I'd like to get to know you, see if I think we can work together. Although I don't need a discussion to know I can work with you, love."

Tasha was back, and she sent Oakley a wry smile. "I bet that's true, but I'm on vacation."

She leaned over and kissed him, announcing to everyone exactly who she was with.

He wanted to drag her onto his lap and feed her himself.

Tonight. He could let his caveman out tonight.

For now, he would play the professional businessman. Oakley started flirting with Tasha.

And Dare began a real conversation with Huisman.

Chapter Eleven

Nate held the door open and Tasha entered the suite, ready to get to the bathroom and remove all of the devices she'd taken from Lou. The last thing she needed was Dare to want some afternoon fun and, oops, she sedated him on accident. Not something that would likely happen. She would have to prime the sucker, but it wasn't unheard of.

"Stay here." Nate didn't actually have to say the words, but he seemed to enjoy ordering everyone around. She'd never seen him play, but she knew he would be a hard top.

She gave him a jaunty salute as he moved through the suite, checking to make sure there wasn't some nasty surprise waiting for them. Or rather pretending to look since they'd bugged the place, and anyone who broke in would have been caught by Lou long before now.

She'd had to be careful with the microdoser. Oakley had hugged her at the end of the lunch, and she'd thought about dosing the fucker just for fun.

But after, there hadn't been time to peel it off. She should have gone to the bathroom, but Dare had hurried her out. He'd been buzzing about talking to Huisman and how the man had plans to change the world.

It did not escape her attention that she should have been talking to Huisman, collecting observations about the man. It was literally why she was here, but instead she'd made the choice to help her boyfriend.

She'd broken Ian Taggart's rule—*Thou Shalt Not Think with Your Pussy.*

Or dick. That one was flexible. It all depended on the gender identification of the operative her father thought was fucking up the mission.

"Damn." Dare stopped in the foyer, staring down at his phone. "I have to go meet a colleague down in the conference hall. He's got some data for me and he's catching a plane in a couple of hours, so I can't put him off. I'm sorry. I was hoping we could spend the afternoon together."

Likely in bed. Which she didn't mind, but the truth was she could use some time to herself. Nate loomed in the background, ready to follow Dare wherever he needed to go. "It's okay because we're spending all night together."

Dare got in her space, his hands coming up to cup her face. "All night, and you're going to get that sweet ass spanked for the way you handled that guard."

"I thought I handled him quite well." She put her hands on his waist. He wouldn't find the recording device attached to the inside of her bra, but there was a small chance he could activate the microdoser. She didn't want to have to explain to him why he'd been tranqued twice in one week.

"You were an incorrigible brat, and you're going to pay." He pronounced her sentence with a sweetness that belied the words. Or rather gave them the meaning she thought he wanted them to have.

It was all play, a way to live out their inner fantasies. "I promise to cry prettily for you, Sir."

It was something she looked forward to. Crying made her feel better. Sometimes a good spanking was the only way to get through all the stress and anxiety she didn't even know she was holding inside.

There was a wealth of satisfaction in Dare's eyes every time she called him Sir. He leaned over and laid a kiss on her forehead. "See that you do. I might be a while. This guy talks forever."

That worked for her. Especially since he was going to have Nate with him. "I might go over to Kara's and pick up a couple of things for tonight."

"The suite's clear," Nate announced as he returned from his walk-through.

"It looks like you're going to get to sit in on another meeting," she told the big guy.

"Brilliant," Nate replied.

Dare looked at her and then Nate, his brain obviously working.

That was not happening. She shook her head. "Nope. He's going with you. I am not the one who was attacked earlier this week."

"If someone is after me, the best way to do that is to get you," he pointed out.

"Everything has been quiet, but the attack happened right here in this hotel. I'm fine. We agreed Nate would watch over you so I don't have to worry." She was serious about this. No lies here.

"All right. Be careful," he said and backed away. He shifted his bag on his shoulder—the one that contained the laptop her team would download this evening. He took it everywhere.

She hated the idea of invading his privacy, but she'd gotten a weird vibe at lunch. When Oakley hadn't been staring at her chest, he'd been watching Dare with an almost predatory concentration.

He was up to something, and she needed to figure out what. She could start by getting the recording device to her team so they could transcribe it.

One more kiss and he was gone, Nate following behind him.

Her cell buzzed.

You make it back okay, cos?

Her sister. Or someone with Kara's phone. The real question they were asking was when are you coming in for a debrief.

She texted back.

Had a great lunch. See you in an hour.

A ping and then a thumbs-up to let her know the message had been received and the timing was acceptable.

She let a long sigh go through her because she knew what would happen soon. She would have a fight on her hands the minute she mentioned she wanted to be honest with Dare. Zach would lose his shit. Kala and Cooper would give her lectures on how important their Agency work was. Tristan would say bitter things about throwing her life away that actually applied to him. Lou would try to use reason.

Kenzie would put a hand to her heart and declare it the most romantic thing she'd ever heard of.

And then she would remind Tasha of how important the mission was.

She wished she could talk to her mom about Dare.

She started to peel off the edge of the microdoser when a chime went through the suite, letting her know someone was at the door.

Probably someone from the hotel. They came up all the time to ensure Dare had what he needed. Sometimes they dropped off snacks or flowers for the room.

It was not a uniformed hospitality professional who stood behind the door.

"Hey, Tasha. Is Dare here?" Brian was in the doorway, and he moved around her like he owned the place.

The man came and went as he liked.

"Sorry, he got called into a meeting." She was surprised Brian didn't know that. Dare tended to text him about anything business. He'd already been in contact with Brian, texting him on the car ride back to let him know he was returning to the hotel. She closed the door behind her and followed him into the room. "He left a minute ago. You might be able to catch him in the lobby. He said he was going down to the conference center."

Come to think of it, she was surprised he hadn't caught him at the elevator. That was odd. Brian had gotten here only a few moments after Dare and Nate had left. They should have passed each other.

Unless Brian had already been up here and hadn't wanted to see Dare at all.

"Excellent. That leaves us free to talk."

She didn't like the sound of that. Her every instinct went sharp. "What do you want to talk about?"

"How did the meeting with Huisman go?" He paced beside the couch but made no move to sit.

She could talk about that, though she wondered why he needed to. She'd assumed he'd been listening in. Lou had made sure they had been the only ones with an actual listening device in the room, but there were ways around that. It depended on how much high-tech equipment Brian had access to. "Fine, I suppose, though I didn't talk to him much. I'm afraid Mr. Oakley monopolized my time."

"So they want to use Manny to get to Dare," he said, almost under his breath. "Did they talk about anything specific?"

"I think you should have this conversation with Dare." She wasn't about to give him intel. If his plans hadn't worked, she wasn't going to serve as his backup. "Like I said, I mostly talked to Oakley, and there was nothing of interest about our conversation."

The conversation had revolved around how rich he was. How he owned three yachts and two airplanes and so many houses across the globe.

"Did anyone mention vaccines?" Brian asked.

This was interesting. She might have something to give her team after all. She might not have gained a lot of clarity concerning Huisman, but she was learning a bit about Brian. "I think there was some discussion about the potential for new vaccines in the future, though they talked about them not being moneymakers. I don't know. The money stuff bugs me. We should be developing vaccines because it's the right thing to do."

"That's a sweet but naïve thing to say," Brian replied. "However, you're right if you're talking about well-established vaccines. There's not a ton of money there. But new vaccines. Well, let's just say the pharmaceutical market made some nice change off of Covid back in the day. As emerging viruses and fungal threats scare the crap out of the public, there will be ways to make billions. Did you hear anyone talk about Tandy Medical?"

Not until now. She made a mental note. Lou and Tris would be doing some serious research tonight while she played. Sometimes it paid to be the operative since usually she would be the one sitting in front of a computer. "I don't remember hearing that name. Is there something going on that I should know about?"

"No." He shook off his tension. "I'm just feeling bad that I didn't go. I know how important this meeting was. You're right. I should talk to Dare about it."

"No problem." The minute he walked out the door, she would change and get back to base. She wanted to know more about Tandy Med and why Brian would call Emmanuel Huisman—who seemed very formal—Manny. Like he knew the man.

Was that why he'd skipped the meeting? Would Huisman recognize him?

Brian stared at her for a moment as though trying to make a decision. "I need to go with you to the club tonight."

Frustration welled. They'd had this discussion. "I told you no. The only reason Dare's being let in is his connection to the club in Toronto. You said you've never been around the lifestyle at all."

He gave her a hangdog puppy look that might have worked on a lesser woman. Or most women, since the man was stunning. "I haven't but I've been reading up on it, and if that's what Kara needs, then I'd like to learn more."

She rather thought he was lying now and doing an excellent job. He said the words with a smooth earnestness. *I'm just a guy who wants a girl. Please let me into your sex club so I can woo her.*

She wasn't buying it. What exactly did he want? There was something different about Brian, something slightly desperate. The situation had changed in some way, and she needed to figure out how. "The man who runs The Station was clear on who we could and couldn't bring in."

"Perhaps I could talk to him. Make him a bit more comfortable," Brian offered.

Why was he so desperate? That was the vibe she was getting from him. A fine edge of desperation. "I don't know that would work. He was very firm. Something you should know about the lifestyle is Doms tend to say what they mean and mean what they say. I'm sorry."

That was the moment his mask slipped, and she saw the man she'd seen in the video the day he'd taken out Dare's attacker. "Well, that is unfortunate."

Despite the fact that she knew how to take care of herself, adrenaline flooded her system, a pure fight or flight response. She was alone with a much larger man, and she didn't have a gun. Calm. She had to stay calm. The best tactic was to get him to go away or to get away herself. If she could avoid a fight, she would. "I can call him and ask again. Actually, I'll have Kara call. He's got a soft spot where she's concerned."

She'd call the base house phone, and then at least someone would know who she was with and that she was worried. They had certain words they only used when there was danger and they couldn't talk freely. Cooper had been tailing Brian. He might still be close. She wasn't sure how worried they would be given the conversation they were having. It could sound perfectly normal on the video feed, but on a call she could make it clear she needed some backup.

"Put the phone away, Tasha."

She glanced up, and he had a gun in his hand. Damn it. Why had she worn a damn thong? If she'd had some granny panties on, she might have been able to carry, but no, she couldn't ruin the line of her designer dress.

Her mom had always said vanity would be the death of them all.

"What are you doing?" She set the phone on the side table. It wouldn't help her at this point.

"You know exactly what I'm doing. I suspect you're the reason I've suddenly got a tail. So tell me, Tasha—if that's your name—who are you working for?"

"I work for my dad." No lies there. She held her hands up, trying to let him see how scared she was. Where was the camera in here? She couldn't remember but there was one thing that they couldn't miss. "Why do you have a gun?"

"For the same reason your people bugged the suite," he replied. "Thanks for that. It saved me the trouble, and I've been piggybacking off you."

"I don't know what you mean." He—or his team—had to be good or Tristan would have picked up on that.

He was moving toward her now. "Let's stop playing games. You're working with a woman known in certain circles as Ms. Magenta."

Fuck. He was talking about intelligence circles. Kara—whether being played by Kenzie or Kala—often introduced herself as Ms. Magenta. It was a joke from their childhood. From the first time she'd met her sisters. She'd only been seven, but she remembered that day so vividly. They'd been in Paris, and they'd snuck to the stairs to listen in on what Dad was doing. The name was joked about when they mentioned the CIA's use of "color" names to protect their operative's real names. When the time had come, Kenzie had introduced herself as Ms. Magenta, and she hadn't looked back.

She had to protect her sisters. No one outside of the Agency knew there were two of them. The fact that they were twins gave them a unique advantage.

"Ms. Magenta?" If he knew that name, then he had intelligence ties no matter who he worked for. He could still be with a mafia, syndicate, or cartel and have intelligence ties.

"Yes, the woman you call Kara. I believe she works for the CIA, or at least has worked with them in the past." He shook his head. "I've misplayed this whole situation, and your team is probably on its way. I think it's time we move this interrogation somewhere else. I've got a couple of hours before Dare will start looking for you. Now we can do this the easy way or the hard way."

Oh, she was going to owe Lou so much. Lou could be paranoid and overly protective, and Tasha was going to have to indulge her every instinct from here on out because Lou was going to save her. She fisted her hands at her side. To him it would look like a frustrated gesture, but she managed to prime the microdoser.

It would be her only chance against him. She'd seen him fight, and he had far more practice than she did. Maybe Kenz or Kala could take him, but Tasha doubted she could best him. "You're scaring me."

"Somehow I doubt that," he replied. "Come on. We need to move out. I've got a car waiting."

So he had backup, and that would way lower her chances of getting away.

"I'm not going to hurt you," he said gravely. "I need some answers. I need to know where the Agency stands on Huisman. You don't know who he really is or what he's capable of. Let's make this a friendly meeting."

"You don't seem so friendly with that gun in your hand." Her cell phone had started buzzing. She could hear it. It was likely her team telling her they were on the way. No matter what he said, she couldn't afford to believe him. She had to give her team a chance to save her—a chance to turn this around and take Brian in instead.

She needed to bring him close. The needle was small. It might not make it through the suitcoat he wore. She needed to get to his skin.

"Would you feel better if I put it away?" He moved in closer to her. "I've watched you. I suspect you're not the operative they intended to use. Was Kara planning to seduce Middleton? I've wondered if it wasn't pure luck that brought you into the pub that night. I knew I couldn't let Ms. Magenta get her hands on Dare, so I gave her the hard sell. Did you know who he was going in? Am I wrong?"

He was way too close to being completely right. "I can't answer you with that gun in your hands. And I'm not some…operative."

Closer. He moved closer. The gun was at his side, though he hadn't put it away. She held her ground. He was coming on her left side. She wouldn't have to pivot, so she didn't move a muscle.

"I don't want to play games anymore. Something is going on here, and I don't like it. You have to have heard the rumors about Oakley," he said as he moved in front of her. There was nothing but confidence in his body language. He knew he could take her, knew he had her exactly where he wanted her. "We'll talk about this when we get to my base. I'm going to assume you have a handler and it's not that bombshell you call Kara. When we get to my safe house, we can call him in."

Every cell of her being was focused on him as he stared down at her. She had to make this work. He was fast. If she made a move, he could bat her away. If the needle deployed, the dose would uselessly fall to the carpet or be absorbed by the fabric of his shirt.

She let her fear show, let tears pierce her eyes. They were true tears because she had no idea how Dare was going to handle the fact that the only friend he'd made in years was playing him. How would he handle the fact that everyone who made him comfortable was lying?

"I'll go with you." She turned and started for the door, feeling Brian move beside her.

When she got to the place where the carpet met the marble of the foyer, she "tripped." Tasha faked a fall, carefully ensuring she came down on her right side. The pain was jarring, but Tasha forced herself to turn and look up at Brian. "I'm sorry. I'm…these shoes…"

She was fine in the shoes. She could run a couple of miles in these puppies, but she was counting on the manly belief that women's fashion anything was silly and fluffy.

Sure enough, he gave her a slight smile. "It's okay. You don't have to be nervous. I'm not going to hurt you. I only want to talk. Let's get you up."

He offered her a hand.

And she took it, slapping her left hand over his and pressing down so the sedative quickly injected into his body.

He didn't react for a moment, proving how small that needle was. It was obvious he hadn't felt it. He helped her to her feet, and she smoothed out her skirt.

The door came open and Cooper moved in, leveling a gun at Brian. "Stay right where you are."

Brian's gun came up, and he oddly moved in front of Tasha as though protecting her was a base instinct he couldn't ignore. "Put the gun down."

"Don't move," Cooper continued.

"He's going to have trouble obeying that command," she explained. It was mean but she wasn't planning on catching him, so she moved out of the way.

"I'm not obey…" Brian shook his head. "What…damn it."

He fell to his knees and thudded to the floor.

Cooper moved next to her, looking down at the fallen operative. "I came to save you."

"Well, you did."

Cooper snorted. "I think you handled him pretty well, Tash."

"You saved me from lower back pain because he looks heavy." She sighed because they needed to move and fast. She lowered her voice to a whisper. "His team—whatever that means—is piggybacking on our bugs, and at least one of them is downstairs in the parking garage."

Cooper nodded and leaned over to pick up Brian, his voice a whisper, too. "Then we need to get a move on. We'll take him straight to the club. He's going to be out for a while, and I'm not about to leave him alone."

It looked like she was in for a wild night.

* * * *

Harry Barton looked utterly delighted as he finished showing Dare the newest data concerning his company's smart inhalers. There were several research groups trying to develop the devices that could revolutionize how COPD and asthma were treated. Up to now the research had been promising, but they were having trouble with integrating the device with smart tech. "So you can see, we're ahead of projections and should be able to bring our device in front of the TGA sometime next year, and the FDA shortly after. All we need is another round of funding."

It seemed they'd solved their problems. The data was excellent, and the potential profits would be phenomenal. This wasn't something he needed to run by his father. "Send me your budget projections for the next year, and I'll be in touch with your CEO. This looks fabulous, Harry. I'm glad you called this emergency meeting."

Harry was his contact with a high-tech Australian firm, and he was all smiles as he closed his laptop. They were sitting at one of the back tables in the largest of the hotel bars. Like most conference hotels the service wasn't great because of the amount of people they stuffed in, but the lack of a drink was fine. He'd had a single beer during his meeting with Oakley and Huisman and wouldn't touch another drop until after they'd played. He fully intended to follow all of The Station's rules. He would give them no reason to not invite he and Tash back.

"Well, I wasn't expecting the data to be that good. I tend to take everything the research group says with a tiny bit of skepticism," Harry admitted as he started to pack up. "They can be overly optimistic, but I think they hit it out of the ballpark this time."

"It was worth missing some time with my girlfriend." He was already considering how he could use the good news to soothe his father. When things were going well, his father could sometimes be tolerable. That was when he could ease the man into a potentially reasonable deal. He could maybe buy himself some time to find a way out of his problems.

What he needed was leverage. Which was just a nice word for

the one he really meant—blackmail.

It was time to start playing dirty when it came to his father.

It was time to dig into the business and figure out where all the secrets were. Because he knew damn well there were secrets and probably some illegal shit going on.

Harry stopped, a startled expression coming over his face. "You have a girlfriend? I'd heard you were completely single. Sorry. Rumors abound. There are some unethical groups that keep information on investors so they can perhaps influence the investors in some ways."

He was aware. He'd dealt with them several times. "I'm happily with someone right now, so I can't be influenced that way."

Though he had to admit that putting Tasha in his world would definitely have worked. He would listen to her and be influenced by her. Luckily for him, he'd met her randomly. Otherwise he might not have trusted the relationship. His Tash had an interest in his business, but only in helping him.

"I'm happy for you, Dare," Harry said. "You should lock her down if you think she's the one. I've been married to my Ashley for almost ten years now, and nothing has made me happier."

More and more he intended to do just that. "It's good to hear. Not all marriages are happy."

"Mine is, and the way to make it so is patience and listening to your wife," Harry said, sliding out of the booth. "Being home on time is important, too. I have to cut this conference short because my daughter's birthday is tomorrow, and there's a petting zoo being put up in my backyard at six in the morning."

"That sounds fun." He actually meant the words. He'd never truly considered having a family, but he couldn't deny that the thought of having one with Tasha was appealing.

Harry's head shook. "Only because you've never been around twenty six-year-olds and a bunch of barnyard animals. And I want to apologize because it's now hitting me that you called this an emergency meeting. I'm so sorry for the confusion. When I talked to Brian, I made it clear this could wait. I was surprised when you texted me and asked me to meet you. I expected we would do a conference call next week."

Brian had been clear. He was still in his meeting, and he needed

Dare to deal with the emergency Harry had declared. "I suppose he was being overly cautious. He knows how important your group is."

They were a mid-level investment. They would likely move up the list with the latest numbers, but Brian didn't know the numbers so he couldn't have known exactly how important it was. Though if Harry had been willing to wait until the conference was over, it shouldn't have mattered. Still, he wasn't about to let Harry know there was a problem.

He wasn't sure there was a problem at all. It could be a simple miscommunication. He needed to talk to Brian anyway, so he mentally put this situation on his list.

Harry waved good-bye and went along to get to the airport so he didn't miss his daughter's birthday. Dare sat back and looked around the bar, wondering if he could catch Brian as he was finishing up his meeting. He'd been with the client for hours. It should be wrapping up by now.

The man Brian had been meeting with was sitting at a table about thirty feet away.

Excellent. They could have a meeting of their own, and he could figure out what was going on. He slid his cell out of his pocket and found Brian's number, dialing it. It went straight to voice mail.

Dare frowned. It wasn't like Brian not to answer when they were working. Actually, now that he thought about it, Brian always answered his calls.

"Everything okay? You want me to get you a drink, Dare? I assure you I can get someone over here." Nate had been standing at the exit, but he moved in now that the meeting was over.

He shook his head. "Nah. I'll save it for after. You said The Station had a nice bar. I thought we could sit and come down after we play."

"An excellent idea. Are you ready to go back to the room or do you have other plans?"

Tasha would already have gone to her cousin's and wouldn't be back for another hour or two. "I'd like to figure out where Brian is. He's not answering his phone."

"Thought he was in some sort of big meeting. Didn't he say that was why you had to take this one?"

"Yes, but the guy he was meeting with is sitting over there and he looks pretty happy, so I have to think it went well from his point of view. It makes me wonder what Brian gave up." He hoped it wasn't enough to unbalance the victories he intended to show his father. That was the problem. He could bring his father ninety percent of what he'd asked for and the man would complain about the ten percent that wasn't possible.

It might be best to figure the situation out now. He stood, picking up his laptop case. It felt a little like a millstone to him. He had to carry it with him everywhere unless it was locked up safely. Luckily The Station's lockers had security on them. And there was the fact that no one knew or cared who he was there. He could pack away all of his troubles and simply be the man he wanted to be.

In a few hours. He was still the son of Edward Nash right now, and he was interested in figuring out how much trouble he was in.

He looked back at Nate. "I'll be over there for a few. Hold the table in case we need it. I'll be right back."

If Brian had fucked up, he might be able to save it. Might. He walked through the throng of people in the crowded bar. Brian didn't fuck up. Brian was solid, so he was probably borrowing trouble.

Five minutes and one conversation later and he realized there *was* trouble. Just not the kind he thought.

"You all right?" Nate asked.

Brian had lied to him. The client hadn't seen Brian all day and hadn't called an emergency meeting at all. He'd been a bit disturbed at the thought, and Dare had been forced to calm him down. "When was the last time you saw Brian?"

One big shoulder shrugged. "Breakfast. The last time I saw him, he was bugging Kara to have lunch with him. They were arguing about it as they went down the lift."

Dare pulled his cell out as it buzzed. A text. From Brian's phone.

Sorry. I'm in the middle of something important. Will explain later. Promise. Have fun at the club tonight.

Was he in the middle of Kara's bed finally? What the hell was going on with him? He was about to write an angry text back demanding some answers when a call came through.

His father. Damn it.

If only it was a call he could ignore. He nodded toward Nate and stepped outside the bar, knowing the big Aussie would follow him. "This is Dare."

"Darren, how did the meeting with Huisman go? And who is the woman?"

He felt his jaw clench. "Huisman seems like a reasonable man, and I believe we can work a deal with him. The woman was there to distract Oakley."

"Is she a hooker?"

He was about to throw his cell across the hotel lobby. "Does it matter? She did her job. I was able to talk to Huisman without interference."

There was a pause over the line. "That was actually quite a smart play."

"You have someone watching me?"

"Calm down, son. I have people at the conference who saw you walking out of the hotel with a woman instead of Brian. You know I don't give a damn what you do with your personal life."

A lie. His father wanted all the control. "She's someone I met here, and she's pleasant to spend time with."

"Good. Get your rocks off all you like, but once you're married you have to be more discreet," his father announced. "There's been talk about you neglecting your duties and running around Sydney with this woman."

"I've done everything you've asked, including getting us one step closer to reeling in the Huisman Foundation. And I sent you the new numbers for the smart inhaler project. I need you to understand that there's only so far a person can be pushed, and I'm almost there."

Another long pause. "All right. I suppose you have done the things I've asked so a little reward can't hurt. You know this life doesn't have to be terrible. You're a stubborn boy, Darren. If you settled down and relaxed into your role, you might find this life quite pleasant. You have the best of everything."

"Except the ability to live my own life."

"If I had another heir who could do the job, I assure you I would take the option, but your brother is a fucking mess. Do you think I want my name carried on by the son of a whore?"

Rage threatened to swamp him. "I'm hanging up now, and you can fuck yourself."

"Darren, stop. I'm sorry." Those were two words he'd never heard from his father unless they were being used ironically. "I'm under some stress here. I shouldn't have said that. You're good at your job, and you deserve some slack. Have fun with the woman you met. Hell, take her with you to the Blue Mountains and maybe she can distract Oakley long enough you can get away with the prize. Huisman is working on some innovative tech, and I want a piece of it. You should, too. Your siblings are expensive, you know. At some point they'll marry and have kids, and they'll look to you to take care of them, too. I know you think I'm some kind of monster, but I do what I do to keep this family afloat. The world isn't a utopia where good wins out in the end. You've got to be ruthless because the only thing anyone cares about is money. When you get back, if you bring me Huisman, we can talk about you having more freedom."

He knew when his father was placating him, but it worked in his favor this time. He let a moment go as though he was seriously considering the offer. He wasn't. All the offer would do was buy him the time he needed. "All right. Maybe we can talk."

"Excellent."

He had a couple of questions, and if his father seemed to be in a giving mood, he would take it. "Did you ask Brian to meet with the Halo group?"

"Brian? Why would I talk to Brian? If Halo needs someone, I expect you to be there. Is something wrong?"

"Not at all. Just a miscommunication." So Brian had lied about a lot of things. "One last question. Oakley mentioned a group we own that he's interested in. One I'm not familiar with. What does Tandy Medical research?"

"Tandy?" His father seemed surprised, and then the line went quiet. "Nothing of import. I believe they're doing some vaccine research. Can't think of a reason Oakley would be interested. He's got enough of that on his own. Don't worry about it. I'll look into it. You concentrate on Huisman."

His father was worried. He knew when his father's voice lost all expression that he was hiding something. There was something about Tandy he didn't want Dare to know about.

Was Tandy his escape hatch?

"Of course. We're going to Oakley's in a couple of days. I'll keep you posted."

"See that you do." His father hung up.

"That seemed intense. Sure you don't want that drink?" Nate asked.

"No." He needed something else. He needed Tasha. He needed his sweet, bratty sub. "Let's go upstairs and get ready for tonight."

And tomorrow he would figure out what his father was hiding.

Chapter Twelve

"Do we have to keep him buckled up like that?" Kenzie paced in the small viewing room at The Station, her eyes on the man in the confinement area.

Brian—whatever his real name was—sat slumped on a modified bench, his arms and legs strapped down. And spread, since the bench had been modified for sex. Not that he was ready for it. He was perfectly clothed, and no one would be taking advantage of the wanton way his hot bod was strapped in.

Not even her sister.

"Uh, did you see the way he took out that guy outside the elevator?" Tristan asked. The team was all here for this debacle. "I think we definitely should keep him restrained. You know what Big Tag says. Restraints are how we show the enemy we love them."

Another of her father's rules. "How long before he's awake? Nate is bringing Dare here in twenty minutes, and he won't want to wait long. He'll get antsy if he doesn't see me."

"Which is precisely why you should have gone back." Zach was a forbidding presence.

They were huddled up in one of The Station's rooms kept for their voyeuristic clients. Brian was in the room where the people would "perform" for the audience behind the two-way mirror.

It had been the best Master Colin had been able to do in a pinch.

They didn't have a place to hold prisoners at the safe house.

And that is why you fail.

Yep. Her dad's voice was playing through her head.

"You would think Colin would be better prepared," Cooper said with a shake of his head. "The man was an operative for twenty years."

"And the fact that he worked with Nate's dad is the only reason he's being patient with us," Zach pointed out. "I assure you this dude would be tied up in the twins' bathtub if Brody Carter hadn't vouched for us. I don't think the man is particularly happy we're using his club as part of an Agency op. He was fine when it was all about making the target feel comfortable, but now that we have an actual prisoner, we need to be careful."

Master Colin had met them with all sorts of colorful Aussie ways to express his disinterest in being dragged into spy games. There was talk of all them being a sandwich short of a picnic. Colin himself was mad as a cut snake. And he'd declared himself knackered by their collective dickheadedness.

There was some other stuff in there, but she'd gotten the message. They were on thin ice, but at least they had a safe space to stash Brian.

The question was how long they could hide him. Dare would have questions, and a lot of them. She'd already had to text with him and convince Dare that Brian had managed to spend some time with Kara, and that was why they couldn't meet.

"Even The Hideout has an interrogation room," Cooper complained.

"Only because you're a paranoid bastard." Kala was in fet wear and a robe, sitting in the back of the room, one long booted leg crossed over the other.

Cooper's lips curled up slightly. "Really? I think you were there giving me directions when I equipped it."

A rare smile crossed Kala's face. "Because I'm a paranoid bitch."

It was good to know having a crisis could bring those two together. "How long do you think before he wakes up, and do we have anything else on this guy? I'm confused about what the hell he wants. He's been embedded with the Nash Group for six months now, but he mentioned Ms. Magenta. Is he a corporate spy or with an intelligence agency?"

"He could be mafia," Kala mused.

"He's not mafia." Kenzie had been the most upset, and not because somehow Brian knew who she was. Half of. She'd been way more upset with how Cooper had manhandled him.

In this case she agreed with Kenz. "I don't think a mafia guy would have treated me the way Brian did. He was trying not to hurt me. He wants intelligence. If he was mafia and he thought I was a rival, he would take me out. There's something going on here we're not seeing."

"He could be a good guy," Kenzie argued.

"Kenz, you heard what the rest of us did." Tristan stood and stared at Kenzie, who was in street clothes. "He knew who you were. He didn't want you to be able to influence Dare, and that is why he pursued you. This is not some love story between the two of you. It's an op. He played you."

Kala held a hand up. "He played me, actually. That's what she keeps forgetting. He pursued me first."

"And he had real conversations with me," Kenzie insisted.

Her heart ached for her sister, but she had to be realistic. "With Kara. Not with Kenzie."

"Kenzie, you are officially off this mission." Zach's lips had turned down. "Kala, you're Kara for the rest of the op. Kenz, you can help Lou. Don't argue with me or I'll send you back to Dallas. You're way too close to this guy, and I don't trust you to think straight when it comes to him."

There were frustrated tears in her sister's eyes, but she nodded and went to sit beside Lou, her arms crossing over her chest.

"He's awake." Lou had been quiet the whole time, her eyes either on her laptop or the man in the window. "He's pretending to sleep, but he's also been testing his restraints."

Tasha moved to the window. Sure enough, Brian's wrists moved slightly against the restraints.

She had some time before Dare would be here. Zach moved to the door.

"Tasha, he knows who you are. I'm not letting him get another look at Kenz or Kala, so it's you and me talking to him," Zach explained. "Lou, keep your eye on the web for any chatter about this guy. I suspect he's a deep cover operative for someone. Hell, the way we're playing things these days, he could be one of ours."

"I don't think so," Lou replied. "I think he's foreign, but I've got some calls in. I'll ID him eventually."

Tasha followed Zach out of the viewing room and into the one that held Brian. She watched as Brian went completely still the minute the door opened. His body relaxed, breathing even. He would look to anyone else like he was perfectly asleep.

"It's not going to work," Zach said. "You won't be able to bust out of the restraints. No one is planning on hurting you, Mr. Peters. If that's your name."

Brian's eyes came open, an icy stare finding Zach. "You're the server from the restaurant."

"You're observant." Zach closed and locked the door. "But then you would be given your profession."

"I'm an account manager for the Nash Group." Brian said the words, but the tone wasn't the Brian Peters she'd known. This was the operative. He might be playing some games, but he was going to show them who he really was under the mask. "Who are you, Tasha? Because I bet you don't work for your dad."

He would be wrong about that, but they didn't give up their familial relationships. "You can call me Ms. White, and refer to my colleague as Mr. Black."

Zach frowned. "You want to go that way? You know all Mr. Blacks are dickheads. Fine."

Brian's stark expression gave way to confusion. "You're CIA?"

"It doesn't matter," Zach explained. "What matters is who *you* are and who you work for."

"It matters if you're Agency," Brian insisted. "Because I'm working with you guys. I need some proof. I'm not saying shit until I see proof. I would say you're lying, but we all know how fucked up the Agency is right now. It's perfectly possible you have no idea what's going on."

She didn't like the sound of that, but it wasn't anything she hadn't already thought of.

"There are no Agency records of this guy." Lou's voice came over the speaker.

Brian frowned. "Is that your sister? That was a lie, too. Tell whoever that is that I'm not Agency but I'm working with them, and I won't say another thing until you let me call my people."

"As we don't know who your people are, I'm not inclined to allow that communication," Zach replied.

"Is he the boss?" Brian asked her. "Is he the one you're working Dare over for? This whole situation is exactly what I thought it was. The boss sent Magenta in to get in good with Dare, but you're the one who ended up with the prize because I distracted her long enough to let you slip in. It wouldn't have worked. He wouldn't have gone for her. She's too cold for him. She's gorgeous, but there's not a lot of soul in there, if you know what I mean."

Damn. She wished Zach had kicked Kenzie out. "I know you won't believe this, but it was pure chance we showed up there. There was no way we could have known you would be there."

"Of course there was. I posted it on social media and an hour later you showed up," Brian replied, and then his eyes narrowed at the silence that followed. "You didn't know. Who suggested the pub, Tasha? I was right. You're not the operative. You're backup for Magenta. Are you her handler?"

Her sister hadn't known he would be there. She would have told her. Kala would never let her go into a situation without every piece of information she knew. Lou would have told her.

The guys would tell her. Cooper and Tristan and... She felt her fists clench. Zach wouldn't have because he would have known exactly what she would have done. She would have held back and let Kala do the job. She wouldn't have talked to Dare at all.

"It wasn't Kara's fault," Zach said quietly. "Or Lou's. Or the guys'. They didn't know. I did. I sent you to the bar. I doubted Middleton would fall for her, but I thought Kara might be able to get to Nash, which would still put us in Huisman's orbit. I saw the post and made the call, and it's my right because I am in charge of this team."

"It's my team, Zach. They're my..." She shut her mouth because she'd been about to say they were her family.

Zach's expression went grim. "And that is why I'm in charge. I never meant for you to get involved, Tash. I thought Nash would take one look at Kara and she would blow him off and then she could play the hell out of him at the conference. You know I never expected anyone to fuck for intel. I wouldn't do that."

"But you'll use it if it's offered to you." A numbness had settled over her. She'd thought they'd been going to a completely random pub. Not completely random. She'd known Kala had an address. She'd thought she'd gotten it off the Internet or a guidebook or something. She'd gotten it from Zach.

"Dare actually cares about you," Brian said.

"Well, he cares about you, too." She wasn't the only one who'd screwed over Dare.

Brian's head shook. "I'm not sleeping with him. I'm his friend. I assure you he'll take my betrayal better than yours. Also, I'm not betraying Dare. He's innocent. He has no idea what's happening."

"What's happening, Brian?" Zach asked.

His jaw went stubborn. "I think I'll keep that to myself. I'd like to speak to your supervisor. You're too young to have any real power at the Agency. If that's who you actually work for. You know there are some naïve idiots out there who get played. Did some guy come up and ask you to help out your country?"

He was trying to push her, but she didn't care if he thought she was a moron. She was in some ways since she'd believed Zach. She should have remembered he was the Agency approved babysitter on this mission. The Agency approved manipulator.

"You can answer my questions here or we can move you to a more...quiet place," Zach said.

She was sick of Zach's games. "My name is really Tasha and I do work for the Agency. We're here on a mission to surveil the meeting between Oakley and Huisman."

"Then they're taking his threat seriously." A wave of relief seemed to go through Brian. "I thought they weren't listening."

"I'm not sure Huisman is a threat at all," Tasha replied. "That's what I'm here to assess. Now you can give me your credentials and we can sort this out before Dare starts asking questions about why you're no longer around or... I don't even know what the *or* is. What's your name and what intelligence agency do you work for?"

His head fell back. "I can't. Let me make a couple of calls, and once I verify who you are, we can talk."

"Dude, you know Kara's code name." Zach's whole body was

tight. "How can you still think we're not Agency?"

"Because my group hasn't verified she is. All we know is she's a player and a rough one. She's excellent at walking out with the prize and making the rest of us fight to get what we were promised. I've been told to make a determination whether she needs to be taken out."

Fuck. Kala had played some games in the beginning before their dad had sat her down and told her she would be benched if she did it again. She'd been trying to make a name for Kara, and apparently she'd succeeded. "She's Agency. I wouldn't try it if I were you."

"I know you Americans think you're the best at everything, but we are taught some rules. Number one is to not believe everything I'm told. I talk to my people or I don't talk at all. You can explain my absence to Dare." Brian settled back down, obviously ready to wait them out.

She started to argue, but Zach shook his head and moved to the door. That was an argument she couldn't have in here. It had been a mistake to let Brian see even a hint of a crack in the team.

The minute the door closed, Zach turned on her. "You set us back hours by showing him you were surprised. I know you are pissed with me right now, but that reaction is the reason I'm here."

The door came open and Kala stood there, leaning against the jamb and looking dangerous in her leather catsuit. "You don't have to be here, Zach. I can make it so you're not here."

"I'd love to see you try, sweetheart," Zach shot back.

Which brought Cooper to the door. "Lay a fucking hand on her and I'll take your head off."

The head Cooper threatened fell back and Zach groaned. "*This* is why I'm here. You're a bunch of fucking hormonal teenagers. I don't care what Tag says. You're not ready. I should have been able to tell you what I needed without worrying about a fight. Hell, I should be able to not tell you shit and still have you do your jobs. I have no idea why Drake thought this would work."

Tasha took a deep breath. She often had to be the voice of reason, and Zach was right about a couple of things. They weren't acting like the professionals they needed to be. They'd taken a simple job and made it infinitely more complex, but Zach needed to acknowledge his part in it, too.

"Why didn't you tell us?" She moved past her sister, bringing the discussion back to the private room where it should be.

Kala shifted beside Cooper, letting Zach inside. "It sure as hell wasn't about me. I would have done my job. If he'd wanted me to go after Nash, I would have."

There it was—jealousy. She didn't like the thought of Kala trying to seduce Dare. Kala wouldn't care about Dare. He would be the target.

Kala wouldn't love Dare.

She loved Dare. The feeling was right there, a warmth she couldn't deny. And she could lose it all.

"I was acting on instinct," Zach admitted. "Honestly, I didn't know what would happen, but I wanted Nash to get a look at Kara and remember her when he saw her again at the conference. That was all. If you'd asked me what would happen that night, I suspected Kala would drink too much. Lou would end up mooning after TJ, and Tash would meet a guy and then get scared off, and all three of you would come back to base having accomplished none of your goals."

Kala cleared her throat.

"Except Kala, of course," Zach allowed. "I never dreamed you would sleep with Nash, and when it happened I thought we could pivot. I'm not trying to be the bad guy here. No one thinks this team can work. They think the Agency is indulging Taggart, which is why we get surveillance assignments when he isn't around. The bigwigs don't trust us, and fucking this op up isn't going to help."

"So what do we do?" Tristan asked. "I can promise you I'll have the data from Nash's laptop in a couple of hours. We can cover for this asshole's absence until morning, but Nash will want some answers after that. Can we use the intel from the laptop to get Langley to give us a longer rope?"

"To hang ourselves with?" Cooper sighed and sank back into his chair. "The only reason they haven't recalled us is they don't know what we've done."

"They know the target changed, but they don't know the twins aren't the ones working him," Zach explained. "They've been informed everything is going to plan, and I sent Tasha's first report on Huisman under the team name, not her own."

"What are they going to do if he's a legit intelligence agent?" Lou asked.

"He is." Kenzie's eyes were steady on the mirror, watching Brian.

"We don't know that," her twin argued.

"The question is what happens if he is and we've got an allied foreign intelligence agent strapped down on a sex bench," Tristan said with a sigh. "That's gotta be against some kind of regulation. At the very least we're in for a 'dumbass' lecture, and I've had so fucking many of those. I can tell you everything Big Tag is going to say to me verbatim at this point. Could I get sent on an op where I get shot? I'm ready for that. I think I'm cool with the sweet release of death at this point."

Tasha's cell buzzed. She looked down, and it was Nate texting them that they were approaching. Another text followed right after. Dare.

I expect my sweet sub to present herself to me in precisely twenty minutes. Any later and punishment will be harsh. Missed you.

Her heart squeezed.

"They're here. I have twenty minutes," she said quietly. "Kala, what are you going to say about Brian?"

"That we had a lovely afternoon and he got pissed when I wouldn't bring him with us and I suspect he's sulking," she replied. "He's about to meet Coop, so he's going to realize things are more complex than they seemed. Brian's off processing that."

That would have to work.

"Magenta." Brian's head had come up, and he was staring at the mirror. "I'm talking to the woman known as Ms. Magenta. I know you're in there, and I know you've listened to everything I've said. I'm going to call you Maggie from now on. That sounds better to me. Maggie, you should understand that this isn't over. Not by a long shot. I'm going to get out of these restraints, and then you and I are going to have a talk. No matter what happens between our teams, we're not through."

Zach cursed under his breath, and Kala rolled her eyes.

But Kenzie's lips curled up ever so slightly.

Tasha pushed through the door and out into the hall that would lead her to the club.

She had a job to do, and it started now. Tomorrow, she would tell Dare everything and likely lose her job and have her whole family angry with her.

For tonight, she would play her role.

* * * *

It felt damn good to be back in leathers. He'd had them delivered straight to the club and worried a bit about the fit. He didn't care about clothes. Normally. He wanted to look good in these. He wanted Tasha to be proud of her Dom.

"You must be Dare," a deep voice said.

He turned and a tall, muscular man stood at the end of the row of lockers Dare had been assigned to. "I am. Are you my guide? You sound American. I thought the owner was Australian."

"Oh, I'm not Master Colin," the man said, holding a hand out. "I'm Cooper. I'm a friend of Kara's and a member of the club. Kara asked if I would show you around tonight."

"Kara's here?" He wasn't sure what this man's relationship with Kara was.

"You thought she was with…" He stopped, seeming to search his memory. "Bryce? Bob?"

"Brian."

"I can't keep up with the guys who follow my Kara around. It's a lot," he allowed, seemingly disinterested in the subject. "But she wouldn't miss tonight for the world, and you and Tash are the only outside visitors allowed in this evening."

What was Brian getting himself into? Maybe there was a reason the man wasn't answering his calls. He was utterly into Kara, and it appeared she had something going with this big American. It wasn't his business. At least not tonight. "Is Kara your sub?"

Cooper leaned against the locker and sighed. "If only it was that easy. We have a complex relationship, to say the least, but it's important to me. Kara won't be playing the sub this evening. Treat her the same way you would a Mistress."

"Ah, so…"

"I'm a Dom," Cooper explained. "Hence the complexity. Don't worry about it. Tonight is all about showing her cousin a good time.

They teach you how the locks work? No cell phones on the dungeon floor."

He wasn't particularly worried about his cell. His laptop was in there, but Nate would be hanging out in here since they'd decided they were comfortable with the security at The Station. "I'm good and totally tech free. I assume my kit arrived."

One more thing he'd ordered.

"It did, and I set everything up in the privacy room you requested. I thought we would do a quick tour of the club and then you and Tash can settle in for the night. You've got the space for as long as you like, but I was going to invite you to spend the last hour of the evening in the lounge with Kara and myself. I find it can be good to have a drink and come down a bit."

From the high of Dominance. From the high of submission. From the high of getting to be whoever a person was for a little while without worrying about the outside world. The idea of sitting in a lifestyle club with Tasha on his lap, talking to people who understood him, seemed like heaven. "We would love that. I thought we could watch a few scenes first. It's been a while since I was in a club."

Cooper straightened up and started toward the door. "I'd heard you haven't been practicing for a while. I hope we meet your standards."

He chuckled. "As long as it's clean and consent is the word of the day, I don't have any standards. I've only been a member of one club, but I know there's a lot of diversity in them. The one I was a member of was small but amazing. It's more about the members than how much money was spent on the equipment."

Cooper held the door open. "See, that's what I keep telling my...friends. I started a club back home, and yes, it is not exactly the most luxurious place in the world, but it's ours. We're working on it. One day, it'll be spectacular."

"Are you going on about that club of yours again?" Kara was standing in the hallway wearing a leather catsuit that molded to her every curve. Cooper moved in beside her, an arm winding around her waist to rest on her hip.

"You know I am, and you know I'm right," he said.

They made a gorgeous couple, and it was clear they were

comfortable with each other.

There was absolutely no space for Brian in there. It made him wonder what games Kara was playing.

"Only if you continue to have excellent advisors," she replied and then glanced behind her. "Tash, hurry up. Your prince awaits, and he looks pretty good."

His heart threatened to stop as Tasha stepped out of the women's locker room, and she looked heavenly in a white corset and thong and heels that he had no idea how she walked in. She was graceful as she moved toward him, her hair flowing around her shoulders, the dark color contrasting with the white of her fet wear.

She was the single most gorgeous woman he'd ever seen, and she was his. She wanted to be with him.

He held a hand out, allowing her to place hers there so he could draw her in. "Hello, beautiful."

Her lips curled into the sweetest smile. "Hello, Sir."

He leaned over, brushing his lips against hers. "In case I forget later on when I'm in full-on Dom mode, thank you for tonight."

"You're welcome, but you never forget, Dare. You always thank me. You always think about me. I can't tell you how much that means to me."

"Do you want to move on to the privacy room and skip all the perverted stuff so you can get engaged now?" Kara asked.

Tasha turned and frowned her way. "You hush."

Cooper shrugged. "I'm with Kara. You two are way too sweet for a club like this."

Tasha moved to his side, still holding his hand. "We are not, thank you, and we want to do all the perverted stuff. We can be sweet and nasty at the same time."

He didn't care that they were making fun of him. He was perfectly comfortable being gooey and romantic with this woman. She was worth any ribbing he got. "Then let's get perverted, sweetness."

She winked his way, and they began their night.

An hour later, he closed the door to the privacy room.

"I think the Aussies are way more hardcore than the Americans.

We need to talk about all those needles because that might be a hard limit, Dare."

He wasn't playing with her. Well, not that way. They'd spent an hour watching scenes and talking about the lifestyle in an intellectual fashion, but now it was time to live his fantasies, and they didn't include talking about her hard limits. He knew them. "Present yourself to me properly, Tasha."

She turned and seemed surprised for a moment, then her expression cleared and she relaxed. The privacy room was small, with a bed and a spanking bench and a long table with all of his brand-new kit laid out. He'd bought every item with her in mind. Her heels clicked along the hardwoods as she made her way to him and then dropped gracefully to her knees, her head tilted down and palms up on her thighs.

"I am so happy to be here with you," he whispered as he put a hand on her head.

"I am, too, Dare. I'm so happy I walked into that pub and found you."

He reached down and brought her chin up. He loved hearing those words, but she'd been tense all evening. As they watched the scenes, there had been a weird distance between them, and he wanted to demolish any walls she was thinking about erecting between them. "I want you to wear my collar."

A brilliant smile crossed her face, and he felt some of the tension leave her. "Yes."

It was so easy with this woman. This was what his college friends meant when they said they'd found the one. He'd never understood, but now he did. Tasha fit with him. She'd so easily become part of his life, one he wasn't sure he could do without. "I promise I'm going to make this work. No matter what."

Her eyes flared, a stubborn look he'd come to love. "I'll hold you to that."

"And I'm keeping the promise I made to you earlier. On the bench, love, and you don't need that gorgeous corset. I've got a robe for you to wear when we join your cousin and her friend." He reached for her hand, helping her up and turning her around so he could unlace her corset.

She was still for him. "You're good at this."

He wasn't. He was fumbling with the laces, but his girl was always trying to praise him. It made him want to be worthy of it. He kissed her shoulder as he managed to loosen the corset. She lifted her arms, and he brought it over her head. "Sweet words won't save you."

"I was only trying to help."

He loved this game.

She turned and her eyes were wide and innocent, and she placed her hands behind her back, making her breasts thrust out. "I didn't know another way to get into the very important luncheon, Sir. I was only thinking of you."

"You were thinking of me when you hiked your skirt up and showed that asshole your legs?" She was still wearing too much. The tiny thong covered her gorgeous pussy, and now that they were alone, he wanted absolutely nothing hidden from him. "Give me the thong."

Her hands went to the band, dragging it down her legs. "Yes. I was thinking about you. I was good at providing a distraction, wasn't I, Sir? You needed a distraction this afternoon."

Such a brat. He took the thong she offered him. "Then let me provide you with one this evening. Go to the bench."

A shadow crossed her face. "Maybe we should talk first."

What was bothering her? He'd thought it was the expiration date he'd placed on them before, but he'd been clear this evening that wasn't happening. "Maybe you should obey me. I have some questions, but we can work this out while you accept my discipline."

Her nose wrinkled sweetly. "My mother told me it would be this way if I ended up with a top. I should have listened to her."

She turned and marched over to the spanking bench, that pert ass of hers swaying and making his cock tighten.

"Your mother told you not to find a top? Seriously?" She'd talked a bit about her parents, but it surprised him every time.

She glanced back as she settled herself on the bench. "Not at all. She just said it would be all spankings and growls about discipline. Lucky for you I like those things. You would be in trouble otherwise."

Oh, he knew. He'd been in such trouble before he'd met her. He'd thought it was because his life was shit, and now he knew it was because none of the other women had been her. He'd had girlfriends he'd cared for, a wife he'd tried to be a partner to, but none of them filled the empty space inside him.

He went to the table where Cooper had done exactly what he'd promised. Dare's new kit was laid out for him. Where to start? He'd been so busy he hadn't had time to spend hours planning out this time with her. That would change at some point. He would dedicate endless hours to thinking up new ways to torture his sweet sub.

Tonight he would start out simple. He laid a slap against her ass and watched a shudder go through her.

"Something is bothering you this evening." Another smack. And another.

He saw her hands tighten around the arms of the bench. This particular apparatus leveled down from her pelvis, leaving her gorgeous ass in the air and her torso on an incline, breasts dangling on either side of the slender bench.

"I'm fine now. I thought this could be awkward, but it was fine. I've never been in a club with my cousin before," she said.

There was something in her tone he didn't like, a certain flatness, but she'd never lied to him so he wouldn't accuse her now. He slapped her ass again, watching her skin turn pink. "Are you worried I'll be angry she's been playing Brian? It's obvious she's in love with Cooper."

She muttered something under her breath.

That earned her a rapid succession of smacks to her cheeks and the fleshy part of her upper thighs. "When we're playing, you're honest with me. No muttering. You say what you need to say."

The words came out between gritted teeth. "I said I wish it was obvious to her, and yes, I'm worried you're going to be upset with me when my cousin breaks your friend's heart. I don't understand her sometimes. She's been in love with Cooper for years, but she won't give in, and she won't let him go. I'm afraid she used Brian to make him jealous."

If the man had been jealous, he hadn't shown it. Another smack. She would be warming up now, giving over to the pain and the release it could grant her. "I don't care what happens between Brian and your cousin. They're adults. They can figure it out. It won't affect the way I feel about you at all."

He let his hand slide up her right thigh to the apex of her legs, his fingers brushing against her pussy. Sure enough, she was wet and getting wetter with every smack of his hand.

"We don't have to think about it for another week or so, Dare. I'll wear your collar. I'll be anything you want me to be. If you still feel the same way about me at the end of the week, we'll need to talk," she whispered.

"I'll still feel the same way." Or he'd be more in love with her.

She shook her head. "I was wrong. We can't talk tonight. I need to feel. Make me feel, Dare. Make me cry. I need it. I need you to manhandle me and fuck me hard. I know my safe word and I'll use it, but otherwise, do your worst."

She was on some kind of edge and he didn't understand it, but he knew a plea for help, and he would never deny hers.

He picked up the paddle he'd bought. It was a nasty piece of business, with holes in it to increase the ache it would bring. Tasha, he'd found, liked a big bite of pain. And a bit of fantasy took her out of her head and let her enjoy the sex more. She needed a nasty Dom. He could give her that. He showed her the paddle. "Did you think you could get away with what you did this afternoon? Your body belongs to me. You do not show it off to anyone else."

She bit her bottom lip, and he saw the moment she gave in to the fantasy. She knew damn well he wasn't some so-called alpha male who demanded she keep her beauty and light hidden so another man could never see it. "I'm sorry, Sir. Please forgive me. I was only trying to help."

"This will remind you who you belong to." He moved back, and her whole body tensed right before he brought the paddle down on the center of her ass.

She yelped but made not a move to get off the bench. In fact, she held on tighter. "Please, Sir. No more."

That was her way of begging for it. He brought the paddle down again and again, the scent of her arousal filling the air and pushing him forward.

She cried, those tears flowing down her cheeks and clinging prettily.

When he was sure she'd had enough, he tossed the paddle away and moved in behind her. The bench was perfectly adjusted to his height, so it was easy to shove his pants down, sheath his aching dick in a condom, and move between her legs.

"Yes, Dare. Yes, please," she whispered.

The fact that her ass was a glorious pink, on the cusp of red, made his cock even harder. She'd needed him. Giving her that discipline she needed to release all her pent-up anxiety had made him feel like a fucking king. He stroked his cock and pressed against her pussy. "I'll always give you this, sweetness. What I said before about your body belonging to me… Well, this is all yours."

He shoved his cock in, holding on to her hips as she gasped and wriggled on the bench. She hadn't moved as he'd spanked her, but she adjusted now, taking his full length inside her. He dragged out again and thrust back in, giving up any attempts at finesse. Lust and love drove him. She was his, a payment from the universe for all the shit he'd been through. For his crappy childhood and even worse teen years. For losing his mom and then his freedom. She was what would make it all worthwhile.

He fucked her as she pushed back, meeting him with a ferocity he hadn't seen in her before. He let it take him, hands digging into her hips to hold her in place.

She cried out as her pussy seemed to clamp down around his cock, sending him right over the edge. The orgasm lit him up like lightning, buzzing through his system and taking over his every muscle.

He pumped his cock into her over and over until he had nothing left to give her.

Tasha was crying again.

Because it had been so much. Because they'd been connected, and this was a safe place for her to do it. He stepped back, dealing with the condom and his leathers so he could move in and pick up his sub, hauling her up to his chest and cradling her there.

"Are you all right, sweetness?"

She nodded, her eyes still filled with tears. "Can I cry for a while, Sir?"

"You never need to ask." He wanted to make that plain to her. "If you need to cry, I'll hold you. Always. I promise. Even if I'm the one who made you cry, I'll be sorry for it and I'll hold you."

She held on to him, burying her face in the crook of his neck and crying against him.

He carried her to the bed and sat, settling her on his lap. He stroked her hair and rocked with her, the motion and sound and closeness soothing him in a way the sex never could. Or maybe it was the combination of the two, the comfort proof that the sex was more than mere bodily function.

After a while she quieted, nestling against him.

"I love you, Tasha." He'd never said those words to anyone but his mother and brother and sister. Not a single living woman in the world had heard them from his lips.

Her head came up, a surprised expression there. "Dare..."

"Hush. You don't have to say anything," he began.

"But I..."

Whatever she'd been about to say was stopped by a loud popping sound.

Gunfire.

Someone was shooting in the club, and his problems might have found him even here.

Chapter Thirteen

Tasha's world tilted at that sound—a loud bang followed by a smattering of smaller ones. A terrible and familiar sound she couldn't pretend to misunderstand.

One minute she'd been safe and warm and in Dare's arms. He'd told her he loved her.

Dare loved her.

She'd been ready to tell him everything and then…

"That's gunfire." She scrambled off his lap. She was naked. Damn it. Her actual clothes were in the locker room.

Her brain started whirling, going over every possible scenario.

"Maybe it's a recording." Dare stood, rushing across the room and grabbing the robe he'd brought for her. "Maybe someone's doing a scene. Fantasy play."

"There would have been an announcement. Colin would never scare his members like this. There are too many ex-soldiers and first responders in this club." That had been a volley of gunfire to get someone's attention, and now she could hear screaming.

Fuck. She had to face the truth. Someone was here and they were either here for Dare, or Brian's team had figured out where he was. Either way, she couldn't let Dare get caught.

She shoved her arms into the robe and tied it around her waist. "We have to get you out of here."

"No, we have to make sure you're safe. I'm not going anywhere until you're safe," he declared, suddenly looming over her. "Does Nate know where we are?"

Nate would have been working with Tristan to download the contents of Dare's system but that should have been finished an hour ago. She wasn't sure where they would be now. "He knows we're in a privacy room, but I have no idea how far away he is. All I know is if the people with the guns are looking for you, they won't stop until they have you."

He shook his head, a stubborn look coming into his eyes. "Then they can take me. Tasha, you stay here and I'll turn myself in. According to Brian, it didn't seem like they were trying to kill me. At least not the first time they tried. I'm not going to put all these people at risk."

It was the worst possible time for him to play superhero. She had to find a way to make him follow her rules. "I'm going to get you out. Nate is probably already making his way here."

"Do you think they're taking hostages?" His hands found her shoulders. "That's the most obvious scenario. Why else would they come inside? Why not wait until I go to the parking lot?"

"Because then they would have to deal with Nate."

"Yes, and here they won't have to because I won't listen to Nate if they're holding a gun to someone's head." He leaned over, brushing his lips on her forehead. "I won't let anyone die for me. They want something from me. I'll give it to them, and they'll let me go. You stay here."

He was being so naïve, and she was not hiding in a privacy room while the op went to hell. "Dare, you are not turning yourself over. I swear that if you do, I'll be right behind you. I'll explain to them that the best way to keep you in line is to take me with them."

He paled. "You wouldn't."

"Try me." He was severely underestimating how desperately she needed to save him. Her team would be out there right now trying to handle the situation. Dare walking out in the middle of it would make things so much worse. "There are several ex-military who are members of this club. I assure you, they can handle the situation."

"Tasha, I'm trying to protect you."

"And I'm trying to do the same for you. So it's your choice.

You can walk out there like a sacrificial lamb and I'll find a way to go with you, or you can come with me and we'll get to Nate and get the hell out of here," she explained.

His jaw went tight. "I don't like you limiting my choices this way."

"I don't like the thought of you being used in some kind of war I don't understand, so suck it up," she shot back as she moved to the door.

He was behind her. "At least let me go first."

This was where it would be so helpful if he knew she was a trained CIA agent, but it wasn't the time to spring that on him. "I'm just going to take a look. They might not know who I am. Stay here."

She slipped out and was surprised to see the hallway filled with a wispy fog. Her nose wrinkled as the scent hit her. Acrid and sulphureous, she knew the smell.

What the hell was going on and could she get to her pants before she had to sneak out? Pants were important.

"What is that smell?"

She started but managed not to shout. "Damn it, Dare. I told you to stay inside."

"Not happening," he admitted. "Why is there fog?"

"Someone set off a flashbang." She moved carefully along the wall. The place had gone quiet, and she saw a couple rush across the edge of the main floor, holding hands with their heads down.

Colin was going to kill them. She would need every hour she had between here and Loa Mali to craft an explanation to her parents about why she'd gotten a friend's club raided, because they would be on the way. Colin would give her father an earful about how the night had gone.

And then there was Brian. What if the fuckers took Brian? Then she'd be responsible for his kidnapping because she'd left him tied to a sex bench.

Calm. She needed to stay calm. The locker room was too far away. There had to be someplace she could hole up with Dare while her sisters and the boys took care of business.

The lights went out.

Lou was at work. The darkness would help unless the fuckers

were a paramilitary group of mercenaries, and then they would have night vision.

"Stay close. We're going to stick to the wall and take a left at the end of the hall." To the right was the main dungeon, and that was almost surely where they would start the search. To the left they could get to the stairs that led to more diversified play spaces, and more importantly, to the opposite of the club where there was a back exit.

She had to hope these assholes didn't know about that exit.

Dare's hand was suddenly in hers. "We're going to talk about this later. You think your ass hurts now…"

She would handle it. If they survived this, she would give him far bigger reasons to spank her. She would take every smack of his hand if he could forgive her. "Come on, Sir. The best thing we can do for everyone here is to get you out."

She crept along the wall, her eyes starting to adjust to the darkness. Not all the lights had gone off. There were neon fixtures parsed around the place, and they seemed to be on a separate grid or likely had to be turned off at the source. The lights twisted the smoke into wispy tendrils of neon light.

In the distance she could hear whispers. Masculine voices were speaking, but she couldn't make out what they were saying. English. She was sure they were speaking English, but she couldn't hear enough to make out an accent.

It didn't matter. Lou and Tristan would make sure they caught these guys on a CCTV. There might not be one in the actual club, but there were plenty in this part of the city. Lou would find them and figure out who they were and who'd hired them. All she had to do was get Dare away from here, and her team would handle the rest.

Of course then the real fight would begin because she had to tell him. She couldn't tell him she loved him too until he knew who she was. It would be okay. They were connected, and he would believe her.

It would be okay. It was all going to be okay.

A dark figure moved across the floor in front of the hallway that led to the stairs. She caught sight of the man in the blinking neon lights and squeezed Dare's hand, stopping their motion. She didn't breathe, her heart pounding in her chest as the figure turned down the hall she'd been planning on using, the shadow of a big gun in his hands.

They couldn't go that way.

She wished she had her gun or her knives. She rarely used them in the field, but she practiced with them often, and she would feel so much more in control if she had them.

Dare tugged her hand, and she could see him pointing forward.

They moved behind the smaller stage, trying to stay low. From there they could make their way to the only place she knew would be reenforced. They could make their way to the viewing room where Lou would be.

It wasn't how she wanted him to find out. She needed to get him in bed and gently tell him. He needed to be able to feel her arms around him when she explained who she really was.

"Stand down, whoever the fuck you are." A familiar voice came booming over an intercom system. Normally it played industrial music on a low volume, but it seemed Zach had pumped that sucker up.

He was in the control room. Lou would be there, too. It meant Kala and Cooper would be moving around the floor, ready to take out the enemy. Tristan would be with them or guarding Brian, while Nate would have one job—looking for Tasha and Dare.

"Stay close." She started to move toward one of the smaller stages, sticking to the shadows.

"I don't know who you are, but you've stepped in it," Zach declared.

She knew what he was doing. He was attempting to manipulate whoever was in the club to get upset and make an angry move. He was also trying to buy time for the team to take them out.

"You are the dumb motherfuckers who've managed to bite off more than you can chew," Zach continued.

She heard a snort to her left and followed her instincts. She kicked out, catching whoever was moving in the leg and throwing him or her off balance. In the low light she saw a man in all black, stumbling, trying not to hit the floor. He held an M4A1 assault rifle in his hands, but those were unsteady, too.

Her eyes had adjusted, and now it was easy for her to sweep her leg out again, catching the guy's ankles and sending him crashing to the floor. But not before she grabbed that sweet rifle.

"Hey, lady," the guy began.

She brought the butt down on his head. The guy slumped to the floor.

"Tasha, what did you do?" Dare asked, standing right behind her. "Who is that?"

She didn't care. Now they had a shot at getting out of here. She gripped the rifle, happy for the familiar weight in her hands. "Let's go find Nate."

"Or you can stay right there. I've got you, bitch," a deep voice said. "Drop that gun and I might forget that you hurt one of my team members."

She stopped because her ears had to be deceiving her. That voice was familiar. Too familiar.

"Chet?"

A deep chuckle. "Holyeeee shit. Tash? Is that you?"

"Tasha?" Another familiar voice came through the darkness. "Damn it. I thought I saw Coop moving in the shadows. Hey! Hey, Lou, baby! Turn on the lights. It's me."

The lights immediately came on, and Tasha was faced with the biggest mistake she'd ever made.

Chet Whittington stood there in the middle of the dungeon, his lean body covered in black fatigues. He looked cool and collected as his lips curled up and his eyes wandered over her. "Damn, girl. You look good. You know I always thought you were sexy as hell with a weapon in your hands."

Dare moved in front of her. "Whoever you are, I'll go with you, but you have to leave her out of this."

Chet frowned, looking Dare up and down. "Who the fuck are you? And I can't leave her out of this since I suspect she's the one who knows where my lost Canadian operative is."

A tall guy with broad shoulders walked in with a tablet in his hands. "He should be right here, boss."

"Tasha, you remember Mike Johnson. I've worked with him plenty of times before," Chet turned to the soldier. "As you can see he's not here. Is there an upstairs? That might be what's confusing the signal."

Her heart threatened to seize because this was absolutely the worst-case scenario. They were here for Brian. It was all about to fall apart.

Dare turned to her. "What is happening? Tasha, how does this man know you?"

"I know her biblically," Chet said with a chuckle.

She thought seriously about using the rifle in her hand.

"I fucking don't know what you mean." Dare's shoulders had squared. "Who are you and what are you doing here?"

Her cousin TJ moved in beside Chet. "I think we can bring the testosterone level down. We're all friends here."

Chet wasn't listening. He never liked to bring the machismo level to a reasonable degree. He just went for it. He sent Dare a smug look. "I'm Chet Whittington, and I work for the CIA. The woman you're standing next to does, too. I suspect I'm going to get called out for ruining whatever play she's running on you." He glanced back at Tasha. "Thought you didn't screw for intel. Guess Daddy's girl isn't as pure as you said you were."

TJ moved in. "I would watch what I say if I were you. I'm on your team right now, but that can change really fast."

"I'm not sure how," Mike replied, obviously standing by Chet. "Don't forget I'm the CO here."

"Fucking Taggarts," Chet said under his breath.

"Seriously?" Kala strode toward them. "What the hell, Whittington? TJ? What is going on? I'm glad I didn't kill the dudes I took out."

TJ sighed and touched his comm unit. He looked a lot like his dad, like all the Taggart men. Six foot three with blue eyes and sandy blond hair he kept in a military cut. "Stand down. We're in friendly territory. I repeat, stand down."

Dare had gone utterly still.

Tasha turned to him. She had to save this. She had to. "Dare, we need to talk."

"Hey, guys. We've got a spot of trouble coming." Nate walked toward them. "I mean real trouble. Like this mess is a bit of sunshine compared to the storm that's coming our way."

Everyone went tense, guns reappearing.

That was the moment the doors swung open, and she realized

she hadn't hit worst-case scenario before. Nope. Not even close. The massive Viking striding her way was worst-case scenario. He was her own personal apocalypse.

Ian Taggart walked right up to her, pointed a finger her way, and gave her a look she remembered from childhood. It was his mad-dad look, and it always made her think twice.

"I said no honeypots," her dad declared.

Tasha wished a hole would open up and swallow her whole.

* * * *

Dare felt numb.

How had the world turned over in a single instant?

One minute he'd been holding Tasha and planning a future with her, and the next he was surrounded by men with guns, and they had zero interest in him. He wasn't even the person they were looking for. It was some kind of weird coincidence.

"Okay, I need for you to remember that we're in the middle of an op," Tasha was saying to the massive man who'd walked in and immediately gotten into her space.

The big blond dude straightened up, and his jaw went tight. "As if I could forget that."

"Oh, I think you did, babe," a soft voice said, and a woman with strawberry blonde hair stepped up next to the scary guy. "We're not alone, and you need to remember that."

She looked like his natural mate. The woman was tall and lovely and reminded him of someone, but he couldn't quite place the familiarity. The two seemed to fit together. Like he'd thought he and Tasha fit. He liked looking in the mirror when she was with him because she seemed to make him look better, as though he was missing something when she wasn't there.

There was a yelp, and then Lou was running onto the scene. The soldier who'd told Chet off smiled and settled his big gun to the side so he could catch her.

Everyone knew each other. Everyone except him. Lou was wrapped around the soldier guy, hugging him like she hadn't seen him in years, and Cooper had joined Kara.

He was so slow right now. It felt like his brain was moving

through molasses. Tasha wasn't who she said she was.

What had that man said? He'd declared he was CIA and then…

I suspect I'm going to get called out for ruining whatever play she's running on you.

Tasha was a spy, and he was her target. He turned the words over in his brain, trying to make sense of them.

"Sorry, Tash. I think Colin called them," Nate was saying.

"Could you put on some pants?" the big guy asked her, his head shaking. "Did you forget everything I taught you?"

"*Eto ne to, chto ty dumayesh*," Tasha said to the guy, who was obviously the boss.

Was that Russian? Tasha spoke Russian?

"*Tak ty ne prosto perespala s obyektom svoyego nablyudeniya, dochka?*" the man replied.

"Ian," his partner said, his name an obvious threat.

The big guy shrugged. "It's all fucked up anyway, baby, and I seriously doubt Mr. Nash speaks Russian. Do you speak Russian, Mr. Nash?"

"I don't think I speak English right now," he admitted. He felt so out of place. "I also don't think I'm needed here any longer. I'll let you people have your reunion."

This wasn't about him. Someone had lost an operative and somehow that had brought these people in to screw over Tasha's plans. What the hell were Tasha's plans?

Pain threatened. He could feel the bitter edge of it, like the knife point pressed against him but it hadn't broken the skin yet. It would gut him if he let it in. Her betrayal would end him in a way nothing else could. Not his father. Not his mother's death. Tasha would be the one who forever taught him he was worth nothing.

"Dare, we have to talk." Tasha stood there, her eyes wide and pleading.

Not five minutes before it would have worked on him. He would have given her anything, moved heaven and earth to get her to smile. She'd had him around her finger so tightly he'd been willing to risk everything for her.

It had all been a lie. She didn't love him. She'd been using him. Like everyone used him.

"We have nothing to talk about…" It occurred to him that he

didn't know her real name. "What should I call you?"

"Tasha. My name is really Tasha," she said, tears shining in her eyes. "I didn't know who you were when we met."

Sure she hadn't.

"I'm going to tell you everything I can, but I have to talk to my team because something's going on here," she explained. "I promise, I'll tell you everything and I'll make you understand."

The key was in that first night. That was when her play had begun. She'd wanted Brian at first. That had been obvious. When had she figured out he was the actual target? All questions he would play through his head probably for the rest of his life.

Shame ripped through him, curdling up like bile in his gut. He was such a fucking fool. He should have listened to Brian. Brian was the only person in the whole fucking world who looked out for him. Brian was his only friend, and he hadn't listened to a word the man had said. Brian had known something was wrong.

A thought occurred to him. She'd been so willing to bring him here. Had that been part of the plan, too? "Did you take photos? Run some film of us playing?"

She knew his background, knew this part of his life was utterly unacceptable to his father. It would be an excellent way to control him.

Tasha looked startled at the suggestion. "No. Dare, why would I do that?"

"He thinks you maneuvered him into this position so you can blackmail him," Kara said quietly. Except this time her Australian accent was gone. She said the words with a flat American accent.

One more lie.

Tasha reached up and clutched his arms. "I would never do that to you. Never. This was for us. Only for…" She bit her bottom lip. "I'm not going to lie to you anymore. I won't ever lie to you again. There was something going on tonight. I have to talk to my bosses before I reveal that to you, but no one else will ever know you were in this club."

Except for all the people who already did, including the asshole who'd obviously had a relationship with Tasha. He stepped out of her grasp, not able to handle having her hands on him. That was when he realized what had happened. "Who downloaded my laptop?"

He always had it with him. It was locked in the safe when he was at the hotel, and he was a pretty light sleeper. He tended to wake up when she got out of bed. She couldn't risk him walking in on her in the middle of the night. That would have blown her cover.

"Sorry, mate. That was me," Nate admitted.

His bodyguard. Of course. That made sense. They'd worked hard to get Nate Carter into position. "Which one of you shot me up with a tranquilizer dart so you could bring in Nate?"

He hadn't been living in reality since the minute he'd met her. He'd been playing a part in whatever drama Tasha needed to keep him close to her. He'd met her, fucked her, and then been so happy to keep fucking her he'd let her steamroll his life. When he was in danger, he'd let her make the decisions so she would feel comfortable.

She was excellent at her job.

"That wasn't us." Cooper stood next to Kara, both of them grim.

Brian was going to be so upset the woman he'd been pursuing turned out to be a spy. "Sure it wasn't."

"It wasn't." Lou still had an arm around her soldier. "We have no idea who tried to take you. I can even show you the video of the attack. It's interesting, to say the least."

"Dare, you have to believe me. Everything I've done has been to protect you," Tasha said, each word a plea.

"Sure." He wasn't giving her anything. "I'd like to be on my way. I need to find my friend. I suspect you have the data you need, so there's no further requirements from me."

He wasn't sure he believed them about the CIA crap. This could be one long con from a rival investment firm. Now they had his data and could outbid the Nash Group on all their open projects, and his father would punish his siblings.

He would have to marry whoever his father chose. If he wasn't cast out after this.

"I'm afraid I can't let you leave, Mr. Nash," the big guy who seemed to be named Ian said. "Tasha is right. We do need to have a private meeting where I can speak freely and we decide how to move forward."

A groan came from Kara.

Ian ignored her and continued. "We'll regroup and figure out what we're doing. What you see here is two different Agency teams working at cross purposes. My group was on a simple surveillance meeting."

"And my group is on a search and retrieve," the other guy said. The guy who looked at Tasha like he owned her.

Thought you didn't screw for intel.

That's what had happened. She'd targeted him, and he'd given it all up. He was probably the easiest target in her whole career. Ian had called it something else. A honey pot. Yes, he'd fallen right into that honey pot and given up everything like the idiot he was. It was time to stop playing her games.

"I don't care what you're doing. I want out. You have the data from my laptop. I assume your spy has been keeping notes of all the things I've told her about my business and my family." He wouldn't look her way. It was easier to engage her boss. "You've gotten everything out of me you're going to get so I suggest you take the win and let me go."

"Dare, you can't go. You're still in danger," Tasha insisted. She reached out.

If she touched him again, he might break. His calm was so close to being blown, and he couldn't. He couldn't. He moved his arm, shoving her hand away. "Don't you touch me."

He actually heard a growl from the boss, and most of the men stepped up.

"*Prekrati, pozhaluysta,*" Tasha said and then shook her head. "I'm sorry. When I get emotional, I sometimes revert to Russian. I asked them to stand down."

"I'm sorry as well. I shouldn't have been so rough." Politeness was a refuge he could hide behind. He needed his calm to get through the next few minutes without falling apart utterly. "But I don't want you to touch me. Please stop trying to touch me. I understand what you've done, and I would like to be through with all of this nonsense. You say you're CIA but you speak Russian?"

"I was born there," Tasha began.

"If you think that's bad, you should hear my Mandarin," Kara said with a yawn as though the world and all its drama bored her.

"Dude, we wouldn't be good spies if we had to ask the enemies for a translation. There's a whole school and everything. Nate, can you watch the prisoner so we can have a much-needed private talk with our…friends. Also, is that one dead? I did not sign up for cleanup duty. Chet, you made the mess. You can clean it up."

Prisoner?

While the rest of the group started arguing about who would take care of the potentially dead bodies, he backed up. Maybe his trouble wasn't over.

Brian would look for him. Brian wouldn't let him disappear.

"Dare, it's going to be all right." Tasha didn't reach for him this time. "Just give me an hour and I'll make everything okay again. I promise."

"I don't care." He wouldn't listen to her ever again. It had been the height of idiocy to listen to her in the first place. He should have known, should have learned. If something seemed too good to be true, it was false.

Tasha had been far too good to be true.

"You should care because she's right," Ian said, his voice deep. "I had eight hours' worth of flight to read over your file."

"I was unaware I had a file." He needed to get out of here. He couldn't be here anymore. It was time to get the fuck out and get back to Toronto and take his medicine. His father could do whatever he wanted. The only people he would care about from now on would be his siblings. He would marry whoever his father wanted, but he would quietly ensure he couldn't have children because he would never put them through his family. For a brief moment, he'd thought he'd found a woman strong enough to fight beside him, but she'd been one big lie. "And again, I don't care. I'm going to get my things and leave, and you can do whatever you like."

He would find Brian and drink himself to sleep.

"And this is why we don't want to work with Americans," a familiar voice was saying. "You work with Americans and end up tied to some weird sex bench for hours. I've got a crick in my neck."

Brian. Brian was coming down a set of stairs, one of the soldiers in all black following behind him.

"It was not my team, Parker," Chet was saying. "We came to find you. Sorry we didn't understand our fellow team was fucking everything up. We would have been here way sooner."

Brian stopped as he caught sight of Dare, his jaw dropping slightly. "Dare."

They'd come looking for a Canadian operative.

Brian was the Canadian operative. Brian, the friendly American who pretended to not know Canadian stuff and needed Dare's help to navigate the ins and outs of Toronto culture. Brian, who wanted to be his friend.

He didn't have any friends.

He didn't have any real family.

He didn't have anything.

"You should have fucking told me he was down here," Brian said, his expression turning stormy. It was an expression Dare had never seen before on his happy-go-lucky friend's face.

But then he was stupid. He was the moron who let all the wolves in and thought they were his friends, his lover.

Brian walked straight up to him. "Dare, we need to talk."

Did they have a prewritten script for what to say when they got found out?

Calm. He needed calm. He needed ice running through his veins, and politeness was the way to go if he didn't want to lose his fucking mind. The need to shout and fight and tell everyone exactly what he thought of them was right there, but it wouldn't matter. They didn't care. Any emotion would put him in a bad position.

His father had taught him that.

"I would like to leave now." He wasn't giving Brian or Tasha or any one of these fuckers a second of his emotion.

He had to tamp that down. Shove it deep and never let it out. If he did, if he let himself feel for a single second, he might never gain control again.

"I'm sorry. You can't," Ian said, and there was an almost apologetic look on his face. "Wait down here with young Nathan, who does not have clearance to be working with anyone unless we've involved Aussie intelligence and there's something his father hasn't told me."

"I'm strictly here to help," Nate replied. "I suppose I'm not getting paid now. Is this a good time to mention I could use a job?"

"Make sure he doesn't get himself kidnapped or killed and we'll talk," Ian promised. "Mr. Nash, I'm sorry for whatever you've been through. I know you won't believe this but my...operative doesn't work this way. Tasha runs logistics for the team. She's not truly an operative at all, and she would never have a physical relationship with you if she didn't have feelings for you. I know your instinct is going to be to avenge the obvious betrayal, but I wouldn't have so many dumbass children if I'd given into that instinct. If she slept with you, she cares about you, and her affection is not something you want to toss away for nothing. Think about that." He turned to address the rest of the room. "My team, Colin has assured me there's a conference room he'll let us use before he chucks us out and never speaks to me again. Actually, he said a bunch of things I didn't understand, but I got the gist."

"The bloke had a right arc up," Nate said, moving in beside him.

"I think I should stay with Dare. There's no need for a bodyguard," Brian offered.

Ian put a hand on his shoulder. "Oh, Mr. Canada, you will be coming with me." He turned to Chet. "Asshole, I expect a report, and before you say something that will make me put a fist through your face, check in with your handler. You'll find everything in both these godforsaken ops has been turned over to me."

Chet's face went a florid red, but he simply nodded.

Apparently this Ian person was the apex predator of the group.

"Dare, we will talk soon," Brian promised.

He ignored the man.

It was way harder to ignore Tasha as she stared at him, the others moving around her. There were tears in her eyes as Ian's wife put an arm around her and started to lead her away.

"Wanna go watch telly in the locker room?" Nate asked. "Maybe get comfy because I think Ian's going to yell for a long time."

He turned and walked away. He would find a way out. Maybe not tonight, but he wouldn't stay here a moment longer than he had to.

His time in paradise was over.

215

Chapter Fourteen

Tasha had to force herself to walk into The Station's conference room and likely wouldn't have if her mother hadn't been right behind her.

The whole time she'd been getting dressed her mother had asked her questions she'd managed to answer in a monotone.

A bit like Dare. Since that moment the world had flipped, Dare had gone stone cold, and she knew what was happening. He'd shut down. He'd closed off his every emotion and shoved high walls up so she couldn't get to him.

She walked in and was surprised to see it was only her team and TJ sitting around the big table.

Had her father finally murdered her ex? She wouldn't blame him. She would help him do the cleanup because Chet was a massive asshole who'd poked Dare in all the worst ways.

"That's all I know, Uncle Ian," TJ was saying. "My group was requested as support for Whittington's op, which was to watch over the Canadian operative during his mission. I don't know all the ins and outs. Whittington isn't Zach. He doesn't bring his military backup into his confidence. We know very little beyond his instructions. We've been stationed in a safe house outside of Sydney for a week now, and the op was supposed to run through next week, though we were moving locations, I was told."

It was easier to focus on the op and where it had all gone wrong than to think about Dare. "I can tell you why. That's when Brian, Dare, and I would have traveled to Oakley's place in the Blue Mountains to spend some time with Dr. Huisman. I'm sure Brian had plans for that. Our only mission was to look around and report back. If we had a shot at gathering any intel on Huisman or Oakley, we were going to take the chance. We were told that Oakley had some unsavory connections when he was younger and a habit of taking over the companies he invests in and keeping the tech for himself. The Huisman Foundation is involved in some research our government is interested in, up to and including potential cancer vaccines and cures that Oakley might keep to himself if he thinks there's more money to be made in treatment."

Her father looked up, his expression softening marginally. "I know the parameters of your mission, *dushka*. I was the one who gave them to you, and by you I mean your sisters."

Kala held up her hands. "Not my fault. Talk to your boy, Zach, who thought Dare would be a better target than the original one. Do we think Middleton's accident was actually an accident at this point?"

"No," her team said in unison.

"Obviously someone wanted Dare to be the one to meet with Huisman." Tristan looked as uncomfortable as she felt. He kept his eyes on the table as though he could avoid a lecture if he didn't meet the boss's stare.

"Or Oakley," Cooper amended. "We can't be sure if TJ doesn't know who the target was. Do we think the Canadian operative took Middleton out so the target moved to Dare?"

"No. He wouldn't do that." Kenzie leaned forward, looking at their dad. "I've spent some time with him. He's not like that."

Her dad's eyes closed, and he went still. Now was one of those times she wished she had a lemony treat to offer her dad. Her mom moved in behind him, putting her hands on his shoulders and rubbing.

"It's okay. Everything is going to be fine," her mom assured him. "Kenz, tell your dad you didn't fall for the Canadian operative and give up all of our secrets."

"I didn't tell him anything, and Kala acts like a psycho around him so he thinks Kara is a complete nutbag," Kenzie complained.

Her dad's eyes didn't open, but his lips curled up slightly.

It was time to point some things out to her sisters. Her dad was entirely too amused with Kala's antics. "It's actually a problem because he has remarked several times how completely different Kara seems on different days. I think now that he's verified Kara is an operative he might just view it as a ploy to keep her target on his or her toes, but you two need to get your act together. Kara needs to be one seamless version of the two of you or it's going to get out that you're twins."

"See, when you talk like that you make sense. So explain to me why you're doing your sisters' job?" He reached up and grasped her mom's hand, gently pulling her until she was sitting on his lap, one big arm around her waist.

This was something she was extremely used to. Her parents' displays of physical affection had been one of the foundations of her childhood. When she'd first come home with them it had been such a weird thing. There had been no physical affection at the orphanage. No hugs or pats on the back. Touching seemed like a bad thing as it only came with corporal punishment. It had been easier to accept affection from the children who had become her sisters and brothers, but eventually she'd allowed Ian and Charlotte Taggart to bring her into their warm hugs, and soon those hugs had become a safe place for her.

Dare was so alone. As alone as she'd been in that orphanage. He'd accepted her affection and soaked it all up and freaking bloomed as a top and a boyfriend.

He wouldn't touch her again. She was afraid he might not really touch anyone again.

She'd done that to him.

"I met him our second night here in Sydney at a pub. I talked to him and liked him and I..."

"Yes, we got that," her father said. "We do not need to talk about what happened next in any detail at all. Let's move on to the 'why didn't you call in when the parameters changed' portion of this discussion."

Her mom gave her a smile. "We'll do the details later. Away

from your father's tender ears."

"There's a reason I said no honey pots," her dad complained.

"It wasn't a honey pot." They needed to understand what had really happened. "It was a 'get back on the horse' situation, and the horse turned out to be the right horse this time. Like the horse I would like to ride until the end."

"We need better metaphors," Lou said under her breath.

TJ chuckled and winked Lou's way. "I think she's doing great. And she's right. Chet was not the right horse."

"He's a giant horse's ass," Cooper pointed out. "And you know why we didn't call in."

"Yes, Zach's already given me the whole sink or swim talk," her father argued.

"It wasn't dangerous," Tasha countered. "Not to us, at least. There was absolutely no way to know that we were working at cross purposes with our allies since the Agency chose not to inform us there were two teams on the ground."

"You would have been informed if you'd called in," her dad insisted. "Drake would have told you. You were on a need-to-know basis, and you didn't need to know until the target changed. I don't blame you. I blame Zach, and I'm going to fire his ass."

"I agreed with him." She wasn't about to cost Zach his job even if she was angry.

"That's some hypocrisy, Uncle Ian." Tristan's eyes had come up.

The uncle in this case didn't denote a blood bond between Tristan and her father. They'd grown up in a big found family, and it had been easier to call the adults who were around all their childhoods by aunt or uncle.

A brow rose over her father's eyes, and they seemed to have gone an icy blue. "Care to elaborate, nephew?"

Everyone in the room seemed to take a step back. Except Tris. "I'm talking about your first solo op. You didn't bother to call in and explain that the man who was supposed to get you into the meeting with the potential bomb maker was murdered the night before your meeting. You simply talked your way in and nearly got killed yourself."

"Yeah, good times," her father said. "And not something you're supposed to know about since that op was highly classified. Have you been on the Dark Web again?"

"I like to keep my skills sharp. If you want to fire me, you should feel free," Tris snarked.

"And let some other team pick you up and use your seemingly never-ending death wish to their advantage? I think I owe your fathers more than that."

It was Tristan's turn to laugh, but there was nothing amusing about the sound. "I think you'll find my fathers might be relieved to not have to worry about me anymore. It doesn't matter. What does matter is the fact that we made the same call you would have made. I've read your files, and time and time again you followed your instincts. Why can't you let us follow ours?"

Her father pointed a finger Tristan's way. "Because your instincts led you to tie a Canadian operative to a sex bench. The least you could have done was get him face down, ass in the air on a spanking bench if you want to humiliate the guy."

"Well, he tried to kidnap Tash," Cooper countered. "We had already suspected he was some kind of plant, but we had to act when he decided to take Tasha in. Were we supposed to let that happen?"

"Of course not. But you didn't call it in. You continued to go it alone. You fucked around and now you're finding out," her father announced. "Your mother and I are taking the op over for both teams. We'll be overseeing the rest of the mission, and understand that you're lucky I'm not canceling the entire thing. Kenzie and Kala, you are not to allow the Canadian to know you're twins. Work it out. I don't care how you do it, but CSIS doesn't know Ms. Magenta is two people, and we're going to keep it that way. Decide now who's staying and who's getting smuggled out of here."

Kenzie held up a hand. "I'll go. I'm attracted to him. I need some space."

"He's Canadian. Did you hear that part?" Her dad asked the question with a desperate air.

"Well, I thought he was American," Kenzie conceded. "Of course he thought I was Australian. Hey, you know Dare is Canadian, too. I'm walking away from my maple-flavored hottie. I don't think big sis is going to do the same."

"Yeah, we need to talk about that. Let's clear the conference room for now. We need to decide how to move forward with this guy. He did not seem interested in hanging around," her father said. "Everyone but Tasha take a twenty-minute break, and then we'll have both teams in along with the Canadian. Kenz, you can listen in, but don't walk around until we're sure the coast is clear. I don't like the fact that fucker Chet knows, but I trust he won't tell. Mostly because he knows I would pull his intestines out of his body."

There was some shuffling about as everyone did what they were told, and in a few moments she was alone with her parents.

"What happened, Tash?" Her father's voice had gone quieter, the usual authority in his tone softened.

"You know what happened." Her mother moved off her father's lap and came to sit beside Tash, her hand going over hers. She squeezed gently. "You are in deep with this guy, aren't you, baby?"

Now that everyone was gone it was okay to let tears cloud her eyes. This wasn't about the op. This was her mom offering help. "I love him, Momma. I didn't mean to, but I fell for him completely, and it's not like it was before."

"Chet was a mistake. He's attractive, and you both work for the Agency," her mom explained. "He made sense to you at the time, and you decided you wouldn't find anyone better. That's not love. That's practicality."

"She's known this guy for less than a week," her father argued.

That earned him a death stare from her mom. "Seriously?"

Tasha sent him her own stare because he was being a hypocrite. "You married Mom within a month of meeting her. You're telling me you didn't know you loved her early on?"

Her father sighed and sat back. "I knew I loved her the night I met her. But we had problems because we didn't take the time to truly know one another. I don't want you to make the same mistakes."

She knew her parents' love story quite well. "I promise not to fake my own death and stay away from Dare for five years and build a business selling classified information. Not that it looks like I'm going to get the chance."

"His father is sketchy," her dad said. "I spent the time on the plane getting to know the family. They're pretty awful."

"His father is terrible. He's insisting Dare marry a woman of his choice and start having kids he'll hold hostage to get Dare to do whatever he wants," she explained. "He's held Dare to impossible standards all of his life. When Dare tried to break free, he started threatening his siblings."

"So he feels trapped, and his father knows he'll need another method of control since the youngest sister is only a few years away from being an adult," her mom mused. "So we need to figure out how to take the father out. We need leverage. Unless you're cool with assassination."

"Mom." The problem was she was fairly certain her mother was only half joking. "It doesn't matter because I seriously doubt he's going to let me talk to him, much less help solve the situation with his father."

"This op doesn't work without Dare Nash," her father admitted. "Our Canadian friend has a big problem he hasn't explained to you yet. Probably because you tied him to a sex bench. So I'm afraid I'm going to have to insist that Mr. Nash do his part, and that means making sure everything looks normal. Do you really love this man? Because I can also pack us all up and head back to the States and leave Chet Bumfuck to deal with CSIS."

"I love him. I can't believe I did this to him. You should know that I was going to tell him everything tomorrow after I'd figured out what was up with Brian. I was going to break my cover."

"If you love him and you trust him, then that's the most sensible thing I've heard you say today," her father said with a sigh and a frown. "Canadian?"

She was not putting up with her father's sarcasm when it came to this. "Is it a good time to point out that Chet is American as apple pie? You better tone down your teasing. He doesn't know us yet, and I won't let you make him feel worse than he already does. He doesn't have a family. I doubt he understands what a functional family can do, so we're going to be nice and normal and not scare this guy off. You will not threaten him with a most dangerous game style hunt, nor will you give him release of liability forms."

"Hey, those came in handy for your sisters," her dad pointed out.

"He's actually right. Anyone who dated Kala could have made a claim," her mom agreed. "But he would never do that with you.

Your father is going to be on his best behavior, and we will be super normal."

"Yeah, a super-normal family where we hide one twin so no one knows there are two of them and our location is often classified and your brother is a moron who should have used a condom and your other brother thinks playing guitar on YouTube is a viable career option," her father snarked. "Sure. Totally normal."

"It's a normal spy family." At least it felt that way to her. "Not that it's going to matter because he's going to say no. I hurt him. I gutted him, and he's stubborn. He won't let me back in. He'll be on a plane to Toronto as soon as he can be."

"You let me worry about that," her father assured her. "My only question is—do you want this guy? Is he worth the trouble?"

"Yes."

"Then talk to your mother about how to soothe a savage beast, and I'll go talk to your guy." Her dad pushed back from the table and rose to his feet. "Charlie, baby, do not start talking about sex until I leave the room. Give me like a minute's head start. For some reason my hearing is still way too good. I keep waiting for old age to kick my ass, but it doesn't."

Her mom grinned. "That's because I make him drink this herbal tea I found at this weird shop. I swear it's got anti-aging properties. And it tastes a little like chocolate. But he's right. Getting that man back is going to be all about sex. Oral is a very good way to go."

Her dad practically ran out of the room.

"It's going to be okay." Her mom stood up, and her arms were open. "If I could get your father back and have all these beautiful years with him, I promise you can convince Dare. You won't have to do it alone. You'll have all of us in your corner."

Tasha wrapped her arms around her mom and let herself cry.

And hope.

* * * *

"I don't want to talk to you." Dare closed the locker door, feeling better now that he had regular clothes on again. He'd felt stupid sitting around in leathers since he wasn't anything close to a Dom. A Dom was in control, and he had none whatsoever.

Nate Carter's presence was proof of that. He wouldn't be allowed to leave this place and go lick his wounds in private. If he tried that, he would be manhandled by the big Aussie and made to look even more foolish than he was right now.

At least Nate was quiet. He'd been grim since following Dare into the locker room. Brian was proving he wasn't as respectful as the guard.

"Good, then you can listen," Brian replied.

He didn't care. He didn't. They could talk all they liked, but he was going to leave. He would not comply.

He walked to the lounge area as Brian started talking.

"I became aware of your father's interest in the Huisman Foundation a year ago," Brian was saying as Dare sat down in one of the comfortable chairs where he was sure the men of the club would sit and watch matches on the big-screen TV.

Dare simply took out his phone and stared at it, scrolling through news sites but not really reading anything.

Brian sat down beside him. "The Huisman Foundation isn't what it seems to be. Emmanuel Huisman is a dangerous man."

"I don't care," he admitted. "That's your business. Not mine."

"It's going to be everyone's business when he starts killing people," Brian insisted. "I think he wants something from your father, and that's why they've been trying to kidnap you."

Brian wasn't a smart spy if he hadn't figured that out yet. "I think it's far more likely that was Tasha's team. They needed to bring a bodyguard in so she wouldn't have to constantly watch me. I'm sure it was much easier to download my laptop with extra eyes on me."

"It wasn't us, mate. Tasha brought me in because she was so worried about you," Nate said quietly.

"And I got to pay for the privilege," Dare shot back before turning to Brian. "I wouldn't worry about some doctor I barely met trying to kidnap me. Do you know how paranoid you sound? Huisman is a doctor. He helps people. He doesn't kill them. Have you even read his book?"

Brian's head shook. "That book is fiction. That book is nothing but another mask he wears. I know Manny. I've known him most of my life, and I promise you he's a monster no matter what happy fairy tale he's selling the public."

"So you have some sort of vendetta against the guy and that's why you're here?"

"I do not have a vendetta. I'm trying to stop him."

"From doing what?" Dare wasn't sure why he was still talking, but maybe Brian could make some sense of the situation.

Brian sighed, his eyes closing briefly. "I don't know, but I don't like that he's in league with Oakley. Oakley has ties to a group called Disrupt Australia."

"I've heard of it. They're a think tank. They try to come up with new ways to do things." Though he'd heard some rumors. Rumors that there was a more extreme group within the organization.

"That's what they are on the outside. What they actually are is a group of anarchists. They see opportunity in chaos," Brian explained. "Huisman is a member. Like Oakley, he's high up in the organization."

There was only one problem with Brian's statement. "Huisman met Oakley for the first time earlier today."

"I assure you they were lying about that," Brian said. "Huisman has met Oakley many times, though they keep their relationship secretive. The fact that they're willing to be seen in public together now makes me think they've got something big happening soon. I believe Oakley's group was responsible for the recent attacks on Jakarta's public transit system. I also think they're funding anti-monarchist groups across Europe, and they've got their hands in a lot of the disinformation campaigns about elections."

"So arrest the man."

"I can't prove it," Brian admitted, "which is why I need you and Tasha in his house in a couple of days."

"That's sad for you because I'm going to be on a plane to Toronto tomorrow morning." That was a proactive thing he could do. He could find a flight home. He didn't care how much it cost or if he was in the last row in economy sitting by the bathroom. He would be out of here.

"We have reason to believe the anti-monarchist groups are planning assassinations in the hopes that they can start World War III," Brian continued. "The attacks in Jakarta caused widespread panic and threatened to destabilize the economy. They almost did it.

They will try again, and if it works in Indonesia, they'll try with other countries. This is the beginning of their offensive. We have to stop them because if we don't, the world will burn. That's what Manny wants. He wants the world in ruins around him so he can take the reins and rule over the ashes."

"You'll have to find another way because I'm not working with you or that woman ever again. I don't want you to contact me in any way." The thought of not seeing Tasha again made his gut turn, and wasn't that stupid of him. Why would he want to see her?

So he could show her how in control he could be. So he could fuck her and enjoy her and take everything from her before walking away.

But he wasn't going to be doing that because he wasn't a fucking monster.

"I'm afraid I'm going to have to insist." Brian's tone went hard. "You have to listen to reason."

"He's not going to listen to reason. He got his ass kicked in every way imaginable this evening, and all he wants to do is take a flamethrower to the world, and I wouldn't be surprised if he's thinking about getting some revenge on Tasha. You thinking about fucking her out of your system and walking away? I know this sounds like a solid plan, but I'm here to tell you that never works out. I tried and ended up married to the woman who betrayed me and raising five kids with her. It's better to give up, but I know you can't think about that tonight."

The big guy named Ian stood in the doorway. He'd been quiet because Dare hadn't even heard it open, much less a six-and-a-half-foot mass of muscle come up behind him.

"You're Tasha's handler?" Brian asked.

"I do have that job," the man said with a sigh. "I take it you're one of Joseph's."

Brian stood and held out a hand. "I work under Joseph Caulder. Ben Parker is my real name."

Well, of course. Everyone seemed to have two names.

"You can call me Ian," Ian offered, shaking the man's hand. "And you can call Ms. Magenta off limits. Seriously, stay away from her. She likes to play with her prey before she devours it whole, if you know what I mean."

"She's making a name for herself in our circles, and it's not always a good one," Bri…Ben pointed out.

"I've talked to her about walking out with intel we've agreed to share," Ian replied. "She'll be helpful in the future. Now why don't you go find that fuckwit Chet while I have a conversation with our friend here. Tell him I want a sit-down soon. I think I'll be able to convince Dare to move forward with the op."

"You won't." Dare had to wonder how this man would try to convince him. Was he in for some actual physical torture? Between this guy and Nate, he wouldn't stand a chance.

And yet he was going to try.

Ian shrugged a big shoulder. "Maybe or maybe not. I can be quite charming when I want to be. Mr. Parker, I'd like to have a conversation with you about your thoughts on Emmanuel Huisman. I talked to Joseph, and he explained that's why you're here, why you asked the Agency for backup."

"Yes, sir. I'll talk to Joseph and request the reports we have on him." Ben was all *sir, yes sir* now and it proved how good the man was at acting because he'd hidden this part of himself for months and months.

Or maybe Dare himself was just shitty and dumb at reading a room.

"Dare, I know you don't want to hear it, but I truly was your friend." Ben moved to the door that led out into the club. "I care about you, and I don't want to see you get hurt, but getting close to Huisman is a bad idea. Manny can't help but hurt anyone in his circle. He's a genuine sociopath. I hope you'll listen. You might be our only hope at finding out their plans before it's too late."

He left, and the man named Ian sat down in front of him, his head shaking. "He's not good at that. He doesn't want you hurt by getting close to Huisman, but he wants to put you directly in his path. See, the logic doesn't work out. This is where I would give you a big old speech about duty to your fellow man and how to help your country." He seemed to think the problem through. "I could go with 'you'll feel all manly and women will want you.'"

"I don't care."

Ian nodded. "Yes, I thought that would be your reply. Nathan, can we have a moment? You can guard the door and make sure

Master Colin doesn't murder me."

"He's a good man," Nate said to Ian. "Go easy on him."

"I'm not here to threaten him. I understand fully what he means to my daughter," Ian said. "I think it's time for me to play fairy godmother again. I'm pretty good at it."

Nate turned his way. "Dare, don't let your anger get in the way of something good. My mum lost years of her life believing nothing good could happen to her. I meant what I said. You're a good man. You deserve good things. Sometimes those things don't show up the way we think they should, but it would be wrong to reject them. And think about it, man. You marry Tash and you have this to hold over her head forever. I think that's what did it for Mum. My dad was kind of an arse and didn't listen to her voice mails, and now she gets to hold it over his head for all of time. You could have that kind of a beautiful marriage, too, if you like. Also, the family's pretty cool. I say that because I want a job in Dallas."

Ian groaned. "I don't know that I can handle having both you and Boomer on the payroll."

"I think you'll make out fine," Nate said with a smile as he left.

Daughter? "You're Tasha's father?"

"The things we do for our kids." Ian sat back, studying Dare. "Sometimes those things seem like excellent ideas at the time, but they don't turn out the way we hope. Your mother thought she was doing the right thing by you, but it didn't work out that way, did it?"

The man had obviously done his research. Or Tasha had a report ready. She'd studied him for a solid week, and he was the idiot who told her everything. "I'm not going to work for you, Mr...Ian."

"It's Taggart if you feel the need to be formal, though I'm going to ask you not to reveal that to Ben. He can call me Mr. Lemon."

Dare was confused. "Why would you hand me a weapon? I could tell him everything. Well, now I could tell him your real last name at least."

"I told you because I want you to know Tasha's last name, though it wasn't always Taggart. She was born Natasha Federova. She should tell you the story, but I want you to understand that if she trusts you, then I have to as well. Lou isn't her sister. Lou is one of her closest friends, but they aren't blood relations, though you'll find my kids love their found family every bit as much as they do their biological family. TJ's probably feeling that right now. Kara is her sister."

He was confused. "Kara's her sister?"

"Oh, yes, and she's both the light of my life and the bane of my existence. That's how kids are most of the time." The man seemed determined to impart a bunch of wisdom. It should be annoying. Dare found it oddly soothing, like this was a real dad talking to him. "Tash, though... She was a gift from the universe. I didn't understand our family wasn't complete until she came to live with us. She's precious to my family, and that's why I'm going to offer you a choice. You can be angry and walk away and not worry about what happens if we don't find the intel we need. That's cool. It's one way to go."

He wanted to walk away. He was almost certain this man wasn't going to torture him. And still he sat there. "It's absolutely what I'm going to do."

"Or you could stay on and help Tasha do the job," Taggart offered like it was a reasonable thing to do. "Now there are going to be rules to follow, and you might not like some of them—the chief one being everything has to look perfectly normal. You have to go back to the suite tonight with her, let the people left at the conference see you together. It would be best if you slept in the same bed since we don't know if they have people watching you closely. That's the kind of shit that can trip a spy up. You forget about housekeeping at your own peril."

"I'm not doing any of this. I don't ever want to see Tasha again." He didn't need to see her. She was emblazoned on his brain, and he would die dreaming about her.

Taggart gave him a look that made it clear he didn't believe him. "Of course you do. Look, lying to me is one thing. I can accept that. You're hurt and I'm part of that hurt, but at least don't lie to yourself. You do want to see her again. You want to do exactly what I said you wanted to do at the beginning of this conversation. Fuck her out of your system. You think showing her you don't care about her will make you feel better. It won't. Nothing is going to fill that hollow place in your gut except letting her back in, and that is scary, which is why that's not what I'm offering you."

This was such an uncomfortable conversation, but he couldn't seem to walk away. "It sounds like you're offering up your daughter on a silver platter."

"I don't have to do that," Taggart said grimly. "She'll do that herself. She'll let you walk all over her, and I'm here to mitigate the damage. Look, if I didn't kill that fucker Chet, I'm not going to murder you. I understand you're the injured party, but you two need to work that out. If I thought for a second you would hurt her physically, this would be an entirely different conversation."

"Who the hell is that guy?" As long as he was here, he could get some of his questions answered. "Fucking Chet. Who names their kid that? He's an ass. First off, he did nothing to hide who he works for. He said it right out in the open. That seems careless. And then there was the way he treated Tasha. You know he basically called her a whore right in front of me."

"And you didn't like that."

Dare took a settling breath. He was getting worked up, and that was a mistake. "It's a triggering word for me. I don't think there's any reason to ever use that word. I was numb at the time. He's lucky."

"Don't underestimate him. He's a well-trained operative, and he doesn't fight fair. At some point in time I'll take care of that fucker," Taggart promised. "If you're still around, I'll cut you in on the action. But let's talk about your problems and how I can help you."

At least they were getting to the heart of the matter now. "Unless you're calling me a ride, I'm afraid there's not a lot you can do. Mr. Taggart, I'm not going to help you. There's a part of me that can rationalize what Tasha did. I can understand the need to protect her country, and hell, it's not like I didn't get something out of it." He winced because he'd told his girlfriend's father he liked having sex with her. Not his fucking girlfriend. "This is a weird conversation to have with her father."

"I'm a weird father. What you're telling me is you would likely shrug this whole thing off if you didn't feel the way you feel, if Tasha had been nothing more than a fun time in bed, but she wasn't. She was more than a good time. She got inside, and that's what you're upset about. She assures me she feels the same. I'm under strict instructions not to hunt you for sport or scare you away with my trademark sarcasm. My daughter is in love with you. Now I argued about timing because from this side of things it seems abrupt, but it was pointed out that I might be hypocritical to question the timing."

He'd needed very little time to fall for Tasha. A single week and he knew he'd never be the same. If only it had been real. "I can't trust her."

"Time and proximity sometimes solves that problem," Taggart offered.

He could see himself getting comfortable, and then she would rip him open all over again. "It won't for me. I won't let her in twice."

Taggart waved a hand. "Then you're safe and you can finish up the op without worrying you'll end up happily married at the end of it. If you don't want to sleep with her, there are various ways to avoid that including not sticking your penis in. I've found that's fairly good advice on a number of levels. Don't stick your penis in."

"Well, I can do that from Canada. Now I'm done with this extraordinarily uncomfortable conversation. If you're going to arrest me, do it, but otherwise I'm leaving." He started for the door, perfectly ready to face whatever beatdown these people were going to give him.

"I'll take down your father for you."

He stopped, his hand on the door, but he didn't pull it open. Taggart had said the only words that could make him stop cold and consider doing something phenomenally stupid.

"I haven't come up with a comprehensive plan yet, but I don't think it will be hard," Taggart continued. "I did a cursory study on the plane. I suspect not all of his business is legit, and it will be important that we're able to prove you weren't involved in that part. Now, the easiest way is to let my wife assassinate the fucker. It's been a while, and she gets antsy."

This whole conversation was surreal. "You wouldn't."

"No, I wouldn't," Taggart agreed. "Charlie totally would, and I would hold her latte. That's a bit extreme, of course, but it's the fastest way to get it done. Like I said, if you can be a bit patient, I can find the leverage I need and force him to do what you need him to. I suspect it might make your life easier if both of your siblings had trust funds he couldn't touch so he couldn't threaten to cut the purse strings. They're the reason you stayed, correct? If I've read the situation wrong and you enjoy working for your father…"

"He's had me under his thumb since I was a child." Dare moved back to the chair, though he didn't sit down. "I can't let him do the same to my siblings. As long as I give him what he wants, he leaves them alone. He wants an heir, to be able to show the world his company will have strong leadership in the form of a son. Johnny is too fragile to live in his world, and he would never accept Gina because she's a daughter and not a son."

"You are his natural heir. You're smart and strong enough to run the business and the family. But he feels the need to punish you because you weren't born the right way. He wasn't married to your mother, and your mother wasn't a person his society would ever accept."

The man had learned a lot about him in a brief time. "He's ashamed of me, but he doesn't have another choice."

Taggart clapped his hands together like he was eager to get to work. "So he blackmails you. Let's blackmail him. Unless you choose the other route. My wife is good at what she does. Hardly even any blood in her head shots."

He had to think this was some of the sarcasm the man had mentioned before. "Why would I trust you?"

Taggart stood, and Dare was reminded how intimidating the man could be. "Because I trusted you with my name, and I'm going to put something else on the line. Girls, I think the coast is clear."

He stopped and stared as Kara walked out from behind the last row of lockers.

Followed by another Kara.

The first Kara gave him an encouraging smile. "I'm Kenzie. Tasha is my older sister and I love her and I'm so happy she's found someone she can love and adore and I don't want to murder all the time. You have no idea how hard it was when she was with Douchebag."

"I'm Kala," the other Kara said.

Twins playing one person. It could give Tasha's team a mighty advantage. "Ben is extremely interested in the woman he calls Ms. Magenta. He would be shocked to find out she's two people."

"And that's why we told you," Kenzie replied. "Tasha didn't ask us to. She would probably freak out, but she trusts you so that means we have to as well."

"And you now have something to hold over my head if I don't help you the way I said I would." Ian Taggart joined his daughters, getting in between them and putting a muscular arm around each. "My children and wife are my whole world. I do not give away my weaknesses lightly, Mr. Nash."

He could be lying. He could not give a damn if anyone found out his main operative was actually his twin daughters.

Or he could be telling the truth and offering him everything he needed to get what he'd dreamed of since he entered his father's house—freedom.

"So if I work this op and you get the intelligence you need, you'll help me take my father down? Even if I don't magically fall in love with your daughter, because that's not going to happen."

Kala snorted. "Sure, dude."

"Yes," Taggart said, ignoring his daughter. "That's the deal. You work the op then your father becomes the op. I think you'll find even if you break her heart, Tasha will still help you."

"If you break my sister's heart I'll help you, too. Into an early grave. I have one picked out and everything," Kala promised.

"You didn't kill Chet," Kenzie pointed out.

"She wasn't in love with Chet. Him sleeping with that MSS operative was a blessing from heaven," Taggart said. "And life is long, daughter. I think that asshole will find his proper ending somewhere along the way. And you won't kill Dare because your sister does love him, and one day you'll understand that when you love someone you want them happy and whole even if they break your heart."

He didn't want to think about Taggart's words. It was a simple exchange. All he had to do was spend some time with Tasha. He didn't have to talk to her when they were alone. He could ignore her.

How would he ever be able to ignore her?

He couldn't be her fool again. He couldn't. But he might be able to be civil enough to get through the op and get what they needed. She would get the lowdown on whatever Oakley was doing. Ben could figure out if Huisman was a megalomaniac out to destroy the world.

And he could be free.

In the end there was no way to walk away from the deal. "I'll do it, and you should understand that no matter how I feel about Tasha, I wouldn't tell Ben or anyone else about the twins. I wouldn't put them in danger no matter how angry I am."

"And that, son, is why I suspect this is all going to work out." He stepped away from the twins. "Kenzie, you know what to do."

Kenzie frowned. "Yes. Hide. And all because I think a guy is cute. And I like Ben as a name way better than Brian. I should have known. He didn't look like a Brian. It's not fair when you think about it. I could help US-Canadian relations. Kala is probably going to start a war." She wrinkled her nose her sister's way, but a bright smile came over her face when she turned to Dare.

One minute he was morosely considering his decision and the next this dude was calling him son, and that felt weirdly nice, and then he had Tasha's sister throwing her arms around him.

"It's going to be okay, Dare. You'll see. Tasha is the best, and we'll take care of you. Promise." If she was bothered by the fact that he was standing stock still, she didn't show it. "I have to hide now. I'm afraid Kara is going to be pretty bitchy from here on out, but hey, if you need anything, Lou and I will be listening."

"Because you bugged my room," he said pointedly.

She nodded, agreeing fully. "Yes." She backed up. "And Dare, a hug goes like this. You put your arms around the huggee and then affection is exchanged. Don't worry. You'll get the hang of it. Someday you will be an excellent hugger. I know it."

While Kenzie slipped out the back, Kala moved toward the door to the club. She shook her head as she passed him. "Sorry about that. She played with a lot of Barbies as a child."

"And you played with knives," Taggart said under his breath.

"Yes, much more fun." Kala disappeared out the door.

"All right, let's go over what I expect you to do on this op." Taggart took a seat again. "It's pretty simple."

"And when it's over?"

"Then the real fun starts," Taggart replied. "It's been a while since I took an asshole down strictly for fun. I think you'll find we'll make it a family project. Hey, my son will probably write a theme song."

He wouldn't be around to meet the rest of the Taggarts. Once this was done, he would insist on conference calls only. Tasha would be out of his life.

But she wasn't tonight, and he had to figure out how to do what Taggart advised. Not put his penis in.

The trouble was his penis was not aligned with his pride. His penis was already trying to justify finding a way in.

But he was going to be smarter than that. He was going to get what he needed and then he would never see that woman again.

Chapter Fifteen

"Y ou know this is going to hurt, right?" her mom asked.

Tasha sniffled and wiped her eyes for what felt like the hundredth time in the last half hour. "It hurts right now. It hurt the minute I saw the look on Dare's face."

"I mean getting him back is going to hurt," her mother said. "It's not going to be as easy as apologizing."

"No, it is not." Kala walked in, followed by Lou. "Dad's doing what he can, though. He's got Dare in the men's locker room. Nate's there to make sure Asswipe can't walk in on them. That's for Asswipe's safety, though."

"TJ's distracting him. They're talking to Ben and the rest of Chet's team. Well, the ones that are awake. I am glad no one died. That would have been a lot of paperwork." Lou sat down across from Tasha. "Cooper is taking Kenzie back to the safe house so we can avoid Ben figuring out Kara is more than she seems."

"Ben?" Tasha asked, a little confused.

"Yup. The Canadian knows how to pick an alias. He's Ben Parker not Brian Peters, and according to Kenz, that name is perfect for him. I'll be working for the rest of the op, so we don't have to worry about Ben at all," Kala promised.

Poor Kenzie. She wasn't the only one who would be hurting. "Ben is only doing his job."

"Bullshit. He was still hitting on me a few minutes ago," Kala replied. "I'm going to make sure he doesn't bother my sister again."

Lou sent Kala one of those stares that always made Tasha think they were having a silent conversation. Lou had been Kala's best friend for over a decade. Despite the fact that Kala had a twin in Kenzie, Lou had always been the one who seemed to truly understand her. Or maybe it was more about acceptance.

Kala's expression softened. "But this isn't about Ben. Are you okay, Tash?"

"Of course she's not okay." Her mother shook her head her sister's way. "Would you be okay if the man you loved suddenly hated you?"

Kala shrugged. "Precisely why I don't intend to do the love thing."

Her mom sighed. "Oh, you've done the love thing, stubborn girl. You just can't forgive him. You're going to regret that, but I can't make you see that he was a child."

"I'm not here to talk about Cooper." Kala went still.

"If you can't be supportive of your sister, you should go and join the guys," her mom said.

Kala's face flushed, and for a moment Tasha thought she would stand up and storm out. It was this way with Kala and their mom at times. Especially when their mom thought Kala was being stubborn. Something had happened with Cooper McKay when they were teenagers. Something happened the night Kala had ended up being kidnapped, but she didn't talk about it to anyone but Lou and their mom.

Lou put a hand on Kala's. "We're both here to support Tash."

Kala's eyes closed briefly, and when she opened them again, the momentary anger was gone. "So what is the plan? Because I know we're not going to shrug and move on. That is not the Taggart family way. Mom, Tash is genuinely in love with this guy, and honestly, I've seen him change in the last week. He was kind of closed off and shut down, and he's come to life. She's good for him and he's good for her. I'm going to assume I'm not allowed to kidnap and torture him until he sees the light."

"No, you're not. He's used to that. It's what his father's been doing to him for over a decade. That's why this hit him so hard,"

Tasha explained. "He's spent the majority of his life being manipulated, and that's exactly what he thinks I've done."

"Have you?" her mother asked.

"No," Lou said. "We didn't go into that pub with the thought of finding a target. Well, not for the op. For Tasha's stress relief, yes, and before you judge you should know that just because we're behind computers doesn't mean the job isn't stressful. Between trying to ensure Tristan stays alive and Kala doesn't kill someone she's not supposed to, it can get really anxiety inducing. Not to mention the fact that Kenz will shut down a mission to save an animal. Or have we forgotten the dog in the Paris sewer systems that nearly cost us the intel about a potential attack on the US embassy in Argentina?"

"I was with her on that one," Kala conceded. "That dog was way sweeter and less smelly than our informant."

"I wasn't judging," her mother corrected. "I know it's stressful. Who do you think put it in her head that she should blow off some steam? You should, too, Lou."

Lou seemed to suddenly realize that she'd acquired the attention of Charlotte Taggart. Her mother could be ruthless when it came to matchmaking. "I'm good with stress. I actually work better under it."

"Mom, focus." Kala was there to help out her bestie. "This is about Tasha. What's the plan? If anyone knows how to get a dude to forgive her, it's you. You literally cost Dad everything and left him for five years, and he forgave you the minute you walked back into his life."

She'd heard the story often. Her dad had known he couldn't waste more time. He'd welcomed her with open arms.

Her mother's eyes rolled. "Okay, so part of my penance was letting your father rewrite history. He was a massive ass when I came back, and he hurt me over and over before he could admit he still loved me. It was a hard process, and I'm afraid Tasha is about to have to go through it, too."

"I knew that story was bullshit," Kala said under her breath.

She'd kind of known, too. Though if there was one person in the world her father could forgive, it was her mother. "I have to make this right. Even if he can't love me. I need to know that I didn't ruin him."

"Of course you didn't, sweet girl." Her mom reached for her hand. "But it does sound like you showed him something beautiful and then took it away from him. That wasn't what you intended to do, but it's the reality of how he feels. I wish you had time and proximity to help this situation along, but I'm afraid all you have is a few days, and then he'll probably walk away."

"Nah," Kala said with a wave of her hand. "Dad's already working him over. He's agreed to help take down Dare's dad."

"He did?" That was news to her.

Her mother nodded. "Yes, he did. For all your father gripes and groans, he knows you. He knew the minute he found out you were sleeping with Dare Nash that you were very likely in love with him. And after reading what Drake sent over, he knew Dare was in trouble. He quickly figured out the familial situation. He knew he would need leverage not only to get Dare to go through with the op once he found out what was going on, but to buy you the time you need to draw him back in."

"I don't know if there's enough time in the world," Tasha admitted, starting to get emotional again. Her parents had been planning how to help her even before she knew she'd had a real problem.

"He's in love with you. Even I can see that, and I don't particularly believe in love. You can get him back if you want to," Kala said. "And we'll help you out. That is a man searching for a family, for acceptance. If it was simply you hopping back in bed with him, I would be worried. I think he can compartmentalize like mad. But Dad is already doing his thing. Mom will be warm and welcoming and weird. Kenzie will do the same. And I'll stay off to the side and try to not say too many murderey things. Though I do not think that man liked Chet. We could bond over that."

Kala wasn't wrong about Dare's need for a family.

"What you have to understand is that men have stages they go through when it comes to a thing like this, and they can be hard on a woman." Her mother sat back. "You're going through the initial stage. It's the worst stage. The world is against him, and he should have known nothing good could come from loving a woman. He should have known the universe was fucking with him, and when he thinks about it, it's all his fault. You see, this stage is hard because what he's trying to convince himself is that he never loved you and you don't matter."

"Yeah, he's definitely in that stage," Lou agreed. "I expected him to yell and seem pissed off, but he's so quiet."

That was a function of his childhood. He had no control, so perversely he placed a whole lot of the blame for any situation he was in on himself. As though that was the only way his brain could handle how little control he had over his own life. "All right. How do I get him out of it?" The answer came before her mom could speak. "How do I get him to accept a D/s relationship with me?"

"Bingo," her mom said with a smile. "That's the second step. I think you'll find if he agrees to work the rest of the op, that you'll have to spend days and nights with him. You'll have to pretend to be a couple in public and in private, if we leave the bugs up."

"Absolutely not. We're taking them out of the suite. There's no evidence that Oakley is listening, so it's only our team and Bri…Ben." Tasha was going to give Dare as much privacy as she could. "Nate is staying with us, and Lou and Kenzie can monitor the hotel. Dare has to have a place where he can be real with me or none of this is going to work."

"I'll let them know," Lou promised. "And if someone's coming your way, I'll send you a text."

"So you'll have to get him talking," her mom advised. "It's not actually all that hard to convince a guy that maybe it's not really the universe that hates him. Maybe it *is* your fault, and you should make it up to him. Now he's going to argue with the making it up part. He'll be all 'I can never trust you again.' Here is where your boobs become important. Men, I've come to learn, can forgive boobs long before they forgive the rest of the woman they love."

Show him her boobs. She could do that. "So my goal this evening is to give him back control. In this case, the control is over me. Convince him that the only way we can get through this op is if he's my Dom."

"That's an excellent start," her mother agreed.

"Is this not another way of manipulating him?" Tasha felt guilt twist inside her.

"You are using that word like it's not something we do every day. What his father is doing is flat out blackmail. What you are going to do is smooth the edges out for Dare. What you are actually doing is compromising and allowing for his pain to be dealt with in a way that doesn't break the two of you forever," her mom explained. "It can take maturity to get through something like this, to understand that you are in the wrong but to let guilt or fear keep you fighting for a relationship that is good for the both of you. Do you truly believe you're good for him?"

She loved him. She knew she was good for him. No one in the world would fight for him the way she would. And that was what she had to do. Fight. She wouldn't be fighting some enemy hiding in the shadows. She was fighting Dare's childhood, his life up to this point and everything he'd learned from it. She was fighting his insecurities and fears. "He will never find another woman who loves him the way I do."

If she didn't win, Dare would likely be alone. Or married off to someone his father chose, which was just as good as being alone. If he had kids, he would try to hold a piece of him apart because they could be taken away from him.

Everything had been taken from him. She had to show him she couldn't be swayed, that she would never allow anything to come between them and she would put him first.

That was what her mom was telling her to do. Put him first no matter how much it hurt.

"It's not forever," her mom said quietly. "I went through this with your father, and my heart ached and there were times I thought it wasn't worth it. Times when he seemed so far from me that being together was an impossibility. I had to consider the fact that he might stay with me so he could punish me, and we would be stuck in some never-ending hell where we wanted each other, knew we loved each other, but his pride wouldn't let us have the life we could."

Kala stood up suddenly. "I'm sorry, sis. I need to go and catch Kenzie before she slips away. I'll see you in the conference room."

She was out the door in a second.

Lou stood to follow her. "Sorry. I think that hit her pretty hard. Sometimes we don't know what we're really doing until it's stated plainly about someone else and we see ourselves. And sometimes it takes watching a friend fall in love to know that what we have is a half-life, and it's time to get out there and find something real. Tash, do what you have to. Even if it hurts. I think taking that pain is something we try to avoid, but if we don't, we can't ever get to joy." She turned to Charlotte. "Aunt Charlotte, when we get back to Dallas, I would like for you to set me up."

Her mom's eyes went wide, and her mouth actually dropped open. Then she slowly nodded. "Yes, I can do that. I know quite a few lovely single men your age."

Lou sniffled and then strode out the door.

"What the hell just happened?" Tasha asked. Lou hadn't dated in years. She'd seemed so ready to sit and wait for TJ to finally wake up.

"I think watching you go through this is making Lou and Kala think about their own lives, and that is a miracle indeed," her mother said quietly. "You can do this, Tasha. Your heart is a mighty thing, and it can overcome the damage done by Dare's father. You have to be patient, and you have to be open and honest with him."

"I won't ever lie to him again. Not about anything important." She would always tell him he was sexy no matter what unsexy things he did.

"Then let me tell you more about these stages you're about to go through and why they're important. You see, men are fragile things," her mother began.

Tasha sat back and prepared for war.

* * * *

Dare sat down at the conference table and wondered how long it would be before Tasha was in the room with him. Five minutes? Ten? He needed to perfect his game face in that time. She'd stripped him so thoroughly of his armor it was hard to think about it being back in place.

Ian had brought him in here and then went off to find his wife. He'd promised they would start what he'd called the "briefing" shortly.

He'd already been briefed. His job was to escort Tasha to Oakley's place in the Blue Mountains and then let her do her thing. Nate would be there as well, helping out, and there would be numerous ways the rest of the team would be watching over them. Spying on him. Oh, it had been put in all kinds of words like protecting and ensuring his safety, but they were still spies. Once they had what they needed, he and Tasha would enjoy the rest of the weekend like nothing happened. In public, at least.

Then they would move on to fucking over his father and getting him free. After that, he would never have to see her again.

He would be free to do anything he wanted, free to be with anyone he wanted to be with. But it would not be her. It would never again be her.

"Mr. Nash?"

He looked up and a man stood at the door, tall and leanly muscled. He looked to be around thirty, maybe a few years older than his Tash.

Than Natasha Taggart. His Tash had never really existed.

"Can I help you? Mr...Ian asked me to wait here." He wasn't entirely sure who knew Tasha's last name and who didn't. He wasn't going to break their deal.

The man slipped inside the room. He wore all black, from his T-shirt to the boots on his feet. "Yes, he told me you were in here. I'm Captain Zach Reed. I'm technically US Army intelligence like our friend TJ, but I work mostly with the Agency, and specifically with the team Tasha is on."

"Okay." He wasn't sure what that had to do with him. "I would say nice to meet you but it isn't."

Zach had broad shoulders and the kind of masculine good looks that would attract almost any woman with eyes. "I can understand that. You're meeting me on one of the hardest days of my life since the man who's been more of a father to me than my own is pissed at me right now. I had a shitty dad, so the idea of him not being proud of me, well, I couldn't care less. Big Tag being disappointed...that hurts, and I kind of thought I was over the whole male mentor authority thing."

He was not going to do some weird therapy with this guy. "Is there something I can do for you?"

"You are going to be hard to deal with, aren't you?"

"Not at all. I fully intend to do anything and everything that is required for this mission. I'll escort Tasha and do what I can to give your team access to whatever the hell you need from Oakley." He held a hand up when it seemed like Zach was going to explain. "I don't need to know. I don't care. He's a bad guy. Go get him. I just want to get it over with."

So he could move on with his life.

Zach put his hands on the top of the chair, considering Dare with a thoughtful eye. "She did not know who you were when she walked into the pub that night. They've explained this to you, right?"

About a thousand times. "It doesn't matter."

"It does," Zach said with confidence. "I'm not sure if Ian explained the way our team works. It's different than you might think. Tasha is the Agency head of this team, but I can overrule her. I outrank her when we're out in the field. It's a special arrangement specifically for this team. There's nothing else like it at the Agency. Someone like Whittington can say he runs his own team, but with the exception of the tech he works with, the members of the team change out on a regular basis. The idea of a team for him is nothing more than constantly changing parts. TJ—Tasha's cousin, by the way—doesn't work full time with Whittington the way Tristan, Cooper, and I do with Tasha's team. It's run that way for a reason. So the operatives never get too close. So the op always means more than the team."

He didn't like the sound of that, like Tasha was a game piece and they moved her around wherever they needed her. Like she was expendable. "Why change it for this team?"

"Well, mostly because Big Tag wouldn't let his kids join the Agency any other way. He's a freaking legend. I joined the Army right out of college. Always planned to. I had an aunt who was my safe place when my dad got angry and the whiskey was flowing. She'd been in the Army for years. It seemed like a good place to be. I wanted to join up after high school but she insisted I get a degree so I could go in on a commission. She worked with Big Tag way back when he was a Green Beret. I heard all kinds of stories and then I actually met the man and all I wanted to do was be as good as he was. And it turns out I'm a ruthless asshole like everyone else. You see, I did know who you were that night. I knew where you would be."

That was news to him. "How would you know? Were you working with the other team? It seems like they were watching me."

"They were watching you because they were backing up Ben Parker. Sometimes we work with CSIS. That's the Canadian equivalent of the CIA. They've ramped up operations in the last few years. They're our closest allies, and we give their operatives ground support when they need it and don't have a Canadian team in place. And no, I didn't have a clue the other team was here, and I didn't know Brian was actually Ben. I bought his cover at that point. But I did think you might be important. I had studied up on everyone at the conference. I knew you were going to be there and that you were actually closer to the head of the company than our original target."

Only because he didn't understand the full story. "I might be closer to the CEO's office than Middleton, but I assure you he probably knew more about my father's business than I did. He keeps me in the dark about a lot of things."

Zach shrugged. "I wasn't aware of that. I decided to hedge my bets and see if I could gather more intelligence, so when Tash said she wanted a night out, I sent her and Kara and Lou to the pub I knew you had been frequenting from Ben's social media. I thought you would go for Kara. I didn't expect anything to happen that night, but I thought you would get a look at her and when you ran into her again at the conference…"

"She wasn't interesting to me. She's a beautiful woman, but there's something cold about her." He didn't think his choice would have changed if Miss Hugs-a-lot had been the one sitting in the bar. He'd only had eyes for Tasha. From the minute she walked through the door. "Besides, Ben was into her. He called dibs. I was left with Tasha and Lou. Lou was very quiet, so Tasha it was."

"Sure. That's how it played out. You picked her because you didn't have another good choice. Keep telling yourself that." Zach pulled the chair out, sitting down across from him. "I didn't think Tasha was serious. It's been months since she correctly broke off that insane engagement of hers. How she thought she could be with that massive ass… Anyway, I never actually believed she would go through with the whole get-back-on-the-horse thing. She didn't ride many horses. Even when she had a horse to ride. I think Whittington was far more interested in having a connection to her boss than in loving Tash."

"Don't you mean her father?"

A long breath blew from Zach's chest. "He told you. Wow. I'm surprised. Ian usually plays things slow."

"I believe he's looking for reciprocity. He needs me to do this job, and he thinks if he pushes the right buttons, I'll be a good boy. One of those buttons is letting me think I'm in his confidence and that he trusts me." He'd known what Taggart was doing. Half his business was selling. A salesperson had to figure out what the buyer wanted, what would motivate the buyer to pull the trigger.

Tasha's father had figured that out very quickly.

What if he hadn't? Now that he was sitting here thinking, he had to concede there might be another scenario. If he couldn't fix the problems with his father, he could force Tasha to go with him. He could drag her to hell because she wasn't the sweet thing he'd thought she was. She could handle herself in hell and then he wouldn't be alone. She could be his solace. Not that he would allow her to ever know that. She would simply be paying him back for the pain she'd caused by making sure he wasn't alone. By sleeping with him. Being with him. He might be able to survive if...

Lucky for him he didn't have to give that option any real consideration. Thanks to Tasha's father, he wouldn't have to see her again. That was probably his point. No matter what the man said, if he knew his history, he wouldn't want the son of a prostitute and a possible criminal to marry his daughter.

"You only say that because you don't know Big Tag. If he didn't care about how you are going to feel about Tasha and his family, you would be tied to something way worse than Ben was. He would find a way to force you to work this op."

It didn't surprise him the man was capable of violence. He had to be. "He sounds like a peach."

"He does what he has to do. He doesn't hurt anyone who doesn't deserve it. They usually deserve it because they've heinously harmed innocent people. He's actually quite kind. A lot like Tash."

He figured out Zach pretty quickly. "Why did you send her in if you're in love with her?"

Zach huffed out a laugh that held not an ounce of humor. "I

didn't think she'd do it. I've always thought she would look up someday and see me. Now I know she always did. It wasn't the same for her as it was for me. I don't know how much of it was real and how much I just wanted to be a part of that family. I've been on teams all my life. When I was a kid it was baseball or football or anything I could scrape up the money to afford and get myself to. I thought I was sports obsessed, but it was about being part of something. I didn't feel like I had a family so I tried to make myself part of one. Now I wonder if I'm going to get fired. None of that is your problem, and I would bet you're not feeling particularly sympathetic."

"You would win that bet." Though there was a part of him that did respond to the words. Hadn't he felt the same way? Hadn't joining that first club and finding his people opened a new world for him?

"I know she hurt you, but you'll be a fool if you let that woman go. She's one of the kindest, most authentic human beings I've ever met. If you let her slip through your fingers, I'll be waiting. I won't be patient this time. I'll go after her and I'll figure out how to make her want me. I'll figure out how to be the man she needs me to be. I'll figure out how to be you."

They would be a lovely couple, and didn't that make him want to put his fist through a wall? "Why would you even give me the warning then? Shouldn't you want me to walk away?"

Zach leaned forward, an earnestness on his face. "Because one of the things I've learned from this team is that when you truly love someone, you want the best for them even if the best for them isn't you."

He didn't want to think about how those words made him feel. "I hardly think I'm the best for her."

"She picked you. She loves you."

Dare had a counter to that claim. "Yeah, well she loved that asshole, too. Maybe she just has terrible taste in men."

"Whittington is charming and good at hiding who he really is. It's precisely why he's an excellent operative. I suspect if you asked him, he would say he loved her. He could compartmentalize. In his head, he didn't cheat on her. In his head, there's the job and his real life. Although I suspect at some point he would have cheated on her

247

outside the job. My point is he seems cool. He's excellent at pretending to be a nice guy. Did you ever pretend with her? Are you hiding who you are?"

"I'm so fucking bad at hiding who I am I had to scramble that first night to keep her from walking away," Dare admitted.

She'd made a big deal out of it. Had she been trying to rope him in? Give him a taste and then see how far she could push him?

If she'd wanted to get close to him, why would she have looked at him with sad eyes and told him she couldn't go through with it?

"Why would she walk away?" Zach asked. "What the fuck did you do to her?"

He shrugged off the aggression. If Zach was in love with her, he would seize any opportunity to protect her. Even if the transgression was in the past. "I wasn't comfortable talking about D/s with her. Not in public. I was somewhat ashamed. She didn't like that. She thought if I was ashamed then I might take it out on her. I wouldn't have, but I understand. She thought if I was ashamed, I would be ashamed of her, too, and she wouldn't accept that."

"And that is why I wanted so much to be a part of this family," Zach said quietly. "They are still fucked up. All people are. We all have our secret pains, and great parenting can't fix some of the horrors the world will visit upon each of us, but that deep core of strength she has… She's a woman who will fight beside you. Who will try hard to never let someone she loves down. Is your shame worth more than the life you could have together?"

He was being misunderstood. "It's not about shame. Why should I feel ashamed? I think we're talking about pride, and I have very little of that left."

"But pride and shame feed each other," Zach insisted. "I'm not talking about the pride you feel that you accomplished something or looking at your friends and being proud to know them. That's the problem with the word. When pride is active it's a good thing. When it's passive, it's nothing but a mask for shame. Think about that, Dare. When you're sitting there telling yourself she hurt your pride, what she did was prick your shame—a thing she would say is not merely useless but harmful."

He wasn't listening to a bunch of therapeutic crap meant to manipulate him. "I already said I would do the mission. That's all you people are getting out of me. And honestly, she's the one who should be ashamed, but you've already pointed out she won't feel that, so no harm, no fucking foul, man."

"Oh, she'll feel it. She'll feel all of it and it will hurt, and she'll try to show you she loves you. I've done what I could to help her. Now I'll sit back and watch you make the biggest mistake of your life, and when you've decimated her, I'll be there to put her back together, and I will not make the same mistake. Enjoy your life, Dare Nash. You're going to get what you really want. Revenge on your father. It's going to be hollow as hell when you're alone."

The door came open and Tasha entered, her eyes widening as she caught sight of him.

Damn, but she was beautiful, even with red eyes and a puffy face. She'd cried off all her makeup. Or had she faked it?

That was a dumb fucking thing to think.

Why would she pretend to cry? He was doing the job. She had nothing else to get from him.

If she was crying, it was because she needed to cry.

Her mom walked in, followed by her father.

"Well at least you're on time, dumbass," Ian Taggart said with a frown as he looked Zach's way.

Zach stood, his body practically going to attention. "That sounds like an excellent reason to not fire me, sir. Always on time."

Ian shook his head as he pulled out a chair for his wife. "If I fired all the dumbasses in my life, I'd have to do everything on my own. But that doesn't mean I won't kick your ass, Zach. Do not pull this crap again."

A sigh of relief went through the man. "I won't, sir." He pulled out the chair next to him. "Tash, have a seat. Can I get you something? A water?"

Asshole. That wasn't his fucking place. "Tasha, come sit beside me."

She practically tripped over her feet to get to his side of the table. She sank into the chair beside him.

He reached over and took her hand, some insane instinct leading him on. "We have to look like a couple. I think we should keep the cover as long as we're in public. This is practice. Nothing more."

Her fingers curled around his. "Of course. That seems like a smart thing to do."

The door came open again, and the rest of the team seemed to be streaming in. Ian took a place at the head of the table, his brow rising as he looked at the two of them and then Zach. He huffed and then opened the folder in front of him.

Ben sat next to the one Zach had pointed out as Tasha's cousin TJ, who seemed to try to catch Lou's eye. She didn't seem to notice and sat down next to the murdery twin. Kala. He should get those names straight.

Tasha's ex took a seat next to Zach and stared at their joined hands.

"Well, that didn't take long," Whittington said with a shake of his head. "I guess she's..."

"Finish that sentence at your peril," Tasha's mother said. "Chet, you're alive because I've kept this team on a leash. Finish that sentence and the leash will be off."

Taggart smiled, but it was a toothy thing, a show of fangs and the hunger of a real predator. "Please finish the sentence."

"Please," her sister begged, looking every bit as hungry as her dad.

"I guess she's really in love this time," Whittington said with a huff. "Good for you, Tash."

"It's only cover," she said, even as she squeezed his hand. "No need for a battle royale. I assure you whatever Chet had been planning to say wouldn't have affected me at all. The leash is still firmly on."

He kind of wished it wasn't. It would be fun to see the Taggart wolves tear that fucker apart.

"All right, let's start." Ian Taggart seemed ready to get down to business. "I've spoken to Langley and CSIS and this is how we've decided to proceed."

Taggart talked but Dare couldn't concentrate on the words. All he could think about was how close she was. How good it felt to have her hand in his.

How they would have to be together for days and days.

How the hell would he keep his hands off her?

It was a question he needed the answer to and quickly.

Chapter Sixteen

Tasha followed Dare into the suite, well aware that the affection of the last hour and a half was about to go away.

He'd been utterly silent in the taxi that had brought them back to the hotel, but when it had stopped, he'd opened her door and helped her out and put an arm around her waist, drawing her close. He'd been stopped by a client, and he'd held her hand while he'd talked to the man. He'd held it in the elevator and as they'd walked down the hall.

He dropped it as the door closed behind them, Nate locking it as he entered last.

"I think I should go to bed and let you two talk," Nate announced. He'd been quiet as he'd sat in the front seat of the taxi.

There had been something of an argument about Nate's ongoing job, but she was almost certain she'd convinced Dare there was a threat. Or her father had.

She'd worried about letting her dad talk to Dare alone. He could be a lot, but Dare seemed way more interested in talking to him than her. He seemed to have convinced Dare that everything needed to stay the same, including how affectionate Dare could be.

"There's nothing to hash out," Dare replied. "Everything is fine. Good night, Nate. We've got three meetings to take and then we'll head out to Oakley's place in the Blue Mountains for the weekend. I've informed them I'm bringing my bodyguard and my girlfriend. Everything is in place, so you can relax."

"I don't think any of us will be relaxing." Nate stepped away and started for the short hall that led to the small room that served as an office. They'd had a cot moved in when Nate had joined them. "If you need anything, I'll be right down the hall."

And then she was alone with the man she loved. The man she was almost certain to lose.

"Dare," she began.

He shook his head. "I meant what I said. We don't have anything to talk about, Tasha."

"I made Coop and Tristan come over and take out all the bugs. All of them." That had been an argument, but she'd insisted. "No one is listening to us. I promise."

He nodded as though accepting good news. "Excellent. Then we don't have to pretend when we're alone in the suite. I'll sleep on the couch. You can take the bedroom."

She hadn't thought about those ramifications. She'd only cared about him being comfortable and having a safe place. "You're not sleeping on the couch, Dare."

"I will do whatever I want." He shook his head. "That was a stupid thing to say. I obviously don't ever do what I want. I do what my father wants. I do what you want. Now I do what your father wants, but at least I'll probably get something out of it."

"Yes, you'll get your freedom, and if my team has anything to say about it, everything your father has." She was all in on the save Dare plan.

"That was a deal I made with your father. Not you. Once we're done here I do not want you to be the go-between. I'll take the scary twin if I have to. Honestly, I think she freaks me out less than the huggy one. I liked it better when you had one very quiet sister."

That stopped her in her tracks. He'd used the plural. And accurately described Kala and Kenzie. "How do you know about my sisters?"

"Well, they threatened me with early graves and weirdly, lessons on hugs."

What had her sisters done?

Trusted her instincts. Believed in her.

But it was so dangerous. Her father had to have okayed the plan. She was floored by the trust they were placing in Dare. "You can't…"

"I'm not going to tell anyone. I'm certainly not going to tell Ben he's trying to court a set of twins. It'll be way more fun to watch his confusion." Dare paced the length of the living area, a tiger in a cage. "Your father offered the information as a way to let me know he's serious about helping me."

He didn't know her dad at all if he could think that. "My father offered the information as a way to bring you closer to our family because he thinks you'll like us and that will make you give me a second chance."

His eyes were fixed on her. "Is that what you want, Tash? A second chance?"

"More than anything."

He seemed to think about it for a moment, and an infinitely sad expression came over his gorgeous face. "I can't. I've spent much of the evening thinking about how I'll stand living with you for the next week. How I can possibly make it through and not let that smile of yours trick me again."

"I'm not tricking you. I promise I will never lie to you again. I'm willing to lay it all bare for you, Dare. I fell for you the first night we met. I did not go into that pub looking for a target. I went looking for solace."

"Because you broke up with that guy?" His eyes flared as though he was a predator and she'd tossed him a slab of raw meat. "That asshole? You didn't merely date him. I heard your cousin say you were ready to marry him. You were going to marry that preening asshole."

Oh, that did not sound like a man who was indifferent to her. All night he'd been cold and untouchable, but that was all an act. Her warm, loving guy was still in there. He was just coming out as jealous guy. This was what her mother had been talking about. Men had trouble dealing with pain and loss. Jealousy and anger were much easier. They were stand-ins for the real emotion.

She had to choose her words, had to give him no reason to think she was still holding a torch for Chet. "It's hard to stop a wedding.

Well, not if you're my brother's fiancée and you decide you don't want to marry a guy just because he got you pregnant. She left us all there at the church after my aunt had worked to put it all together in record time. I didn't get that far. I was having second thoughts before I realized Chet was a cheating asshole."

He pointed her way as though she'd made his point. "His name is Chet. That should have been your first second thought, Natasha. Chet. Who the fuck names their child Chet?"

"You sound a lot like my father right now."

"Well, he makes sense," Dare admitted. "Your father is good at giving advice. Do you know what he told me to do if I wanted to stay out of trouble?"

She winced because she could make a pretty good bet on what he'd said. "Did he offer you a condom? You have to understand. He's a sex-positive guy, and he's always been open about safe sex. And did I mention that my brother's ex-girlfriend had his baby and dumped the kid in a car seat with the receptionist at my father's office? Being a grandpa wasn't something he was expecting for a couple of years. He's sensitive about condoms right now."

"He did not offer me protection. He told me not to put my penis in you."

She felt a smile cross her face. "Then he likes you. Wow. He really likes you."

Dare frowned. "He does not like me. He basically told me to stay away from you."

"He does like you. I can tell because he knows you probably will put your penis in me, and he didn't even tell you to wrap it." Her family had been supporting her all night even as her dad had yelled at the team and probably threatened to demote Zach. "He's willing to get stuck with half-Canadian grandkids."

Dare stood there as though trying to figure out what to do next and utterly failing. "I don't know how to handle this. I don't... I've spent so much of the last few years of my life reacting that I have no idea how to act. Tonight was weird and traumatic and I want to talk to you about it. I want to share it with you and have you help me through, but you caused it, Tasha."

Her heart threatened to crack. "I am so sorry."

"I don't know that I can go through this again. It hurts too much."

She wanted to cross the space between them and wrap herself around him, but he wouldn't accept that from her at this point. "You won't have to. I promise. No more lies."

"I can't." He shook his head, weariness coming over him. "I can't trust you again. I can't be in your world. Your world is nothing but lies. I understand it's necessary, but I don't want to be a part of it. You're all wolves. I need some fucking peace in my life."

"It's not all lies. It's not." If he was scared he would be drawn into her dangerous work world, she could fix that misconception. "Normally it's fairly boring. It's watching over my sisters as one of them picks up a dead drop or does surveillance on a potential terrorist. I have to watch over them. They can be reckless, and I don't know how I would live if something happened to them and I wasn't there."

"You do what you have to for your family," he said grimly. "I understand, and that's what I'm doing here and now. If your father can be believed, I have a shot at getting my brother and sister out from under my father's thumb. Hell, I want to get my stepmother free. She's not great, but no one deserves my father. I'm only allowing you to use me for them."

"I'm not trying to use you. The op and our relationship are two separate things."

"They aren't, and that's not my fault," Dare argued. "You might not have slept with me the first night because I was the target, but you damn straight did all the other times knowing I was. You didn't come to me and ask me if I would help. You didn't sit me down and say hey, Dare, I'm totally into you but oops, you're in the middle of some grand conspiracy and I'm a CIA operative."

"I was going to." That was the hardest part. She would never know how he would have taken the truth if she'd been the one to tell him, to hold his hand and make him understand that he was the most important thing to her.

Her admission didn't move his expression one bit. His eyes were still frigid as he stared at her. "After you had what you wanted. That information was more important to you than I was."

"It wasn't. It's not. I was going to tell you everything. It was just bad timing."

His head shook. "You can't even admit it. We can't solve the problem if you don't think there is one. You think it was okay for you to spy on me, to manipulate me. It was okay because you were going to tell me. I'm supposed to believe you? Do you know why I liked your dad? He was the only one all night who didn't make me feel like the bad guy. Like I'm supposed to forgive you immediately because you had a couple of tears in your eyes."

"It was more than a couple." It had been a torrent, and she'd had to shut it down because she'd known it wasn't fair to bring that kind of emotion to the conference table.

"I'm sure you're good at crying. Acting seems to come naturally to you."

He was so wrong about that. "It doesn't. That's what you are not understanding. You're assuming I'm some sort of deep-cover operative. I'm not. I'm the logistics girl. I'm the go between. Most of my time is spent sitting in a safe house with Lou. I'm not good at acting. I've never done this before."

"Well, you were spectacular at it, sweetheart. You should get out in the field more because I know I, for one, was absolutely willing to give up everything I had to get in your panties."

"Now you sound like Chet."

"I did not call you... Damn it." He stopped, taking a long breath. "I'm sorry. I don't know how to deal with this because I feel fucking used. You would think it would come naturally to me, and yet here we are. Go to bed and maybe in the morning I'll be able to be civil."

"You don't have to be civil. I can handle a few words. I would rather you got it all out and let us talk about it. I know it doesn't make sense, but I did not sleep with you so we could get access. They just sort of went together. Even as I say the words I know how stupid they sound. I know none of it makes sense and I'm going to have to deal with the fact that I'm the bad guy here, but I also know that I'm not willing to let you go. I'm never the bad guy. I'm the sensible one. I'm the one no one ever worries about because Tasha Taggart never goes wild. She always makes the right decisions for the right reasons. She's never selfish. I'm selfish about you. Only you. I went wild and made bad decisions for you. I know you've walked a tightrope all your life. I did too. I did it for years, and I know how careful it can make you. I held myself apart from everyone for a long time after I came to America. I was the weird kid with the thick accent who didn't know how anything worked here. I knew the only way I could fit in was to be helpful and to not cause trouble. My parents loved that out of me for the most part, but that little girl was still in there. That kid who got left at an orphanage after her mother was murdered."

His face had flushed. "Do not trauma dump on me."

"I'm not. I promise." She tried to ramp down the emotion. "I'm not trying to make you feel sorry for me. I'm trying to help you understand me. Deep down. It's an integral part of my personality to not make waves. I made them for you, Dare. I made them because you are worth the trouble. Even if my family had been against it, I would have told you. I wish I'd been smart enough to do it earlier, but I was scared, too."

He went quiet for a moment. "I can't love you, Tasha."

"I think you can. I think you do. And if you can't then you've lost nothing by talking this through with me, by taking this time we have and trying to see if we can make this work."

"I lost the you I thought you were," he argued. "I lost the me I got to be with you. That's not nothing."

She was going to lose him. If she let him sleep on the couch tonight, he would lie out here and build up his walls. He would build them so high she couldn't possibly climb them. Her mother had told her exactly what she needed to do. "Sleep with me, Dare. Use me the way I used you. Hell, sleep with me because it's never been as good with another person."

His jaw tightened. "It wasn't good with Chet?"

The fact that he kept going back to Chet gave her some hope. "Not as good as it is with you. Chet is an asshole, and we should stop talking about him because he is the least of our problems."

"There is no *us*, but I am willing to admit that I don't see a way I don't fuck you again if you let me. Do you want me to use you? That's all it will be. Sex. Nothing more. You won't get anything else out of me."

"That's a risk I'm willing to take."

He stared at her for a moment as though trying to imprint his will on her. "I'm making you a promise."

She could do the same. They were at war now—one she didn't want to fight, but she meant to win. They should have the battlelines drawn clearly. "And I promise when you want to come back to me, I won't give you any trouble. I'll let you in without a fight because I know something you don't. I know I love you and I'm what's best for you, and you'll see it."

"Don't say you love me."

She shrugged. "Just because I don't say it doesn't mean it's not true. You have never been properly loved, Dare Nash. You've never had a family that could support you. I'm willing to bet you're going to like it."

"I don't have a family."

"You could. You could have mine." Her mother was right. She might have to take some harsh words, but the man was already bending. He was already bargaining with her and himself to get more time with her.

Time. It was all they needed.

"I only want the help your father promised. That's all." He turned and started for the bedroom.

She followed.

"If you're coming in here, take off your clothes." He pulled his shirt over his head and tossed it aside.

Ah, they were moving on to the second stage. Her mom had explained there were four stages of aggrieved masculinity. Stage one was a whole lot of yelling/freezing out. Stage two was rage sex. She'd been warned this was the truly dangerous stage, the one that could make her feel like shit.

But she could get through it.

"Are you planning on using me, Sir?" D/s was a language they could agree on. It was what he could accept right now.

His face was all hard edges as he glanced back at her. "Yes. I am. You can consent or I can go sleep on the couch. It's your choice."

Yep, they were fully in the rage-sex stage. She needed clear parameters. "I would like to set my expectations. During your use of my person, will I be getting an orgasm or will leaving me unsatisfied be part of the punishment?"

He seemed stumped by the question. "I don't mean it as

punishment."

"Don't you?"

His eyes narrowed. "Fine. You will serve me and then go to bed, and you will not pleasure yourself. Is that understood? Since you've forced me into this position, I'll make some rules of my own. One of them is you don't get any relief I don't give you. Outside of the parameters of the op, you will obey me. The only way I will have any kind of a relationship with you is as your Dom."

She wanted to hug him because he was diving deep into stage two. She didn't because her mom was right. He needed this time to get his feet back under him and find solid ground again. "Yes, Sir. I understand."

His expression went stark. "Tasha, don't do this. I'll cut you up. If you let me, I'll tear you apart."

He might, but she was resilient. "I think you're worth the risk."

His eyes closed, and when he opened them she saw the resignation there. "Then strip. You don't wear clothes when you're here. You're to be naked and ready to serve me when you're in this suite."

"Yes, Sir." She quickly got out of her clothes, folding them before standing in front of her Dom. This was likely to be somewhat brutal, and she was ready for it.

He needed this. If she thought this was about anything but working through his pain, she would refuse him. But Dare didn't understand that a person could fuck up and still be loved. He'd been taught to trust no one and that he always had to be perfect.

"On your knees."

Yep. Brutal. The good news was she had a safe word, and she would bet he wouldn't make her use it.

She dropped to the soft fabric of the carpet and sat back on her heels, well aware that her nipples were hard and her hair flowing around her shoulders. Allowing her knees to open slightly, she gave him her biggest, subbiest eyes. "Like this, Sir?"

His cock strained against his slacks. "Yes, Tasha. That's perfect, and I should remember that. You're too perfect to be real, but I'll take what you're so willing to give me. I won't feel bad about walking away from you when this is done."

She had to pray he was wrong about that. "Understood."

"Take my cock out."

She undid his belt and carefully eased the zipper down. In seconds he was spilling out, filling her palm with his hard flesh. She stroked him once and then twice as a pearly drop appeared from the slit of his dick.

She leaned over and swiped her tongue across his cockhead.

His hand found her hair and twisted to the right side of pain. "I didn't tell you to do that, sub. If I wasn't worried about my state of mind, I would spank you right now. Another rule. You don't touch me unless I tell you to. I told you to take my cock out, not to lick me."

There was the ache again. He was putting walls between them. He would take pleasure from her, but only on his terms.

"Yes, Sir." She sat back. Her first instinct was to go as cold as he was, to protect herself. But she'd done this to him. He would welcome her coldness. It would prove to him who she was, and that was bullshit. She was Tasha Taggart. She didn't melt in the face of some pretty reasonable irritation. She would never let him walk all over her, but she could take a bit of punishment if it bought them the time they needed. So instead of chill, she looked up at him, a warm smile on her face. "What would you like me to do, Sir?"

"I'm going to fuck your mouth," he admitted. "I'm going to use you. The only thing you need to do is tap my leg if you can't handle it."

So he was going to be a little brutal. It might be fun if they weren't so emotional. They could play raiding Vikings. Or she could have been forced into a hot alien breeding program. Her mom had let her read way too many romance novels at a young age. "All right."

"Why are you doing this, Tasha?" There was an ache in his voice.

Oh, she was doing this because he was still asking the question. She would do it until the answer was imbedded in his soul. "Because I love you. Because I screwed up, but I won't let that stop me from fighting for us."

He shook his head and his hands twisted in her hair again as though the very words had sent some unnamed emotion through him. Unwanted emotion.

She vowed to make him want it.

"Take me," he ordered as he shoved his cock against her lips.

Tasha let her submissive side take over as she opened her mouth. That big, gorgeous cock of his invaded and filled her. He wasn't playing. He shoved his cock in until she gagged and then brought it back out only to thrust in again. Tears pierced her eyes, not from pain or discomfort, but from the real hurt rolling off the man she loved.

That hurt made it easy to let him fuck her mouth, to thrust in and pull out until she swallowed around him and he filled her with every drop he had.

"You take it all," he ordered. "Don't you lose a drop."

She swallowed, his cock softening as she licked him clean.

Now he would praise her and likely move to the bed.

Dare stepped back, buckling his slacks. "I'm going to take a shower. You can sleep in here or on the couch. I don't care."

Now tears pierced her eyes for a different reason. She'd been sure they would end up in bed together.

"Did you think one blow job would fix all the damage you did?" His voice had gone low, almost sympathetic. "I hate to disillusion you, but I've had better. Go to bed. That's all you're getting out of me tonight. If you feel like you need something more, you can go through my phone and get some intel. That should be payment enough."

She watched as he started to walk away from her, tears rolling down her cheeks. She'd thought for sure she was cried out, but the humiliation opened something new inside her. They were only words, but she couldn't help the hollow they unlocked inside her. She would have bet the world he couldn't be that cruel to her.

A sob began but she cut it off, clapping a hand over her mouth so he wouldn't hear her.

Maybe she should let him win tonight. On shaky feet she stood, trying to hold it in. She was going for a robe when a strong arm wrapped around her waist, hauling her back against him.

"I promised," he whispered as he wrapped his arms around her. "I promised I would hold you when you cry. Even if I'm the reason for it. I promised."

She turned in his arms. The day had been awful, and all she'd wanted was to be right here.

He picked her up as she cried and carried her to bed, and she held him, hoping she never had to let go.

* * * *

Dare came out of the best dream of his life into the harsh light of morning.

In the dream he and Tasha were married and his brother and sister were happy and fulfilled. He strangely worked for her father, having destroyed everything his own father had built. He'd given the money to his siblings and then burned the fucker down. He'd happily taken over running part of Tasha's father's business.

They'd been happy. So fucking happy.

And now he was awake and she wasn't even in bed with him. Now he was awake and yesterday flooded into his system.

She'd lied to him. She'd fucked him over and then begged him to forgive her and he couldn't.

Except when he'd realized the shitty things that had come out of his mouth the night before, he'd come back to apologize and she'd been crying. She'd been trying so hard to hold it in, but her shoulders had shook and he'd known he'd devastated her. It wasn't an act. If it had been an act, she would have cried openly to get his attention. His words had struck and hard. He'd wanted to hurt her and he had, and then he'd given into instinct. He'd wrapped his arms around her and made good on his promise.

Because I love you, Dare. Because I screwed up, but I won't let that stop me from fighting for us.

He wanted to believe her.

"Do you want some coffee?"

He practically bounced out of bed because that hadn't been Tasha. He pulled the sheet around his mostly naked body. He'd shoved himself into boxers the night before hoping that would keep him from going back on his promise to not stick his dick in her. Now he realized how dumb that had been because if she'd been in bed with him, that thin material wouldn't have been a deterrent. The extra person in the room totally was. "What the hell are you doing here? Whichever one you are."

One of Tasha's pink-haired sisters was sitting in the chair near the desk. She was dressed down in jeans and a plain T-shirt, all that cotton candy hair in a ponytail on her head. "Can you guess?"

From the way her eyes flared with mischief and the lack of threat in her tone, he could. "Kenzie."

She grinned. "Bingo. You're already good at this. Though you should know I do a mean Kala. If I hadn't wanted you to know, you wouldn't. Or I could be Kala and I'm tricking you because I do such a good Kenzie."

The weirdness never stopped with this one. "Aren't you supposed to be hiding somewhere?"

She nodded and gestured around the room. "No one will look for me here."

He moved toward the dresser where Tasha had folded and placed his slacks. "I think Ben could come through here at any moment."

"I'm sure he will, but he won't find me. After all, you didn't know I was here. I'm excellent at hiding. Lou came over to bring Tasha some things, so I hopped a ride. She does know I'm here, but Nate doesn't. I snuck in through the ceiling in your bathroom. It's easily accessible from the staff room."

"Staff room?" He wasn't aware there was one. The suite was big, but he was pretty sure he hadn't missed a whole room.

"Yes. How do you think they service this floor?" Kenzie asked as though it should be apparent. "They don't come up the pretty elevator, and they don't store things on another floor. Rich people want their mineral water replaced right away. And their fancy towels. There's a whole cabinet of fancy towels. I know because I climbed it to get to the ceiling."

He was so confused. "Why didn't you come through the door with Lou?"

Her eyes rolled as though the answer should be past obvious. "Because then Nate would know I'm here and I wouldn't have been able to sit and watch you sleep. You can learn a lot about a person from how they sleep. You don't even sleep with a gun. You are a very secure person. Or you don't have a lot of people trying to kill you. It's one of the two. I'll figure it out. Also, you have the lightest snore. I found it somewhat soothing."

He had so many questions, but he settled for the obvious one. "Why?"

She groaned and twirled around in the chair. "It's boring in the safe house. It's much worse since now we've got Asswipe's team bunking down with us. It's not so bad for me because it's only me, Kala, and Lou in a room, but I have to listen to Tris and Coop complain about sharing with four other dudes who are used to staying in sniper positions for days. They do not mind bodily smells, if you know what I mean."

He stepped into his slacks. "I do not. Nor do I care to."

"The only thing that's fun is the drama." Kenzie grinned. "TJ is trying to get Lou's attention, and for the first time in her life, she's kind of ignoring him. He doesn't even know she's planning on letting my mom set her up. I can't wait until she tells him. That was the shock of a lifetime. See, Lou's had this thing for TJ since we were kids, and he's been stringing her along forever. It's not fair. She's had one boyfriend, and I'm pretty sure he broke up with her because TJ threatened him. I think he likes knowing Lou's always there, but I hate the fact that Lou's letting her life slip by. She should be out finding the nerd of her dreams, not mooning after my dumbass cousin."

He didn't care. Or rather he didn't want to care. The truth was he was kind of interested in Tasha's family. But he wasn't indulging in his curiosity. TJ and Lou seemed very opposite. Not that it mattered. Because he wasn't asking.

"Why are you really here, Kenzie? And where the hell is Tash?" He should have been more specific in his rules. He could see that now. Last night he hadn't put in enough thought. He was in a hardcore, if temporary, relationship with her. He got to make the rules. They'd only gone over sexual servitude the night before, but how could she service him sexually if she wasn't in bed with him? She wasn't allowed to leave their bed without permission.

His bed. It was *his* bed. He simply allowed her to be in it with him. That was the key. Always reminding himself that he was in charge and she was only here for the op. And he'd only held her last night because of his promise. She might have lied to him, but he wasn't going to turn it around on her.

Yes, she'd placed herself in his care because there was no other way to get him to cooperate. Except there was, and it was rapidly becoming hard to come up with any excuse except that Tasha wanted to be with him.

"I told you. She's talking to Nate and Lou," Kenzie replied as though that should have been obvious. "And I'm bored. It's a small safe house and the walls are pretty thin. Tell me something, Dare. Do you like listening to your parents go at it? Because I don't. And they do not care. When I bring up the fact that they are old and could use some discretion, my father tells me I was conceived in loud sex and I should find the sound comforting, and it's awful. So here I am. Do you like all your friends knowing your parents have sex to nineties hair-metal bands?"

"My parents had sex in an exchange of services for cash. I don't think they listened to music." He could be wrong about that.

"Dude, your mom was a sex worker? That explains why she would give your dad the time of day. I've been studying those files and I have questions. He's an asshole, and he's super not cute and she totally was. You must get your looks from your mom. Being pretty would probably help in her profession." Not a single bit of judgment came from Kenzie's mouth. Well, not for his mom. "Let me tell you, I wish my parents could be professional about sex. High school was hard on me. All my friends' parents were doing normal things like protesting books that mentioned genders and hinted at anything vaguely sexual like a kiss, and my parents were like 'come to the club and learn how to not get an STI or pregnant.' My friends all got normal experiences like crying in the bathroom because they thought they might be pregnant from kissing their boyfriends, but not me. I knew how everything functioned. It was terrible."

Somehow he got the idea she was joking. "My father tossed a box of condoms at me and threatened to kill me if I got the wrong girl pregnant. But also told me I better have sex or I couldn't consider myself a man."

Kenzie's eyes lit like she looked forward to the challenge of whose parent was more embarrassing. "My father left books about sex around the house in case we needed information. One of them was about safe anal sex. He left it in my brother's room because he wasn't sure if Seth was gay, and he didn't want to leave him out."

Dare winced. "That's pretty bad."

265

"It's okay. Kala took it and read it at the table at my dad's next big family dinner, and he did not do that again," Kenzie said with a shake of her head. "He just sat down and sighed and said touché. It was one of the greatest moments of my childhood."

"Is he?" There was that curiosity again.

"Is who?"

"Is your brother gay?"

She shook her head. "Nah, but he wouldn't talk to Dad the way the rest of us did. Seth likes to communicate via song lyrics, and my dad is bad with song lyrics. He assumes everything is about sex. So when Seth sang about being isolated and not knowing how to tell people who he is, Dad went straight to 'my son's gay and I gotta show him I love him.' You'll like Seth. Do not listen to my dad. He's a great songwriter, and he's got a nice voice."

"I'm sure he's good."

"And then there's my dumbass brother Travis, who didn't use a condom. That's his name now. My dad is getting it legally changed."

That man did not look old enough to be someone's grandpa. "Tash mentioned something about a wedding that got canceled."

"Oh, I'll show you the video. My aunt Grace was trying her hand at wedding planning, and she had a videographer there. You can see the moment my brother's soul leaps back into his body when he realizes he won't actually have to get married. I've never seen Travis so happy."

"But now he's a single dad," Dare found a T-shirt and pulled it over his head.

"Turns out he's pretty good at it," she admitted. "He's had some help, but for the most part he does the work. He's balancing taking care of Colton with working and going to law school. I don't know what disappointed my dad more, the unplanned pregnancy or the lawyer thing. I think it's the lawyer thing. I, for one, am happy he's going to learn how to get Kala's ass out of jail because it *will* land there one day."

"Your dad doesn't like the kid?" The thought of a kid being unwanted rattled him. Like he'd been.

Kenzie snorted. "Yeah, sure. You've obviously never seen my dad around kids. He carries Colton around and calls him his little buddy and is already teaching him stuff he shouldn't. My father is a menace."

He didn't seem like one. If Ian was telling him the truth, he was doing everything he could to make sure the op ran well.

Or to make sure his daughter ended up happy.

He didn't want to think about this. He shouldn't be talking to Tasha's sister about anything except the mission. He didn't need to know more about her family.

"Zach and Chet got into it big time last night," Kenzie revealed.

Shit. Tasha's sister knew how to reel him in. "They did? What did that fucker say about her? Chet, not Zach."

"Zach would never say anything bad about Tasha. Tasha is a saint in Zach's eyes."

"Because he's in love with her."

Kenzie's eyes went wide. "What?"

Oh, so he knew something she didn't. Wasn't that fun? It actually was. It was really fun. "He's clearly in love with her. I got the whole 'if you hurt her, I'll kill you and then run away with her' speech, though the kill you part was mostly implied."

Kenzie seemed to think about that for a moment. "Holy crap. That makes so much sense now." She looked up at him, a gleam in her eyes. "You are good at collecting information. Now do Tristan. Figure out why he's being a big old scaredy cat when it comes to marrying Carys and Aidan. Mostly Carys, I think, but Aidan's in there somewhere."

So. Many. Questions. "Did Chet get his head taken off?"

"Dad cooled everyone down," she said with a sigh. She studied him for a moment. "All right. I'll tell you the reason I really came over. I needed to see if you hurt Tash."

He frowned. "Of course I did. I lashed out at her and said some shit I shouldn't have and I made her cry because I'm an asshole."

She got the softest look on her face and stood up, crossing the space between them.

This was the point where she would either hug him or gut him, and he wasn't sure which he was more scared of.

She put her hands on his shoulders. "You are a good man, Dare Nash."

"I told you I was mean to her."

"And yet she slept in here and she's obviously following directions since she's walking around naked. She wouldn't do that if you'd devastated her. It's okay. Mom says the rage-sex phase takes some time. You'll get to bargaining soon."

"I'm not going to barg..." His brain processed the words Kenzie had said. "What do you mean she's walking around naked?"

Kenzie patted him and stepped back. "Naked. Without clothes. Probably because you went for the whole 'I can have a D/s relationship with you and not risk my heart, and here are a bunch of kinky rules.' Tasha is good at following rules."

Rules. He'd told her she had to be naked here in the bedroom.

In the suite.

Damn it.

He grabbed a robe and started for the door. "Natasha Taggart!"

Surely she wasn't sitting in the living area of the suite completely naked. She would know he didn't mean for Nate to see her like that.

She was sitting on the couch, a cup of coffee in front of her and a towel under her gorgeous, naked ass. Just sitting there like it was a completely normal thing to be naked in front of people who weren't her lover. Just hanging out because that was how comfortable she was with herself.

He was going to have such a freaking talk with her father. What the hell had he been thinking?

"Put this robe on right now." He was well aware he sounded like a school marm from some Regency novel complaining about an ankle showing.

Tasha frowned. "You told me..."

"I meant the bedroom. I obviously meant the bedroom," he insisted.

"No worries, mate." Nate was lounging on the couch across from the ladies. "Tash's like a sis... I'm not going to say that because I've tried hard to never see my sister naked. Elodie feels the same. We would never go to the same club. Tasha's like a friendly fellow club member."

"That is a completely different thing." A club was a fine place to be naked in. He wrapped the robe around her awkwardly, backward, really, because everyone could see her breasts and her breasts were his for the time being.

"Oh, did I miss something?" Fucking Ben walked in the door like he owned the place. "Are we doing the club thing again?"

He kind of wanted to punch Ben in his overly perfect face. It was hard to forget that Tasha had wanted him first.

"Sir, if you'll allow me, I'll put the robe on the proper way," Tasha offered, a hint of amusement in her tone.

He was glad she found it funny. If she put the robe on the right way, Ben would see her. Nope. He tugged his damn shirt off and started putting it over her head.

Tasha huffed and managed to get her arms through the proper holes. When her head came out, she was frowning his way. "You know I was only following your clearly stated rules."

"I told her that wasn't what you meant," Lou said with a shrug. She was properly dressed in jeans and an overly large sweatshirt that hid her body altogether.

Good for Lou.

"There are rules?" Ben asked. "Is this that D/s stuff? You told Tasha she had to walk around naked?"

"I told her she should be ready to service me sexually at any time." If she could be naked and proud, then he could be an assholey top. He could be the possessive assholey top he was deep down inside.

"Here I am, baby." Tasha stood, and his shirt hit her midthigh. He needed bigger shirts. "Ready to do my Master's will. Another part of my Master's will was that I was to be naked whenever I was in this suite. Not the bedroom. In this suite. The definition of a suite…"

He was not going to handle her sarcasm with grace this morning. "Finish that sentence and we'll go back in the bedroom for a non-erotic spanking."

Her mouth closed.

Why did she have to be so pretty? "Let me clarify. I want you naked when we're alone and there's every reason for us to believe we're going to stay that way. Although now people come in from the ceilings, so there's that."

"Or at the club," she replied with a nod.

"We won't be together…" He growled. They wouldn't be

together long enough to go to another club. He seriously doubted they would be allowed back in The Station. Still, arguing would make him sound foolish. It was easier to go along with her. "Or at the club. Now will you please go and put on some clothes so we can talk to our guests in a civilized fashion?"

"Yes, Sir. I would be happy to," Tasha agreed.

Ben shook his head. "I have no idea what's going on. Is there more coffee around here?"

Nate stood as Tasha walked into the bedroom. "Come on, mate. They set up some breakfast in the other room. I could eat."

"So could I. The safe house we're staying at is full of testosterone. I had to get out of there early," Ben said, slapping a hand on his gut. "I'm glad to be back in my hotel room. So much less drama. I think Maggie has something going on with that Cooper person. Way to lead a guy on."

There was a squeak from overhead, but Ben kept walking.

When he was safely out of sight, Lou's head tilted up. "You are going to be in so much trouble."

"Should I do something?" He didn't want to be the reason the twins got found out.

Lou shook her head. "Nah, she's going to go and wait in the car, and when we get back, I'll let her help me do some online shopping. I need a makeover."

Another squeak, this one infinitely happier.

"I know how to soothe a Taggart beast," Lou promised. "Have Tasha go over the new reports we pulled. We've identified a couple of projects at Tandy Medical that Oakley might be interested in. I'd love your thoughts. I'm going to go. Tash looks good. You didn't take it out on her."

She was wrong about that. "I did."

Lou gave him a grin. "I don't think you would know how. You said some words to her and then you held her while she cried. You're moving nicely through this phase."

"Why is everyone going on about phases? I'm not in a phase."

"Sure you are. You're in the rage-sex phase. Soon you'll be bargaining. This is all according to Charlotte Taggart, who is the ultimate authority." Lou picked up her big bag and started for the door.

Well, if someone knew his future, he would like in on the secret. "What am I bargaining for?"

She turned at the door. "According to the expert, somewhere in all the rage sex you'll start to think you can keep doing this because Tasha owes you. You'll think you can keep her because she should serve you for longer. It's really punishment."

Damn it. He was already there. His rage-sex time should have lasted longer. He should have made way better use of it. "And then what happens?"

Lou bit her bottom lip as though keeping in a laugh because she could read his damn mind. "Then you wake up one morning and you're not so mad and you're part of this weird, wonderful family. It's a good bargain, Dare. My mom made it a long time ago, and she's been happy ever since. And Dare, you should know you look good, too. That is a very manly chest you have there."

"Hey." Tasha came back out wearing a sundress that covered everything it should. She tossed his shirt at him. "What are you doing, LouLou?"

Lou shrugged, opening the door. "You know Doms need to be told they're pretty, too."

Tasha was having none of it. "Goose. Gander. Cover it up, Sir. Bye, Lou. I'm going to get some breakfast. I'm hungry all of the sudden."

He was left in the middle of the suite, pulling his shirt on and all alone. At least he thought he was. For all he knew the whole Taggart clan was in his ceiling.

Strangely, the thought didn't scare him the way it should.

Chapter Seventeen

Tasha sipped her coffee and thought about how she was going to murder her sister. She wouldn't make it hurt. She would consider it more of a putting Kenz out of everyone else's misery. Everyone thought Kala was the hard one. Sometimes Kala had nothing on her shiniest sister.

She glanced around the small kitchen. Ben and Nate were out on the balcony making their way through massive plates of food and discussing what Oakley could possibly want from Dare's father. Dare had gotten dressed and joined them. She knew she should be out there, but it hurt too much to sit across from him and pretend nothing was wrong.

It was easier to plot her sister's murder.

"You all right?"

She started, shocked anyone could sneak up on her. Her game was nowhere close to being on today. She barely managed to not drop her mug. Setting it on the counter, she turned Dare's way. He had a mug in his hand. "Is the carafe empty? I can fill that up for you."

He put his mug down next to hers. "When I told you to serve me, I didn't mean like that. I mostly wanted to know where you'd gone. Now that Ben's not hiding his true occupation, he talks in military terms way too much. He and Nate seem to have a whole different language I don't understand. And then there's talk of how many 'roos are in a paddock, and none of us understand that. I thought I'd see what you were doing."

"Planning my sister's murder." She'd promised she wouldn't lie to him again.

"Ah, maybe I shouldn't have told you. If it helps, I think she was trying to make sure I hadn't hurt you."

"She was being reckless." She lowered her voice. "And Ben is here. He could have caught her."

"Only if he was looking up in the ceiling. Do I snore?" He was surprisingly calm.

"Only a little. I find it soothing."

His lips quirked up slightly. "That's what your sister said. She watched me sleeping. That's weird, right?"

Yep, she was going to murder her sister. Still, she could think of worse scenarios. "Be happy it wasn't Kala. She would have woken you up with a knife to your throat and warnings about hurting me. I'm sorry. Kenzie shouldn't have done that. I'll talk to her about leaving you alone. And I'm sorry about the misunderstanding."

Dark eyes narrowed on her. "Did you misunderstand?"

There might have been some malicious compliance in her actions this morning. He *had* given her instructions. "I was following your rules, Sir. You said…"

He moved into her space. "I know what I said, and I know what a reasonable human being would do. I'm planning on telling your father exactly what I think about his parenting methods. He didn't shame you enough."

The man obviously hadn't figured her family out. "He didn't shame me at all. He overuses the word *dumbass*, but it's all love for him. You seem awfully calm about my sister sneaking into your bedroom."

He moved away, leaning against the granite countertops. "I was surprised, and then I have to admit I found her amusing. I don't understand your family. My siblings wouldn't think to try to protect me. I promise you won't ever find my brother or sister climbing out of the ceiling to make sure I'm okay."

"Only because they probably think you're indestructible. I would bet you don't ever let them see you being vulnerable." It was hard to think his siblings didn't appreciate what he'd done for them.

"Maybe, but if it's true, it's because I had to." He turned slightly so he could look out the small window. "I wonder how they'll feel when I burn down everything around them. I'm not looking to save my father's business. If your dad finds a way to save the legitimate parts, I intend to sell it off, split the profits between my siblings, and start over again somewhere new."

Dallas is nice. That's what she wanted to say, but he wasn't ready to hear it. "You wouldn't keep part for yourself? You've earned that money. You would run the company well."

"I don't want it, and I think giving it all to them might make me feel less responsible for them. I don't actually know if my brother and sister like me. Isn't that a kick in the gut? The only time they truly interact with me is to ask me to fix something for them. It's not the same with your family. You know each other. Really know each other."

There were big differences between their relationships with their siblings. "We grew up together. I'm only a year older than Kenzie and Kala, and our brothers are a few years younger. You're so much older than Johnny or Gina. You were more like another dad to them than a sibling. I wouldn't judge them harshly for that."

His eyes narrowed. "Why not? You know it would be easier to manipulate me if I thought you were the only one who cared. Why would you try to ease my mind this way?"

His brain might always go to that place. She had to find a way to show him she was different. "If my goal was to control you then yes, cutting you off from people who love you would be an excellent way to go. If my goal is to be a person who truly loves you, then I can't think of a worse way to go."

"I would think they would teach you better in spy school."

She was tired, and it wasn't merely from her lack of sleep the night before. Her mother had told her it would be hard and she had to suck it up. She wasn't going to give up on him. "Only because you don't understand my team at all."

"Zach said something about this team being different than other teams."

"The word *team* being the operative term." At least he seemed to be interested. The night before he hadn't wanted to talk to her at all. "There's not really teams of intelligence agents. It doesn't work that way. An operative is guided by someone hirer up, and they rely on whatever support services are convenient in the area they're working in. They often don't know the men and women helping them, and those people sometimes don't even know the operative's real name."

"Like Ms. Magenta?"

She nodded. "Yes. Once again, my sisters like to play around with tradition. Personally, I've gone by Ms. White on occasion, usually with foreign operatives. Had I known Ben worked for CSIS, I would have introduced myself differently. I get the feeling he's going to be a pain in my ass."

"I don't know about that. He seems upset that Kala and Cooper have something going. I think he's feeling like she used him," Dare mused. "It might make him stay away. He has no idea Kala's not the one he's interested in. At least I think so. Anyway, what you're telling me is your team is different because you have ties to each other, a history together. That's what Zach told me. It's also probably why you get the shit assignments."

She'd thought about that a lot, but she wasn't willing to change things. They had to prove they could do the work. This op would not help them move that meter forward. "Probably. We're an experiment, and one not everyone at the Agency wants to see work. They would rather have fifty Chets who'll do anything for the mission."

His jaw went straight. "Another rule. His name doesn't leave your lips."

His jealousy was something she could hold on to. "That's easy enough. I don't think about him much."

It wouldn't be the same with Dare. She worried she would think about Dare the rest of her life.

"I am sorry for what I said to you last night, Tasha," he admitted, his eyes on her again. "Those words were meant to hurt you. They weren't fair because while you lied to me, you never once said a thing meant to make me feel small. You did the opposite. You made me feel better than I have in a very long time. That's my only real excuse. I hated that it was a lie."

Tasha tamped down her frustration. "It wasn't, but I'm not sure how to make you believe me. I tried to put myself in your position, and I don't know that I would believe me either. Nothing in your whole life prepared you for this. Or rather it prepared you in the worst way. If I were you, I would look at me and think I was like everyone else who's let you down."

"Well, all those other times I didn't get mind-blowing sex out of the experience. Tash, I'm tired. I've had conversations with half your family about how I should save everyone the trouble and marry you and be happy. I can't do that right now. I can't even consider it, but what if we don't fight about it? What if I accept that you thought you were doing the right thing and you accept that I don't know if I can have a relationship with you outside the parameters of this mission? What if we agreed to just be for a while?"

"To be?" She wasn't sure what he was saying.

"To be together while we're together, and then we go our separate ways. That was the plan in the beginning, after all. We were going to have a couple of glorious weeks and accept that was all we could have."

Now she could see that she'd never meant to accept that deal. "But we could be more."

"How?" Dare asked with a shake of his head. "Am I going to join your team? I don't think so. It could take me years to deal with my family. You have a job that requires a lot of travel and leaves little time for anything else."

"You would be surprised." She wanted to argue with him, but he was dangling a lifeline. It might have an expiration date, but it was something. Her mother had told her patience would win this battle. "I can agree to your bargain."

He winced. "Can you not tell your mom this is a bargain? I think she's going to be way too proud of herself."

Her sister had been talking. "I can agree to it if you concede one point to me."

A wary look came into his eyes. "What's that?"

"Can you believe that I care about you? That I did not sleep with you for the mission."

"Can you admit that the mission was part of it?" Dare asked. "Not all of it, but part of it."

She was so glad they'd gotten to bargaining. "Yes. I can agree that I jumped at the chance to see you again. Everyone freaked out that we would have to change plans, and I was secretly excited because there was nothing in the world I wanted more than to have time with you."

He held a hand out. "I can agree."

She reached out, thinking he would shake her hand, but he tugged her close. He wrapped his arms around her, hugging her like she was a comfort to him.

He was such a comfort to her. She laid her head on his chest and breathed him in.

His hand ran up to her neck and then into her hair, fingers moving over her scalp. "So you and Zach run the team."

She nodded, not moving because he hadn't let her go. It felt too good to be in his arms. She would stand here forever if he would let her. "He's our military liaison."

"And he cares about you," Dare said slowly, as though contemplating the words. "That's the point. To have a team that cares about each other."

"We're friends."

"Did your father hire him knowing he would try to get into your panties?"

She gasped and stepped back. "What are you talking about? Zach is a friend. Nothing more."

Dare reached out and brought her into his arms again. "I'm sure he seems that way to you, but I happen to know the truth. He should understand that if he tries anything, I might not have a military background, but I can be ruthless, too. But you should be gentle with him. He seems to be an okay guy. See, I could understand you having a thing for him. That would make sense. Chet is awful. He's like the comic villain in a bad rom-com, the one the whole audience knows is a douchebag. Only the heroine thinks he has any value at all."

She hugged him tight. "I'm a foolish and impatient heroine who should have waited for the right man. When you think about it, you should probably spank me for that."

A shudder went through him, one that had nothing to do with distaste and everything to do with anticipation. "I don't have any idea what to do with you. I'm so fucking lost."

She hated she'd put him here. Patience. It was the word of the day. "Then let's just be."

If she could give him peace for the time being, she would. And then she would fight like hell. The truth of the matter was she might have to choose him. She might have to choose between a life in the Agency and a life with him.

Her family would understand if it came to that.

"Let's just be." He lowered his mouth to her, kissing her with a slow hunger.

That was when a chime went through the suite, letting them know someone was at the door.

Dare groaned. "It's probably more food. I swear that Aussie is going to double his costs in food alone."

"I'll get it." She went on her toes and pressed a kiss against his lips. "You go and find a way to get rid of Ben. I don't need another briefing on how dangerous Huisman is."

She strode to the door, throwing it open to let in whatever staff member was bringing them food or towels or…her dad.

"Hey, Natasha. I'm afraid we've run into a bit of a problem." Her father stood there, a grim expression on his face. The fact that he'd called her Natasha let her know they weren't giving away their family ties. It was a shorthand to let her know how to behave.

"What's the problem, boss?"

"I'm afraid he's talking about me." Emmanuel Huisman stepped into view.

Yep, that was one big-ass problem. She opened the door and let the men in. It looked like unwinding would have to wait.

* * * *

Dare stepped out of the kitchen, expecting to see Tasha letting in someone from the staff. Likely someone who had no idea their staff room had been used as an access point earlier in the day.

He wished he didn't find the whole family so amusing, wished he could find a way to be cold to all of them.

Instead, he found himself staring at one of the aforementioned family. Ian Taggart walked in.

Ah, there was the man he wanted to harass. He was a man who

seemed to not have a problem talking about embarrassing things. Well, they were going to test that theory. "Hey, we need to talk about the lackadaisical way you have chosen to raise your children. Did you know what…"

"Dare, we have company." The expression on Taggart's face stopped him cold. "I'm afraid we'll have to talk about my parenting skills later. Dr. Huisman came to visit. Me. In a house he shouldn't have known about."

Dare felt his eyes widen as Dr. Huisman walked in, passing Tasha.

"I'm afraid I have my own security, and when I realized what was happening with Oakley, I could stay silent no longer. Especially not when I realized the Agency was involved. We have a connection, Mr. Taggart and I. I thought I could avoid this trouble, but I worry I'm being painted as a villain. Normally I can handle it. I might even deserve it in some people's eyes, but I need to make you listen to me. Mr. Nash, you are in danger."

What the hell was Huisman doing here? Huisman was one of the people they were gathering intel on. Well, Tasha and the team were gathering intel on. The man wasn't supposed to walk into his suite with Ian Taggart.

Why had he gone to Taggart in the first place? "I don't understand. If you think I'm in some sort of danger, why wouldn't you come to me?"

Tasha walked past Huisman, taking a place at Dare's side, her hand sliding into his. "That's an excellent question. I'd also like to know how he found my boss."

"Your boss?" Huisman seemed confused for a moment and then he shook his head, his expression clearing. "Yes. Mr. Taggart is your boss. Of course. I wasn't aware you were in his employ."

Taggart's eyes narrowed. "You know."

Huisman flushed. "I know many things, but I would never blurt them out. I understand the delicate nature of your work and that you might want to keep your relationships private. And that is all we need to say about that. I told you, Mr. Taggart, I'm here to help you. I have no intention of obstructing your investigation. Not when I've recently discovered how dangerous Mr. Oakley is."

"I don't understand what's going on." Dare didn't want to admit that fact, but he couldn't stand being in the dark. Something had turned. He could feel it. A simple op had gotten extremely dangerous.

"Is our Canadian friend here?" Ian asked.

"He's on the balcony. He can't hear us," Tasha replied and then turned Dare's way, her voice going low. "I think what my father is trying to say is Dr. Huisman knows about our relationship. And I find that interesting."

"As I stated, I have a connection to your family," Huisman reiterated.

Ian crossed his arms over his broad chest. "A man who worked for me a long time ago was there the day his father was killed."

"Owen Shaw did not kill my father, though I know he had reason to," Huisman explained. "It was a man named Levi Green who murdered my father as I watched from the staircase. However, as I grew older I must admit to a fascination with everything that happened that day. I needed to understand, so I studied everyone who was there and who had a hand in shaping the day that shaped me. It led me to Shaw and his wife, Dr. Rebecca Walsh, and then to McKay-Taggart."

"Apparently Dr. Huisman has made a study of our whole family." And Ian Taggart wasn't amused by that fact.

"I know your connections to the CIA and I would have happily left it all alone if not for two events," Huisman explained. "I discovered Auggie Oakley isn't the man I thought he was, and I figured out that Benjamin Parker infiltrated your group and his goal would be to poison you against me."

"Why would he do that?" Dare asked. It was pretty much exactly what Ben had done, but it looked like Tash and her dad weren't giving away information they didn't need to, and he was going to go along with it. They were the experts.

Even as he said the words, he heard the door to the balcony opening and he turned.

"What the hell is he doing here?" Ben stood in the doorway that led to the balcony, a stark look on his face. "Dare, why did you let him in? I told you. He's not who he seems to be."

A long sigh came from Huisman. "Benjamin. It's been a while."

"Not long enough." Ben stalked into the room.

Nate followed behind him, moving in close to Dare and Tasha. Dare wanted to tell Nate to protect Tash because suddenly this felt like a dangerous situation. There was an almost palpable hate coming off Ben. Huisman watched him with wary eyes.

"I believe I told you Manny is a dangerous person. This should prove it to you," Ben said, crossing his arms over his chest. "He has connections you can't imagine. I would bet he found you. Have you asked yourself how that happened? Unless you went to him."

Taggart frowned, and it was easy to see how tense the man was. He was walking a fine line, trying not to give away names and ties and dots that Ben could connect. "I did not."

Huisman frowned his way, but there was an almost sympathetic feel to the expression. "I have security, too, Ben. You made certain I needed it. When I found out you were likely here in Sydney, I asked my security team to check into everyone around Mr. Nash, and that led me to discover the Agency was in town. I suspected you were behind that, and I called in some favors so I could talk to the head of the team myself."

Ben nodded as though the doctor had made his point. "You mean you called your cronies, the politicians you own."

"I called the ones I work with, Ben." Huisman's head shook like he was frustrated. "I have to work with them to get the foundation's research in the best position it can be in. I know it's distasteful, but that's how the world works. I have to deal with governments if I want to get critical research done, research that will help humanity."

"I see through you," Ben declared. "I know exactly who you are. You cannot fool me but please, let's keep the charade going. What are you doing here, Manny? What's the con this time?"

Huisman sighed. "Con? I thought I was a murderer. Or a terrorist. I believe that is what you told your bosses at CSIS. You need to figure out which type of criminal I am and stick with it."

"I think you're all of the above," Ben said with grim surety. "So what's the play this time? Are you trying to cut Oakley out so you can take over the group?"

"What group?" Huisman seemed at a loss.

"I'm talking about the group behind Disrupt Australia." Ben stood mere feet away from Huisman, creating a real threat that he could attack.

Taggart moved closer, as though getting ready to step in if he had to.

Huisman's head shook. "I've partnered with them on a couple of projects. They're doing interesting work when it comes to dealing with problems. They've made some innovations that I find helpful. As we move into the future, it's important to find new solutions. I don't know how I would take over. I'm not even on the board."

"God, you're a good actor." Ben turned to Taggart. "Did you read the reports I sent you on the group?"

"I did." Taggart seemed to be choosing his words carefully.

Ben's face fell. "But you don't believe me."

"I think we need more evidence," Taggart allowed.

Ben huffed. "I should have known you wouldn't believe me. I guess Huisman owns enough American politicians that it doesn't matter what the truth is. Are you going to listen to him now?"

Ben was being unreasonable. Even Dare knew they should listen to the man. "I think we should."

Even lies would give them something. If they could catch the doctor in a lie, that would be evidence.

"Yes, I'm going to listen to what he has to say, Ben." Taggart had a grim expression on his face as though he knew what kind of trouble his words would bring. "I think you should go back to your room or you can go to the safe house. I'll try to make sure you're in on the briefing I intend to give your bosses."

"You'll tell them I'm crazy," Ben said with a shake of his head. "I thought you might be different. Do you know how tired I am of trying to warn the world about him? Maybe I should let him show you exactly who he is. Maybe I should let the snake bite you and then you'll believe me." He turned Dare's way. "Watch your back. It's obvious Manny's already working with these people. They'll give you up if he wants them to."

Could Ian Taggart be Huisman's pawn? Somehow he couldn't see it. Did he trust these people? He had instincts, and they were flaring up now.

"You could come with me," Ben offered. "This whole op is blown. We won't get anything out of it. Come with me and I'll make sure you're safe."

And there was his answer. Ben was offering him everything he should want. Safety with his own government.

He wasn't going to do it. He was going to stay with Tasha. He was going to make his bet.

"I can't." He squeezed Tasha's hand. "I have to see this through to the end."

He couldn't leave her now. It would have to wait. That heartache… It wasn't for today.

She leaned against him as though deeply relieved.

Ben nodded as though he should have known he would be alone. "Then you've made your choice. Good luck with them, Dare. I think I'll go home. It's easy to see I'm not needed here."

"Or you could go back to the safe house and wait for me," Taggart said in a way that let everyone know that was the correct path.

Ben shot the man the bird and walked out.

"All right, I'm going to need to know how you and our Canadian friend are connected." Taggart locked the door behind Ben and then made his way to the sofa.

"It's a long story, and I'm afraid I don't come out smelling like a rose." Huisman looked weary as he sank down in the chair across from Taggart. "Am I able to speak freely around Mr. Nash's bodyguard?"

"He's a friend of the family," Taggart explained. "Tasha, Dare, take a seat. Nathan, I suspect you should keep an eye on the door."

Nate nodded and moved into place.

Dare sat down, gently pulling Tasha beside him. "Where is your security, Dr. Huisman?"

"I chose not to bring them. Against their wishes. I'm not a man who likes to walk about with an entourage. Despite what Benjamin will tell you, I prefer a quiet life. So I only use bodyguards when I believe I'm in grave danger."

"It looked like Ben would take you out if he could," Dare said.

"I think if Ben truly wanted me dead, he would have done it by now." Huisman seemed to shrink a bit. "That is not Benjamin's plan. No. He doesn't want me dead. He wants me to suffer."

"How do the two of you know each other?" Taggart asked.

"We were childhood friends. Ben was my best friend. He was a kind child. I was a bit awkward, and my father did nothing to curb those tendencies. He wanted me to be a wunderkind. When my IQ tests came back at a genius level, he put me in all kinds of extra classes. I was not allowed to be a child. Except when I was with Ben. His family lived on our street and we were in the same classes, though I'm a bit younger than he is. I think if my father had lived he would have moved me through school more quickly and our friendship would have waned."

"But he died when you were seven." That didn't seem like a lot of time in school.

"And I entered first grade when I was barely five," Huisman explained. "I was reading at three. My father wanted to have nothing but tutors for me, but by that time he and my mother were divorced and she insisted I go to a school. I met Ben the first day, and we were close after that. As you can imagine, it was hard for such a young child to fit in. Ben was kind to me. We seemed to fit in a way I didn't with anyone else. His parents were the ones who came for me the day I watched my father die. I stayed at their house until my grandfather came to retrieve me. Then I didn't see Benjamin for a few years. We reconnected in high school and things were good between us. We were the best of friends."

"When did they go bad?" Dare was curious. He was seeing Ben from a different perspective.

Huisman flushed, a light pink staining his cheeks. "We went to two different colleges. The young lady he was dating at the time ended up attending Harvard with me. Ben stayed in Canada. Time and proximity brought Deanna and I closer together, and I'm afraid Ben was hurt when we could no longer hide our feelings for one another."

"So this was all because you started dating his girlfriend?" Tasha asked.

"There's more," Taggart said, his voice tight.

A brow rose over Huisman's eyes. "So you've been doing some research on me. I suppose I shouldn't be surprised. Benjamin would have made certain you were concerned. Mr. Taggart is correct. Benjamin refused to accept that Deanna and I were in love. He came to Massachusetts and confronted me. We fought. I said some things I shouldn't have said, but I was in love with her. Deanna...she couldn't handle the tension. She offered to go somewhere quiet and talk to Benjamin. I never saw her again. Not alive. She died in an accident. Ben survived. I sometimes wonder...no. It was an accident."

"There was a question?" Dare asked.

"It seems Benjamin was driving quite recklessly that night," Huisman answered. "There were witnesses who said he took corners far too quickly. I've dreamed about how frightened she must have been. He blames me, of course."

"Why would he blame you if he was driving?" Tasha asked.

Dare knew. "She wouldn't have been in the car if he hadn't gotten involved with her."

"It's worse," Huisman corrected. "Benjamin believes I tampered with the vehicle. It was a car he'd rented. She wasn't supposed to be with him that night. He believes I sabotaged his car so I could get rid of my rival for her affections. I didn't need to get rid of him. I know this isn't well done of me to say, but I could provide Deanna with a much more luxurious life. His parents had lost much of their wealth by this time. Deanna was a pragmatic woman. I loved her, but I also understood why she chose me over Benjamin. Ben was exciting and I was stable."

"The police don't believe there was any tampering. According to the reports I read they found no wrongdoing. Deanna Fisher's death was ruled an accident," Taggart said. "But I'm sure Ben would point out that police can be bought."

"Yes. My grandfather came into town the next morning and spent some time trying to figure out exactly what was going on. Benjamin decided that he paid the police to hide the fact that the vehicle had been tampered with." Huisman leaned over. "It was...a hard time. I said things to Benjamin I wish I could take back. I know how hard all of this was on him, but it's been years and he's still trying to take me down, as he puts it. He accuses me of all manner of crimes. Why exactly is he coming after me this time?"

Taggart looked his way, nodding, which Dare took as permission to explain the situation. He was surprised Taggart would allow him to be a part of this conference, but he was game. "Ben believes you're a member of the leadership behind Disrupt Australia, a group of powerful people who want to truly disrupt the world. There was a cluster of attacks on Jakarta's public transportation system a few months ago."

"Yes, I remember," Huisman said with a nod. "It nearly took down the country's government."

"He believes Disrupt Australia was behind it," Dare explained.

"That's ridiculous." Huisman stood, pacing. "They're economists and scientists. It's a think tank. They're not terrorists. Mr. Taggart, does the CIA believe DA is a terrorist group?"

"That's what we're here to determine," Taggart admitted. "I'd certainly like to ask you a few questions about what you know about the group and how you came to be involved."

Huisman stopped. "I will answer any questions you have. All the Agency ever had to do was ask. I will cooperate in any way you need, Mr. Taggart, but first you must listen to me. Mr. Nash, I approached Mr. Taggart because I've learned that Oakley is planning to kidnap you in an effort to get your father to give him a sample of something dangerous one of your companies is working on."

Tasha's hand tightened slightly around his, the only reaction she had to the words. Her calm helped Dare keep his own.

"Excellent. And what is that?" Ian sat up as though they'd finally gotten to the part he'd been waiting for. "I've brought you here. You're in the same room with Nash. I've given you what you want. Tell me what we're dealing with."

"Nothing less than the potential annihilation of millions," Huisman stated. "From what I've learned, Tandy Medical is working on biological weapons."

"What?" His hand tightened around Tasha's. "I can believe my dad is stealing money or selling stuff he shouldn't, but developing biological weapons? Tandy works on vaccines."

"Yes, and one of those vaccines is for anthrax," Huisman explained. "There are several terrorist groups who have been experimenting with anthrax delivery systems. Inhalation anthrax has an excellent rate of death. Even with aggressive treatment it's roughly fifty fifty. It would be far less if this strain was let loose in the undeveloped world."

"Which is why we're trying to develop better vaccines." Dare felt floored. He'd thought he could believe anything of his father, but this was a lot.

"But as you develop the vaccines, the scientists at Tandy are also working on a better anthrax."

Huisman's words sent a chill through Dare. For the first time, he felt anxiety begin to thrum through his system. His father wouldn't do that. "Why would anyone want better anthrax?"

"That's a naïve question, Dare," Taggart said, but his tone was softer than it had been. "There's money in a better anthrax. The same way there's money in building bombs and running guns. Dr. Huisman, I do not believe that Dare is involved in his father's illegitimate businesses."

Huisman nodded. "I had made that assessment myself, but at the very least Oakley believes his father will be willing to trade the weaponized anthrax process for you."

"I'm not sure he would actually do that." His father would definitely weigh a cost analysis versus losing his eldest son.

"I believe that's a correct assessment," Taggart countered, speaking to Huisman. "He needs Dare in order to look like he's got someone ready to take over. His father doesn't think anyone else in the family is capable of handling the business. He's put a lot of time and money into Dare. He won't let him go easily."

"My father hates me." Dare felt like that should be clear, but no one was getting it.

"I don't think your father knows how to hate or love," Tasha added. "I think he views everyone as a chess piece to move around and sacrifice if needed. You are an important piece to him. There's a reason they aren't trying to get to your brother or sister. Your father wouldn't care. They aren't important pieces except they are an excellent way to manipulate you."

He wasn't going to argue with her. Especially since when he looked at it with an unemotional eye, she made sense. His father was concerned with having a male heir. So much so he would force an unacceptable one into the role. But there were other problems to deal with. "Why do you think Oakley is planning to kidnap me?"

"Because he already tried," Huisman said grimly. "A few days ago I believe he sent someone to take Mr. Nash. It was right before we met, correct? You didn't have a bodyguard when you first came to Australia. Did Benjamin stop him?"

So it hadn't been a ploy by Tasha to get him to hire Nate. He'd pretty much let go of the idea, but it was good to know it for certain. "Yes. There was an incident Ben had to save me from. I was sedated, so I don't remember much. You didn't answer me. How do you know if you claim you're not close to Oakley?"

He wasn't certain about Huisman. Not that he was sure of anything at this point. Who the fuck was he supposed to believe? He was living in the moment when it came to Tasha, but he wasn't going to do the same with Huisman or Ben. Listening to Huisman, Ben sounded like he wanted revenge.

Sometimes there were good reasons for revenge.

"I've been spending time with him," the doctor replied. "That was the point of me coming down here. Oakley wanted to meet, and he tempted me with financing for a pet project of mine. Despite the rumors, I do not rule the Huisman Foundation with an iron fist, and my personal money is not limitless. I have some projects my board isn't interested in funding, hence I've come out here. I would have spoken about them to you this weekend, Mr. Nash."

Would have? "I thought that's exactly what we were going to do. Are you worried Oakley will try again?"

"I know he will." Huisman frowned and hesitated, as though he wasn't sure he should say whatever he was going to say next.

"Dr. Huisman, did you have someone placed in Oakley's organization?" Tasha asked. "Or did you start paying someone who was already there?"

A light flush stained Huisman's handsome face. "I became worried about Oakley when I learned of Mr. Middleton's convenient accident. I knew from briefly talking to him before that he would prefer to have Mr. Nash join us. I told him to simply invite who he liked."

"I wouldn't have come," Dare admitted. "I wouldn't have stepped on Lance's toes like that. It was his territory. My father wouldn't have asked me to go, either. He wanted Lance working with Oakley. It only changed when Lance died."

"That was when you got suspicious?" Taggart asked.

"I suppose I was always suspicious," Huisman admitted. "Oakley is a big personality. Maybe *suspicious* isn't the right word. Maybe it's *concerned*. I was concerned he would take over anything he touched. I was concerned if I allowed him to invest the way I wanted, that he would warp my projects. So I wanted some insight, and I was willing to pay for it. Oakley is a man of his class. He doesn't even notice lower-level employees when they do their jobs. But he doesn't pay them enough to keep them loyal. I bribed his housekeeper. I offered her payment for any information she could give me that might let me know whether or not I should allow Oakley to invest."

Dare thought there was more to it, but he wanted to stick to the important facts. "And she told you he tried to kidnap me?"

"She informed me that she'd been instructed to get a guest room ready at Oakley's hunting lodge. For the week of the conference. She thought it odd since she knew he planned to be at his penthouse here in Sydney and then in the Blue Mountains. The hunting lodge is a place he goes when he wants to be alone. It's in the… She called it something. Yes, the bush. She called it a shack in the bush," Huisman explained. "Very isolated. She also noted that he'd ordered his helicopter pilot to be on call all week despite the fact that he had nothing on his calendar that would have him leave Sydney."

"All of that is circumstantial and easily explained away," Taggart said.

"But his meeting with a man named Jeremy Kye was not," Huisman countered. "I'm going to send you a file with all the information I've gathered. Once I was suspicious I worried it was me he might be after. I had a private investigator follow Oakley, and he caught him meeting with a known mob associate. Kye specializes in getting witnesses to change their testimony. His MO is usually to kidnap them and change their thinking via torture."

"I'd like to read the reports," Taggart agreed. "How did you find out about Tandy?"

"I have tapes of the conversation with Mr. Kye," Huisman admitted. "They discuss what he wants from Tandy."

"Why not go to the police?" Tasha asked.

Huisman sat back in his chair. "Because Oakley owns a good portion of the police and the politicians here. You'll notice that they also speak around the subject, but I figured it out. I knew Benjamin was watching. I also know that he's joined the CSIS. I know because they opened an investigation into me and my family's foundation shortly after."

"You say family," Tasha began, "but you are the last Huisman. Your grandfather died a few years ago, and you never had brothers or sisters."

"I was not blessed with siblings, and my few cousins are gone now, too, but the foundation is my family at this point." Huisman sighed. "Once I considered Benjamin family, but that is over now, and I knew when he was here that there would be support from either CSIS or the CIA. You can imagine my relief when I learned it was Mr. Taggart and his team who were here. I know you have no reason to believe me, but I hope you will choose to act on the information I've gathered and save Mr. Nash. And perhaps many, many more. I chose to come to you because I believe the Agency will have more luck getting Australian intelligence and law enforcement to believe in the danger than I would."

That made sense, but they still had a problem. If Huisman was correct, then someone was coming for him. "I think Tasha should..."

Taggart held out a hand. "Stop. I need you to consider the next words that come out of your mouth, son. You seem to have started processing the whole betrayal thing, and that is great. You're moving along nicely, and you don't want to piss off your woman by playing into gender roles that have no place here. None. I assure you if Tasha's brothers were the ones in trouble, they would ask Tasha to please help them deal with the situation."

Because Tasha was trained and deadly. Because Tasha had a job to do.

One that would probably be so much easier if he just let her do it.

She was frowning his way. "What were you going to say, Dare?"

"I think Tasha should figure out how she wants to handle it." He knew when he was wrong. He was excellent at sales, but he did not know how to handle his own potential kidnapping, and in this case the little woman didn't need protecting. The little woman *was* the protector. It made him feel...useless again. If they were attacked, Tasha would defend him, but he might be able to do the same for her. He turned to the man who seemed to have all of the answers. "I want an extra service in our deal. You have to train me so I know how to fight."

Taggart's lips curled in a smile, a satisfied expression. "I can do that." He sat up and turned to his daughter. "What's it going to be, *dochka*? Fight or flight? I'm leaving this to you."

Tasha's shoulders squared as she nodded her father's way. "I'll make that decision in private, if you don't mind. Dr. Huisman, I appreciate everything you've done for us but..."

Huisman stopped and put his hands up as if in concession. "You don't know me, and you've only truly heard what Benjamin has said. He's been your friend so far. Believe me, I know how nice it is to be Benjamin's friend, but I warn you what can happen when he decides it's over. I believe I'll head back to Toronto this evening. I'll let Oakley know I won't be meeting with him. Tomorrow. I think it's better I tell him from the safety of my own home. And Mr. Nash, I do hope you find a way to deal with your father. He's involved with dangerous people."

The doctor started to walk away.

"Dr. Huisman," Taggart called out.

Huisman stopped and turned.

"I'm grateful as well. Please feel free to call me if anything else comes up," Taggart said with a nod.

Huisman's shoulders straightened, his head coming up. "I shall. And please tell Benjamin whenever he is ready to talk, my door is open. For old time's sake."

He disappeared out the door and neither Taggart nor Tasha's eyes left it for a moment. They both stared.

"*Chto ty dumayesh, dochka?*" Taggart asked.

"*Ya dumayu, chto on interesnyy chelovek,*" Tasha replied.

He was not getting cut out by the polyglots. "No Russian. Not until I understand it."

Taggart's brow rose, and he looked awfully amused.

It wasn't so surprising. He should learn an extra language. He'd always wanted to, and Russian would be...not helpful in any way in his business, but it would be if he wanted to fit in with the Taggarts. Which he didn't.

Tasha turned Dare's way. "He asked me what I thought about Huisman, and I said he's an interesting man. I meant that he's interesting in a way that we should watch him and be careful."

"But he helped us," Dare argued. "Or do we not believe him?"

"Oh, I believe him about what could happen to you," Tasha explained. "And we're going to talk about that. But I need more information before I decide whose side I come down on when it comes to Huisman and Ben."

"Huisman does a lot of good in the world." He wasn't sure why Taggart and Tasha would question the doctor. He'd come to help them. "He's very philanthropic."

"That would be an excellent mask." Taggart stood. "He looks good on paper, and Ben right now looks like a loose cannon. I don't like either. We'll keep an eye on both and try to stay out of Ben's orbit."

"That might be hard," Tasha said. "I think keeping my sister out of his orbit will be the real challenge. And if I have to pick between fight and flight, we're going to fly, Dad."

Her father pulled out his cell phone and stepped away.

It looked like he was going on the run.

Chapter Eighteen

Tasha had known she would get Dare out of Australia the minute Huisman showed up at their suite with her dad. The only question was how to do it and still have any shot at getting some important intel. Evening was coming on quickly and they had decisions to make, so she'd called the team together. After all, running with Dare instead of going to Oakley's would affect them all.

"And we trust Huisman?" Kala asked. "I don't like the fact that he showed up here. Our location is classified."

"He wouldn't need to read classified docs to find us," Tristan argued. "All he would have to do is follow Kara."

"You've been sloppy," Chet accused.

"No one followed me," Kala countered. "Maybe the problem was another whole team showing up to fuck with everything."

"Maybe you should have figured out you were literally working with a foreign operative," Chet shot back. "This is not our fault. We were ordered to sit back and let the Canadian do his job. We haven't been surveilling because Ben was worried Oakley's team would pick up that something was wrong. If we had been, trust me, none of this would have happened. I would have called Langley and let them know the baby team needed a diaper change."

She was ready to let them hash it out in a ring somewhere. Her sister would murder Chet and that problem would be over with, and Kala might be chill for a day or two.

Her mother sat at the end of the table. She'd been perfectly silent up until now, allowing Tasha to lead the discussion. Now she cleared her throat as if to say "move this along, daughter."

She was right. Kala killing Chet would be a whole lot of paperwork. "Whether we trust Huisman or not, we have to consider his intel is real. Someone did try to kidnap Dare a few nights ago."

"And would have succeeded if not for Ben Parker," Chet pointed out.

"Did you get anything out of the guy?" Tasha asked. "Where are you holding him?" She sighed at the look on Chet's face. "Tell me he died after you got what you needed."

One shoulder shrugged. "Parker was too rough with him. He was a corpse when we got there. I kind of wondered if he'd already talked and the Canadian killed him. He's not being real open with us, if you know what I mean. We could have avoided all of this if he'd given us Tash's name to run a check on."

"Understood." She didn't need him to tell her how fucked up things were. Tasha put both palms on the table, ready to explain how things were going to go. "I will be taking Mr. Nash out of Australia this evening. We're going to drive to a small airfield outside of Sydney. We'll fly to New Zealand, and from there we're taking a private jet and we'll make our way back to the States where we'll figure this out from there."

She would take him back to Dallas where they could watch over him.

"You can't take Nash out of the country. You're blowing the whole op." Her asshole ex sat across the table in the safe house along with TJ, who had a blank expression on his face. It was what she liked to think of as his soldier face, the one he used when he wasn't giving up a thing he was thinking.

"Our op was blown the minute the target was killed in an accident." Cooper sat back with a shrug.

Tristan shook his head. "Nah. I would say we've completed our op because we now have new intelligence on both Oakley and Huisman. Our op was to surveil and report. We have watched and gathered, and I'm ready to write a report that states everyone is fucked up. So we're done here."

Her team was seated around the dining room table in the safe house. They'd retreated after Huisman left. They'd walked out like they were going for an afternoon in the city, but Tasha knew they wouldn't go back. Nate and one of the guys would collect their things after Dare was safely away. They would hole up at Sanctum and decide what their next move should be, but one way or another Dare was going to be out of this.

"You are not done here." Chet sat across from her. He'd made sure he was directly in her line of vision, asking TJ to move over before he'd sat down. He'd stared at her like he could enforce his will. "You have already cost me an important ally."

When they'd arrived at the safe house, Ben was gone. Her father had gotten a call from Ben's handler who'd explained that Ben was coming off the op.

"I'm not sure why Ben was so important," Zach argued. "He was never going to be able to walk into Oakley's place. What was he thinking? Huisman would recognize him, so he would have to pull out of the op at this point anyway."

"I'm not sure Mr. Parker is capable of being rational when it comes to Dr. Huisman," her mom said quietly. "It might be for the best that he's not here."

"It might be best for you and your team, but it's shit for mine." Chet ran a hand over his barely-there hair. He kept it in an almost military cut. "I needed Parker, and I doubt he'll help us out again."

"I would have thought you could talk Ben into staying," Kala said. "After all, you're the one who's been working with him."

"Maybe if you'd been nicer, we wouldn't have this problem," Chet shot back.

"She's not going to fuck someone to make your life easier." Cooper had sat up, his eyes going steely.

"Well, Tasha fucked someone and made my life harder," Chet replied.

"Hey," Dare began.

Tasha put a hand over his. "He's not worth it."

Zach was leaning against the wall, not far from Chet. "I don't know. I think he could be worth it."

"You stay the fuck out of it, you pathetic twit." Chet stood, turning Zach's way. "Do you honestly believe I don't know? Everyone knows. I would think you would be on my fucking side. Maybe if that dumbass gets killed, you'll get another shot at Tash. Isn't that what you want? Do you think I don't know you're the one who sent her looking for me that day?"

Zach's shoulders had straightened, his eyes narrowing. "Well, it was better for her to figure out what an asshole you were before the wedding."

"And you thought you could slip in." Chet seemed determined to taunt the beast.

"Now is not the time to have this discussion." She was rapidly losing control.

"Wait, what are they talking about?" Tristan asked.

"Zach has a thing for Tasha, apparently." Cooper seemed to catch on. He looked at Kala. "Did you know about this?"

Kala shrugged. "Nah. I do not put my nose in that shit. It's hard enough to watch the crap that goes on between Lou and TJ. I don't need more longing looks in my life. I stay away from feelings. I'm sure Kenz knew, but she's still hiding out."

"Nah, she's screaming at me through the glasses." Lou winced and seemed to try to turn them down. "She wants to put a twenty on Zach."

"I will not take that bet," Cooper said. "Zach looks ready to eat Chet's innards."

"There's no crap between me and Lou," TJ protested, losing his stoic expression. "We're the best of friends. She's the only person in the world who actually knows me."

"Does Big Tag know you blew my op because you couldn't let Princess Tasha go?" Chet taunted.

Zach's lips curled up in a smirk. "Who do you think gave me the intel?"

She heard her father snort from behind her but didn't turn around because she couldn't take her eyes off those two.

Well, that fit a narrative. "I think we should get back to the problems at hand."

"The only person who knows you? Are you kidding me?" Kala faced off against TJ. "She might know you, but do you actually know her or do you use her to feed your never-ending ego?"

"Hey, TJ and I are friends. I don't know that I'd say we're best friends," Lou hedged. "Kenz, stop shouting. I can hear you."

"Seriously?" TJ was focused on Lou now. He had a kicked-puppy look on his face. "Is this because I wouldn't kiss you the other night? You have to know how much I want to. I told you why I thought that was a bad idea. Baby, I adore you on every level, but I'm not in a good place to settle down."

"You'll never be in a good place to settle down," Kala argued.

That was the moment Tasha realized Dare had moved. He'd gotten up and joined her dad, who was standing in the doorway that led to the kitchen. Her dad was leaning against the jamb and had a bag of chips in his hand. He offered some to Dare, who whispered something to her dad that had him explaining.

They were enjoying the drama.

Men.

They would be pulling out the beers next.

She didn't want to think about the fact that Dare seemed to fit in with her dad.

"Let's get back to the question at hand." It was time to take charge.

"Should you be talking?" Tristan directed the question Kala's way. "Dude, that is the pot calling the kettle black."

"Tris," Cooper warned.

Kala's brow rose in that "Taggart is about to explode" way of hers and their father's. "Really?"

"You think TJ's been stringing Lou along?" Tristan asked. "What have you been doing since we were freaking fifteen years old? You chased and chased him, and the minute he wanted you, you froze him out."

"I'm surprised you haven't found a way to get rid of the new guy," Chet was saying.

"I'm not going to get rid of him. Tasha loves him, and he's good for her," Zach replied. "I got rid of you because you're not good for anyone."

"I don't know that I would call it stringing me along," Lou said, biting her lip. "TJ's been clear about the fact that he doesn't like me that way."

"I do like you that way," TJ countered. "I just don't think it's the right time. You know you're the only girl in the world for me."

"Then why are there so many others?" Lou finally seemed to find some fire.

"To get back to…" Tasha began.

Her mother held out a hand. "No, I'd like to hear what he has to say."

Her mother was a menace, too.

"There hasn't been anyone who meant a damn thing to me," TJ replied. "Why don't we go somewhere and talk?"

"So you can convince her to give up more of her life for you?" Kala asked.

"The way Cooper does for you?" TJ turned Kala's way. "I'm there for Lou. Half the time you pretend like Coop doesn't exist. You know he built that whole fucking club for you."

"Hey," Coop said, standing and leaning over. "How about we not talk about this in public."

"I would watch your ass, Dare," Chet was saying, pointing Zach's way. "This guy will do anything it takes to get what he wants."

Dare looked up. "Should I get a mirror? I'm not sure how I should watch it. Zach, are you going to shoot me in the ass? I would suggest somewhere else. I think an ass can probably take a bullet pretty well."

Her father laughed and nodded her way. "I like him, Tash. You did good."

Tasha had enough. She stood up and slammed her fist on the table. "Stop it, all of you. It is obvious to me that you are all screwed up in numerous ways, but I'm not going to allow any of you to threaten this mission. TJ, Lou is going to start dating. Stay out of her way. Kala and Cooper, everyone knows there's way more to whatever fucked-up mess you have going, but you're both too stubborn to talk about it, and until you're willing to, keep it to yourselves."

"I'm not the one who mentioned it," Kala began with a frown.

Tasha wasn't done. She turned to Tristan. "You have zero room to talk about anyone. You are literally going to let the woman you love marry your best friend because…none of us knows.

That's your misery, brother, because you won't share it, but stay out of everyone else's drama if you don't let us in on yours." She turned to the worst of them all. "Chet, you slept with someone else. You knew damn well I wouldn't be okay with it. You fucked around and I found out. Zach saved me a lot of time."

"He could have saved me some money by telling you sooner," her dad interjected.

She pointed a finger her father's way. "You hush. You are not going to turn this into a soap opera for your entertainment."

Her father gestured around the room. "I don't have to. It plays out in front of me every day."

"He's right about that, baby," her mom said with an apologetic wince. "It's hard not to watch."

She gathered all of her willpower. "I am not leaving this open to debate. I am taking Dare out of here. The fact that Huisman is leaving the country will change Oakley's plans and potentially tip him off that something's gone wrong. It's time to pull up stakes and report back."

"You should have done that in the first place." Chet had his arms crossed over his chest. "If you had, we wouldn't be in this position. You're thinking with your pussy, Tash. And honestly, you're doing this as payback. You don't have to. When you're willing to admit you made a mistake, I'll be willing to discuss getting back together. You've had your fun with that asshole. I get it. Anything more is playing the whore."

"You want to deal with him?" Zach had gone a nice shade of red. He was staring Dare's way. "Or should I do it?"

She rolled her eyes and wished there was something she could do to lower the testosterone level in the room. Lou needed to get to work on a new device.

"I don't think either of us should fight him right now." Dare sounded perfectly reasonable.

"Thank you." Maybe they could get back to business.

"I think we should wait a while. Until he's forgotten this moment entirely and he thinks I don't care that he used that word in my presence and about someone I care about. A year or two should do it. Then we track the fucker down. I bet he ends up in dark alleys from time to time. We sneak up and slit the fucker's throat. I don't care if he's in pain as long as he's dead. See, I think the pain part is where most people screw up. Just get to the killing," Dare said.

"You are not allowed around my father anymore." She knew damn well who'd put that idea into her sweet man's head.

Her father held a hand up. "I swear to… Okay, we might have talked about it, but this is mostly his idea. I'm proud of you, son. Though a little pain wouldn't hurt if it was properly planned. See, this is where knowing a lot of people with BDSM clubs comes in handy. There's usually a torture room somewhere close."

"And kinksters are excellent when it comes to cleaning up," her mother added. "They know how to get blood out of anything."

"This is why no one thinks this team can ever work," Chet announced. "Sure, let's threaten to kill me. Let's not care about the fact that it's your fault we won't get the information we needed. I will make sure this goes into my report. You guys have a fucking blast playing at being operatives. You're a bad teen drama. Let's get out of here, TJ. I'm still your boss until we get back to the States."

"Come on, man," TJ protested. "I can't leave Lou like this."

Chet proved he was a dick. "You can and you will unless you want me to explain that your whole team fucked up and get every single one of you fuckers back on regular duty. Think they'll like losing the extra pay? I know Mike won't, and he's in control of your ability to be promoted."

TJ stood, his body at attention. "I'll get the team ready to move out." He glanced over at Lou. "Don't think this is over, LouLou. Not even close."

Lou didn't look at him as he strode out, but Tasha noticed she'd taken the glasses off. Likely because Kenz wouldn't stop talking in her ear.

Chet walked out, and they would probably have to face some nasty music when they got back because of him, but that was a problem for another day.

She took a long breath, hoping they could all calm down now.

"We need to decide how we're going to move out. I don't know that we should tip off Oakley if we don't have to," she began. "I do think we should talk to the Canadians about what's going on at Tandy, and we should do it before Dare's father gets a heads-up."

It occurred to her that this might be a good start to bringing Dare's dad down. They could do a lot of the work from Dallas, and if he was worried about his siblings, well, she would bring them to Dallas, too.

"I've already talked to Parker's boss." Her father took a seat at the table, which led Dare to retake his own.

"They're going to raid Tandy this evening. They're sending in a small team and trying to keep it as quiet as possible," Dare explained.

She should have known something was going on when her dad had taken Dare aside.

"The quiet as possible part is only to keep Oakley from hearing about it," Dare continued. "I've been assured if there are biological weapons being made there, the justice system will come into it. This might take my father out at the knees, and I won't ever have to deal with him again. He could be arrested by this time tomorrow. Quietly, of course. The CSIS agent promised me he could handle everything."

Her stomach threatened to take a dive. She'd thought it would take longer.

If his father was handled, there would be no real reason for Dare to stay in Dallas. If he was arrested later this evening, they wouldn't have to work together.

In fact, he would need to go home to deal with the fallout. There would be every reason for him to be in Toronto and stay there for a long time.

"So our problem now is keeping Oakley from knowing his plans have gone awry," her mother mused. "According to Huisman, at the very least, Oakley is trying to get a copy of the research they've done on the weaponized anthrax. He won't want CSIS to know about it. He could use the proof to force Dare's father to be on his side."

"Which would tip Tandy off, and they could hide the research," Cooper concluded. "So Oakley needs to believe this is going as planned. He's going to know Huisman is gone when he doesn't show up tomorrow afternoon. I'm worried if he figures out

Huisman is leaving that he might send someone to check in on Dare. Dare's the prize here."

"And we know the man doesn't mind showing up uninvited." Tasha shook her head. "I'm not risking it. If he shows up, he does, so you should work fast."

"I don't know if I like the idea of losing this chance to take down my father," Dare argued. "More than that, shouldn't we be concerned that there are people out there weaponizing anthrax? If anything Ben says is true, shouldn't we take the chance to avoid the possible attacks that could come from this?"

"CSIS and the Canadian authorities can deal with it," she explained.

"Unless they aren't able to," Dare replied. "I think I should stay around. We know he doesn't want to kill me."

"Don't be naïve, Dare." Cooper was calm again. "He might not want you dead, but if he thinks you're a threat in any way, he'll kill you."

"We're only trying to cover Dare leaving, right? We need Oakley to believe Dare is still in the suite getting ready to move out to the Blue Mountains tomorrow," Tristan mused. "So we take him in the front door and lead him out the back. We put him in a car with a bodyguard and drive him out to meet the plane. He's on his way in a few hours. Meanwhile, Tasha shows her face around the hotel. She orders room service for two, so if Oakley has eyes around, everything looks normal. She can answer the door wearing something that lets the staff know Dare is walking around naked somewhere in the suite and questions won't be asked. Not until the next morning when Tasha exits stage left and we all head home. Except me. I'm going to London to help set up the London office's new network."

"Sure," her dad said with a shake of his head. "Because the London office can't find anyone else to do it. You won't be able to hide forever, Tristan. But you do make a good point. If we can keep the fact that Dare isn't where he's supposed to be from Oakley, we might have a shot. I happen to know Oakley's got a cleaning crew going into his place in the mountains in a few hours."

"He knows that because we bribed the manager to let us put

one of our own crew on the team," her mom admitted. "Who's up to clean some toilets and download some files?"

Lou held up her hand. "My accent is shit, but no one expects me to talk anyway."

Zach frowned. "I don't think that's a great idea."

"We can't send one of the twins in. Oakley's seen them, and if he's got facial recognition on any of his security cameras she'll be screwed." Tasha wasn't thinking about the implications of Tristan's plan. She wouldn't be on the plane with Dare. She might not ever see him again if he decided he didn't want to. "Lou knows what she's doing."

"And I'll have Kenz watching over me." Lou stood and grabbed her glasses again. "If Tristan can take over the CCTV cameras at Oakley's place, we'll have good coverage, and I'll know if it's safe to make a try for the data. We can't send the guys. They don't look like they belong on a cleaning crew. I'm the best bet here. I can do it."

"I know you can," her father said. "Go and get ready. Tell Kenz to get her ass back here. Kenz and Tristan will monitor from here. Kala will drive Lou out and be ready if she needs backup. Cooper, you head to the airfield now. I want you to make sure the plane is ready to go and we don't have any surprises. I would go with you, but I need to be close to a secure line. The op with CSIS is going down in a couple of hours, and I'm coordinating for the Agency. I need to stay here so Zach can drive Dare out." Her father snapped his fingers. "Damn it. I think we should leave someone with Tasha. Someone who looks somewhat like Dare in case one of Oakley's people gets a glimpse of him."

She was about to protest that she could handle herself, but Dare stepped up.

"It should be Zach." Dare had a grim resolve on his face. "Zach looks a little like me and he'll protect her."

"It should be me," Zach agreed.

"Dare is not driving himself out to the airfield." Tasha reached for the only argument she could make. Things were going down way too fast, and she couldn't handle it. Not ten minutes before they'd had days, if not weeks, to sort things out, and now it was over and she might never have another moment alone with him. He was stubborn. He was set in his world view, and time away wouldn't fix things for them. If he left, they would likely be over.

Her mother slid her chair away from the table. "I'll do it. It's time to get back to my little nugget anyway. Travis is probably in a fetal position by this point, and my little guy needs his babushka."

"Travis should have worn a condom," her dad grumbled. "I'll fly back with Tasha and the rest of the team. All right. We all have our assignments. Tasha and Dare, you head to the hotel. Zach, make the switch away from prying eyes. Charlie will be waiting in the garage to take you to the airfield. Lou and Kala need to leave. Lou's shift starts this afternoon. Everyone else, we move out in twenty."

Twenty minutes and then a fifteen-minute drive and he would ride away forever.

She watched as everyone started to move, but she and Dare seemed stuck in their places.

This was it. The end, and it had come far sooner than she'd thought.

She stood and moved to Dare, taking his hand.

If this was all the time they had, she intended to make it count.

* * * *

Dare's head was still reeling when Tasha held her hand out.

He would be on a plane home soon. He could be out from under his father's boot in less than twenty-four hours. The Taggarts were making all of his dreams come true.

So why did he feel like he was standing at the edge of a cliff, ready to completely fall off?

"I need to talk to you." Tasha started to lead him out of the kitchen.

"Is there anything to talk about?" He wasn't sure more talking would help them. He knew what he had to do and what he owed his siblings. What he owed himself. "I think the parameters of the mission are clear."

There were tears in her eyes as she turned to him. "This is not a mission for me. Please. We don't have any time."

She would ask him to stay with her. Or ask if she could go

with him. Would she do that? Would that be a proper sacrifice to make up for her betrayal? To give up the job and family she loved.

How could he take her away from her family? Did he even want to? He wanted her but he wasn't sure he should. Her life was all about lies and subterfuge. She'd deceived him. Could he trust anything about her?

Still, he followed her through the small house, past the living room where her parents were talking, past the space where Zach was checking his weapons, getting ready to head out.

They were a better fit. He'd wanted Zach on Tasha duty because he knew damn well the soldier would take a bullet for her. Zach would do anything for Tasha, and one day she would look up and the handsome operative would be there and she would know it was right. Zach and Tasha made sense.

Dare would be nothing but a memory by then. He would be a vague memory in her head because her whole life was an adventure. He would be nothing but a bump in the road.

She would be the only thing in his memory, in his heart, because she was the only adventure he would ever have, the only one he would ever want.

She seemed to be maneuvering them to the back of the house, likely to step out on the patio to talk, but he suddenly didn't want to talk. They had so little fucking time. He found the door to what appeared to be an office and tugged on her hand, dragging her back and inside.

He slammed the door and locked it, turning her way.

"Dare," she began.

There was no reason to talk. There was nothing he hadn't already said, and he wasn't good at talking things through. He was a stubborn ass and he wasn't sure he could change, so this might be the last chance he had to show her how he felt, to have any space in her head and heart over the long and lonely years.

He slipped his hand around her neck, cradling it as he lowered his lips to hers.

Her whole body seemed to go on alert, and she pressed herself against him, her breasts crushing against his chest. She wrapped herself around him, holding on like she never wanted to let go.

A million scenarios played through his head. He hadn't had

enough time with her. He wanted to spank her, to tie her up and play with her ass and then force her to take his cock in her mouth. He wanted to spend hours torturing her, clamping her pretty tits and flogging her until her skin was pink and her arousal was the only scent he could smell. He wanted to take her to clubs and show off his sub and be so fucking proud to be her Dom.

He wouldn't get any of those things. Or the more dangerous things he wanted.

He wanted to hang out with her family and be a part of them. He wanted to know if Lou was going to smack TJ at some point, and if Kala would get her head out of her ass long enough to see how Cooper looked at her. Maybe Ben would show back up, and how fun would it be to watch him think he was dealing with one woman when it was actually two? One who actively loathed him and the other who was half in love. He wanted to sit next to his father-in-law at family gatherings and eat popcorn while the sparks flew.

He wanted to marry Tasha and be happy.

He wouldn't do any of those things. He would stay in Canada and take his place at the head of his family, and he would do it alone.

Like he'd always been alone.

He pressed her against the door, need surging through him.

"Dare, please," she whispered.

He had no intention of playing games with her this afternoon. He let his tongue surge into her mouth, stroking against hers as his hands found her breasts. He cupped them, memorizing the feel of them. She was so fucking soft and yet strong at the same time.

His cock lengthened, the sensation causing him to move his hips against her belly. The feel of her against him had him groaning.

He pulled at the hem of her skirt. He wanted to take his time, but that wasn't happening. Their last encounter would be quick and overwhelming emotionally.

Like their whole relationship.

Her hands clutched at him, running down to cup his ass as she kissed him back with everything she had. One leg ran up his, opening herself to him. He slid his fingers over her panties and wasn't surprised to find she was already hot and wet. She responded so beautifully to him. No other woman would ever respond to him the way she did. Like she'd been made especially for him.

Like they'd been made to fit together with a perfection that could only have been planned.

The minute he touched her pussy, his brain went on the fritz, only one thought in his head. *Bind her to him.*

Nothing mattered but being inside Tasha.

He somehow got his slacks undone, freed his aching cock. He pressed her against the door, pinning her. There wasn't time to get her out of those panties, so he simply shoved them aside. She shouldn't wear them. She should always be ready for her Dom. She should understand that he could want her at any moment—at every moment.

Her legs came around his waist as he drove up inside her. Pure pleasure threatened to swamp his brain. She was so fucking perfect for him, so tight and slick and hot. This was his home. Deep inside this woman, her body wrapped around his. This was as perfect as his life would ever get.

Tasha held on, tightening around him as he fucked her against the door, thrusting inside over and over again.

He wanted it to last forever, wanted to stay in this moment with her.

He kissed her as he felt her tighten around him, her orgasm sending him into his own.

He kissed her over and over again even as they came down from the high of pleasure. Even as reality crept in again. He kissed her because he couldn't think of anything else to do.

He kissed her until there was a knock on the door.

"It's time, Tash." Her father's voice came through.

She closed her eyes and hugged him. They were bright with tears when she opened them. "Dare, we don't have to go through with this."

But they did.

His body and brain were at odds as he stepped back, settling her on the floor again. She was the picture of passion, her hair and clothes disheveled. She was so fucking gorgeous it hurt to look at her.

"We'll be right out," he said as he zipped up his slacks.

Her eyes closed again, and she straightened her dress. "I'm going to clean up before we leave."

She opened the door and slipped out, and he was left with a judgmental-looking Ian Taggart.

"Bet you didn't even wear a condom," Taggart said with a steely gaze. "Don't think I'll let you get away with it the way I did that ditzball my son impregnated. Canada isn't big enough to hide your ass."

Taggart stalked down the hall as the words settled on Dare's soul, and he wondered if subconsciously that wasn't exactly why he'd done it.

Chapter Nineteen

Tasha closed the door behind her, locking it with a hollow pit in her gut.

He was gone.

Nate would make sure Dare made it downstairs to her mother, and then she wasn't going to see him again. They'd held hands in the car and then made a few public displays of affection as they'd sat in the bar and had a single drink. The conference was coming to a close, and Dare had several people who wanted to follow up with him next week when everyone was home.

Though they hadn't seen Oakley, they'd made sure everyone had seen them.

And then they'd walked up here and he'd strode away toward the stairs with Nate.

No good-byes.

She could still feel him moving against her, his passion pinning her to the door as she held on for dear life. Her last memories of Dare would be stamped on her brain forever. She would go to her grave wanting to be right back there where he couldn't hold out on her, where he'd shown her everything they could have had.

Had those final moments been her punishment for lying to him? Was he smiling because he knew he'd gotten back some of his own?

He hadn't used a condom. Even as he'd shoved her against the door, she'd known he wasn't thinking and she'd done nothing to stop him. Now she wondered if he'd done it out of spite, so he could leave her pregnant and alone.

Joke was on him since she was on birth control. A part of her wished she wasn't, wished she could hope to keep a piece of him with her always. She was so desperate and it was pathetic, but she couldn't help it.

"You okay?"

She started at the sound of Zach's voice. She'd known he would show up but not that he was already here. "How did you… Kenz told you about the ceiling."

Zach had the saddest look on his face as he stood in the doorway that separated the living space from the bedroom she'd shared with Dare. "I thought it was better than coming through the door. Now answer me. Are you all right, Tash? Anything he said to you… He doesn't understand the kind of work you do. You don't have anything to be ashamed of."

"I don't know about that." She felt infinitely tired now that it was over. She walked to the couch and sat down. Only nights before she'd lain on it with her head in Dare's lap as they'd watched a movie, and then he'd picked her up and carried her to the bedroom. All of the adrenaline of the day was gone, and she was sad. "I could have been honest with him."

Zach sank down beside her on the other end of the couch, a careful distance between them. "I would point out all the ways that would have been a bad idea, but I suspect you won't listen to me. You should know that I support everything you did. When we're standing in front of Drake and the big bosses, we'll present a united front."

She didn't even want to think about that upcoming torture. She was sure Chet had already filed a report on all the ways she'd fucked up. "I don't know. I've started to wonder if I'm right for this job."

"You're wondering if you can make things better between the two of you if you give up everything for him. You love your job. You believe in it. If the only way to be with him is to give up who you are, then he's not as good for you as I thought."

She'd considered this very subject as they'd driven back to the hotel. Dare had a career, too. "Wouldn't I be asking him to give up who he is if he moved to Dallas?"

"Who is he right now?" Zach asked. "He's under his father's thumb. The situations aren't the same, Tash. You love your job. He hates his. He doesn't have a big group of friends and family around him. He could. He could have your family. Don't think I didn't see how Ian took him under his demonic wing."

It was a joke in her family. Aunt Chelsea still called her dad Satan from time to time. "I don't think Dare's going to let himself love me, much less my family. I think he's going to bury himself in dealing with his siblings. You don't think being willing to move to Toronto would sway him to at least talk to me?"

She knew she was fooling herself. Dare might not have verbally said good-bye, but his body had. He'd given her everything in those final moments, and after, they'd been like zombies, all emotion spent. They'd moved with only the need to get through it.

"Darlin', if he can walk away from you, he doesn't deserve you." Zach's voice had gone low. "I know you don't want to hear that and especially from me, but it's the truth. I have no idea how he walked away. You lied to him, but you had a reason, and if he loved you, he would find a way to stay. He would spank you and you would be tied up at The Hideout for much of the next couple of months, but he wouldn't be able to walk away. Tell me something. Is there anything he could do that would make you leave him?"

There were plenty of things, but none that Dare would actually be capable of. "No. I would fight it out with him."

"I can go get him. I can knock some sense into him."

She had to deal with the Zach revelation. It appeared she wouldn't be leaving her job anytime soon. After all, it was all she had. She turned to him. "Zach…"

He held up a hand, his deep brown eyes trained on her. He really was a heartbreakingly beautiful man. If only she felt the same spark for him, her life might be easier. "We don't have to talk about it. I know it's never going to happen. I've had over a year, and you've never once looked at me the way you do Dare. Hell, you don't look at me the way you do Chet." He grimaced. "I don't regret that, Tash. I knew he didn't deserve you."

"I didn't realize how you felt about me. I always thought you viewed me like an annoying little sister," she admitted.

"I think I hid it pretty well, but no, I never once saw you as a sister," he admitted. "I thought you were green in the beginning, but you figured the job out quickly. You're gorgeous and loyal and smart, and you don't scare me the way your sisters do. They are utterly terrifying, and I'm not just talking about Kala."

She had to laugh. "Kenzie hides it well, but she's every bit as intense as Kala. I'm sorry, Zach. I don't feel that way about you. I care about you. I see you as a friend."

"And I'm happy to be your friend. Don't think I'm going to pursue you. I gave up on that. I didn't tell you about Chet because I thought breaking the two of you up would make you fall into my arms. I did it because you would have been miserable with him."

"I would have been. Dare is different. I really do love him. I don't know what to do." She sat there while Dare was in a car driving away from her. It felt wrong.

"You give him some time," Zach said with a sigh. "Maybe time and space will give him a different perspective. Of course, I could beat some sense into him."

"Absolutely not." She shook her head and took a long breath. Unfortunately, she thought Zach was being optimistic. Time wasn't going to solve this problem. Distance would only harden Dare's resolve. The only shot she'd had was staying close to him, giving him as much love as he could handle, and softening him up with warmth and sex and family. That was gone now. "We should order some food and make this look good. I would swear Dare and I had some eyes on us downstairs. I think Oakley might have one of his employees watching us."

"There are only a couple of people on this floor, so if we have food for two delivered, they have to think he's still here. Besides, we'll get a heads-up if anything goes weird. I know Tristan and Kenz are supposed to be watching Lou, but they'll still monitor the cameras here at the hotel." Zach stood and stretched his muscular body. "Is it too early to get some food?"

She glanced at the clock. It wasn't dinner time, but she could justify ordering early. After all, they would need to get an early start. "We'll call it a late lunch and get a snack later. What do you want?"

"Get me a steak and potatoes. And have them bring up a couple of beers. We're still on Dare's dime, so order dessert, too. We can watch a movie or something. I know this is rough on you, but you're not alone."

"Thanks. It's good to know I have my team. Well, I have them until the Agency decides we're bonkers and cuts us loose. I wish we hadn't aired all that dirty laundry in front of Chet," she admitted, getting up to grab the room service menu.

"He knew it all anyway," Zach replied, grabbing the remote.

"Yeah, but now he'll try to use it against us." It was good to think about all the other ways her life was fucked. It wasn't merely losing the love of her life. She might lose her career, too.

"I think you'll find the Agency will give your dad a lot of leeway." Zach turned on the big TV. "They know damn well he'll be out of here if his kids aren't working for them. I wouldn't worry about it too much. Well, not now that Big Tag slapped me upside the head, told me he'll kill me the next time I don't call him, and then went about his business. I figure that was his way of telling me I'm not fired."

"He was never going to fire you." She dialed room service and put in their order before rejoining him on the sofa. She probably wouldn't eat any of the pasta she'd ordered, but she had to make it look good. Tomorrow they would call for the bellman and look to the world like they were heading out to join Oakley. If Dare got a call from him, he would handle it, not letting the man know he wasn't where he was supposed to be.

In less than twenty-four hours they would be back to something like normal.

"What do you want to watch?" Zach asked.

She didn't care. "Anything but a romance."

She settled in and stared at the screen, not really seeing anything but Dare's handsome face.

Forty minutes later there was a chiming through the suite. Zach was already in the shower. The door to the bedroom was open, and he would pick his moment to move across the room, letting the room service attendant see that a big, dark-haired man was in the room.

He looked enough like Dare that if he didn't show his face, the attendant shouldn't question it.

She opened the door and allowed the man with the cart in.

He started to set up the elegant table, uncovering the well-presented meals for her approval.

"Dare, food's here," she called out.

"Be right there, babe."

She checked her phone while the waiter was fussing over making everything perfect. It was odd because she didn't have any bars. They hadn't had trouble with the signal while she'd been here. "Babe, you might check your phone."

It was likely nothing, but she couldn't let it go. If they didn't have signal then the CCTV cameras in the hall would be out, too. They were on a wireless network.

She forced a smile on her face as she signed the check and handed it back to the attendant. She'd been right. She didn't want to eat. It had been a mistake to not order a bottle of wine. That held some appeal.

"Thank you so much," she murmured, following the man to the door so she could lock them in. She would feel safer then. She would use the landline to call Tristan and figure out what was going on.

Zach would be pissed, but they were not touching that food. They were going to be on protein bars tonight. She wasn't risking it. All it took was one domino to fall and they were screwed.

The attendant left and she turned, ready to deliver the bad news.

Zach stepped out of the bedroom, wearing nothing but a towel, his hands in the air. "I think it's safe to say someone is jamming our signal. And they knew about the ceiling. Which I find interesting. Tell me something, Mike, what did you do with TJ because I know damn well he's not involved in this."

Her heart seized as she realized there was a man in all black behind Zach, holding a semiautomatic to his back. He had a mask over his face, but Zach had obviously figured out who he was.

"Where's Dare Nash?"

Fuck and double fuck. She had to save this. She held her hands up. "He's not here. What's going on, Mike? You're the operations sergeant for my cousin's team, right? You do understand we're on the same side."

"How the fuck would I understand shit when no one cares about my rank because my last name isn't Taggart," the burly man said. "Do you know how it feels to have that dipshit sit in on briefings I should be in? And we're not on the same side of this. Not in any way. Isn't that right, boss?"

"Did I catch you in the act, Tash?"

Chet. She would know that self-satisfied tone anywhere. Damn it. She turned, her hands coming down.

"You finally giving Zach what he's been begging for?" Chet moved in. Like his teammate he was dressed in all black, though he hadn't bothered with a mask. "I did not think you were quite this much of a whore, baby. I should have known because you were always so hot in bed. I do miss that part. As to the TJ question, I sent that asshole home with the rest of the team. They think I kept Mike back because technically he's the head of the team and we're the ones who are going to have to explain what happened. So don't think your cousin is coming to save you."

"I think TJ has an accident coming in his future," Mike proclaimed with a humorless laugh. "So sad, but it's a dangerous job."

"What the fuck are you doing, Chet?" Tasha asked.

"I'm saving my ass. You blew up this op, and my career was already on the line because your father's been badmouthing me. My boss is all over me right now, and I know why."

"Because you're sloppy and you rely far too much on what you think is your charm and looks?" She was so done with Chet.

"Because your father wants me out. Well, guess what, sweetheart, there's a faction at the Agency who wants him out," Chet said, his voice a silky threat. "Taggart is old school, and there's a new wave coming. He's going to hold us all back, and I can't have that happen. I think the old guy might think twice about his precious angels working for the Agency if his oldest gets herself killed."

"Hey," Zach began.

Oh, this was far more dangerous than she'd imagined. At first she'd kind of thought Chet was just preening. This was serious. "Zach, stop. Chet, killing me isn't going to do anything but send my family after you. Do you want that? You think my father's the problem, but you have no idea what my mother is capable of."

"I've heard the stories. I don't believe any of them," Chet admitted. "Your mom is a nice piece of ass, but she's not some killer. She'll cry and start taking a shit ton of valium and beg her husband to save the daughters she has left, and that will be the end of this stupid fucking experiment. Without a team behind them, I suspect Cooper will go back to flying brass around in a helicopter and Tristan will burn out. We all know that fucker has a death wish. I will have solved all the problems, and I didn't even have to marry you to do it."

"You touch a hair on her head..." Zach began.

Chet reached out and grabbed her hand. She wanted to fight but she had to stay calm if she was going to have a chance to save Zach.

Chet pulled her back against his body, his arm snaking around her waist. "I've touched her, Zach. Doesn't that kill you, you pathetic piece of shit? I've touched her everywhere. Maybe I'll touch her again before I let Oakley kill her. He'll be pissed I didn't bring him Dare, but I think that fucker will come running from wherever you've got him hiding once he finds out Oakley has you. And then Oakley will give me everything he has on Disrupt Australia, and I'll be a hero. Your father will go after Oakley, and he'll find that disturbs some people at the Agency. And CSIS."

Ben. "Ben told us Oakley was dirty, too."

"Our friend Ben only cares about taking down Huisman. Do you want to know the funny thing? Still have no idea if that doctor has anything to do with it. I think Parker wants revenge, and he'll do whatever it takes to get it," Chet explained. "Now we only have a couple of minutes before whoever's watching figures out I jammed the signals. Mike, do what you have to."

Tasha pulled away, trying to send her elbow up and back, but Chet held her tight, and she felt something burn against her neck.

Immediately her vision went blurry, but she heard the ping of a weapon going off.

In the distance she heard the sound of a siren even as blood bloomed across Zach's chest. His eyes met hers as he fell to the carpet.

"Fuck. Let's go. I would bet those cops are coming here," Chet was saying, but his voice sounded far away even though she knew he'd picked her up. She was being held in his arms as they started to move out. "Fucking Lou. She would have called the minute she realized the signal was down."

It wasn't Lou, but she couldn't correct him. Lou was at Oakley's getting the intel they needed, the intel that would prove he was dirty and he was working with Chet. Her team would figure it out.

But it would be far too late for Zach. Too late for her.

She prayed her mom protected Dare as the world went dark.

* * * *

"So I should update you. The CSIS team is planning on raiding Tandy in the next two hours. We should know something concrete by morning." Charlotte Taggart looked cool and chic as she drove down the road that would take them out of Sydney.

They'd been driving for half an hour without much talk. First they'd dropped Nate off at the safe house where he was going to watch over Kenzie and Tristan, who were planning tomorrow's op at Oakley's big cabin. Lou would "clean" Oakley out of any information that might seem useful, and then they would all be leaving Australia by tomorrow night.

Tasha would be back in Dallas. Or DC? "Is the team going to Dallas or do they need to go to DC?"

A brow rose over Charlotte's blue eyes. "I tell you they're raiding your father's facilities and you want to know where Tasha's going?"

He shouldn't have asked. But damn it, he wanted to know. Still. "I asked about the team."

"Sure." Charlotte expertly maneuvered the Mercedes sedan onto the freeway. "You're concerned about the team. Well, the team will be back in Dallas, and we'll get called in on some ferocious conference calls. We don't actually spend a lot of time in DC. We've got a conference room at the office with some high-tech security measures when it comes to the Internet. It's next to impossible to hack that particular system, though we do go out to Langley if the big bosses are paranoid enough. I doubt that will happen this time."

"Is she going to be in trouble?"

Charlotte waved him off. "It's nothing for you to worry about. Oh, I had to tell the flight crew what we wanted for dinner. I hope you like lasagna. It was the best they could put together on short notice. If we were in Dallas, I would have my brother-in-law send over some food. You haven't lived until you've had Sean's...well, everything."

He didn't want to talk about dinner. "How bad could it get for Tasha? Can that asshole mess with her career? I'm surprised he's still walking around."

"If I allowed my husband to kill everyone who annoyed him, there would be very few people left on earth," Charlotte replied cooly. "I know everyone thinks he should be this crazed alpha male who bashes the head in of anyone who looks twice at his daughter, but that's not a realistic way to live. Tasha made a mistake. I'm glad we figured it out before she was married to him. Chet's a dumbass, and I doubt very much he'll try to do something to get her fired. That *would* attract my husband's attention. Although sometimes I think he wouldn't mind. It's hard to know our girls are out there risking their lives."

"You could tell her no."

She chuckled. "I don't think you've ever tried to tell her no. She doesn't take it well. I mean, she's fine hearing a no about something like 'do you want to eat now' or 'did you like that movie.' The no doesn't work so well when it's about her future and her career. Women tend to like to decide that stuff for themselves. This job wasn't Tasha's dream job. She took it on because her sisters were going in. And Lou. Those four were always together. I'm glad their cousins Devi and Daisy didn't feel the need to save the world. Anyway, I'm not sure Tash had a dream job. I think mostly she wanted to take care of the people around her, to be part of whatever her family was doing."

"She could have done that in the security company. She could have answered phones or something," he muttered. It made him nervous that she was still out there. He'd thought having Zach protect her would ease his mind, but it wasn't. He couldn't get it out of his head that she would be in danger and he wasn't there to protect her.

Not that he would be great at it. She knew more about physical combat than he did, but he should be there to throw his body in front of hers.

"I don't think Tasha would like the receptionist job," Charlotte mused. "We've been through a few since our last long-term receptionist left to get married. Maybe Tash should think about taking the job. It seems to be an excellent way to get married."

"She doesn't want to get married." Tasha seemed to want to have fun, to have adventures. "She's nowhere close to settling down."

"Uh, I think I know my baby girl. Trust me. The whole Chet thing wasn't about falling for him. She was attracted to him and convinced herself she could love him. She wanted to start her life. I told her more than once that she was being impatient. My daughter wants to start her family. Maybe now she'll take another look at Zach."

"Why? If she hasn't up until now, there's zero reason to think she'll fall in love with him." Hadn't he been thinking about this scenario an hour ago? He'd tried to tell himself he would be okay with that outcome, that those two kind of belonged together.

He shouldn't care. He should be focused on what was happening in Toronto.

"Tasha is resilient. She'll figure it out. She'll mourn you for a while, but my daughter will move on with her life. If you're feeling guilty, you shouldn't. She'll find a way to build the family she wants. Zach is perfect, when you think about it. He knows who she is and what her work requires. He fits in well with her family. He's a solid guy."

He didn't like a word coming out of Charlotte's mouth. Every single one rankled. And he wasn't feeling guilty. He didn't have anything to feel guilty about. "But she doesn't love him."

"No, but the man she does love has chosen poorly, and there's not a lot we can do about that."

Ah, so Tasha's mom was trying to put him in his place. "Chosen poorly? She lied to me. Actually, everyone lied to me."

"I don't recall lying."

"You weren't here. Would you have?"

"Absolutely. We're on a mission, Dare. It's an important one. I also would have given Tasha the go-ahead to bring you in after I'd studied you for a few days," Charlotte admitted. "I would have told her to trust you. If she'd told you, how do you think you would have reacted? Would it have been different if she'd told you herself?"

"I don't know." He hadn't really considered it. He'd been far too involved in what had happened to think about hypotheticals. What if Tasha had come to him of her own accord? What if she'd held his hand and told him everything and explained what she needed from him, told him she cared for him and didn't want this to change their relationship. It would still have been a lie. He would still have felt foolish and surrounded. "I want to say it would have changed something, but I can't. I would still have looked around and realized I was surrounded by people who lied, by predators."

"Predators?"

"Isn't that what you are? You're a pack of wolves, Mrs. Taggart. As much as your husband amuses me, I recognize how dangerous he could be. I'm surprised he didn't beat the shit out of me this afternoon."

"For the condomless sex? You'll catch hell for that for the rest of your life," she admitted. "Well, you would if you stuck around. I guess that's a good reason to go. Don't worry about it. Tasha's on birth control." She looked his way. "You didn't like that."

"What? Of course I do. I'm glad we don't have anything to worry about." Except he'd kind of held on to that worry. He would have to talk to her at least one more time to make sure she wasn't pregnant.

And if she had been, he couldn't leave his child fatherless.

Like that would happen. Tasha would have ten men stepping up to the plate. She wouldn't be alone for long. Her mother was right. She would briefly mourn him and move on.

"You call us wolves, and that seems to scare you," Charlotte began, her tone softer now. "Are you hesitating because of anything my husband and I have done?"

Charlotte couldn't fix this problem. "You are wolves. No matter how you wrap yourself in designer wear or Ian plays the laid-back sarcastic guy. Kala is an obvious predator, but Kenzie's one, too. The world you move through is harsh, and I don't think there could be a place for me there. I've spent my whole life with a wolf at my throat."

She laughed, though there wasn't a lot of humor behind the sound. "No, you haven't because your father isn't a wolf, and he's never been. Your father is a jackal. He's a shark. He's a lone predator who thinks of nothing but his own hunger. You fundamentally misunderstand what it means to be a wolf."

"So you don't deny it?"

"Absolutely not," Charlotte declared. "I'm not sure I was born a wolf. I don't know if I would have become one had my father not murdered my mother and taken my sister and I back to Moscow. He was the head of a syndicate. He thought it would be fun to have a teenage girl assassinate his enemies."

"I would think that's an excellent reason to become a jackal."

"Ah, but I already had a pack," she corrected. "I couldn't fight my father because he used my sister against me. He hurt Chelsea to punish me. I had to protect her. Like you have. You are a wolf. You just haven't found your whole pack yet. You're a young wolf protecting even younger wolves, and no one taught you. You had to figure it out yourself. That's the difference. The jackal is alone and likes it that way. The jackal uses those around him to feed his own hunger, never thinking of anything but himself. The wolf pack protects its own. You could have a pack. You've done so well on your own. You've protected them since you were a child."

"It sounds like you did the same. Didn't you choose your sister? How can I choose myself?"

"There's no choice to be made here. Your siblings are welcome in our pack. One way or another your father will go down," Charlotte promised. "If you need to be in Toronto for a while, I think you'll find Tash would go with you. There's a time to pick your siblings and a time to form your own pack. I had to make that decision long ago. I had to pick my husband. It didn't mean I left my sister behind, only that every decision I faced had to be made with him in mind, with him at my side. If it helps, my sister is still in my life. She's still my closest friend. She will never admit it, but her life started when I made that choice."

A pack. A family. His father had never cared about family except how his looked to society. "I don't know what I would do. Sit around and wait for her to come home?" He shook his head, realizing how that sounded. "Not that women haven't done that for years. I don't want to bring Tash to Toronto. I want to be done with everything my father built. I want something new. Her career is important to her."

"Oh, you are coming along nicely," Charlotte said with a satisfied smile. "It just so happens that a new position has opened up at McKay-Taggart. We need a head of sales and marketing. I bet there would be a lot of travel involved. See, jobs make excellent cover for an operative and her husband. No one would think twice about Tasha being in Europe if her husband is taking meetings."

He could be her cover.

She wanted a life of adventure, a life with her family. He could be part of her family. Part of her pack.

He wouldn't have to be alone. Ian and Charlotte Taggart could teach him how to protect his own pack when the time came.

"Don't let stubbornness cost you both. When Tasha says she wants you, she's not pretending. She's not lying or manipulating you. She says it because she loves you, and if there's one thing my daughter knows how to do it's love someone. She is loyal and steadfast. You will never find another woman who can love you the way she will," Charlotte said quietly.

"You drove me so you could sell me, didn't you?"

"Did it work?"

He was a wary man, but he was a man who knew damn well a good deal when it was sitting in front of him. "I was serious about the physical training. If I'm going to be her cover, then I need to be her backup, too. And turn this fucking car around. I'm not leaving without her."

Charlotte swerved across two lanes to take the exit that would bring them back into the heart of Sydney. "I'll have to call Ian and let him know persuasion won. I'll take you back to the safe house. Call Tasha and let her know you'll meet her there in the morning."

He pulled his cell out and dialed her number.

"Hello, Dare."

That wasn't Tasha's voice.

"Who is this?"

Charlotte kept driving, but her hands tightened around the steering wheel.

"Who do you think it is, boy?" The man had a thick Australian accent.

"Oakley. What are you doing with Tasha's phone?"

He heard Charlotte curse under her breath, and she pulled over at the first parking lot she could find.

Dare put the phone on speaker.

"Well, I sent my friends there to pick you up, but they only found your girlfriend. She's already here. I had her brought to me by helicopter," Oakley said. "You can come to my place and trade yourself for her or I can kill her."

Terror wound around his heart. He'd taken Tasha? What had happened to Zach? "I'll come. I need to know where it is."

"I'm sending you an address," Oakley replied. "I expect you to be there in an hour, and if I get a hint that you're not alone, I'll put a bullet in your bitch. Is that clear? You can make it through this. If your father gives me what I need, I'll send you on your way. But she won't live if you don't show. Am I plain?"

"Yes. I'll be there."

The phone call disconnected.

Charlotte was immediately on her cell, calling her husband.

"Charlie, baby, I have to call you back. We've got a situation," he said. "Someone jammed the wireless at the hotel. I don't like it. I'm making my way over now, but traffic sucks and I can't get Tash on the line."

"Because Oakley has her." He didn't wait for Charlotte to speak. She was Tasha's mom, but he was going to be her husband. He had to take the lead on this. Not when it came to planning. He would leave that to the experts, but he had to make it plain that he wouldn't be left out. "He'll trade her for me, but you need to send an ambulance because I can't imagine Zach let her go without a fight. If he isn't already…"

Had Tasha been forced to watch her friend die? He'd done that. He'd insisted Zach be the one to stay with Tasha. He'd fucking done it because he'd known Zach would do anything for her.

"Kenzie sent police to the hotel the minute we realized someone was jamming the place," Ian admitted. "I'm going to find out what happened. You get back to the safe house."

"I can't. I have to be in the Blue Mountains in an hour. Oakley is willing to exchange Tasha for me, but I can't bring anyone with me." Now that he was thinking about it, that part made no sense. Unless Oakley had other plans. "He's going to kill Tash no matter what, isn't he?"

It made his blood run cold.

"Yes, and when you're sitting there telling yourself you shouldn't have left her, understand if you hadn't, she would likely already be dead. You're a prize to trade back to your father. They don't need Tasha except to draw you in. They will keep her alive until they're sure they have you," Ian explained. "Once they have you, there's no reason to keep her alive."

"Dare, you have to know we can't let you go alone," Charlotte began.

Did she think he was dumb? He'd learned. "I won't be. I suspect my pack can take this asshole down. But you should know Tasha comes first. No matter what happens. Tash comes first."

"I'm not letting my first son-in-law die," Ian said. "You're the first time she's had good taste. I'm not risking another Chet. Charlie, baby, start driving. I'll send you a meet spot. Be careful."

"I love you," she said and hung up.

Dare programmed the address from Oakley's text into the vehicle's GPS and sat back, his heart still thudding in his chest.

"Hold on. I think we can make it, but it's going to be tight," Charlotte said and started out of the parking lot. "The good news is Kala is already there. She and Lou went out to his cabin this afternoon. If Kala can get her out, she will."

And if she couldn't, it would be up to him.

He would save Tasha. If it was the last thing he did...

Chapter Twenty

Tasha lay on the cold floor, trying to keep her panic level to a minimum. She had no idea where she was or who was watching her, but she could hear voices coming from her right. Not close. She would bet whoever was talking was standing right outside the room.

"What do you expect me to do with her?"

Fucking Chet. Her head throbbed as it all came back to her.

Zach. They'd shot Zach. Zach was dead. She was in Chet's custody. Or Oakley's, perhaps.

She was on the floor, cold concrete against her cheek. Her hands were bound behind her back. She would bet it was zip ties. Her legs were free, but it was hard as hell to run when her arms were tied.

"I expect you to take care of her before we bring Nash back," Oakley demanded. "You'll take video of her as proof of life. I'm certainly not dragging her out in the field. Anything can happen out there, and I believe in mitigating my risks."

"I thought you would…" Chet began.

At least the fucker was having second thoughts about actually killing her.

"Do you want what I have on the rest of the group? Do you want the truth about the Canadian?" Oakley asked.

She could practically hear Chet standing up taller. "I'll get it done. But you better give me what I need. You have no idea what her father will do if he ever connects me to this. I was careful. I know CCTV didn't pick me up, but if he even gets a hint… All I'm saying is that fucker is dangerous."

He should be more worried about her mom and sisters. Her dad was a freight train they would all see coming. Her mother would smile and cry prettily and then stab that motherfucker in the back, but only after she'd fed him his own balls.

They were going to kill her. Her parents were going to kill her. Her sisters would never let her live this down.

If she survived.

She had to get away. If she didn't show, Dare would run. Dare was with her mom. They would have a plan, but it would work far better if she wasn't there to be a distraction.

Or would that mean they lost the chance at Oakley? She couldn't exactly go on the evening news and testify that he'd kidnapped her. The Agency would want her to protect her identity.

"Guys, she's awake," another familiar voice said.

She groaned because she hadn't realized Mike was sitting a couple of feet away.

There was nothing to do except sit up. At least now she could start to get her head clear. Her arm ached as she moved.

That asshole. Chet had taken out her locator chip. She'd had it implanted in her upper right bicep when she'd joined the Agency.

"Hurts like hell, doesn't it?" Chet stared down at her. "It's so much better to simply have your tech override the system and show you're on a plane back to the States."

"My father will still find me. Do you think he can't put two and two together?" She wasn't sure what the fucker was thinking. Damn, her arm ached. There was a rudimentary bandage around it. "TJ knows you're not on the plane."

"TJ can fuck himself. He thinks I went on another plane because I'm heading to Langley and he's going back to his base. And I won't worry about him for long. Like I said, I have an accident planned for your cousin," Chet said with a shrug. "I always knew I would either be a part of this family and enjoy the privileges that come with being a Taggart, or I would destroy you all. You chose my path when you broke off our engagement. I know your father's been messing with my assignments. What I'm coming back with will put me on top, and no one will be wiser. I'll have brilliantly done my job and your dad will have gotten one of his operatives killed. And a target, since I doubt Nash survives the experience."

"I planned on giving him back to his father." Oakley stood beside Chet, towering over the man. "But I think that's likely impossible now. He'll tell Taggart I'm the one who took his daughter."

Chet had a smirk on his face, one that just dared her to tell.

He was such an asshole. He hadn't told Oakley anything. Chet had to have a good idea that a member of her family was watching over Dare and would likely be there when Oakley showed up. Chet and Mike would be gone once they got the intel.

"Don't you want to know what he's planning on stealing from Dare's father?" She couldn't tell Oakley her parents would likely be at that meeting with Dare.

Chet was playing a dangerous game. He was counting on her father taking Oakley out before he could give Chet up. If she and Zach were dead, no one could tell her dad Chet had anything to do with it. The records would show he was on a plane heading over the Pacific at the time of her death, and there wouldn't be anything her dad could do legally. He might not even suspect Chet since up until this moment she wouldn't have thought he would be capable of doing something like this.

"I don't care." Chet looked down at his watch. "You should get going if you're going to make the meeting with Dare. Mike, didn't you say you caught his car on CCTV?"

Mike nodded. There was a laptop on what looked like a big stack of some kind of fertilizer bags. "Yep. I got him coming down the A32 a couple of minutes ago. He's going to be on time. Should be turning onto the road that leads to your land any minute. He had to have driven like a bat out of hell. You're looking for a white Mercedes."

Oakley stared at him for a moment as though trying to figure out what was wrong with the scenario. Likely intuition was telling him his American "friends" were up to something, but he couldn't figure out what. He pulled out his cell. "Hey, Willie, you see a white Mercedes coming up the road?"

Whatever Willie said had Oakley nodding and hanging up.

Chet and Mike looked at him, calm expressions on their faces.

She had to admit. They were good. She wished so badly that she could tell Oakley everything and watch the bloodbath that would ensue, but that would merely blow up whatever plan her parents had implemented.

Dare was coming for her.

Or maybe he wasn't and they were putting Tristan or Cooper in his place.

Had he cared at all? Or had he been grateful it was over?

"I'm going to pick up Nash," Oakley announced. "You stand by with the phone I gave you. When you get the signal, livestream her as proof of life. Before I take Nash with me, I'll send you the coordinates to the intel I promised. Do not let that bitch say a word, do you understand?"

"I think I can handle it," Chet promised. "You'll get your proof of life, and we'll take her body with us. You have to deal with Nash."

Oakley started for the door of what seemed to be a large gardening shed. "I'm taking him someplace safe. I'll handle it from here. You be gone by the time I get back. I don't want to see your face again. If you don't use that material the way we agreed on, you'll discover I can find you no matter how hard you try to hide."

"No worries, mate," Chet replied with a jaunty salute. "I'll happily take a cushy desk job and let the idiots of the world put their lives on the line, and you can feel free to kill as many people in Third World countries as you like. Have fun, man."

Oakley left, slamming the door behind him.

She had maybe ten, fifteen minutes to figure out how to get away from two trained operatives. "He doesn't know Dare was with my parents."

Chet's smirk kicked up a notch. "Nope. Idiot thinks Dare wasn't in the suite at the time. Doesn't have any idea I put Zach out of his misery. He has no idea Zach even existed. He thinks you're exactly what you presented yourself to be—a girl trying to make her way in the world by fucking a rich dude."

"My father is going to kill him, but you're counting on that," she said.

"I am," Chet agreed. "You see, when I go to my bosses with the intel Oakley's handing over, I'll be untouchable."

Somehow she doubted that. "My father won't take things at face value no matter how carefully you've covered your tracks. He'll want to know how you got the intel. If it leads back to Oakley, he'll definitely have questions. My father is dangerous when he's curious."

"It won't matter. I'll have brought the Agency invaluable intel about a group of anarchists who are planning an attack on a vulnerable government in Southeast Asia. I'll stop that attack, and I'll be the golden boy," Chet promised.

"Meanwhile, Oakley gets weaponized anthrax he'll use to kill hundreds of thousands," she said.

That stopped Chet. His expression shuttered. "You can't know that."

So her asshole ex didn't know everything. "I know what he wants from Dare's father. He wants either the anthrax itself or the protocols for how they enhanced it."

Mike shook his head. "Taggart will take the asshole out before it gets that far."

A long breath went through Chet. "That's right. Look, Mike, why don't you give me a moment with my ex?"

A brow rose over Mike's dark eyes, and then his lips quirked up in a knowing smirk. "Sure thing, boss. You only have about ten minutes before I expect Oakley will call in. You sure Taggart won't take him out before he sends the coordinates?"

"Big Tag will want proof of life," Chet assured him. "We send that, get the coordinates, and we're out of here."

And she would be dead.

Mike put his laptop aside and walked to the door, closing it behind him.

She was alone with Chet, and she had to figure out how to get away.

"I wish you weren't so pretty," Chet said with a shake of his head. "I know everyone talks about how hot your sisters are, but you really are a work of art."

His hand came out, tilting her chin up.

"Yeah, well somehow you're not as attractive as I thought you were."

He stared at her for a moment. "I wonder what you could have been if you hadn't been saddled with that asshole of a father."

Her father was the best man she knew, and Chet didn't deserve to breathe the same air.

Dare had immediately taken to her dad, like he'd known Ian Taggart could be the kind of father he'd always longed for.

"This isn't going to work out the way you think it will. My dad won't simply be upset about my death. He'll want to know what happened to Zach, too. His body wasn't left at a place Oakley owns. There will be some trace of you."

"I was careful, baby." He smoothed back her hair like they were lovers. "He'll think what I want him to think. I do wish I'd had more time. I could have put another couple of bullets in that asshole. You do know I never wanted this to happen, right?"

She noticed Mike was standing at the window, his back silhouetted against the opaque glass, proof that even if she could handle Chet, she would have another problem standing in her way. "I don't care."

Chet sighed. "She didn't mean anything. You are the only woman I've ever loved."

"And you're about to kill me."

"Well, it turns out I love me more. But you should understand that I'll think about you forever, Tash. He had you a couple of times, but you're going to be mine forever."

"Are you going to take my body and keep my corpse close?" She wouldn't put anything past him.

She could headbutt him from this angle if she could get to her knees.

"Baby, I'm leaving your body here for your family to find. I'm not dumb. I do understand forensics. It's why I'm not going to do what I want to do. I want one more time with you, but I wouldn't put it past your dad to be thorough when it comes to investigating your murder. I just wanted to be the last man to have you."

He'd never seen her as anything more than a possession.

She was about to tell him what she thought of him when she

noticed Mike's head jerk and then his body slide down the wall.

Like he'd taken a very quiet head shot.

Like her team hadn't needed a locator chip to figure out where she was.

She needed to give whoever was out there as much of a chance as she could.

That meant giving Chet a little bit of what he wanted. Out of the corner of her eye she could see the door beginning to open.

She tilted her head up and gave him her biggest, widest eyes. "Do you think I wanted to leave you? I loved you, Chet. I knew my family hated you, but I still chose you."

He was staring at her lips.

He really was a dumbass because he wasn't paying a lick of attention to the woman sneaking up behind him.

"And then you left me," Chet murmured. "Baby, if I thought there was any way I could keep you…"

Lou put a gun to the back of his head. "Don't make me vomit. I'll have to clean it up myself."

Because she'd been playing the maid at the main house. Now Tasha knew where she was.

Chet went still. "Hello, Lou. I'm surprised they sent you."

She could see him calculating how to move to throw Lou off. The only problem was Lou wasn't alone.

Kala had her SIG trained on Chet. "And me. Hey, asswipe. Long time, no see. So you're a traitor. Guess you should have stuck around longer. You would have found out my pops got Lou a job on the cleaning crew at the big house. And he didn't have to kill someone to do it. Just paid the guy off. Unlike Oakley, who definitely had Middleton killed. We got that intel. He's not as smart as he thinks he is. And now we have you."

"I don't know what you're talking about, Kala. I was about to cut Tasha loose." Chet stood, his hands up. "I came to save her the minute I heard the rumors Oakley was going to try to take her today."

"Tasha's right there," Lou said. "She can tell us what happened."

"He thinks he can call me a woman scorned and get away with it," Tasha explained as Lou holstered her weapon and moved to help her up. She knew exactly what was going through his head. "He knows I can't let you kill him because we should get the intel he sold us out for, but he thinks he'll be able to negotiate. He's thinking the Agency will call it a he-said, she-said and wash its hands. After all, Mike's dead, and so is Zach."

Kala snorted. "Zach's not dead. He's a tough motherfucker. Not only did he manage to write Chet's name in his own blood in case he didn't make it, he was halfway down the hallway when the police found him. I'm not messing with Zach anymore. He had a hole in his chest and was still making his way to the elevator. From what we understand all he kept saying was that they had to save Tasha. He's in surgery, according to Tristan. We'll have plenty of ways to send your ass to jail."

Relief flooded Tasha's system. Zach wasn't dead. They hadn't taken the time to make sure because they'd heard the sirens. Her team had saved him. Zach could still make it, and she would do anything she could to help him find the future he deserved. "You are so lucky, Chet. The fact that he's not dead might save you."

Kala looked her way. "Seriously, you're not going to let me kill him? That seems like such a waste. I have good bullets. If you want to keep it quiet, I have excellent knives."

Tasha stretched her arms, the circulation starting to flow like fire in her veins. "I want to know what Oakley was sending him. He said something about information on the Canadian. I want to know if he's talking about Huisman or Ben."

Kala grimaced. "So I have to choose between the deep satisfaction of murdering Chet or the potential joy of finding out Ben's a terrible piece of shit and holding that over Kenzie's head for all of time. It's a hard choice."

"It's not." Lou was always reasonable. "You can kill Chet later. I'll help. I got some great cleaning tips this afternoon. Those guys really know what they're doing."

Tasha turned to her ex. "What do you say? Should I let my sister pick your fate? Or do you want to tell me where they're going to meet with Dare? You might have a shot at the Agency not wanting to put you in jail. They might just fire you."

Not that her father would let that stand, but she wasn't about to mention that. Her parents wouldn't be satisfied with Chet being unemployed.

"If I tell you, you'll turn me over?" Chet asked, his voice low and tight. The expression on his face was the one he got when he knew he'd been caught, a blank look that meant he was trying not to give away a single emotion.

"Yes." She meant what she was saying. Her sister didn't need more blood on her hands. "I promise. You tell me where they're planning on meeting Dare and I'll make sure you get back to the Agency in one piece. I won't let my father or my sisters hurt you."

"The field a half a mile behind the main house. He's got a helo pad there. I think he plans to move Dare to another location. He thinks it's clear enough that no one can sneak up on him, but your dad will likely have a long-range sniper rifle on him. There's woods not a quarter of a mile away. They're perfect to hide a sniper," Chet admitted. "He wanted my opinion, and I told him it was a good meet spot."

He'd planned this well, she had to admit it. Chet had set it up so there would be no one left to speak of his betrayal. He'd thought he'd killed Zach. He'd set it up so he did away with her himself, and then her father would take out Oakley and Chet would be in the wind, presumed innocent and in good with his bosses because he would have the intel they all wanted.

But she would be the one to walk away with the prize this time.

She nodded her sister's way. "Deal with him. I don't want to break a nail. I have a man to save, and I want to look good when I do it."

Chet started to back up, but Kala was quick. She brought the SIG down on his head, and Chet crumpled to the ground.

"Are you sure I can't take his balls like a prize of war?" Kala asked. "There's a nice set of shears right over there. I bet they're super sharp. I need some new jewelry."

"No. But we should tie him up," Tasha admitted. She stared down at Chet's unconscious body and felt absolutely nothing but tired of dealing with him. What had she been thinking? Dare would hold this asshole over her head for all of time. She suddenly knew it because she wasn't letting him go. If she had to follow that man to Toronto, she would. She would give him all the space he needed, but in the end they would be together because he was the right man for her and she was good for him. "Lou, can you handle him? Check his phone. He's supposed to be getting a location from Oakley about where the data is. Try to get him to send it before you give him proof of life. Mostly because you won't be able to. I need to get to the meet spot. If Dad sees me, he'll know he's got a go to let Mom take Oakley down. We have to risk not getting the intel because I'm worried he'll get away with Dare if Mom can't work because she's not sure where I am."

There was no question who would have that sniper rifle in her hands. It would be her mom.

"I'll text him that I changed the deal and he gets nothing without the coordinates. Chet's an asshole. It's a believable play." Lou nodded and started to hog-tie Chet with the precision of a Master. She liked to practice and her dad lived on a farm, though no piglet on Boomer Ward's land would ever be treated the way Lou was treating Chet. "He'll survive the experience. Just come and pick us up when you're done. We still have to deal with the body outside, though there's minimal cleanup there. Kala's gotten good with the head shot."

Kala gave them a little curtsey. "I practice."

Lou shook her head and proceeded. "I think all of Oakley's security detail is with him. It's why it was so easy for us to get here from the big house. We searched all of the outer buildings once your dad called and told us you'd been taken. He figured you wouldn't be far from where Oakley was meeting Dare."

She started out of the gardening shed, which was more like a small house. She found herself in the middle of a beautiful yard, the main house in the distance and surrounded by mountains. "Who's playing Dare? Cooper's too tall."

"Dare's going in. He wouldn't let anyone else do it," Kala admitted.

Dare was here? She'd been sure he would let her parents handle it. He had come for her, and while she knew her parents would watch over him, he wasn't trained for this. Anything could happen to him. Anything. He would have to walk out there alone.

And then she heard the sound of gunfire echoing in the distance.

Tasha took off running, her sister at her side.

* * * *

"The minute you see Tasha, hit the ground, son. Charlie will start shooting. She'll give me cover and I'll get Tash out. Cooper will come for you," Ian Taggart said.

It was weird because Taggart wasn't anywhere close to him and yet it sounded like he was standing next to Dare.

Cooper had been the one to teach him how to place the small communication device in his ear. It was flesh colored so it blended, but he'd been told if someone got close enough they could see it.

He wasn't supposed to let anyone get close enough.

They were all here, even though he couldn't see them. As he'd driven in, Ian had been on his cell explaining everything that was going to happen. Kenzie and Tristan had come out with the rest of the team, and they were monitoring the situation from the back of Taggart's vehicle, but they wouldn't stay there. The minute they saw Tasha, everyone would come running.

Should they?

"Why don't you let Oakley take me?" He turned the corner onto the dirt road he'd been told would lead him to the meet spot. Five minutes before, he'd dropped off Charlotte Taggart, who'd gone from worried mom to cool and confident the minute her husband put a massive rifle in her hands. "I'm worried Tash will get caught in the crossfire."

That was the plan he preferred. Tasha would be released, and he would go with Oakley and whatever happened would happen. They could try to get him back or let his father negotiate. Except, according to the Taggarts, his father was likely to be arrested soon.

Damn it. It didn't matter. All that mattered was Tasha. Now that he was here he realized how dumb he'd been. Nothing mattered except her, and it hadn't from the moment he'd met her. His life had changed when she'd walked into that pub, and he wouldn't allow his pride to get in the way of his happiness.

There was a moment of quiet over the line that let Dare know Taggart was trying to figure out how to handle him. "Because Oakley is going to kill her either way. That fuckwit she almost married needs her dead, too. He doesn't know Zach was alive when he left him. Chet is counting on Oakley killing Tasha and then

Charlie killing Oakley. Those are the dominos he needs to fall if his plan is going to work."

That was a gut punch. Of course finding out Chet had anything at all to do with it had been another. The man had claimed to love her, had planned to marry her, and he was going to kill her? Who could kill his sweet, strong, and loyal Tash? Who couldn't love her? "He promised he would let her go. Oakley doesn't know who she is. Why not let her go? Can't he override Chet?"

"He needs her dead, too, whether or not he knows she's Agency. I would bet no. Chet needs Oakley in the dark or he might be more careful than Chet wants him to be. Look, Oakley is playing a dangerous game. He's counting on a couple of things. What he wants from your father is highly illegal and would damage both their reputations if it came out," Taggart explained.

"So my father won't talk." Dare got that. "And he thinks my father will have enough control of me that I won't. But Tasha is the wild card."

"And he's going to burn her," Taggart concluded. "I'll be surprised if she shows at all, to tell you the truth. Lucky for us we had Lou and Kala already out here. They're searching the whole property for her. It makes sense that he would have her somewhere close. I have to hope he's kept her alive so he can at least show you some proof of life in order to get you to turn yourself in."

He was going to be sick. Tasha was somewhere close, and he couldn't do anything to help her. Not even turning himself in would change her fate. How many times had he had this feeling in the pit of his stomach? The one that told him he was useless, impotent to change the fate of the people he loved. He was one man, and he was so fucking alone.

He'd only felt that loneliness abate when he'd met her.

"Dare, I need you to hear me," Taggart said. "Tasha is going to be okay. She's smart and capable, and her sisters will not let her down. Her mother and I will not let her down. Say it. Say it out loud and make it happen."

"I will not let Tasha down. Tasha will live through this, and we'll be together and we'll build a family and be happy."

"Yes, you will. You will do those things and so much more." There was nothing but steady confidence in Taggart's tone. "Cooper and I are in place. We can see the helo pad, and there's a pilot walking around doing a check."

So they definitely meant to take him to another location. He had to pray Taggart was right and Tasha was still alive, that they had some kind of chance at saving her.

He wasn't alone this time. This time he had a whole pack behind him, the wolves who welcomed him because he loved one of them.

"I love your daughter very much, sir, and I am asking your permission to marry her." It was a stupid time to ask. Everything was on the line, but it felt right.

It felt like hope.

"I think you'll find my Tasha doesn't need permission, but you have my blessing and gratitude," Taggart replied. "We'll get through this. Stay calm and do everything I tell you. I can see you."

He'd turned again, and he could see a big field and the helo pad in the distance. The woods he'd left the Taggarts in were across from him. Oakley would be between them. Charlotte was at the edge of the woods, up in a tree.

His future mother-in-law was a badass who'd shucked her designer shoes and hauled herself up a tree and settled in.

They wouldn't let him down.

"How close should I get?" Up ahead he could see a big SUV coming over a hill. From the map he'd been sent and studied in the car, there were several structures on the property leading up to the main house, situated at the base of one of the mountains.

"Stop now. I want you away from that helo," Taggart replied. "Walk about halfway between the car and the helo, and try to keep some distance between the two of you. I don't see Tasha with them. Demand proof of life before you offer to hand over your weapon."

He had a gun, a big one Taggart and Cooper had tried to show him how to use, but he was pretty sure all he'd gotten was how to click off the safety and pull the trigger. He had to stay calm. Tasha needed him.

He parked the car and eased out, seeing Oakley's big body in the distance. He was surrounded by five burly guards, each of them armed to the teeth.

There was no sign of Tasha, and he was pretty sure Chet wasn't with them either.

Had Chet taken off with her? Was he going to hide her away or kill her? Dare prayed it was the former. No matter what happened, he could hold her and help her heal. *Just let her be alive.*

He took a deep breath and tried to remember what he'd learned about the property. The main house would be roughly half a mile north. The helo pad was far closer to the big building Taggart had described as the caretaker's storage. It was where all the landscaping equipment was kept. If he needed a place to hide, it was closest, and if he remembered correctly a bit behind him. The road branched off in two directions, the one that led him here and to the main house, and the one that wound back to the storage house.

Where would Tasha be held? Was she even close? They'd carried her out of the hotel alive, but that was all he was certain of.

Oakley started to walk toward him.

Move. He was supposed to move. Meet him halfway was what Taggart had said, but not too close. *Don't let them put hands on you.*

"Where is Tasha?" Dare let the gun hang at his side, showing them he was armed but he wasn't pointing it anyone's way yet.

Oakley stopped midfield and put a hand out, stopping the men around him. "She's fine."

"I doubt that." Dare stopped, keeping yards between them.

"She's alive," Oakley replied, staring at him for a moment. "I didn't expect you to come armed. I guess you're more your father's son than I thought. I rather bought into the whole 'I hate my father' thing you have going."

"I can hate him and still want his business." He was going to play to Oakley's expectations. "What are you planning to do with the anthrax? Not that I care. What I care is you're stealing it instead of fucking paying us. Do you think we made it for fun?"

A brow rose over Oakley's eyes, a clear sign he'd surprised the man. "I thought you didn't know about your father's more interesting side businesses."

"I know everything. I'm the man's heir. We might not see eye to eye on a lot of things, but we both like money. If you'd come to me, I would have made you a deal. I'm a salesman, after all, and I know there's nothing that's not for sale."

Except the pack. The pack would never sell each other out.

Never. The pack would sacrifice and suffer for each other. They would celebrate each other. They would live all of life together.

"Well, I've tried to talk your father into it," Oakley admitted. "I guess I should have come to you."

"You could kill my father and put me in the CEO spot," Dare offered. "But I need proof my girlfriend is alive. She's the one thing that's not negotiable. I want to see her."

"Let me take you to her. She's a short helicopter ride away," Oakley promised.

A lie. Tristan had monitored Oakley's helicopter. It had flown straight from an office building in Sydney to this place. No stops. They had CCTV footage of Chet carrying Tasha on that chopper. She was here. They wouldn't have had enough time to get her here and then drive her somewhere else. It made sense that she was in one of the buildings on the property. "No. I don't move until I see her and she's released. That was the deal. We can make another one, you and I, if you like, but her release will be part of it, too. You want that anthrax, you can have it, but she's my payment."

"A little closer," Taggart said in his ear.

Dare moved forward a couple of feet.

Oakley sighed. "Fine. I'll show you that she's alive." He pulled out his cell and punched in some numbers. And frowned because no one picked up the line. "She's here. She's alive. I can take you to her."

He'd had a plan, and part of it was someone picking up the other end of that line.

Had Chet fucked Oakley over, too?

Or had Kala and Lou found Tasha?

"Dare, Lou has her," Taggart said in his ear. "I just got a text. They've got her secure. Get down."

A shot rang out but Oakley had moved, and Charlotte's bullet went wild, hitting one of the other guards.

Oakley ran back to the safety of the SUV. "That was a mistake."

Dare felt something hit his right shoulder, and fire exploded across his system. That was a pain unlike anything he'd ever felt. Shot. He'd been shot.

"Move, Dare. I'm coming," Taggart assured him.

But he wouldn't be there in time. Dare realized it in that moment. Oakley had moved faster than they'd expected. Dare felt tied to the earth, his feet not moving as he processed the pain. He watched as two more of Oakley's men went down, but his stare was fixed on Oakley. He'd reached into the SUV and pulled out a rifle.

Oakley was protected. Charlotte had a whole SUV between them, but Oakley had an excellent shot at Dare. He wouldn't be fast enough, he realized. He would have to get behind the back of the car to have any chance at all.

He was here, where he'd always thought he would be, and he was reacting the way he thought he would. He was letting it happen because for so long it had seemed like his only way out.

It wasn't now, and he suddenly, ferociously wanted to live.

Dare moved as he heard Taggart shouting, coming up from his right. He picked up the gun in his other hand and held it up, pointing toward Oakley, who fired.

And that was the moment Tasha ran from behind him, her hand coming out to pull him back.

He watched as Oakley's head twisted. Charlotte had taken him out through the window of the SUV, a neat head shot that had the man slumping over.

Dare caught Tasha.

Why was she falling? His heart caught as he saw the little circle of blood beginning to grow from the center of her chest.

"Tash?" He dropped to his knees, carrying her down with him. "Baby?"

She looked up at him, her eyes slightly glassy. "Dare? Are you okay? Did he hit you?"

He had, but the pain was a million miles away now. All he could see was her. "I'm fine. Baby, I need you to hold on."

Kala was suddenly beside them. She was pale as she stared down at her sister. She looked up and started yelling. "Cooper! Cooper, we need to take her to the hospital! Cooper!"

Taggart knelt down beside her, his eyes grim. "Tash, you stay with us. This is nothing. Look, baby girl. There's a helo right there, and Tristan's going to find a hospital. Dare, I need you to let me take her now."

He wasn't about to give her up. Did Taggart think he couldn't do this? He could do anything for her. Dare stood, forcing his muscles to work. He had to keep her still. The bullet was lodged in her chest. He needed to move it as little as possible. "Come on, baby. We need to get you to the hospital."

Kala had run ahead and was helping Cooper by forcing the chopper pilot to his knees. The man handed over something to Cooper, who immediately got into the pilot's seat. The whir of blades moving started up.

"Careful," Taggart warned.

"I've got her." Dare moved as quickly as he could without jostling her. How close was that bullet to her heart? How long did she have? The world seemed to be moving in quick and slow motion all at the same time.

"Yes, we're bringing in a gunshot wound." Kala had her phone to her ear. "We're bringing her in on a helicopter, and we're ten minutes out. I need a trauma team to meet us."

The helo was small. Only four seats. Taggart hopped into the back.

"You'll have to give her to me, Dare," Taggart announced. "You're losing blood. I know you want to keep her, but let me take care of her. Get in the front and let me stabilize her."

Taggart was right. He didn't want to let go. If he let go, he might lose her. He couldn't lose her.

"I love you," he whispered.

Her lips curled up. Her face was so pale. "Love you, too. Dare, be happy, baby. Don't…"

"Absolutely not." He wasn't letting her go. "You have to stay. There's no happiness without you. None."

Kala moved in, helping him settle Tasha in her father's arms.

Dare forced himself into the last seat, beside Cooper. As the helo started to take off, he saw Charlotte Taggart running across the field toward Kenzie, who was already hopping into Oakley's SUV.

"Tristan, get to the landscaping shed. Lou's got Chet there. You and Nate take care of him and call this in to Drake," Cooper said as he expertly handled the chopper.

The beauty of the Blue Mountains came into view, but all Dare could do was pray.

341

Chapter Twenty-One

Dare stood in the waiting room of the small hospital, the doctor's words not quite penetrating his brain. While she'd been in surgery, he'd allowed them to stitch up the small wound Oakley's bullet had caused. The one he'd given to Tasha was having a much more devastating effect.

Coma. Tasha was in a coma, and she might not wake up.

He heard the words *massive blood loss that had come during surgery*. They'd had a hard time getting her blood to clot, and they couldn't find the reason. They'd stabilized her, but her brain function was showing that she was in a coma, and they weren't sure how the loss of blood had affected her brain.

Tasha had a rare blood type, and none of them had been able to donate. They'd brought blood in from Sydney, but they didn't know that it would work.

Time would tell.

Time was the enemy.

Kenzie had cried and Kala had walked off, Cooper following after her.

The Taggarts had held on to each other.

And he sat.

They'd given him a chair at her bedside, and the days seemed to flow into each other. There was light and darkness, and someone brought him meals he wouldn't eat. He stepped out only to give her family time with her.

If she died, he wanted to go with her. He wouldn't, of course, but he knew he would spend the rest of his life waiting to see her again.

Three days seemed like three years.

"Dare, you need to shower, man," Taggart would say.

Charlotte would gently force him to drink water.

They'd updated him on his father's situation. Ben had called and told Dare how he'd been allowed in on the raid, and they'd found what they needed to arrest his father and the majority of his board.

He didn't care.

His siblings called, worried. He'd assured them they would all be okay.

He'd lied because nothing mattered if Tasha didn't wake up.

Why wouldn't she wake up?

He stared down at her. She looked so peaceful. Like she was sleeping.

"Dare, we're going to have to talk."

He hadn't heard the door open. He glanced back and Taggart was standing there, a grim look on his face.

Dare didn't like that look. "She needs more time."

Taggart walked in. He looked like Dare felt. Haggard. Beyond tired. A little hopeless. His sons had made it in the night before, and they'd both begged their oldest sister to wake up.

"We can give her a few more days, but at some point we have to make decisions," Taggart said.

"Can we take her back home?" He'd thought a lot about this. "Maybe if she was home…"

"We can if that's the decision we make. But, Dare, we're past the point where the odds are in our favor. She lost so much blood. I have a friend who's a neurologist. She's going to come in and consult. She thinks Tasha's brain was deprived of oxygen for too long."

"She's not brain dead."

"Not technically," Taggart agreed. "But she's losing function every day. Rebecca is sending some experimental drugs she's been working on. They should be here sometime today, and she'll be here shortly after. If these don't work…"

He didn't want to even think about the possibility. "They'll work."

"If they don't," Taggart began.

Dare shook his head. "No. You don't get to do that to me. You're the fucking alpha of this pack, and you are the one who taught me. She will wake up. The drugs will work. She will be awake, and we will deal with anything else. I'll take care of her no matter what. There might not be anything legal, but she's my wife and she won't leave me."

Taggart's eyes closed and he reached out, putting a hand on Dare's shoulder. He took a long breath. "She will wake up. She will be okay."

Dare woke up deep in the night. A big man in a white coat stood at the end of Tasha's bed. "Doctor?"

The man turned, his dark eyes flashing just for a second. "Hello. You must be Tasha's boyfriend. I'm Doctor Federov. I'm going to administer a special medicine for Tasha. I think this will help."

Dare stood. "The medicine Dr. Rebecca Walsh sent?"

"Yes," the doctor replied. He had a syringe in his hand. "That medicine. It's experimental, but you shouldn't worry about it. Give it a few hours and she should wake up."

Something about the big guy made him calm. "How does it work? You're the first doctor to give me hope."

"It will reopen the neural pathways that were damaged by the lack of oxygen to the brain." The doctor pushed the plunger. "It's not anything that's on the market, but I assure you it's safe for Natasha." The doctor turned and stared down at her for a moment before looking back Dare's way. "I wish you both a happy life."

"My life will be perfect if she'll just wake up," Dare admitted.

The doctor seemed to shake something off and slid the syringe into the sharps container. "You know you won't hurt her if you slip into bed beside her. It might be good for her to wake up warm and safe."

It was what he'd wanted to do for days. Hold her. Sleep beside her.

He climbed into bed beside her, easing her into his arms, and for the first time in days, he managed to get to sleep.

* * * *

Tasha came awake, the weird dreams she'd had of her father falling off slowly. The fact that she'd dreamed of her biological parents told her she'd slept hard. Her dreams were mostly normal. She was trapped in a giant shoe store and had to navigate around in seven-inch heels. She was sitting in a briefing with the head of the Agency and she didn't have any clothes on.

But when she saw her bio dad, she knew something was off. She was sick or drugged, as though her subconscious sought a safe place to heal.

What had happened? She knew it wasn't a normal "wake up in her bed and smell the coffee Kala made before her morning run" kind of day. She wasn't in the little house she and her sisters and Lou rented in a Dallas suburb, the one they'd been so proud to decorate, though they'd fought over whether or not knives were good home décor.

She went still because the last thing she remembered was Chet. Chet had shown up and Zach was…no…Zach wasn't dead. Something else had happened.

Why was she so warm?

Tentatively, she opened her eyes and realized she wasn't alone.

Dare was asleep, his body curled around hers, head cradled against her neck. He held on to her like she might drift away if he didn't.

"Tash?" a soft voice said.

Her sister. Kala scrambled out of the chair she'd been sleeping in.

"Kenz, Tash is awake." Kala leaned down, her voice still low as she put a hand on her twin's shoulder.

Kenzie was asleep on the floor, a jacket rolled up as a pillow beneath her head.

Kenz sat up, wiping a hand across her eyes. "What?"

"Call Mom and Dad," Kala said. "They're at the hotel with Trav and Seth. I'll go wake up Lou and the guys."

"Wait." Her sisters were moving too fast, and they were still too loud because Dare shifted slightly against her, his arm tightening around her waist. "What happened? Where am I?"

Kala stared down at her. "You took a bullet for Dare, dummy. One that probably wouldn't have slammed into his chest the way it did yours."

"Hush." Kenzie got to her feet. "She was trying to save him."

"That's my point," her grumpiest sister argued. "He could have taken that bullet way better than she could. He would have had a gut shot. I dress it in the field, we call a real ambulance instead of having to stuff you in a chopper."

Yup. This was reality. Not a dream. In her dreams her sisters weren't so obnoxious. "So I had surgery?"

It was weird because she actually felt pretty good. If she'd had surgery a couple of hours ago, shouldn't she ache?

"You've been in a coma for almost a week," Kenzie stated, tears in her eyes.

A week? Well that would explain why she didn't feel like she'd just had surgery.

"You nearly died because you bled so much. It caused your brain to be deprived of oxygen. That's what put you in the coma," Kala explained. "Dad's friend, Rebecca, had the doctors here give you an experimental drug a couple of hours ago. He thought you would wake up sometime in the next twenty-four hours, so Kenz and I snuck in when we realized Dare was asleep. You're only supposed to have one visitor overnight, but we wanted to be close."

"He wouldn't leave you for more than a couple of minutes," Kenzie said.

"That's why he smells so bad," Kala added with a nod.

"Is Zach okay?" Memories of the day were coming back. "Did he make it through surgery?"

"Yes, he's a tough one," Kenzie replied. "They wanted him to stay at the hospital in Sydney, but he insisted on transferring here. It gave us a place to stash the guys. I think this hospital will be happy when we leave."

"Tell me what happened to Chet, and did we get the intel we

346

needed?" She wanted all the bad stuff out of the way. Zach was alive. Dare was here with her. She wanted an update, and then she could focus on him. The fact that he was here, holding her like he would never let go, gave her hope.

"Lou got all the dirty stuff on Oakley, though Mom killed him, so it's not like his ass is in jail," Kala explained. "Chet is back in Virginia being held in a CIA interrogation facility. We got everything we needed on him, and I've already been cleared for killing Mike. TJ would be here but he's on assignment again, and I can't figure out where he is or if he even knows what happened."

That was intelligence work. "Did we get the intel Oakley promised? He said it had information on the Canadian."

Kenzie's head shook. "I think the plan got screwed up in the chaos, and Tris, Lou, and I have gone through Oakley's cell and the laptop we found. We have nothing. He was serious about hiding the intel. But I have to believe that info was about Huisman."

"She believes Ben. Surprise, surprise," Kala groused.

Dare started to stir.

She didn't want their first moments to be surrounded by her sisters arguing. The rest of their lives would likely be just that.

"Go call Mom and Dad. Give us a minute," she said.

"Tash?" Dare's head came up as her sisters were slipping out the door. His eyes widened. "Tash? Baby, are you awake? Am I awake?"

He was so beautiful, even though his clothes were wrinkled and his hair was going twelve different ways. He sat up.

She shifted on her side, being careful with the IV in her arm. She felt remarkably good for being half dead for the last week. She would have to thank Rebecca for all her hard work. Tasha was sure she was in for about a million blood draws to figure out how the drugs had affected her system, and she would smile through each one.

Because she was alive. Because she was with Dare.

"You're awake. I'm awake. Are you okay, baby?"

He stared at her for a moment, like she was some kind of miracle. His hands came up and gently traced the lines of her face. "I thought you were going to die. I couldn't…"

"I'm tougher than that," she promised. "And I'm not fragile. I feel strong, Dare."

He wrapped his arms around her, holding her close. "I love you. I love you so much. I don't care how we started. All that matters is that we end together."

A shudder of relief went through her. "I love you."

He pulled back, and his face went stony though his eyes were suspiciously bright. "You will never do that again."

This was the danger zone. "Do you mean saving you or working?"

He huffed. "I mean stepping in front of a bullet and nearly dying, Tasha. That's what I mean. You will never do that again. There are going to be so many rules from here on out."

She was sure there would be, and they would all fall away when he was more comfortable. This was bargaining at its finest stage. "Yes, Sir."

That seemed to mollify him a bit. He sighed and leaned in, his lips brushing hers. "I don't know what I would have done, Tash. Don't ever leave me."

That was one rule she could follow.

The door came open and Lou rushed in, followed by Tris and Cooper and her sisters. She was told her mom and dad and brothers were on the way. Zach stood in the doorway, his big body in a hospital gown and an IV at his side. He sent her a smile.

Her team was here. Her love was here. Her family would be here soon.

All was right with the world.

Epilogue

Dallas, TX
Three weeks later

Ian Taggart loved having a sleeping baby on his chest. If anyone asked, he would tell them it was because a sleeping baby was a good excuse to take a nice nap, but it was more than that. He put a hand on his grandchild's back and sighed.

Travis was an idiot, but damn he loved this kid.

There was a huff as a big canine joined them, putting his fluffy head on Ian's thigh and joining the all-male nap fest that occurred most Sunday afternoons. Ian liked Sundays.

"Pops?" Said idiot who he also loved way too much but who didn't listen to sound advice was staring down at him. "You want me to take Colton?"

Travis was the last of his kids still at home. He was also the last of his kids still in school. Law school. It made Ian shudder, but at least the kid would likely be able to support his son at some point. All the rest of his kids were out in the world. Kala and Kenz lived with Lou in a house that was both frighteningly clean and filled with weapons, and a strange set of pop culture toys. Seth had an apartment he shared with his cousin Lucas, and Ian knew not to go over there without prior warning because those two boys knew how to go through a box of condoms. Between the singing thing and the fact that Lucas was an up-and-coming chef, they kept women churning through that place.

"He's fine. We're napping." He was laid out on the chaise on the patio in the backyard, the sound of the pool soothing. Colton was easy. Colton merely wanted someone to hold him and shove a bottle or spoonful of food in his mouth and make sure his diaper was clean. That was all. Colton didn't jump in front of bullets and damn near tear his father's heart out.

Travis sank down to the seat beside him, the one where his Charlie usually sat, but today she was out looking at condos with Tasha and Dare.

Dare. The new VP of sales for McKay-Taggart. He was going to handle the whole sales force across all the branches, and Damon and Ten already loved him. In the week he'd actually been on the job, he'd taken charge and streamlined processes and generally made everything work better. It was good to have him around the office, but even better to see the way he made Tash smile.

"I think I'll be able to move out soon," Travis announced.

Ian opened his eyes and looked at his youngest. Travis looked tired. Being a third-year law student and working at his uncle's restaurant and part time at McKay-Taggart while taking care of a five-month-old was weighing on the kid, and he probably hadn't been helping. He liked to say sarcasm was his love language, but sometimes earnestness was needed, too. Sometimes a kid needed to know he was still welcome at home. "I think that would make your mom sad. And me. I know I've been hard on you, but you have to know how proud I am of you stepping up and being a good dad. Stay. Let us help you with Colton."

"You already help," Travis said. "Everyone helps. I feel like I should be... I don't know. Further along, I suppose. Tasha's getting married. She's moving out on her own. Dare seems so competent. He walked in and everyone did what he said. People still roll their eyes when I try to take control."

"Dare's got a couple of years on you, and he's had to be in control," Ian replied. "You're doing great, Trav. Keep up with your grades and you'll have a job waiting for you. For now, stop worrying and enjoy the help. Your mom and I will enjoy having Colton around. I suspect your sister and Dare won't wait too long to give him a cousin. Besides, someone has to take care of the pups when your mom and I are gone."

He'd thought he would be done with dogs when he was done with kids, but two years before Charlotte's cousin Dusan had sent them a Black Russian Terrier puppy as an anniversary gift. The fucker. Bear was the smartest dog he'd ever owned and now was a ninety-pound security system who loved cuddles with his mom's Cavalier King Charles Spaniel, Lola. And the twins had Bud 2, Even More Bud, a big rescue mutt they adored but who needed a sitter when they went on an op. Trav was great with all of them.

"I would love to stay." Travis ran a hand through his way too long hair and smiled. "Well, if you're sure you can handle him, I wouldn't mind studying more."

He closed his eyes again. "Be gone, son. Let the young and old be lazy and enjoy the afternoon."

"Will do. Love you, Pops. Let me know if you need me to take him." Travis stood and smiled. "Hey, Mom. How did the hunt go?"

"I think they're going with the three bedroom in Uptown." His whole world strode out, Lola prancing beside her. "It's beautiful and has great light, and they can have both an office and a guest room for when Dare's family comes to visit. They're taking the whole 'Dad going to jail' thing well. I guess that's what happens when you're a dick. No one cares. Dare's got all the finances already in order, and his stepmom has taken control of the house and is apparently doing really well with Johnny and Gina. They're going up to Toronto soon to visit." Travis nodded and walked back in the house as Charlie turned to Ian. "How is my little nugget? My heart squeezes every time I think of him. Did you tell Trav we want him to stay while he's in school? He's worried about it."

She sat down beside him.

His baby was so pretty. Even more gorgeous than the first day he'd lain eyes on her. He couldn't help but remember how gorgeous she'd been when he'd spanked her at Sanctum the night before. He'd spanked her and used a violet wand on her, and then they'd performed the real scene. His baby still liked everyone to watch.

"He's staying through law school." He would never have

allowed Travis to leave. Travis was still in school. He didn't have the same fallbacks the other kids had. His young adult struggles had become serious the minute that baby had been left with the receptionist.

It was one thing to watch his kids start their lives and have to deal with normal adult things like eating ramen noodles for dinner and having to play at a truly terrible DIY club, but another when they would really be struggling. He would step in if they were really having trouble. Especially the little guy on his chest.

It wasn't Colton's fault his dad forgot the condom.

"Okay. So now that the kiddos are settled in for a while, I have some hot and horrible gossip." She slipped off her shoes and lay out on the chaise next to his.

This was what he lived for. Long afternoons with her at his side, all being right with the world. "I find myself strangely unmoved by gossip today."

He was in a live and let live kind of mood. He let his eyes close again. He could nap the afternoon away and then he'd grill some steaks for dinner and he and Charlie could destroy Alex and Eve tonight while they played Spades. His younger self would be so disappointed that his version of a perfect way to finish a weekend was playing cards, and not for money or intel.

His younger self had been dumb. Life was pretty perfect.

"You'll want this gossip." Charlie's voice went low. "I got a call from Drake while I was out. I wanted to talk to you before we tell Tasha. Chet was found dead in his cell today."

Oh. He opened his eyes and tilted his head her way. She was right. That was good gossip. "Do they think it was me?" It could have been if Tasha hadn't made him promise not to murder the asshole. Another thought hit him. "Baby, was it you? You can tell me."

Her pretty blue eyes rolled. "No, I did not somehow find the time between playing at the club last night and meeting Tash and Dare this morning to fly to and from DC, break into an Agency holding facility, and mysteriously exsanguinate our daughter's ex."

"But you could have," he prompted.

She seemed to think about that for a moment. "It would be tight, but yes."

"Exsanguinate?" It was an interesting way to assassinate a dude. A bit showy for his tastes. He would have gone for something simple like strangulation or evisceration.

"He lost ninety percent of his blood volume, and it wasn't on the floor," Charlie explained. "They think someone has a new weapon. I think someone didn't want Chet to talk. I have to tell Tash."

"Maybe leave out the blood volume part," he advised.

His security system pinged, letting him know someone had entered the house. Bear's head came up and his tail started wagging, telling him he didn't need to get up because whoever was coming their way was a friendly.

"Dad! Mom!"

One of the twins.

Charlie stood up. "We're in the back."

Colton's head came up, his tiny mouth yawning like a baby lion. He looked at his grandfather as though asking *what the hell?*

Ian wanted to know the answer, too. He shifted, sitting up as Kala and Kenzie raced out the back door.

"Dad, Cooper just got word from a friend of his in Army intelligence," Kala said, a little breathless.

It was bad if Kala was panicking.

Charlie moved in, opening her arms. She took Colton as Ian got to his feet.

"What's happening?" The nap would have to wait.

"TJ's unit came under heavy fire," Kenzie said. "I don't have all the information, but TJ's been taken. Cooper's friend is saying that brass isn't sure they want to risk a rescue."

"So Lou's already planning it," Kala concluded. "She'll go with or without us."

Yep. His nap was over.

It was time to get back to work.

Lou, TJ, and the whole team will return in *Live, Love, Spy*, coming March 5, 2024.

Live, Love, Spy
Masters and Mercenaries: New Recruits, Book 2
By Lexi Blake
Coming March 5, 2024

Life can often be awkward when you're a child genius. For Louisa Ward, that came in the form of meeting her one true love at the age of 12. TJ Taggart was perfect. But being a year younger and a full grade ahead of him in school always made things weird. Working in the CIA has turned her into a strong and capable woman. Until TJ walks into a room. Fifteen years later, she still gets butterflies every time she sees the gorgeous soldier, but she's tired of waiting and ready to find love, even if it can't be with him.

TJ Taggart always knew he wanted to be a soldier. But joining the Army would require a sacrifice. Since meeting Louisa, TJ knew she was the one for him, but they had different paths in life. Lou was meant to change the world at some prestigious research job or maybe teach at an Ivy League school. There would be a chance to sweep her off her feet when his time in this dangerous life was done, and their happily ever after could begin.

On a top-secret mission, TJ's unit is ambushed by an unknown adversary. No rescue is coming. As he waits to die, all he can think of is the time he wasted and how badly he wants to be with Lou. He's more than a little surprised when his sweet, quiet girl shows up leading a CIA special ops squad to bust him out. Back in Dallas, it's time to claim the woman of his dreams. He has a plan to win her over, until the adversary who almost killed him returns to finish the job.

Author's Note

I'm often asked by generous readers how they can help get the word out about a book they enjoyed. There are so many ways to help an author you like. Leave a review. If your e-reader allows you to lend a book to a friend, please share it. Go to Goodreads and connect with others. Recommend the books you love because stories are meant to be shared. Thank you so much for reading this book and for supporting all the authors you love!

About Lexi Blake

New York Times bestselling author Lexi Blake lives in North Texas with her husband and three kids. Since starting her publishing journey in 2010, she's sold over three million copies of her books. She began writing at a young age, concentrating on plays and journalism. It wasn't until she started writing romance that she found success. She likes to find humor in the strangest places and believes in happy endings.

Connect with Lexi online:

Facebook: Lexi Blake
Twitter: authorlexiblake
Website: www.LexiBlake.net
Instagram: authorlexiblake

Printed in Great Britain
by Amazon

28179921R00202